# LIFE, LOVE and the PURSUIT of HAPPINESS

A Bell Sound Novel

# SANDRA HILL

AVONBOOKS

*An Imprint of HarperCollinsPublishers*

LIFE, LOVE AND THE PURSUIT OF HAPPINESS. Copyright © 2019 by Sandra Hill. All rights reserved. Printed in the United States of America. No part of this book may be used or reproduced in any manner whatsoever without written permission except in the case of brief quotations embodied in critical articles and reviews. For information, address HarperCollins Publishers, 195 Broadway, New York, NY 10007.

First Avon Books mass market printing: July 2019

Print Edition ISBN: 978-0-06-285410-0
Digital Edition ISBN: 978-0-06-285409-4

*Cover design by Nadine Badalaty*
*Cover illustration by Shane Rebenshield*
*Cover photographs by Shirley Green (couple); © Mariusz S. Jurgiele-wicz/Shutterstock (rock beach); © pkline/pabradyphoto/deputyrick/Mustang_79/Serg_Veluseac/iStock/Getty Images (five images); Charles Carlson/Adobestock (background)*

Avon, Avon & logo, and Avon Books & logo are registered trademarks of HarperCollins Publishers in the United States of America and other countries.

HarperCollins is a registered trademark of HarperCollins Publishers in the United States of America and other countries.

FIRST EDITION

19 20 21 22 23  QGM  10 9 8 7 6 5 4 3 2 1

This book is dedicated to my granddaughter Jaden, who recently started her first year of college. Like my heroine, in this, the second book of my Bell Sound series, Jaden is launching a new beginning, in a different place, far from everything that is familiar to her. A little bit scary, but an adventure, to be sure. And, oh, so many exciting possibilities! I wish you all the best in your journey, sweet girl. Life, love, and the pursuit of happiness.

# LIFE, LOVE and the
# PURSUIT of HAPPINESS

# Prologue

*The bigger they are, the harder they fall . . .*

*T*he first time he saw her, she was wearing a tool belt.

The second time he saw her, she was wearing leather and riding a Harley, her ice-blonde hair blowing in the wind.

The third time he saw her, she wore nothing at all. *Hoo-yah!*

Merrill "Geek" Good didn't stand a chance. He was in love. Or lust. Or both.

Didn't matter that the ex–Navy SEAL, soon-to-be treasure hunter had been around the world a dozen times, seen amazing things, done amazing things, been wounded five times, almost died once, screwed so many women he should be called De-Walt, could bench-press two hundred and thirty pounds easy-peasy, measured 150-plus on the I.Q. meter, and had a million or two in stocks due to an erotic invention he sold on the Internet. *Don't ask!*

Nothing in his colorful life had prepared him for this woman. Love at first sight didn't begin to describe the wallop she packed.

Unfortunately, Delilah Jones didn't reciprocate his feelings.

### *Prison makes good women horny . . .*

The first time she saw him, she was blasting the rust off an old metal diner with a power tool—and was so disconcerted she almost bored a hole straight through. *Holy-frickin'-moly!*

His light brown hair was cut short, military style.

He wore a uniform of some kind, probably Navy.

Whiskey-colored eyes smoldered as he watched her work.

The second time, he was standing on a street corner in a ratty Metallica T-shirt, cargo shorts, and flip-flops as she passed by on Uncle Clyde's motorcycle.

He lowered his sunglasses halfway down his nose and peered over them to watch her almost hit the car in front of her.

The third time she saw him, it was by moonlight. She'd been skinny-dipping in Bell Sound, the bay behind her property, and he was standing on the rocky shore, which she'd thought was private.

It was a devilish situation. She was new in town and needed to make friends, not enemies, for business and other reasons.

Even so, that's when Delilah decided to put on the brakes, slam the door, raise the wall, amp up her usual snark factor a notch or two, do everything in her power to keep the man away. Merrill Good might be sizzling, bone-melting, pure temptation on his size twelve hoof to most women, but that was the one thing a female ex-con couldn't afford now that she was finally free.

Still . . .

# Chapter 1

*Two roads diverged in a yellow wood,*
*and he chose . . . the bay . . .*

No regrets?" Navy SEALs Lt. Commander Jacob Alvarez Mendozo, aka JAM, asked Merrill as they sat with their buddies at a round table in the ballroom of a mansion called Chimes in Bell Cove, a small town on the Outer Banks of North Carolina. The room was festooned with Fourth of July decorations. They were inhaling beers and raising an occasional champagne toast to the newly married couple, Christmas tree farmer Ethan Rutledge and ex–female SEAL Wendy Patterson. A lethal combination! The alcohol mix, not the happy couple or the overabundance of odd-for-a-wedding red, white, and blue paraphernalia.

"Not so far," Merrill answered, knowing that JAM referred to the abrupt turning point he was taking in his life, leaving the exciting life of the teams a month ago and moving here to Bell Cove. He would soon be starting a shipwreck salvaging and treasure hunting company, a different kind of exciting, he hoped. Even so, he admitted, "I am feeling a little disoriented, though. It'll pass, eventually, but for the moment, I'm not sure who I am, or where I fit in, neither fish nor fowl, if you know what I mean. Hell, I'm like a dickhead addict going cold turkey after my fifteen-year fix in Special Forces."

Merrill was surprised at himself, that he could put that many words together, considering the state of his inebriation.

"Same as me. Sixteen damn years! Which is like a hundred in frog years," JAM quipped, "not to be confused with dog years."

They grinned at each other. SEALs had been known as frogmen from way back when most of their work had been done on boats or in the water. Ribbitting was a joke among the guys when someone called them animals.

Yeah, sometimes the only thing that would do was a good ribbit. It was as popular as the traditional "Hoo-yah!" in some instances. Or if you asked a SEAL who'd been out on a mission too long if he was feeling "froggie," as in lascivious, the answer would be a loud and bodacious ribbit.

"I still say you should join me in treasure hunting," Merrill said. "The first meeting of my crew will be held on Monday. You could stick around an extra day or two and see what we're about. I could use you, man."

"I'm tempted, but no, I'm not ready to leave the teams." JAM shook his head for emphasis. "I know it's crazy, but I feel as if there's something important I'm destined to do yet, as a SEAL."

"You mean like a God-ordained thing?" Merrill asked, and he wasn't kidding. JAM had studied to be a priest at one time.

"Maybe." JAM shrugged.

"You're full of shit."

"Probably." JAM paused. "Don't shut the door on me, though, buddy. I might change my mind down the road a ways."

"Anytime," Merrill assured him.

When JAM went to the men's room, Merrill glanced around and realized that another reason he was feeling so off balance today was that he sat at a table with a handful of his SEAL buddies in full white dress uniforms, while he was in civilian attire. Yeah, it was a tux, since he was a grooms-man at this hokey-ass, Independence Day–themed wedding, but it was a white tux, which was not the same thing as white formal military duds. Not at all! He knew from vast experience that women went gaga over men in uniforms. Not so much men in tacky white tuxes with pink ruffled shirts and pink boutonnieres to match the bridesmaids' attire. Ethan's preteen daughter by an earlier marriage apparently had a thing about pink.

The whole town of Bell Cove had shown up to support Ethan and Wendy, their native son and daughter, who'd finally gotten their acts together, a celebration of what they called "a forever kind of love." *Did I mention hokey?* The event was being held at the mansion owned by architect Gabriel Conti, descendant of the Conti Brothers who founded Bell Forge, for whom the town was named, more than a century ago.

Even though the Fourth of July was a few days past, the theme of the nuptials was a red, white, and blue extravaganza, complete with flags and rockets and sparklers—the whole patriotic stars-and-stripes works, thanks to local do-gooders who'd taken over the festivities, making it as much a town event as a personal celebration of love. In fact, a marching band had led the wedding party from Our Lady by the Sea Church to the mansion on the bluff overlooking the Atlantic Ocean on one side and Bell Sound on the other. Some couples have a wedding march, these dodo bird townies insisted on "Yankee Doodle Dandy."

The reception was being held both indoors, via the open French doors, and under a massive tent outside with panoramic views of the water for the overflow crowd. The caterer's serving staff wore Uncle Sam and Betsy Ross outfits. *I kid you not!* Not to mention punch with red, white, and blue vodka ice cubes. There would be a fireworks show later over Bell Sound.

When Ethan and Wendy had protested the extent of the patriotic decorations and themed activities surrounding their event—*How much was this stuff costing anyhow?*—the mayor and town council had told them not to worry, that lots of the decorations were left over from the Fourth of July celebration and, in fact, could be saved and reused for the newly planned Labor Day Lolly, or Lollypalooza, not to be confused with the music festival by that similar name, although it was a town known for its bells and bell music. So why not? Also, maybe some of these decorations could even be incorporated into their second annual Christmas Grinch celebration come December, the mayor had mused. *"Grinch what?" you may ask. Hah! Suffice it to say, you do not want to be "grinched" in Bell Cove.*

All of this was cornball to the max, but kind of nice, in an innocent Aunt Bee/Sheriff Taylor/Opie/Barney/Goober kind of way. *Yeah, I'm an Andy Griffith Show fan. So shoot me!* Which was probably why Merrill had decided to settle here in small town, USA. Being estranged from his own family for so many years, he was probably looking for family in this community. That was more important at this stage in his life than leaving the adventurous life of the teams. How pathetic was that?

Not that he was giving up adventure. Not with a new shipwreck salvaging/treasure hunting company. Still, his motives for this big move would be fodder for a psychiatrist's couch.

In any case, Merrill's mellow mood was helped by the six "dead soldiers," i.e. empty longneck bottles of beer sitting in front of him, two empty champagne glasses, and the sight of the vision which just appeared in the far doorway. A late arrival.

Even with all the loud music, the town square bells could be heard ringing out the hour. The two churches, the town hall clock tower, and God only knew what else. Everyone and everything here came with bells. Right now, it was as if the bells were announcing a personal alert to him: Hot Babe on the Horizon.

Delilah Jones.

*Oh, boy!* Ever since the babe had put the deep freeze on him, he'd decided to cut his losses. No more passing idly by the 1950s-style diner and motel she was renovating. No late-night beach visits. No more looking for a sighting of her around town. Nope. Instead, Merrill was devoting all his time to the launch of his new business enterprise. And he'd almost succeeded.

Until now.

"Oh, boy!" someone said aloud, reiterating his thoughts. It was another of his longtime friends, Captain Luke Avenil, who sat on his other side at the circular table. "Slick," the senior of his old teammates, had to be close to forty now, which was old for a SEAL. But then, Merrill was thirty-five. Not much difference. Slick elbowed him and asked, "She the one?"

Merrill ignored Slick's question as he watched the blonde bombshell in a white halter sundress edged in red, with a shiny red belt, and white high-heeled sandals walk across the dance floor. She was heading toward the dais, carrying a gift-wrapped package, presumably to greet the newly married couple. The band Nostalgia, a popular Outer Banks classic rock group, was playing that old Springsteen song, "Born in the U.S.A.," and, without doing anything overtly sexual, Delilah's stride kept beat to the music.

*Boom-chick-a-boom-boom-boom. Born-in-the-U-S-A.*

*Boom-chick-a-boom-boom-boom. Born-in-the-U-S-A.* That's all Merrill's brain, and eyeballs, registered. But then, he was more than a little bit buzzed, from alcohol and unrequited lust.

The Boss's rendition marking Independence Day in his own inimitable fashion was not your usual wedding song, but then this wasn't your usual wedding celebration. And, yeah, it wasn't really a song about patriotism, but the people of Bell Cove, who'd taken over the planning for this wedding reception, probably didn't know that—or care.

Belatedly, he responded to Slick, "The one what?"

"Don't play dumb, Mister Genius. Your one and only," Slick replied. "In other words, the one you've had a hard-on for the past three weeks."

"How would you know? You just got here yesterday."

"News travels fast."

*No kidding!* The gossip grapevine in Bell Cove was remarkable, but it was nothing compared to the SEALs and WEALS—Women on Earth, Air, Land, and Sea, the female division of SEALs—both of whom made minding each other's business an art form.

"Is she the one who's got you dragging your tail and sighing with luuuuuve," added another of his table mates, Navy SEAL Ensign Hamr Magnusson, a former NFL quarterback called "The Hammer." With mock seriousness, Hamr wagged a forefinger at Merrill. "You're gonna give SEALs a bad name, buddy, even if you're not in the teams anymore. Women chase us—we don't chase them."

"Bite me," Merrill offered, and tossed a handful of USA flag–foiled Hershey's Kisses at Hamr's grinning face.

Hamr grabbed a few, midair, and lobbed them back at him.

Everyone at the table, including JAM, who was back, turned to assess the subject of Merrill's affections as she stopped to talk to some big blond guy in a dark suit with a white shirt and blue tie (as compared to a dork in a white tux with pink accessories). It was Karl Gustafson, a local guy who owned a convenience store and gas station. She was chatting with him in a way she never talked to Merrill.

"Holy crap! Is that . . . yep, it's Goose," Hamr said.

"What?" several guys asked.

"Goose Gustafson. Remember him? Linebacker for the Cowboys before his knees gave out."

On those words, Hamr stood and walked over to join Chatty Cathy and the blond god, who apparently pumped more than gas.

"Well, shiiiit!" Merrill muttered, feeling an unfamiliar tug of jealousy. Bad enough that she'd given him the cold shoulder, so far, but did she have to be all nicey-nicey with the Viking stud? Yeah, he'd pretty much given up the fight, so far, and yeah, he had enough on his plate at the moment without wasting time on an affair that would probably go nowhere. Still . . .

"This is the first I've heard about you biting the big one, Geek. I don't recall meeting her when we were here at Christmas," JAM mentioned. "What's her name?"

"Delilah Jones," Merrill answered, reluctantly, knowing what would come next. "She just moved here this spring."

"Her name is Delilah . . . Delilah Jones?" Slick sputtered. "Sounds like a porn star to me."

"Me, too," Merrill said. "And I might have made the mistake of mentioning that the first time we met. Which is probably why she avoids me like crotch itch. One of the reasons, anyhow. I don't know what else I've done that could have pissed her off so much."

"Did you know there's a website that tells women, and men, what their porn star names would be?" interjected Master Chief Frank Uxley, aka F.U. He was the rudest, crudest Navy man to ride the waves, and that was saying a lot. "Mine would be Frank Bonier. Get it? Bone Her."

"Shut up," Merrill ordered F.U., who sat opposite him.

"Up yours," F.U. retorted with a smile, not at all insulted.

Merrill ignored F.U. and went on to explain to JAM and Slick his various encounters with Delilah and how not into him she was.

"When I asked her out on a date, she looked at me like I had three heads."

"What are you, like fourteen?" Slick asked. "Even I know that people today don't date. 'Friends With Benefits,' my man!"

"You guys are full of it. 'Friends With Benefits'

is so 2016. The correct term is 'Netflix and Chill.' It's the new 'Friends With Benefits,'" explained Ensign Marcus Weller, new guy on the teams. And young for a SEAL, too, at only twenty-two. "Stream *Ghost* and you're in like Flynn." He waggled his eyebrows with meaning.

"Oh, that's just great. I walk up to a woman and say, 'Wanna watch some flicks and fuck?'"

"Whatever works," advised JAM, who tended to lose his priestly attitude after a few beers. Never in a million years would JAM approach a female in that way, though, drunk or sober.

"Personally, I haven't approached a woman in years," Slick said. "Connections in a bar work for me."

"That's because you've been burned by your ex-wife so many times, you're afraid of commitment," Merrill said.

"Who died and named you Dr. Phil?" Slick countered.

"Flash used to swear by the Gospel According to Hank Williams," contributed Lt. Cody O'Brien, who still mourned the death of his close friend, Travis "Flash" Gordon, who died in an explosion last year in Baghdad. In their decade-long stint as partners, Flash and Cody had been notorious for their continual arguments over the merits of country over rock, Johnny Cash over Steven Tyler. "Everything you ever wanted to know about love could be learned from a country song, according to Flash. 'Tequila Makes Her Clothes Fall Off,' 'Trashy Women,' 'Ain't Much Fun Since I Quit

Drinkin',' 'Girls Lie Too,' 'She Thinks My Tractor's Sexy,' 'She Only Loves Me For My Willie.' No shit! A Willie referring to Willie Nelson, not a cock, though I prefer the latter."

They all stared at Cody. Not just for his long spiel about his partner, whom he'd avoided talking about for months, but that he could remember all those song titles in a genre he hated.

Understanding their confusion, Cody shrugged and said, "The asshole bequeathed me his country music collection. Fuck!"

Into the silence, they all thought about their fallen comrade and then gave their attention to the babe who'd started this whole line of conversation. The babe who was now chatting with not one but two Norse god ex–football players.

"Well, Geek, my man, she had me with the tool belt and the Harley," Slick said.

*Tell me about it!*

"And she *is* hot in a Marilyn Monroe kind of way," JAM added.

*Scorching hot!*

The other men at the table nodded their heads in agreement.

"In fact, that dress looks just like the one Marilyn Monroe wore in that Billy Wilder classic comedy, *Seven Year Itch*. The scene where she's standing over a subway vent," Merrill said. "It sold at auction a couple years ago for almost five million bucks, as I recall."

They all looked at him with amazement. He had

a fool habit of reeling off data his brain amassed like a computer encyclopedia. "I'm just sayin'."

Not surprisingly, F.U. asked, "Do you think those hooters are real?"

"Shhhh!" Merrill and several others cautioned F.U. when it appeared he might be overheard by some women nearby. That's all Merrill would need—the female viewpoint on his love/lust interest. Seated at the next table were some former SEALs, who'd served with Wendy, accompanied by their wives. Zachary "Pretty Boy" Floyd and his wife, Britta, Torolf and Hilda Magnusson, Justin "Cage" LeBlanc and Emelie. Commander Ian MacLean, who still served as the senior officer at the Coronado base, was there with his wife, Madrene. WEALS member Camille Dumaine had come with her husband, Harek Sigurdsson, a computer guru whose I.Q. was almost as high as Merrill's, or so he claimed. Other WEALS teammates of Wendy's, Diane "Grizz" Gomulka and Delphine Arneaux, were in the "Pretty in Pink" wedding party up on the dais, where Merrill should be, as well, actually.

Excusing himself, he made his way around the dance floor, making sure his path didn't cross with she-who-hated-his-guts. Wendy's aunt Mildred and her senior dance club were demonstrating "The Shag," a dance step that was made popular back in the sixties and continued in the Carolinas to this day. They were really good! Especially at their ages, or maybe because of their ages and all those years of experience. Ranging from sixty to eighty, they were proving that age was relative with moves that were almost professional.

With the intricate footwork and hand gestures, they soon had the wedding attendees on their feet, clapping to the beat of that old song "Sixty Minute Man," some of the men calling out crude suggestions to the groom related to the lyrics. Finally, the crowd joined in and there was a pathway down the center where individual couples danced, or rather shagged, their way through the gauntlet.

Merrill saw Gabe Conti leaning against the wall, watching the dancers, and went over to join him. Gabe looked just as miserable as he was in a matching white tux and pink accessories.

"Do you think if we live here long enough we'll be shagging our asses off like that?" Merrill asked.

"I can shag. Hell, I was raised in the Carolinas. It's a rite of passage to learn those dance steps."

"So?" Merrill raised his brows in question. "Why aren't you out there?"

"I don't like to dance, and I feel like an idiot when I do," Gabe slurred out. "Besides, the only reason men . . . most men . . . dance is because they view it as a form of foreplay. As in 'I'll do the friggin' dance if you let me do you later.' I don't expect to be so lucky tonight."

Whoa! That was a mouthful for the usually reserved architect. Merrill guessed that Gabe had imbibed as many adult beverages as he had, if not more. Good thing this was his home. He wouldn't have to worry about a DWI.

"What's with you and Laura? I thought you two

were the new hot item." Merrill was referring to Laura Atler, editor of the local newspaper, *The Bell*.

Gabe shrugged. "I got tired of her ordering me around." At Merrill's look of disbelief, he laughed and said, "She dumped me."

They both watched Laura smiling flirtatiously as she danced down the center pathway with Hamr. How had those two connected already? Hah! Hamr was known for his smooth moves, and, yes, he was looking smooth on the dance floor, too. Who knew Vikings could shag! The dance, not the other kind of shagging, which was an inborn trait, according to all the boastful males in the Magnusson clan. Hamr's brother Torolf was a SEAL, too. Merrill knew the Magnussons well.

Something occurred to Merrill then. "Good Lord! My tongue is numb," he remarked.

"Mine, too," Gabe said.

They both probably looked like idiots then as they tried to stick out their boozy tongues and look at them.

Then Gabe had a sudden inspiration. "Do you think we should try sucking on those vodka ice cubes?"

"Good idea!" Merrill saluted Gabe's suggestion with a high five.

They both pushed away from the wall and almost fell forward. Laughing, they headed toward the bar where the punch bowl was laid out.

But then, a vision in white stepped in front of them, smelling of lemons and sex.

Okay, the scent of sex was probably a fantasy of

his alcohol/testosterone-loaded brain, but he definitely detected the odor of lemons, which he happened to love.

"I need to talk to you," Delilah said.

Merrill twisted to see who she was addressing and leaned a little too far to the left, finding the damn floor was suddenly slanted. Blinking to regain his balance, he decided it must be someone behind him she was talking to.

But no, she was looking right at him, oozing lemon sexiness. And wearing moist-looking red lipstick in a color that could only be called Crimson Slut. Not that he meant *slut* in a bad way. No, this was good sluttiness.

His numb tongue got a sudden hard-on, just taking in her mouth. *No joke! A tongue hard-on. They ought to put me in* Ripley's Believe It or Not. *I wonder what I would get if I saw something more blatantly sexual, like maybe her tongue peeking out with a Hey-Howdy welcome.*

"Did you hear me, Mister Good? I need to talk to you," she repeated.

*Mister Good? Is my father around? No. That's impossible.* "Me?" he asked dumbly.

Meanwhile, Gabe was laughing his ass off at his dumbness. The architect walked off, calling out, "See you later, Geek," at the same time he gave a good luck sign over his shoulder.

"Why did he call you Geek?"

"It's my nickname." When she frowned with confusion—*and, by the way, even her frowns are sexy*—he explained, "Because I'm really smart."

*Could I say anything less smart?* he asked himself, mentally bitch slapping his woozy head.

She arched her brows. "How smart is it that halfway through the reception you're drunk off your ass . . . I mean inebriated. Forgive my language. Can't hold your liquor, huh?"

"I hold my liquor just fine, thank you very much," he said, then spoiled the effect by belching. "'Scuse me."

She rolled her eyes. Then she suggested, "Let's sit down?"

*We better, or I might fall down and topple you to the floor with me. Flatten you into a pancake, an anatomically correct pancake with breasts and a vee-mound and knobby, lickable knees and everything. But, no, we would fit together perfectly. Like a tongue and groove. Tongue again! Oh, crap! Please, God, don't let me have said that out loud. I didn't? Hallelujah! But, man, I am so skunked.*

Unaware of his mental breakdown, she sank into a chair at an empty table and set down her stemmed glass in which a lemon slice floated on top of a murky liquid. A lemonade margarita, he guessed. Ah, that accounted for the lemon scent, but how about the sex scent?

*Aaarrgh!*

*What is it about this woman that makes me into a bumbling sex addict, or rather, sex idiot? She could say algebra, and I would think sex. She could be wearing a tent, and I would think sex. She could be shoveling shit, and I would think sex. No, no, no! That last was crude. What the hell is wrong with me? I can be as smooth as the next guy. Where is my smooth now?*

Merrill eased himself into the chair next to her, carefully.

She was running a fingertip around the rim of her glass, over and over.

Even in his fuzzy condition, he recognized the nervous gesture. *Why is she nervous? Around me?* "What exactly did you need to talk to me about?" he asked. "Especially since you've made it more than clear you want nothing to do with me."

"Money," she said bluntly. "I need money. Ten thousand fucking . . . I mean, flipping dollars. At least. Hopefully."

Merrill blinked. Not the answer he'd been expecting. Not at all.

*Sex for money? Is that what she's saying?*

*And whoa . . . ten thousand George Washingtons! That must be some sex!*

*But I've never paid for sex in my entire life.*

*Would I now?*

*In a hot damn, Crimson Slut minute.*

"Um . . ." His tongue hard-on got harder, just picturing what those Crimson Slut lips could do, which prevented him from speaking for a moment. Good thing because Delilah had more to say, which didn't quite fit in with his Crimson Slut scenario.

"I've heard that you're hiring people for a ship-wreck salvaging operation, and I need a job, like right away."

*Oh! That's what she means. Damn! That's better, of course. But, damn!* He tried his best to hide his disappointment.

To no avail.

"Did you think . . . oh, Lord, you *did*!" She started to stand, a flush rising in her cheeks.

He reached out and pressed a hand on her forearm as the fog in his head began to slowly dissipate. "No. Don't go. I didn't mean to offend you. My only excuse is I'm a little bit snockered. Okay, 'drunk off my ass.'" He tried to smile but was pretty sure that only one side of his mouth turned up. He probably looked like an idiot.

She studied him for a moment before sinking back down. Taking a long swig from her glass, she waited for him to speak.

"Are you a diver?" he asked.

She shook her head.

"Historical antiquities expert?"

She gave him an incredulous look, as in "Are you mocking me?"

"Computer mapping? Boating skills? A mechanic? Nursing? Accounting?"

With each of his questions, her shoulders slumped lower. In truth, he had all the crew he needed, and they were all experienced. "I thought you were working to restore the diner and motel."

"I am, but that requires a shitload . . . well, more money than I have at the moment. It could be months before I open for business."

He shrugged. "You could always get a waitress job or something in town, as a temporary solution. I hear the tips are generous here on the island."

"I could also be a stripper . . ."

He blinked, unable to come up with an answer

that wouldn't put him in the Horndog Hall of Shame.

". . . which isn't going to happen since my tassels are all worn out."

He blinked several more times.

"I'm just kidding. Jeesh!" She shook her head decisively. "I'm not *that* desperate, even though I do need a big chunk of money, up front."

"You think I give advances on earnings? Sign-on bonuses? Hell, salvaging is a gamble at best. The pay is scarcely above minimum wage, the attraction being a piece of the pie for all the crew if we ever actually discover the pie."

"I have basic carpentry and renovation skills, like painting. I can clean like nobody's business. And I can cook. Really well. I know that's not the kind of pie you mean, but don't you need someone to provide meals when you're out on the water? When I open that diner, it will be a huge success. I know it will. But I need a new commercial stove and a propane tank before I can think about lighting a fire."

"Is that what you need the money for? Equipment?"

"No. It's something else."

The flash of fear in her blue eyes was a clear signal to Merrill. He'd been involved in undercover intelligence for too many years not to recognize trouble, and he didn't mean an overdrawn bank account. "What?"

"None of your damn business," she snapped. Then softened her tone when she realized her attitude wasn't helping her prospects. "I'd rather not say."

"I beg your pardon. You want a job, and an advance, with, let me guess, no references, but you won't tell me why you're so desperate." He put up a halting hand and continued, "No, don't try to tell me that you aren't desperate. I might be three sheets to the wind, but I'm not brain-dead. You have to be aware that I have the hots . . . rather, an attraction for you, but you've made it more than clear on every occasion that we've met that I am repugnant to you. So, even though you're not stripper-desperate, I figure you must be really desperate to come to me for help." He arched his brows in question. "Right?"

"Repugnant? I wish!" She cast him a sideways survey. "You are so hot you make my toes curl."

*Whaaat?* He thought about asking her to repeat that remark, but he'd heard her loud and clear. Besides, he didn't want to chance her taking it back. "Then why the cold shoulder?"

"The last thing in the world I need right now is a relationship, for all the obvious reasons . . . a new town, a new business, no time, yada yada . . . but some other reasons, as well."

"Same here," he agreed. But that didn't stop the sap from rising, as his Viking friends were wont to say, and other things from rising, as his SEAL pals were wont to say in a much more graphic fashion. "I thought it was because I offended you with my stupid comment about a porno princess name when we first met."

"Everyone says that. No biggie!" She waved a hand dismissively. "If I've been rude, it's nothing personal."

"It feels fucking personal."

This time she did stand and put her hands on her hips. With her chin raised sky-high, she declared, "Never mind. Forget I asked. It was a fu . . . freakin' long shot, coming to you about a job. Sorry to have bothered you."

There was still that nervousness about her fidgeting hands, and the fearful expression in her eyes. "Are you in trouble?" he asked bluntly.

She closed her eyes for a moment before opening them to look at him directly. Terror stared out at him from the caramel depths before she whispered, "Big-time," but then she raised her chin even higher and asserted, "It's not your problem. I'll figure something out. I always do."

And that cinched the deal! Before she could make a hasty exit, he blurted out, "Okay, you're hired."

Even as he said those words, he felt kind of like Marie Antoinette must have before she stepped up to the guillotine. Ironically, the band morphed into a new song, "Another One Bites the Dust."

"Lilah! I swear, you're enough to give a girl pal-
pitations. I've been sitting here in my living room
with the shades pulled down since Friday night
waiting for your call," said Salome Jones, best
known as Sal by her pals around the casino circuit,
the Slot Machine Fruitcakes, as in "Three cherries,
anyone?" Yes, her grandmother was addicted to the
one-armed bandits, as well as having a fifty-year,
chain-smoking nicotine habit, which she'd kicked,
partly, a few years back by satisfying her cravings
with secondhand smoke in the casinos and puffing away herself on those annoying e-cigarettes.
And, yes, she still considered herself a girl at a
self-proclaimed "youthful sixty-four."

"You mean, you missed church?" This was alarming. Her grandmother never missed church, even
when she'd been on an all-night slot bender.

"For the first time in fifteen years," her grandmother said with disgust. "Didn't want to chance
Jimmy the Goon breaking my legs on the way
home. And you know how important my legs are."

Delilah rolled her eyes. At one time, her grandmother had been an exotic dancer. Not to be confused with a stripper, she was always quick to
add. In fact, she'd been a Las Vegas showgirl, before returning back in the 70s to Atlantic City and
the family home. The vintage row house, with
wide, steep steps rising to a front porch and a brick
two-story dwelling, was located on one of the side
streets leading to the famous boardwalk. Once a
desirable neighborhood. Now borderline skid row.

Her grandmother probably exaggerated the danger she was in. At least, Delilah hoped the situation hadn't progressed in the past few days from serious to life threatening. James Goodson, aka Jimmy the Goon, was eighty-five if he was a day.

"I told you I'd call as soon as I had news," Delilah said.

"And do you?" Delilah heard the sound of puffing as her grandmother vaped between words. In the background she could also hear the song "It's a Hard-Knock Life," and knew that her almost five-year-old daughter, Magdalene Jones, was probably eating breakfast on a TV tray, watching that old *Annie* DVD, the original, not the remake. Maggie adored the songs and knew them all by heart. It had been Delilah's favorite movie as a child, too. She wasn't sure why. Maybe because being raised by a single grandparent as she had herself been and being raised by a single great-grandparent as Maggie was, felt a little bit like being an orphan.

Which about broke Delilah's heart.

It was no kind of life for a kid to be glued to a TV, instead of running around the neighborhood. But Atlantic City was no Mister Rogers' Neighborhood these days, and hadn't been for a long, long time. Better TV brain freeze than playgrounds marked by drug dealers or stray bullets.

And better *Annie* than her grandmother's third addiction, reality TV shows. There was *Real Housewives of New York City, Real Housewives of Beverly Hills, Real Housewives of Atlanta*. With a sigh, Delilah assured her grandmother, "I'll be wiring you the money tomorrow." *I hope.*

"All of it? Ten thousand dollars?"

"Yes." *I hope.*

"Thank you, Jesus!"

*No, thank the guy who's advancing me the money and for which I will be indebted for months. But, yes, thank Jesus, too, because He probably influenced Merrill Good's decision to help me.* Delilah sighed again. She could berate her grandmother for getting in so deep with a loan shark to the point where she was three months behind in rent and utilities and her gambling debt was rising by leaps and bounds at 33 percent interest per week, but the old "girl" already felt bad enough. Besides, Delilah owed her grandmother too much, not just for raising her after her mother died in a drunk driver hit-and-run when Delilah was only six but for taking custody of Maggie when she was born two months into Delilah's five-year incarceration in the Edna Mahan Correctional Facility for Women in Clinton, New Jersey.

Five months out, and Delilah still shuddered over the mere thought of that place.

"Promise me, Gram. This money pays off your damn debts."

"I thought you gave up cussin'."

Delilah had developed quite a potty mouth in prison, which she was trying to clean up, for the sake of her daughter if nothing else. "Damn isn't a swear word."

"You sure about that? I should ask Father Sylvester."

"Aaarrgh! Stop changing the *damn* subject. None

of this money goes into the casino for a quick double-or-nothing. Promise?"

"Absolutely. Cross my heart and hope to die. I've learned my lesson."

In the old days prior to her clean language vow, Delilah would have gone on a tirade, chastising her grandmother, "When have I heard that before? For cripe's sake, Gram, grow up and get your ass in shape. Stop wasting your money in the fucking casinos." Instead, she said, "It's time to make some changes in your life, Gram."

More puffing and more "Hard-Knock Life" could be heard before her grandmother continued in an obvious attempt to avoid a commitment to change. "How's the diner renovation going?"

In one ear and out the other! It was useless trying to change her grandmother at this stage, Delilah realized. All she could do was try to curb her impulses. So, she answered her question. "Endless! I spent all morning outside, cleaning and reconditioning the red vinyl covering on the stools. All twelve of them! A bitch of a job! I have no fingernails left, and the skin on my hands looks like red, wrinkled prunes. Next I'll have to work on the booths."

"Whatcha been usin'?" Puff, puff, puff.

"GOOP. That waterless hand cleaner. I saw it on YouTube. Rub it in real good, hose it off, and let it dry in the sun. Even the cracked vinyl comes back to life."

"Delilah Jones! You know what you gotta use, don't you?"

"Don't tell me," Delilah said with a laugh. "Skin So Soft."

"You know it, honey."

Aside from being an exotic dancer, and a restaurant hostess when the dancing gigs ran out before she was old enough to collect social security, and a gambler, Sal Jones was a noted Avon Lady from way back, selling the beauty products on the side. Acquaintances used to duck and hide when they saw her coming down the street. On the other hand, many people became bosom pals and welcomed her monthly visits for the conversation as much as the products. It was the non-Internet version of social media.

Of all the items Sal schlepped around in her big purse, the bestseller was the famous, or infamous, Skin So Soft, a bath oil product that supposedly had a thousand alternative uses, everything from bug repellent to treating head lice to spot remover to fabric softener to hoof polish for horses. Besides that, her grandmother had a ginormous collection of vintage Avon perfume and aftershave bottles in the shape of cars, animals, figurines, even a pistol, which she believed would be worth a fortune someday. Too bad she couldn't have sold that for ten thousand dollars!

There was even an Elvis figurine, for chriss—for heaven's sake! Now *that*, Delilah might borrow to put on display in the motel office. If she ever waded through the piles of paper and debris enough to clear a shelf!

". . . and not just that. Every time someone sits on

those seats, they'll get a little whiff of that heavenly scent."

Delilah realized that her grandmother was still extolling the virtues of Skin So Soft while her mind had been wandering.

"Why don't you come down here and show me how it's done, Gram?" she suggested. It wasn't the first time she'd invited her grandmother to move here, and she knew what the answer would be.

"Sorry, sweetie, but I'm used to my own things, and my friends here. Squatters would probably move in if I left the house empty for more than a few weeks. They'd be rummaging through my Avon stuff, looking for drugs. Besides, it will be easier for you to get things in order without me and Maggie underfoot. She'll be there soon enough."

In other words, her grandmother wouldn't leave the casino neighborhood. And she'd be bored out of her gourd without cable TV, which Delilah had yet to connect, an unnecessary expense. No use anyhow since the circa 1990 sets in the eight motel rooms were not only not smart TVs, nor flat screens, but they were mini-size. Some might even be black-and-white.

"Have you registered Maggie for kindergarten there yet?" her grandmother asked, clearly changing the subject.

"Not yet. I need to regain parental rights, legally. First step is having you release guardianship, but, in order to do that, I have to establish a suitable residency here for a young child. That means a home with a separate bedroom for her, running water, a working kitchen, everything that makes a place a home. My parole officer is adamant about that."

She glanced around the small efficiency behind the motel office that she was using for an apartment. It was barely habitable, her efforts being focused more on getting the diner operational, and after that the motel rooms. She could just see the CPS officer checking this out and sniffing, not just at the smell of mildew and mice, but years and years of neglect. So many things to do! First off, she'd bake some cinnamon rolls to mask the odors.

Her grandmother sighed or puffed out a vapor. Hard to tell which. "Well, it better happen soon."

"Because of school starting in seven weeks?"

"That, and Jimmy the Goon. It's not safe here."

"Gram! Son of a bitch!" *Oops!* "If you're worried about danger, even after you pay off the loan, you better hightail it down here, too, at least for a few months." *You can do without the fucking . . . um,* darn *slots that long.*

"Maggie wants to talk to you, hon."

More changing the subject.

After some shuffling noises, Delilah heard, "Hi, Mommy."

"Hello, sweetheart."

"Can I have a puppy?"

This had been Maggie's constant refrain, which hadn't worked with her grandmother because of her working so much and Maggie being in day care. No one to train or take a dog out to do its business during the day. But, sensing Delilah's guilt over not being around for her daughter these past five years, she'd amped her requests, steering them in Delilah's direction, and added a bit of whine factor.

"Maybe when you're a little older."

"But Nancy Fulton has a dog, and she's only four. And Freddie Cole got two puppies." *Sniff, sniff!* Definitely a whine with a little fake sob tossed in.

"We'll see when you get to Bell Cove." Time for Delilah to change the subject. "I heard you watching *Annie.* I can't wait to watch it with you."

"Annie has a dog. Sandy. I'm going to name my dog Sandy."

Delilah refused to fall for that bait.

So her devious daughter switched bait. "Did you find us a Daddy Warbucks yet?"

Delilah laughed. It was a make-believe game she and her daughter played. Every time Maggie asked when she could come live with her, Delilah would say, "As soon as I find us a Daddy Warbucks." In other words, as soon as she had enough money. "Bald-headed rich guys are hard to find."

"Mom-my!"

"Just kidding. Guess we'll have to make our own fortunes."

"Stop teasing, Mommy."

"Okay, but don't you be worrying, Miss Mag-Annie. We'll be together pretty soon. Have you been marking the days on the calendar I sent you?"

"Yep. I can't wait. I'm gonna go to school in a town made of bells where everyone is friendly and there are no bad people and we're gonna open a restaurant with peanut butter and banana sandwiches and I'm gonna have my own bedroom with Annie wallpaper and betcha there will be a dog just waiting for me to—"

"Whoa, whoa, whoa. One thing at a time."

Once Delilah clicked off, promising to call again the next evening, she sat for a long moment, staring into the distance. Normally, Delilah was not a list maker, but she pulled out a notebook now.

Her first list involved her daughter, Maggie, and everything she needed to do for her move to the Outer Banks to take place:

—Diner running.
—Furniture. Maggie's bedroom. Living room.
—Regain legal guardianship.
—CPS home inspection.
—Parole meeting.
—Kindergarten registration.
—Sell motorcycle.
—Buy used car & child's booster seat.

Heck, while she was at it, she might as well make a list for the diner. It was probably unrealistic, but she hoped to have the diner open for business before Labor Day. But before that, she needed to:

—Finish vinyl restoration.
—Replace Formica countertop.
—Electrician: cooktops, ovens, fridge, freezer.
—Spray-paint the diner.
—Call food suppliers.
—Design & print menu.

   —Jukebox repairman?
   —Business license. Food permits.
   —Hire staff.

Delilah didn't expect to get to the motel renovations until winter when business on the Outer
Banks would come almost to a standstill. It was a
shame, too, because there was almost no lodging
for tourists in Bell Cove. But before she could open
the eight rooms, she would need:

   —Interior & exterior painting.
   —Plumbing & electrical updates.
   —Mattresses, drapes, bedspreads, linens, shower
   curtains, towels, toiletries.
   —TVs.

If she let herself dwell on the immensity of the
task she'd set for herself, she would want to give up
before she even started. A miracle would come in
handy about now, or at the least a Daddy Warbucks
as she'd teased Maggie about.
*Can anyone say sugar daddy?*
*No!* She wouldn't even joke about something like
that. She would do this on her own, or not at all.
She set her notebook aside and walked outside,
inhaling deeply of the fresh, salty air. Across the
dunes and rocky shore, she could see the pure
blue sky over the sparkling waters of Bell Sound.
A beautiful sight. But one Delilah could hardly see
over the haze of her misted eyes.
But, no, she would not cry! The last time she'd let

tears flow was five years ago when she'd learned how her high school sweetheart, Davie Zekus, had betrayed her, flipping for the Atlantic County prosecutor. His reward: life without parole for murdering the convenience store clerk. Hers: five years' incarceration for accessory to armed robbery and murder. There had been lots of time during the years she'd been trapped in that notorious women's prison when she'd wanted to break down and give up. But she hadn't, and now, well, she was a different person. Not so naive. Never again would she trust her future to another person. She stood on her own.

She was jarred from her reverie by a noise emanating from around front. The clatter of metal. Walking over to the side of the building, she looked and saw Merrill Good approaching after having apparently tripped over the three ten-foot chrome metal tubes that comprised the diner's counter kick bar. She'd been polishing it yesterday and needed to store it under a tarp until she was ready to reinstall it inside. Of course, it had to be her boss who practically killed himself over her "debris."

"Oh, sh—!" she started to mutter, changed to, "Oh, shazam!"

Talk about perfect timing! Not! And talk about the wrong man in the wrong place at the wrong time. She did a mental fanning of her heated face. The man oozed sexiness, even with his bloodshot eyes and day-old whiskers, sweaty T-shirt and shorts and athletic shoes that probably cost as much as the "lightly used" high-end commercial fridge she'd been eyeing on eBay. He was six-foot-three of pure temptation.

Her very own Daddy Warbucks.

Sort of.

Minus the bald head.

Good thing Maggie wasn't here yet. She'd be asking Merrill if she could shave his scalp.

*Actually . . .*

*Nah.*

*I must have inhaled too much GOOP.*

# Chapter 3

*He would be her kryptonite, or die trying . . .*

$D$espite his hangover and despite his instincts not to come on too strong, Merrill showed up at Delilah's property on Sunday morning. There didn't appear to be anyone around, so he decided to explore a little bit. On the other hand, maybe he should escape before she ever knew his pathetic self was on the premises.

He opted for pathetic.

The vintage motel and diner were marked by the hokey names of Heartbreak Motel and Rock Around the Clock Diner, but then this was a town that celebrated hokeyness. Every friggin' business and home had its own distinctive bell or chime. Bats in their belfries, for sure.

Take the business names, for example. The town square was a testament to kitschy monikers. The Cracked Crab. Hard Knocks Hardware. Happy Feet Emporium. Styles and Smiles. Blanket-y Blank, a quilt store. And the Christmas Shoppe, often mispronounced as Shoppie.

Hell, it was a town that invented a Grinch contest

last Christmas. The ultimate in schmaltz. In fact, the billboard outside of town read: "Get Grinched! Welcome to Bell Cove." And it was home to the ugly Rutledge Christmas trees, Charlie Brown look-alikes that were popular throughout the Outer Banks.

Truth to tell, Merrill loved Bell Cove *because of* all its quirks and oddball characters. Why else would he have relocated here?

But it wasn't the schmaltzy Elvis connection that struck Merrill now as he gazed around Delilah's site. It was the run-down condition of the diner, which fronted Bayside Road, and the once bright blue motel, which was set back about sixty feet, closer to the dunes on the Bell Sound side of the island. Admittedly, it was a good location for a business, on a corner lot along a thoroughfare leading to town, which would be busy in high season, and there would probably be a nice view from the rear of the motel, but, frankly, the two structures looked like teardowns to him. It would take a hell of a lot more than ten thousand dollars to get these dumps back in shape. Not that Delilah had said she would use the money for that purpose. Nope, by the looks of things—the sanded rust spots on the diner, the ladder and tools, paint sprayers and paint cans sporting the neon red, neon blue, and silver colors of the diner, the wet vinyl counter stools drying in the sun next to a gallon container of something called GOOP—she intended to use elbow grease to single-handedly bring Elvis back to life.

Good luck with that!

Just *his* luck, he tripped over a couple of metal pipes creating a god-awful clatter. He righted himself but before he had a chance to duck and head for cover, he noticed Delilah peeking around the back of the motel. *Busted!* And she was pissed at first sight of him, if the hands on hips and the scowl on her face were any indication. But then, she quickly wiped away the scowl, probably figuring it wasn't a good idea to annoy the gift horse, meaning him, who was definitely feeling like a horse's ass.

Normally, he was not such a clumsy, uncool guy. Maybe he was suffering some kind of PTSD or withdrawal from the military kind of thing. Maybe he was going to turn from G.I. Joe to Forrest Gump. Maybe Delilah was Merrill's "Jenny." Maybe he would start running across the country like good ol' Tom Hanks. Maybe now would be a good time to start.

The scowl might have left Delilah's face, but she kept her hands on her hips. An unconscious attitude statement. Obviously, she was not a fan of Forrest Gump, or him. In the chocolate box of her life, he was one of those hated, blah cream fillings. Who wanted that when they could have caramels, or cashews, or his favorite, cherries?

*Yep, PTSD!*

"Hi!" he said, *lame as Forrest on his best day*, walking up to her, quickly adding, "Don't worry. I'm not going to start hanging around, or anything. I was out for my morning run," (*Can anyone say Forrest Gump?*) "and thought I'd drop by and give you the check." He patted the pocket of his shorts.

"Oh." Her face heated with color and her hands dropped to her sides.

And he felt like even more of a horse's ass. Shiiit! The last thing he wanted was to embarrass her over the money, or to make her be nice to him only because she needed to.

"I thought you'd be hungover this morning," she said.

"My head clears when I run. Comes from years of five-mile runs in the morning and in the evening with the teams." He flinched at his running mouth, then conceded with a rueful shrug. "But, yeah, there's a mother of all sledgehammers pounding inside my head right now."

She smiled.

*I'm in!* Sensing the tiniest break in her armor, he did a mental fist pump in the air and returned the smile.

"Would you like a cup of coffee? Or a cold drink?"

*Definitely in!* Two fist pumps now. Really, Delilah had this wall around herself where he was concerned. He pictured it as some super-strong translucent material that only a certain person or weapon could penetrate. Hell, there wasn't a weapon in the world he didn't know inside out and backward. Besides, if he could break down a steel-reinforced door in an Al-Qaeda hideout with just the kick of his boot, he could handle this, even if it meant chipping away one sliver at a time. Piece of cake! "I would love a cup of coffee, Delilah," he said with the innocent flutter of his eyelashes he'd perfected over the years.

"You can call me Lilah. Everyone does," she conceded then.

"Um. I think I prefer De-li-lah, if you don't mind. It's different. Plus, it sort of rolls off the tongue, nice and smooth." *Like a hot, slick French kiss on a first date.*

She eyed him suspiciously, then motioned for him to follow her. Which was no chore at all. Her back view was almost as good as her front one. And she wasn't even dressed in anything sexy. Just a pair of cutoff denims, a black tank top, and white sneakers. Her blonde hair, more silvery than gold toned, was piled on top of her head with one of those claw combs. Her waist was small, her hips flared out, and she had a rounded ass that would just about fit in his big hands. Not to mention she was above average in height for a woman, five-eight or five-nine, which meant long, supple legs that gave a guy ideas.

*Face it, I have way too many ideas.*

They went through an old-fashioned—and decrepit—wooden screen door at the back of the motel office into a large room that served as a combination living room and kitchen. Off to one side was a small, separate bedroom and a tiny bathroom with a shower stall, no tub. Very basic. In fact, shabby. And not shabby chic, either. But it was clean, and livable, he supposed. Plus, there was a delicious, sweet smell in the air. She must have been baking.

God forbid that he should mention his thoughts because her chin was raised defensively, as if just waiting for his criticism of her humble abode. But then she went over to the small bar dividing the kitchenette from the rest of the room and poured coffee into two mugs from an old-fashioned electric percolator, the metal type his grandmother used to have, and raised her brows at him. "Sugar? Milk?"

"Neither," he said, walking up and placing the envelope on the counter. Best to get this out of the way, up front. "The check is drawn on a local bank, made out to you. If you need cash right away, you can cash it, or get a cashier's check. Whatever you need."

"Thank you," she said, not bothering to open the envelope. Clearly, she was embarrassed. And proud. "When do I start work?"

He took a sip of coffee, and then another. It was good. "Can you be at a meeting tomorrow afternoon at our office? Two p.m.? It'll be the first meet-and-greet for the group I've put together."

She hesitated before nodding.

"Is that a problem?"

"No. I just need to plan my time so I can work on the diner during the off hours. No biggie."

It was a damn big biggie, in his opinion. He thought about suggesting that she hire someone to help, but then realized she wouldn't be asking him for a loan—rather an advance—if she had any extra cash. "Some of your work, especially in the beginning, can be done here or at our office. You'll need to plan menus, order food supplies, assess what cooking supplies are on board currently, that kind of thing. But you'll be a housekeeper, as well, or rather a boat keeper, meaning cleaning, laundering towels and bed linens."

"Oh, shit! I mean, oh, boy! I didn't think about the fucking sleeping arrangement. Oops, I mean freakin' . . ." She shrugged at another of her failed attempts to clean up her language.

He grinned. "No fucking there. Too close proximity unless you go for that sort of thing. No, *Sweet Bells* sleeps up to fifteen people in a pinch, ten comfortably, in four closet-sized bedrooms and two pullout cots in the salon or break room. But don't be picturing anything fancy. It's a sixty-five-foot former tramp steamer refitted into a diving boat."

"In other words, not a yacht."

"Hardly. Anyhow, aside from cooking and cleaning, I figure you'll be a Jack of All Trades . . . or Jill of All Trades, filling in wherever you're needed. Any problem with that?"

"No problem. I'm a hard worker, and I really am a good cook." She smiled tentatively at him. "*Sweet Bells*? Is that the name of your boat?"

"Yep. It used to be *Sweet Jinx*. Named after the Jinkowsky family that founded the original treasure hunting company, Jinx, Inc. *Sweet Bells* seemed like a good change, in light of our headquarters being here in Bell Cove and us sharing space and a wharf with Bell Forge."

She probably didn't understand what he'd just said, but she didn't ask for clarification. Instead, she wanted to know, "How many people will I be cooking for?"

"Just eight, including you. Some will only be part-time, or as needed."

"Will I be full-time?"

"Whenever we go out, yeah."

She nodded her acceptance of that news. "I read about your first project . . . the one involving the three saint shipwrecks. It's only about five miles off-shore. Does that mean you'll return every night?"

Her question was telling. Was she thinking that she could get a few hours of work in on her diner after working all day on a salvage boat? "No, we won't return to base every night. We have to protect our site once we start. If we leave it unguarded, even just overnight, especially when we've located a wreck, someone else could move in and steal whatever they can grab."

"Pirates?" Her tone suggested disbelief.

"Oh, yeah!"

"Dangerous?"

"Maybe. Probably not."

"Well, let's hope they look like Johnny Depp in the *Pirates of the Caribbean* movies."

*A joke? From the woman who usually treats me like the devil incarnate.* "Or Zoe Saldana."

"Touché!"

She grabbed a plate of frosted pastries that looked like cinnamon buns, the obvious source of the sweet scent that filled the room, and, without words, they walked outside with their coffees and sat on folding chairs beside a rusted white patio table. She shoved the plate toward him, which was his cue to try her offering. One bite, and his eyes widened with surprise. He wasn't big on sweets, but this pastry was exceptional. "Wow! What *are* these?"

"Cinnamon buns. With a twist. I call them Delilah's Delights. These are caramel-apple flavored."

"Delilah's Delights, huh? Well, I'm . . . delighted."

She smiled. "I told you I'm a good cook."

While he devoured the rest of his pastry, and then another, they sat in silence. It was only ten a.m. but the sun was hot, promising a blistering, over 100-degree day. For now, there was a slight breeze off the water to relieve the heat, but it wouldn't last long.

"This really is a nice property," he remarked. "Have you considered selling and buying a place needing less work?" Waterfront land, even one with a rocky shore like this one, would sell for big bucks to a developer in a condo minute.

"I wish," she said, "but not possible. My uncle Clyde . . . actually, my great-uncle . . . left this place to me on the condition that I get the diner and motel up and running within a year, and that I keep it going for at least five years."

"Otherwise?"

"Otherwise, it goes to some Veterans for Elvis type organization."

"Are you serious?"

"As a heart attack."

"Where you from?"

"New Jersey."

"Really? So am I." Wouldn't it be ironic if they'd

lived in neighboring towns and never met? "I grew up in Princeton. How about you?"

"Atlantic City, which is like the other side of the world compared to Princeton. Caviar and boardwalk hot dogs different."

"I don't recall my parents ever serving caviar at the innumerable faculty parties they held. More like cheese and crackers washed down with lots of wine." Truth to tell, they were imported cheeses, like pule which was made from the milk of Serbian donkeys, or precious slivers filled with crap like truffles that cost as much as filet mignon. And crackers—oh, Lord! The crackers could only be purchased from some specialty shop in Manhattan. And the wines were shipped by the crate from their favorite California vineyard.

His parents were intellectual snobs, traveling in a crowd that basked in their PhDs and academic scholarships. Imagine their shock and dismay when he'd chosen the military over some "higher" calling. But they also considered themselves food connoisseurs. Imagine what they would think of an Elvis-themed diner and a menu that probably depended on oil—a lot of oil, for frying everything from burgers to pickles.

Whatever! He'd stopped caring about his parents' freely offered opinions a long time ago.

"Do you have any brothers or sisters?" she asked.

Oh, crap! He did not want to delve into that old history. Especially . . . Oh, what the hell! "I have a brother, Ben, who's about thirty-seven now. Two years older than me." For a second, his chest hurt, like his heart was being squeezed, just thinking about his brother, whom he hadn't seen or spoken to in five years, ever since the last big blowup with his parents. Ben, who was doing research in biophysics at Johns Hopkins last time he'd heard, something to do with brain injuries following head trauma, had sided with his parents against him.

"You're thirty-five?" she asked, homing in on the least important part of what he'd said, or thought. "You don't look any older than twenty-five."

"The bane of my life," he said, forcing a grin. "I've always had a baby face, which was a good and a bad thing. I got away with murder because of my seeming innocence, but I got carded until I was thirty, which was embarrassing and a pain in the ass. Eventually, I grew into my face. At least, I hope I did. I'd hate to look like a teenager when I'm seventy with white hair and wrinkles."

"Women would envy you. I envy you."

"For looking young. Pff! If you looked any better, the female population of three states would put a hit out on you."

She stiffened up, like always when he made some comment about her appearance.

So he changed the subject. "Do you have any family around?"

"In Atlantic City?" she asked, then went on before he could elaborate. "My grandmother is still there. She raised me after my mother got killed by a drunk driver when I was only five."

He was about to ask about her father, or any

other family, but she stood and said, "Thank you so much, Merrill, for bringing the check over here today. Please know how much I appreciate your consideration."

He didn't know about consideration so much as his own pleasure. "You don't need to thank me. I expect to be paid back."

"That's not what I meant. You bringing the check here this morning knowing I need the money right away . . . it speaks to your sensitivity."

"That is just what a guy needs to hear. That he has a sensitive side. Next you'll be mentioning my inner female."

She asked him the strangest thing then. "When you were in the military, did you ever shave your head?"

"Yeah. When we did survival training in a jungle setting, with all the bugs and crap, being hairless was a lot more comfortable. Why? Do you have a thing for baldies?"

"No."

"That's good because, instead of looking like a hot Dwayne Johnson, 'The Rock,' I look like Humpty Dumpty before the fall."

"I doubt that sincerely," she said. "On your worst day, you are about a hundred on the hottie meter, hairless or not."

Which just about made his day—or year.

# Chapter 4

*The Welcome Wagon was unwelcome . . .*

*P*eople were being nice to her.

*Dammit!*

Too nice.

*Dammit!*

Even when she was borderline rude to them, they persisted in being neighborly. In other words, nice.

*Dammit!*

Delilah needed to maintain her privacy if she wanted to hide her sordid past. Niceness led to neighborliness, which led to friendships, which led to confidences, which led to open books.

What would all these people think if they knew her open book—the real Delilah Jones? Convicted felon. Unwed mother. No education except for a prison GED. Granddaughter of a gambling grandmother. Trailer park trash without the trailer.

Oh, her secrets would come out eventually, she supposed. At least some of them. Maggie, for example, would be coming here next month. Delilah wasn't ashamed of having a child. Not one bit. But she didn't want to reveal that her baby had been born in a prison clinic where she'd been badgered by officials to give her up for adoption, something she'd adamantly refused, finally signing over guardianship to her grandmother. That decision had not endeared her to some prison sadists who'd undoubtedly had potential adopters in line, for a fat fee.

If there was anything she'd learned in prison, it was to trust no one. People would be all nicey-nice and friendly and helpful, and before you knew it, you were being turned in to authorities by them for some minor transgression. Or they would be expecting some favor in return for their niceness. Everyone was out for themselves.

Delilah shook her head to rid her mind of the horrible memories.

More important, people here were bound to ask where she'd been working in recent years. Did she have job experience running a business, or better yet, as a chef? Hah! Working in the prison kitchen hardly qualified her as a budding entrepreneur or to be a Cordon Bleu anything, but she had read constantly—cookbooks, of all things. Comfort food for the hungry soul.

After two years into her incarceration, a new kitchen superintendent arrived who grudgingly allowed Delilah, a model prisoner, to practice her recipes during her free hours. Her Sunday-night dinners became a treat for many on the kitchen staff. Her flavored cinnamon rolls were especially popular, and she planned to feature them in the diner. Delilah's Delights, she would call them, as she'd told Merrill. She was still experimenting with her recipes, but so far she decided on: Peachy Praline Cinnamon Rolls, as well as Strawberry Walnut, Cream Cheese Pecan, Ginger Apple, Orange Marmalade, White Chocolate Chip Raspberry, Honey Pistachio, and today's Caramel Apple Cinnamon Rolls. Best of all, in honor of Uncle Clyde's passion, there would be Peanut Butter and Banana Cinnamon Rolls, both crunchy and creamy.

Delilah had known while she was still in prison that the diner and motel were going to be bequeathed to her by a bachelor great-uncle, her grandmother's brother, whom she'd only met once, as a child. She'd also known that Uncle Clyde had cancer, having exchanged letters with him starting with her conviction. He had empathized with her, having served time himself as a young man. Thus, she'd been informed when he passed away last year. But that meant that the businesses had been closed for more than six months when she'd finally arrived here on the barrier island. Only then had she discovered that they'd been closed half the time before that, while her uncle suffered through years of cancer treatments.

After her initial shock at the mess she was facing and the conditions of Uncle Clyde's will, Delilah realized that quitting was not an option. First of all, she'd let the restaurant become her dream. Secondly, finding another job would be difficult if not impossible. Checking off "Have you ever been convicted of a felony?" on a job application doomed her prospects to failure.

And so, she established a plan for herself. Live frugally. Work to get the diner open first. Bring Maggie to live with her. After that, renovate the motel. Depend only on herself. Trust no one.

Therefore, what she did not need was a bunch of people hanging around, being all welcome-wagoney, peppering her with questions, pretending to be her new best friends, probably with ulterior motives. Even those who were sincere in their overtures posed a danger to her plan.

Every day of the five months she'd been in Bell Cove so far, someone—often multiple someones—invaded her privacy with offers of advice or friendship or just plain nosiness.

She soon found out that today, the day after the Independence Day wedding reception, was going to be no different. The Sunday from Hell had started off with Merrill Good, who was a godsend to her in some ways (*like a ten-thousand-dollar godsend, thank you very much*), but a devilsend in others (*like what angel has bedroom eyes that tempt good girls to do bad things?*).

After sharing a coffee with her, Merrill stuck around for more than an hour, insisting on helping her to unscrew the vinyl seats off the booths and carrying them outside for her GOOP treatments. If he hadn't made previous plans to meet some of his military buddies for lunch before they returned to California, he probably would have stayed all day.

*Yikes!*

His ulterior motive was glaringly obvious to her.

The guy looked at her and saw sex on a stick. And he didn't even try to hide the fact that he wanted her, which was commendable. In a way. In terms of honesty. And, in terms of wanting her but putting himself on a short leash. Restraining himself from hustling her hard probably had ulterior motives, though; he must fear crossing the line in today's tenuous employer/employee sexual harassment environment.

Little did he know she wasn't about to sue anyone. That kind of publicity she did not want or need.

Besides, he'd done nothing wrong, except for being too damned nice, even as he cast those smoldering looks her way.

*Niceness . . . bah humbug!* Too bad she hadn't been around last Christmas when they'd held that Grinch contest. She would have won hands down.

After Merrill left, another vehicle pulled up. Surprise, surprise!

A gray-haired woman, who couldn't be more than five feet tall, got out on the driver's side, then took a metal walker out of the backseat. Hobbling over to where Delilah was hosing off the vinyl booth seats that she'd already gooped an hour ago, the woman greeted her warmly. "Well, hello there, dear. Looks like you've been a busy bee today."

"Yep. A lot of work, but the old vinyl is starting to look almost new."

"It certainly is. I remember when Clyde first installed them. Back in the 1970s, I think, after he returned from Vietnam. Forgive me for not coming around sooner, but I'm still recovering from double knee surgery last winter. I'm Ina Rogers, secretary for Our Lady by the Sea Church."

"And I'm Lilah Jones," Delilah said. After the way Merrill reacted to her name, perhaps her nickname would be more appropriate, attract less attention. "Ironically, I grew up going to a church called Our Lady Star of the Sea."

"Really? Where was that?"

*I stepped into that one.* "Atlantic City."

"You're Catholic?"

*That one, too.* "Lapsed."

Ina waved a hand dismissively, her attitude being like that of Delilah's grandmother, *Once a Catholic, always a Catholic.* "You're welcome to attend anytime, Lilah, and of course I'm in the church office every weekday morning if you want to register."

"Maybe later." Delilah figured that she would probably go back to church again once Maggie was here. A good example. In fact, she found herself disclosing, "My daughter will be here with me soon. I'm sure we'll see you then."

"A daughter? How nice! How old is she?"

"Four and a half."

"Oh, good! She can join the children's bell choir."

"Maggie would love that."

"Is your husband coming, too?"

"No husband," Delilah said, and declined to elaborate as Ina's gray eyebrows rose in question. To Ina's credit, she didn't appear judgmental, just interested.

Delilah realized that, by tomorrow, word would

have spread around town that she had a daughter and that she was a single parent. Oh, well. It would have to come out sometime. Maybe it was better this way.

"I knew your uncle Clyde very well, you know." Ina was already off on another subject. "Oh, the stories I could tell!" Her faded blue eyes twinkled at some presumably naughty memory.

*Good heavens!* Was this old woman implying . . . ?

Delilah pulled two web-type lawn chairs from her junk heap and ended up serving Ina a glass of iced lemonade and a cinnamon bun on a turned-over tomato crate covered with an Elvis place mat. There were about two hundred of them in the storage shed, celebrating his various movies. She might frame a few later on.

Ina oohed and aahed over the pastry, while Delilah pumped her for juicy details on Uncle Clyde, who'd apparently been a notorious ladies' man, "handsome as the devil" in a ducktail hair-style, which he sported right up till the end. Her uncle's funeral had been quite the local affair with a guitar-shaped coffin and Elvis music on the church sound system, rather than hymns, al-though there had been a poignant Elvis rendition of "Amazing Grace" that had brought the house— rather, church—down.

*Good grief!* Delilah wished she could have been there.

Before she left, Ina managed to finagle a trip in-side Delilah's quarters on the pretext of a potty visit, but probably to snoop around. After her snoop fest, Ina insisted that Delilah accept the gift of a convertible sofa bed and matching chair in a "lovely teal blue" that were just sitting in her basement. Oh, and she might have a roll or two of matching teal-and-white-striped wallpaper, left over from a bedroom she'd redecorated ten years ago. It would make a lovely "accent wall," according to Ina, who watched a lot of HGTV when she wasn't working at the church office. Ina would have Eddie Van Hoy, the town's taxi driver/delivery person, bring the furniture over later this week.

In the end, all Delilah could say was, "That is so nice of you." *Dammit!*

Ina took an orange-ginger cinnamon roll wrapped in plastic wrap home to have for a snack later. Delilah figured it would be good for business. Word-of-mouth promotion, literally, before her grand opening.

Delilah had barely hosed off the booths' vinyl seats when a pickup truck pulled up in front of the diner. There was a logo on the side for Hard Knocks, the local hardware store, where she'd done some business, mainly odd supplies and tools that weren't available in Uncle Clyde's arsenal.

Frank Baxter, the owner, emerged and immediately began unloading commercial-size cans of paint onto a dolly, which he rolled up to her and asked, "Where you want me to put these, honey?"

From Frank, who was in his sixties and sporting the world's worst comb-over, rather comb-forward, of orangish-brown hair, which was clearly dyed, badly, it was hard to do anything but smile at his endearment. He was just being nice.

"What's this, Frank? I didn't order anything?"

"Was cleaning out my warehouse and discovered all these paints your uncle ordered before he got so sick. Figure no one else is gonna want neon red, neon blue, and silver high glossies."

"Frank, I can't afford to buy these right now. There must be at least two hundred to three hundred dollars' worth of paint there. Maybe later if you can hold on to them."

Frank waved a hand dismissively. "No problem. Besides, it was a special order, and, like I said, no one else is gonna buy these metallic colors. Consider it a welcome to Bell Cove gift. No, you don't have to thank me. Just buy your other supplies from me, instead of that blasted Internet, like some folks around here do."

"You can be sure of that, Frank." She surprised both him and herself when she almost reached up and gave him a hug. Usually, she avoided physical contact of any kind with people. Instead, she shook his hand.

Still, she thought, *Nice, nice, nice!*

*Dammit!*

Before he left, she asked, "How do you feel about cinnamon rolls?"

Thus, two more of her pastries hit the road. Apple cinnamon and pistachio lime.

Eliza Rutledge, whose grandson got married the day before, came by, too, with two high school boys who worked for her at the Rutledge Tree Farm and Landscaping business. Eliza brought a dozen flowering bushes, some bedding flowers, and a pile of mulch to "pretty up the front of the diner." When Delilah tried to protest, Eliza scolded her, "I know pride when I see it, girl. Just say thank you, and let it go."

"Thank you," Delilah said. Within an hour, the bushes were planted, and the diner, as dilapidated as it still was, did look better.

*Could a person die from niceness?*

Eliza also left with a cinnamon roll for her afternoon break. A plain one, iced with raisins.

Next up were Stuart and Barbara MacLeod, owners of Blankety-Blank, Historic South Carolina Quilts, who arrived in a white panel van decorated with hand-painted quilt patterns, which they probably used to cart home the products they bought at many estate sales throughout the South. At least, that's what Delilah had heard from a volunteer at the local library, where there was a display of several of their coffee table books.

She hadn't met them yet, but she had passed by their shop on the square, and their displays were exquisite. Way beyond her means!

They introduced themselves to Delilah, urging her to call them Stu and Barb, to which she offered her nickname of Lilah. Supposedly, they'd been history teachers at some Charleston community college and retired here five years ago to share their passion in a commercial way, again according to the library volunteer.

Delilah had to smile. The gray-haired couple, in their late sixties, looked like they still lived in the sixties, *the 1960s*, overage hippies from another era. She with long hair hanging loose to her waist and he with a single braid, both with matching, twisted leather headbands, but his across his forehead. She wore a loose, ankle-length skirt with a peasant blouse. He had a tie-dyed T-shirt with a peace emblem tucked into bell-bottom denims embroidered with flowers along the hem. They both wore Birkenstocks.

"My dear, you are such a welcome addition to our little town," Barb said, holding on to Delilah's hand after she shook it with both of hers.

Delilah tried to pull away, discreetly, but Barb, despite her age, had a grip like a Wall Street power broker.

"We didn't know your uncle well, but we loved the idea of a vintage diner and motel the first time we visited Bell Cove. Even though Elvis hated hippies, according to that letter he wrote to Nixon. How could anyone hate a generation that celebrated love?"

"Now, hon, that was probably just the press twisting things," Stu said to his wife. "Remember, we decided to forgive Elvis. Any man who could sing like he did had to be pure of heart. His rendition of 'Love Me Tender' was quintessential love."

"Or 'Are You Lonesome Tonight?' My favorite." Barb sighed. "We made love for the first time on Laguna Beach to that song. Remember, darling?"

"Remember? Hah! I had sand where the sun

don't shine for days afterward, sweetheart. And a rash on my ash. Ha, ha, ha."

They gazed at each other lovingly.

*TMI*, Delilah thought.

Stu turned to Delilah again, took her right hand (Barb still held her left hand), and gave her a quick kiss on the cheek.

Delilah cringed inside at that additional physical contact. Why did people, especially strangers, feel the need to touch?

"Despite Elvis, we were great fans of your uncle's Thursday Night Meat Loaf," Barb was saying. "Do you intend to continue that offering?"

"Well, I don't know. Maybe."

"Cheap ketchup, that was his secret ingredient," Barb told Delilah.

"Now, Barbie, you don't know that for sure," Stu said. "Personally, I think it was the herbs he used." He told Delilah, "Rumor was he grew a little of his own herbs out back, if you get my meaning." He winked at her.

*What? Pot-infused meat loaf? Was that possible?*

By now, Stu and Barb were off on another subject. The motel.

"Would you mind giving us a tour, dear?" Barb asked. "We have some ideas that might help."

*Uh-oh! I sense an incoming nice attack.*

The motel unit was painted blue, or had been at one time. Now, the once-sky-blue color was faded and peeling in spots. The eight rooms had been an homage to Elvis songs, each with blue in the title, each with its own brass placard: BLUE

SUEDE SHOES, BLUE MOON, BLUEBERRY HILL, BLUE HAWAII, BLUE CHRISTMAS, BLUE RIVER, MOODY BLUE, and G.I. BLUES.

The rooms were actually fairly large with two full-size beds, bedside tables with lamps, and a dresser. But there were also sitting areas with miniscule television sets facing sliding patio doors through which could be seen magnificent views of Bell Sound. There was no way to get down to the rocky shore, unless some enterprising person, meaning her, installed steps at some point in the future—the distant future. Back inside, some of the framed Elvis movie posters and memorabilia were still intact on the walls, but mostly the rooms were a gut job. On the other hand, the bathrooms weren't too bad. The cast-iron tubs would need to be reglazed, and tile walls required regrouting, but the bathrooms themselves were larger than the tiny facilities found in motels today.

"Here's what we were thinking," Stu said, gazing around with a surprising admiration. "Barb and I deal in antique quilts, of course, but we also have access to new fabrics and products. For example . . ."

Barb pulled out several swatches of cloth from a macramé shoulder bag she carried and handed them to her husband. First was a quilted material in varying shades of blue that gave the appearance of ocean waves. "This ombré method of shading from one tone of the same color to another would be wonderful in a quilted bedspread over heavy batting," Stu said.

"Then, a cotton fabric with the same blue wave

ombré design could be made into curtains for the front windows. And this . . . don't you love this sheer?" Barb held out an almost-transparent material that shimmered with the varying blues. "It would make great panels for the sliding doors."

"If you used these materials, which aren't too busy, as your base, then you could work the Elvis theme in each unit around them," Stu explained.

They *were* beautiful, just the kind of thing she would like, but Delilah knew she could never afford them. "I appreciate your thoughts. I really do, but honestly, I'm on a really tight budget. And, besides, I need to get the diner operating first."

"Oh, my goodness, sweetie, we didn't mean right now," Barb said, squeezing Delilah's hand. To her husband, Barb whispered, "We were being intrusive."

"No, it's not—" Delilah started to say.

But Stu was squeezing her other arm. "It's important that you use quality materials in a commercial operation. Anything cheaper would fall apart after five washings. But what we failed to say is that we have access to wholesalers. We could get all these things for you at cost. And maybe even at a significant discount below cost. When you're ready."

"And I'll bet there's someone locally who could sew them up real cheap," Barb added.

They both stared at Delilah for a long moment before giving her a final squeeze and saying, as one, "We just want to help."

Which was all well and good, but another speed bump in Delilah's journey to be independent and private. Once again, Delilah realized that she was being undermined by niceness.

*Dammit!*

Stu and Barb left with her last two cinnamon rolls. An experimental apple honey oat mix with cream cheese frosting.

Which was ironic because no sooner had they left the premises than Sally Dawson of Sweet Thangs, a bakery and ice-cream shop, arrived with a bone to pick with her. Well, a cinnamon roll, not a bone. And there was not a cinnamon roll to be had.

"What's this I hear about you trying to run me out of business?" Sally asked right off, hands on hips.

Sally was about the same age as Delilah, but looked like a teenager with her brown hair cut short in a pixie style and freckles dotting her makeup-free face. Despite her youthful appearance, Sally had three young sons she was raising alone since her soldier husband had been killed in Afghanistan.

"Huh?"

Sally gave her a fierce scowl, then laughed. "Just kidding. I've been hearing raves over your cinnamon rolls, and just wanted to make you an offer. If you'd like to sell them at my bakery until you get the diner going, I'm game."

"You would do that for me? The competition?"

Sally laughed some more. "Not really competition. We would be partners. I'd only charge a little percentage for profit at my end, but once your diner and motel open, I would expect you to put out some brochures for my bakery. Maybe even sell some of my products. Hey, you could offer Continental Breakfasts to motel customers. Just basics. Croissants, pastries, cinnamon rolls, with coffee and tea."

"That sounds good, but it'll be a while before the motel is ready."

"And my offer to sell your cinnamon rolls in the meantime?"

"I'd love to do that, but I'm not sure how much time I'm going to have. Starting tomorrow, I'll be working for Bell Cove Treasure and Salvaging. I need to earn some extra cash to complete my renovations here." That wasn't quite a lie.

"Really? You'll be working with Merrill Good, that hot Navy SEAL?" Sally grinned, exposing one slightly crooked incisor, which was oddly attractive.

"I don't think he's a Navy SEAL anymore. Besides, how do you know he was a SEAL? They don't go public with that, do they? Maybe he was just Navy."

"Oh, he was a SEAL all right. My husband was Delta Force, and, believe me, I can recognize one of those bad boys at fifty paces. Doesn't matter if they're Green Berets, Deltas, SEALs, Rangers, or whatever. Badass to the bone."

*Okaay. Merrill is a badass. Well, I knew that, didn't I? Just looking at him makes my toes curl.* "Um . . . if you think Merrill is so hot, maybe you should make a connection. Or . . . have you already?" For some reason, that idea bothered Delilah. A lot. She wasn't sure why.

"Not a chance! One military man was enough for me. When . . . *or if* . . . I ever get involved with another man, he's gonna be safe and boring. An accountant, maybe."

Delilah was the one to laugh now.

But not for long.

"I understand you have a daughter. How old is she?"

Well, that was quick. The Bell Cove grapevine at its best, just like the prison grapevine, or gossip networks everywhere. The juicy tidbit was passed on today by Ina Rogers, Delilah presumed. "A little girl. Magdalene Jones, or Maggie."

"Magdalene, what an unusual name. Pretty."

"My family has a warped sense of humor. Biblical names for the women, but bad women of the Bible, not the saintly ones. Like Mary Magdalene, Delilah for me, my grandmother is Salome or Sal, and my mother was Jezebel, or Jezzie. There was probably a Bathsheba early on."

"I love it! My husband had been certain we'd have all boys, they run in his family, and he wanted to name our boys Matthew, Mark, Luke, and John. Unfortunately, we never got around to a fourth son, a John, before he died."

Delilah sensed Sally's pain over the loss of her husband, even though he'd been gone for several years now. But she didn't want to add to her grief by asking questions about his death. Instead, she remarked, "So, your sons are named Matthew, Mark, and Luke?"

"Yep. Luke is about the same age as your Maggie. Maybe they'll become friends, although I must warn you, he's a terror on a dirt bike."

"Maggie is more into the movie *Annie*, although she might become more adventuresome once she's here and out of doors more often." That was another thing Delilah would have to add to her lists. Buy Maggie a bicycle.

Sally didn't ask her about Maggie's father, or where Maggie was at the present time, which Delilah considered a blessing. There were only so many secrets she wanted to dole out at one time.

After Sally left, Delilah covered the refinished booth seats with several tarps, not wanting to reinstall them until the interior of the diner was completely clean and restored. Besides, it looked like a summer storm was about to hit, one of those sudden flash rainfalls that came down fast and furious on the beaches and were over almost as soon as they started.

The day had been unsettling for her, with all the visitors, jarring her with all the things she would have to add to her "To Do" lists. How naive had she been, thinking that she could open a diner and motel on a barrier island, lickety-split, and then move her daughter here with no complications? And Merrill Good was going to pose the biggest complication of them all. She just knew he would.

Delilah did what calmed her most then. She baked in her small kitchen. Two dozen cinnamon rolls. Ginger apple and peach pecan. The mindless gentle kneading of the batter. The repetitive motions of rolling the dough. The sweet scents that filled the air. The immediate gratification of cleaning up afterward.

To Delilah, baking was a form of prayer.

She prayed for new beginnings on this island.

She prayed that her past wouldn't catch up with her in a negative way.

She prayed that the niceness of her new neighbors wouldn't erode her independence and turn to hostility once they found out about her past.

She prayed that time would be on her side in terms of opening the diner before winter ended the tourist season.

She prayed that Maggie would adapt to life in a strange setting with a mother she barely knew.

And, in the midst of all these worries, she prayed that she would be able to resist that "badass to the bone" Merrill Good, who made niceness seem like erotic foreplay.

*Dammit!*

## Chapter 5

*There are all kinds of highs . . .*

**M**errill was excited on Monday afternoon, the first official opening of Bell Cove Salvaging and Treasure Hunting. And not just because this was the launch of a new venture. Merrill was more than familiar with the adrenaline rush that marked the start of an active op in the military. Same thing, sort of.

The difference here was Delilah Jones, the added spark to his excitement. No question his testosterone went on red alert at first sight of her in his space, and his blood pressure amped up a point or two or ten.

She was already there when he arrived for the meeting at the building he shared with Bell Forge. For a moment, he just leaned against the door frame and watched as she moved around his office setting up a coffeemaker. *Where did that come from? And mugs? Who knew I had eight matching mugs?*

She was also arranging pastries—big honkin' cinnamon buns, to be precise—on a fancy tray. *The place smells like a friggin' bakery. Not that that's a bad thing.*

*But holy crap! She must have gone out and bought these things for me, first thing this morning. And just how did she do that?* he wondered. *On a motorcycle, which is the only vehicle she owns, as far as I know.*

No matter.

She turned and noticed him, with a start of surprise.

"Hey, De-li-lah," he drawled out, still leaning a shoulder against the door frame, arms folded over his chest, legs crossed at his booted ankles. "You've been a busy bee, I see."

"Shhh. Don't do that," she cautioned, glancing over his shoulder at some of the others who were approaching.

"Do what?"

"Say my name like you're kissing air."

Now there was an image he liked. Kissing. Her, not the air. He grinned.

"And stop grinning, too."

"Happiness is a sin now?"

"It is when you look like you've been up to no good."

"Darlin', there hasn't been nearly enough 'no good' in my life for a long time."

"That's another thing. You can't be calling one of your employees *darlin'*."

"I don't really consider you an employee. More like a team member. We're all partners in this enterprise."

She arched her brows with disbelief at his mincing words.

He shrugged and pretended to zip his lips as some of the guys he'd been having lunch with passed by into the room where they immediately did double takes on seeing Delilah.

And she wasn't even dressed sexy. White, calf-length pants, with white sneakers, no socks, and a sleeveless red-and-white polka-dot blouse. Her platinum blonde hair was tied off her face with a red ribbon into a loose ponytail. No makeup to speak of, though women had a way of hiding that. He had a girlfriend one time who spent an hour in the bathroom making up her face only to emerge looking like a young Taylor Swift.

Now, if only she'd added that Crimson Slut lipstick from the Rutledge wedding reception! But, no, he wouldn't want her broadcasting her sexuality to one and all. Just him.

And, to his chagrin, he noticed that "one and all," those of the male persuasion in the room, were noticing her plenty now that the room was full. Even with Bonita Arias, who was a classic Spanish beauty, in attendance, as well.

Soon they were all sitting around his office, which was small but open onto a long warehouse space, which was empty for the moment, leading to the immense garage-style doors, which they shared with the forge. Luckily the forge wasn't operating today—down for repairs—otherwise, it would be unbearably hot in here, even with the air-conditioning running full blast in the back office. The doors were up now at his side of the bay, and they could see from this distance the newly refurbished wharf (*ca-ching, ca-ching*) and the deep waters beyond.

Everyone was sipping from mugs of coffee and wolfing down cinnamon buns, as if they hadn't just had big lunches at the Cracked Crab. Delilah was still bustling about, offering more coffee and pastries, being hospitable but not overly friendly— her usual reserved manner.

"Okay, folks, welcome to Bell Cove Salvaging and Treasure Hunting," Merrill started off. "Gabe Conti, owner of Bell Forge, a silent partner in this operation, couldn't join us today. He's an architect, for those who haven't met him yet, and he had to be in Durham on a job site today. You probably won't see much of him anyway.

"Also missing are K-4 . . . Kevin Fortunato . . . who still has a few weeks left on his military commitment. He just let me know last night that he'll be joining us. K-4 is an experienced diver and knows a little bit about research, which might help with other upcoming projects. K-4 and I worked together on Navy teams for years, so, I can vouch for his skills, especially intelligence gathering." Merrill didn't mention that the teams were SEALs. Intel best left unsaid. Besides, folks here had heard or deduced that fact on their own.

"Most of us know each other, but not all. So, let's introduce ourselves. I'll start. Merrill Good, project manager and primary stockholder of the company. I still answer to the name Geek, my military nickname, but 'Boss' will do for those so inclined." He grinned, knowing some guys would call him "Boss" over their own dead bodies. "Just kidding on the boss crap. As I've said before, we're all partners on this operation. Anyhow, I'm a certified diver but my skills will be best deployed on the electronic equipment we'll be using—computerized mapping systems, scanners, magnetometer, and so on. No robots yet, which cost as much as a jet plane, but I can only wish, after our first successful mission."

"I'll second that . . . the wish for a successful treasure hunt," Bonita said, "but personally I'd rather buy a Tiffany diamond tennis bracelet with my cut."

Others mentioned a Lamborghini, a boat, a new home, and a vacation.

Once the hubbub died down, Merrill continued, "I expect to make our first run out to the site on Wednesday . . . if everyone's cool with that." He glanced around and saw lots of nods.

"One of the first things we'll do is gather random samples from the ocean floor so I can run them through a gas chromatograph mass spectrometer . . . try saying that real fast . . . to measure any differences that might suggest the presence of a wreck."

Delilah looked dazed.

"Anyhow, that's it for my introduction." He motioned to the fifty-something guy, maybe late forties, on his right to take over. He was dark haired (probably dyed), with an olive complexion denoting some Latin culture. His wicking T-shirt fit his body like a glove. He was probably attractive to women in an older stud sort of way.

"Adam Famosa here. Professor of Oceanography at Rutgers University, a proud citizen of the USA, but a Cuban expatriate from when I was a kid. I've taken a leave of absence for the fall semester to help in the transition from the old company in Jersey, Jinx, Inc., which Geek recently bought out. I worked for Jinx off and on for fifteen years."

"Glad you could join us," Merrill said, and he meant it. "We look forward to hearing how things were done at Jinx."

"My pleasure," Famosa said.

Next up was an elderly gentleman in a wheelchair. "I'm Harry Carder, retired financial consultant, the old fart on this team. I'll be handling all the bookkeeping, payroll, office kind of things. Unless you need a deadweight to anchor your boat, I don't expect to be out on any of the ocean treks with my constant companion." He patted his wheelchair for emphasis.

Everyone laughed at his self-deprecating humor.

"I can attest to Harry's expertise, wheelchair or not," Merrill said. "I first met him on a visit to the Outer Banks last Christmas, and his advice has been invaluable."

Harry's face flushed but Merrill could tell he was pleased at the compliment.

"I'll second that about Harry. I know him well," said Bonita. "Harry lives at the same senior citizen boardinghouse as my father. Dad is a samba aficionado, nuts about any kind of dancing, really, and

Mildred Patterson's place here in Bell Cove is notorious for its dirty dance club . . . and its nuts." With a wink at Harry, who was still blushing and about to protest the description of his place, she laughed.

Actually, Merrill was staying at the Patterson house, too, for the time being, until he found more permanent accommodations, which were hard to come by in Bell Cove. The town tried its best not to become a commercialized tourist mecca and therefore didn't have many rental options. Wendy Patterson, Mildred's niece, owned the house. He knew Wendy from SEALs back in Coronado, Wendy having been a member of the female SEALs division known as WEALS, Women on Earth, Air, Land, and Sea. Six degrees of separation, or something like that.

Bonita continued, "Anyhow, I'm Bonita Arias. I'm an oceanographer, too. Rather, a marine archaeologist, to be more specific. I live in Ocracoke and have worked on several shipwreck salvaging operations."

Bonita was a classic beauty with ebony hair that hung straight down her back. Of medium height, aided by a pair of high wedge sandals, her slim body more than filled a sky-blue halter top and matching shorts.

Bonita was hot. Just not to him.

"I've been working for the U.S. Fish and Wildlife Services, but I'm on a leave of absence, hoping to receive my doctorate soon from UNC at Chapel Hill," Bonita continued. "So, I might not be here on-site all the time."

"We'll appreciate all the time you can give us,"
Merrill said.

"I don't have any fancy degrees, or experience as
a diver," interrupted the next member of the team,
as opposite from Bonita and Delilah as any woman
could be. "I'm Charlotte LeDeux from Lafayette,
Loo-zee-anna, praise God and pass the gumbo,"
the person in men's coveralls and a New Orleans
Saints baseball cap said, as if impatient with all
the niceties of introductions and wanting to get
on with the real work. It was hard to tell whether
she was thirty or forty or older. "You kin call me
Charlie or Captain. Frankly, I don't wanna become
best buds with any of you. Talk about! And I expect
you'll soon feel the same way about me."

"Why don't you tell us how you really feel?" Famosa said, probably trying to tease her into more
pleasantness.

"Bite me, Casanova," she replied.

*So, I'm not the only one who pegged Famosa as a tomcat.*

"Casanova? I'm not *that* old," Famosa protested
with a laugh. "Lighten up, sweetheart. I was just
teasing."

"Tease this." Charlie flicked Famosa the bird,
then explained to the others, "I'll be manning the
wheel of the salvaging boat, and there isn't anything I don't know about boat motors. My family
ran a commercial fishing boat on the Gulf for five
generations, but went out of business after the last
hurricane, combined with all the environmental
poison being dumped by the devil's spawn, the
fucking oil companies who are raping our land and

waters. And that's all I have to say on that subject. I need to earn a shitload of money to buy back our company. So, let's get on with this treasure hunting crap." She tugged the bill of her cap down with a jerk, letting them know loud and clear that she was done talking.

"Okaay," Merrill said with a grin, enjoying the rather stunned expressions on some of the faces. "Next?"

"Well, then, you're probably going to hate me, Captain Charlie," the big blond Norseman sitting next to her said, giving her a playful elbow nudge. "I sell gas here on the island."

"That figures," Charlie said, and elbowed him back, hard. "You damn Vikings were born raping and pillaging."

Said Viking just grinned. "I'm Karl Gustafson, but you can call me Gus or Goose or Damn Viking, although I can't recall the last time I pillaged. What the hell is pillaging anyhow? I played linebacker for the Cowboys for about fifteen minutes a few years back before my knees gave out. Maybe I pillaged there, come to think on it. Came back to the Outer Banks with a wife who also lasted about fifteen minutes when she realized I wasn't gonna be the next Joe Namath or Joe Montana in retirement. Anyhow, I opened Gus's Gas and Goods, a convenience store, and I'm living the good life here with my mama, who will run the business when I'm here working for Geek. I'm an expert diver and looking forward to new adventures." He waggled his eyebrows deliberately at Charlie, as if she was an adventure he would like to explore. He probably did it just to pull her chain.

Charlie looked at him with disdain, but some of the others viewed Gus with admiration as they realized who he was. "The Goose" had been on his way to the Hall of Fame as one of the best sack leaders in the NFL during his two years with the Cowboys, not fifteen minutes.

"Hey, Gus, didn't I see your mug on the cover of *Sports Illustrated* at one time?" Merrill asked. "A little false modesty, maybe?"

"You should talk. I hear you're an Internet sensation with that invention of yours. A penile glove, I think it's called." Gus cast a gotcha smirk his way.

"What's a penile glove?" Delilah asked, immediately followed by, "Never mind. Holy moley, you folks are a bunch of bleepin' celebrities while I'm just a nobody. I'm Lilah Jones, and I'm gonna be a jack or jill of all jobs. Cook, dishwasher, fetch-and-goer."

Merrill didn't consider her a nobody, and he noticed that she identified herself as Lilah and not Delilah, probably because of his earlier teasing her about her name.

"I'm a nobody, too," Charlie said, and Harry claimed the same.

"If those cinnamon thingees I just scarfed down are any indication, you can be my cook anytime," Gus contributed.

"Actually, I'm renovating the diner and motel in town. When they're done, you can buy them there anytime you want."

"So much for self-promotion," Famosa commented, reaching for the last of the pastries on the tray, followed by a wink at Delilah.

A wink Merrill did not appreciate at all.

"That's it for our team. For now," Merrill said. "Let's talk about our first project. The Three Saints." He stood and walked over to the laptop he'd set up attached to a projector. Clicking it on, an image immediately flashed onto the opposite wall which he was using as a screen. "Delilah, could you pass out these folders?" To the others, he explained, "There are copies of each of the slides for you all to study later. Any questions, just yell out."

Famosa murmured, "Delilah? Who's Delilah? Oh." He grinned.

*The lech!*

Delilah immediately did as Merrill asked and scowled at Famosa's grin.

*Good girl!*

"As you can see on this first slide, it's an aerial view of the salvage location. The perimeter highlighted is about one square mile, slightly more than that in nautical miles. Those boundaries are stipulated on our salvage license. We don't go one inch over those lines without being in trouble."

"Appears to be about five miles out from here," Charlie noted. "Has the area been searched before?"

"Never. Lots of places close by, but this is a virgin site. The locals say that the shoals out there can be wicked under the best of circumstances, but during or after a storm, the shifting sandbars are brutal. Add to that, you have two strong ocean currents that collide near Cape Hatteras and have a ripple effect out to our site."

"Hmpfh! No wonder so many ships wrecked here then!" Charlie mused, studying the slide that showed up next listing the hurricanes that had hit this coastline in the past three hundred years. "No wonder this whole blasted area off the Outer Banks is known as 'The Graveyard of the Atlantic'! I thought Loo-zee-anna was a magnet for hurricanes, but this is ridiculous!"

"There are still three million shipwrecks sitting on the bottom of the world's oceans and seas, you know." This according to Famosa, ever the professor. "And that's no bullshit. Three frickin' million!"

"Do they all have treasure?" Delilah asked.

"Nah! Lots of them carried perishable goods that have long melded into the sea floor. And the ships were wooden. Can anyone say shipworms? Not that those wrecks don't have historical value in themselves, but no treasure."

"The interesting thing, though, to us Outer Bankers, anyhow," Gus interjected, "is that there are still three thousand shipwrecks uncovered off our coastline alone."

*Three thousand!* Delilah mouthed silently.

It *was* an amazing number.

"What do we know about the three ships in question?" Famosa asked.

"I can answer that," Bonita said. "A trio of Portuguese ships supposedly went down in 1862. Called the Three Saints . . . the *St. Martha*, the *St. Cecilia*, and the *St. Sonia*."

While Bonita talked, Merrill clicked to a slide with drawings depicting the three ships and the little bit of history about their voyage.

"The ships carried weapons and gold bullion, worth millions. This was before the Yankees had taken control of this region in a number of big battles. The three ships managed to evade Northern offensives, but not the notorious Outer Banks storms."

"So, we're looking for historical weaponry and gold," Famosa concluded.

"Bingo, but there's also a rumor that one of the ships carried some Spanish princess betrothed to a wealthy Savannah sugar planter," Merrill said. "Aside from all the gold, her dower chest contained museum quality jewelry, or so the rumors go. The other two ships were escorts."

"God bless rumors," Famosa remarked.

"You wouldn't believe what rumors say about my physical endowments," Gus interjected with a grin.

"Like anyone cares," Charlie said.

This conversation was going nowhere fast. Merrill reined it in by continuing his slide show and a description of the first phase of their salvage mission. When he was done and answered some questions, a surprising two hours had gone by. He told the group, "Let's meet again tomorrow morning. Bring all your gear for inspection, and we'll do a run-through on schedules and duties on the initial run."

Excited chatter followed, and Delilah started to

# *Chapter 6*

*One step forward, two steps back . . .*

$A$fter Delilah gathered a pad and pen from her handbag, Merrill led her through the warehouse toward the open doors, across the wharf to the gangway connecting it to the sixty-five-foot former tramp steamer. The temporary ramp, which hung about ten feet above the deep water, was shaky at times and he put a hand to the small of Delilah's back to steady her, but immediately drew back when he felt her tense up.

*Whoa! Talk about uptight!*

Realizing that she might have overreacted, she said, "Sorry. I'm a little nervous when tightrope walking."

Rope? The metal ramp was at least four feet wide, and there were side rails. Maybe she wasn't as comfortable on the water as she'd led him to believe. Or maybe he'd lost some of the few points he thought he'd scored yesterday in getting closer to Delilah.

And, frankly, if anything was a tightrope, it was dating today. A tightrope of shark-infested waters—the sharks being all the ways a guy could trip. He had to be very, very careful that he didn't lean too far in either direction. Be a wuss or be a predator. A balancing act, for sure.

If Merrill wasn't a born competitor, he might consider giving up on this pain in the ass seduction.

*Is seduction a taboo word today?*

*Probably.*

*Or am I overthinking this?*

*Probably?*

*See. Tightrope.*

But then he considered the prize. Delilah. Definitely a pain in the ass. Definitely worth the pain.

Unless the question he needed to ask her brought an answer he couldn't live with. Then she would be out of his crosshairs faster than he could say adultery.

He couldn't wait any longer. Once they hit the deck, he asked, "Are you married?"

"What? Where did that come from?"

"I heard this morning that you have a child."

"And?"

"It takes two people to make a baby . . . usually."

"But not two *married* people."

"Which means . . . ?"

"Yes, I have a child, an almost-five-year-old daughter, who will be moving here later this summer. But there is no husband, never has been. You have a problem with that?"

"Not a bit." He was practically doing a Snoopy dance in his head.

"You're grinning again," she pointed out.

*No fuck!*

He didn't take much time showing her around up top, knowing she wouldn't be interested in the actual salvage equipment, especially when she observed, "It's not very pretty."

"I told you it was no yacht."

"Yeah, but you didn't say it was a rust bucket."

"Hey, this 'rust bucket' has all the bells and whistles needed for a salvage operation."

"In other words, don't judge a book by its cover?"

*Or a person by her sexual history?* Which he wasn't about to ask out loud. Instead, he chose the safer: "Or a boat by its rusty patches."

"Right. I've become an expert on rust, y'know, refinishing that diner of mine. Maybe in my spare time, I could work on prettying up *Sweet Bells*."

*I have other plans for your spare time, baby.* "Go for it," he said. "I'd love to see you hanging over the side on a rope scaffolding."

"Maybe not." She laughed. "I was just kidding, anyhow. About how the boat . . . ship . . . whatever . . . looks. What I know about water-going vessels of any kind, including a rowboat, wouldn't fit in a thimble."

"What's a thimble?"

"Seriously?"

He grinned. Some more.

Going down the narrow staircase of the hatch to the cabin, he waited for her to follow and then showed her the salon, a large rectangular room with wide, cushioned window seats that provided storage and could serve as beds in a pinch. A long counter with four high stools screwed to the floor divided the lounge area from the kitchen. Off to the right was a dining table, also attached to the floor, with benches.

Delilah immediately went to the kitchen and began opening cabinet doors and peering into the stainless steel range and fridge, both of which were commercial size.

"You can see that I bought basic, nonperishable food supplies, figuring I would get the fresh stuff as late as possible. I assumed that all of us team members would share cooking duties, which probably would have been a disaster. So, your offer to cook really was opportune."

She just grunted as she continued to examine the goods on hand.

"If you need extra fridge space, there's a unit off the engine room, intended for fish, but I guess it would serve any purpose."

She was already making notes as she counted plates and cutlery and cooking supplies. "Despite the basics already here, it looks like I'm going to have to do some shopping, more than I expected," she remarked, running a finger over one large frying pan and grimacing. Apparently it wasn't as clean as it should be.

He sat down on one of the stools and pulled his wallet out of his back pocket. Laying a credit card on the counter, he said, "Use this for anything you need to buy. Keep receipts and hand them over to Harry, but in the meantime get whatever you think we need."

"How long will we be out on the boat at any one time?"

"Hard to say. At least a week. A cabin cruiser is available for emergency transport of anyone needing to get to shore quickly. We're only five miles out, but I don't want people going back and forth every day. It would cost too much, be disruptive to our routine, and leave us undermanned in the event pirate salvagers show up on the scene."

"Hard to believe, in this day and age, that pirates still exist."

"Oh, yeah. In fact, the smaller boat stays on-site at those times when we need to come into the pump station to empty waste, or to the warehouse to replenish our fresh water tanks or food supplies."

"And the number of people on board?"

"Plan on eight, but there might not always be that many."

"Bulk ordering makes sense for nonperishable food, of course. Lots more than you already bought. Can boxes be stored in your warehouse?"

"Sure."

"At some point, a large freezer might make sense, too. For the warehouse. Would save on trips to a supermarket. And be more cost efficient."

"Let's put that on the back burner, for now. There's another issue we need to discuss. Your transportation."

"What?" Just like that, she tightened up again.

*Does she ever loosen up? Relax a little. Have sex? Oops, I mean have a hobby or something?* "How did you get the coffeepot, coffee, milk, sugar, pastries, mugs, and stuff to the office today?"

She blushed. "On my motorcycle."

He arched his brows.

"A backpack, side saddles, and a little ingenious shelf I rigged to the back fender."

"That's what I thought. I appreciate the effort, by the way, and so did everyone else. Your buns are outstanding."

She nodded an acceptance of his compliment, although she wasn't altogether sure which buns he referred to.

He wasn't, either.

"Okay, here's the deal. For the next few days, you and I are going to do a swap. My pickup truck for your cycle."

She started to protest.

But he raised a halting hand. "No, don't worry about me. I'm willing to make the sacrifice. You get a vehicle to cart all the supplies you need, and me"—he sighed dramatically—"I'll just have to suffer on a 1978 Harley FLHS Electra-Glide."

She laughed. "Okay. For a few days."

"Anyhow, go peek in the three sleeping quarters and the head. You'll see stacked berths for four in two of them, what are usually called bunk beds, and a double-size alcove berth in the 'captain's quarters,' which I have every intention of claiming for myself. You and Charlie and Bonita will share one room. Up to four of the guys in the other, unless someone wants to sleep in the salon."

"Is there a washer and dryer on board?"

"Nope. That means we'll need at least two sets of bed linens and a bunch of towels. I did buy some, but you'll need to check them out."

She quickly added linens and towels to the growing list on her notepad.

"By the end of the first week, we may all be smelling a bit ripe, although a quick dip in the ocean should handle that." At the look of horror on her face, he added, "For some of us."

"I can swim, before you ask," she said defensively, "but swimming with the sharks . . ." She shivered in an exaggerated fashion.

He hummed the tune of *Jaws*, just to tease her. "Dun dun . . . dun dun . . . dun dun dun . . . dunnnnnnnnnnnnnn!"

"Very funny! Not!"

"Actually, shark attacks are rare off the Outer Banks. Although I hear there's been an odd boom in baby bull sharks this year in some of the bays, including Bell Sound. Probably due to climate change. But not to worry. The babies don't bite, and, in fact, are really cute."

"Pfff! Cute or not, if babies are being born, Mama and Papa have gotta be close by. Nope! I do not enter any water with sharks in them. Period."

"Got it," he said. "Delilah stays on the boat."

While Delilah explored with her notebook and pen in hand, he went up on deck, where he could hear footsteps. Charlie was raising the floor hatch under the wheelhouse, accessing the engine room. She was obsessive about safety, with good cause, of course.

Gus and Famosa were pulling neoprene dive suits from built-in storage chests and laying them out on the deck for inspection. Although many divers liked to use their own equipment, there was standard gear for everyone on the boat. It was always good to have spares.

"So, is she off-limits?" Famosa asked right off.

Gus grinned.

Apparently "she" had been the subject of discussion between the two of them before he showed up.

"Who?" Merrill asked. After all, Famosa could be referring to Charlie or Bonita. But Merrill knew. He just knew.

"Blondie," Famosa replied.

*Why don't you refer to her that way, to her face?* Merrill was about to say, but stopped himself. Let Famosa learn the hard way. "Off-limits? I wish! But I have no first rights or anything. Go for it. A little advice, though. Delilah is shy. You might have to be a little aggressive. Hustle hard."

When Merrill went down below again, he couldn't find Delilah, at first. When he called out her name, though, he heard a muffled sound coming from the captain's sleeping quarters. He found her on her knees, face down to the floor, her rear end in the air, running a broom or something under the bed.

For a long moment, he just enjoyed the view.

But then, he hunkered down beside her to see what was going on. "What the hell are you doing?"

Apparently she hadn't heard him enter the room because her head shot up at the same moment his went down. They butted heads, hard.

"Son of a . . . ouch, ouch, ouch!" she hollered. "Are you trying to kill me?"

"Me? I think you cracked my skull open."

They both tried to rise at the same time and hit heads again. This time he went down, backward, with a crash.

He didn't lose consciousness, but he *was* dazed. Not so much that he wasn't aware of her kneeling over him, touching the rising bumps on his forehead with tentative fingertips.

"Merrill, are you all right? Do I need to call an ambulance?" Her face was so close, he could feel her breath on his lips. Like a kiss.

*A breath kiss?*

He liked the sound—rather, the thought—of that.

And so he did what he shouldn't, but what he'd wanted to do since the first time he'd seen her. He put hands on either side of her face and tugged her the few remaining inches closer. Then he locked lips with her in a kiss that was sweet and seeking and innocent as a hello.

But, hello, her lips were parted in surprise . . .

*Yay, me!*

. . . and because fifteen years on the teams had taught him to grab any window of opportunity before it disappeared . . .

*Seize the day!*

. . . or because maybe she'd been wanting this as much as he had . . .

*Okay, that's a stretch.*

Well, for all those reasons, and then some, the sweet kiss turned wicked. Wicked good.

*Sometimes bad is good, and good is bad. Didn't Masters & Johnson, or Einstein, or Dr. Ruth, or some frickin' expert on Oprah say that one time?* Merrill mused, his Mensa brain always at work, like a bloody encyclopedia. *Hey, I can multitask. Kiss and think at the same time. Can't I?*

*No, that's stoo-pid! Get your brain out of your dick, sailor! Or your dick out of your brain.*

*I am so losing it!*

The sweet kiss turned molten—a moist, hungry burn of the senses.

And she was hot damn kissing him back.

*I've still got it!*

In fact, there might be tongues involved. Yes, definitely tongues.

*This has got to be the second-best reason why God invented tongues.*

*Sweet, sweet, sweet!*

*No, hot, hot, hot!*

*Am I breathing too hard?*

*Did she just moan?*

He moved his hands from cupping her face to cupping her buttocks.

*WHAT?*

*When did she crawl on top of me?*

*Who the friggin' hell cares!*

*Forget the fucking window. This is a door. And I'm in!*

He explored her body with wide sweeps of his palms, from her shoulders to her waist and the small of her back, over her buns, and down her thighs. She was soft and cushy everywhere. Not fat. No, she didn't have an ounce of extra fat on her body, but she wasn't hard muscled or toned like the athletic women he was usually involved with, either. A delicious change. He wanted to sink into her creamy skin and lap it all over.

Needless to say, he had a hard-on that would like to swim in that cream, too. *That is so crude. Hope I didn't say that out loud.*

For the sake of his sanity, or before he went monkey ass trigger-happy with a premature ejaculation, he rolled them both over so she was flat on her back and he was looking down at her. Her blue eyes were smoky with passion. Her lips were rose hued and kiss-swollen. In other words, blonde bombshell personified. Every red-blooded man's wet dream.

Which they both woke from with a start when Charlie, who had a voice like a megaphone, could be heard yelling from above, "Hey, boss, the UPS driver needs you to sign for a delivery. You up for that?"

He was up, all right. In more ways than one.

Jumping to his feet, which caused the two bumps on his head to begin a drumbeat behind his eyes, he helped Delilah to her feet. She had two matching bumps on her forehead, which probably hurt just as bad as his did.

"I knew this would happen, I knew this would happen," she was muttering as she pulled a long-handled feathery mop out from under the bed. It was loaded with dust bunnies, an old sock, and a bunch of other clingy stuff. That's apparently what she'd been doing when he came in. Mopping under the bed. Why, he hadn't a clue. "I just knew this would fu—freakin' happen."

*Oh, great! She's having regrets. Already.*

"I'm sorry. I never intended to do . . . *this* when I came in here," he apologized.

"It's not your fault."

*Excuse me?* "It's not?"

"You can't help being so hot a girl can't resist you."

He started to smile, but stopped himself just in time. She was serious.

"Can't you do something to make yourself less attractive?"

"Like?"

"Get a bad case of bad breath. Belch. Tell dirty jokes."

In the meantime, she was standing there, leaning on her mop, looking bed-mussed and sex-flushed. Her hair was half in, half out of its ponytail. One of the buttons on her blouse had come undone, exposing the edge of a red lace bra. *Red?* His favorite color, next to flesh.

Yeah, he was going to do his best to repel her attraction. Not! "On the other hand, we could just go with the flow," he suggested.

"You mean, have an affair?"

"For a start."

She looked at him as if he'd just crawled out from under a rock.

*So much for my hotness!*

"That's it. I quit. Don't worry about the money you advanced me. I'll pay you back, even if I have to sell my motorcycle."

Merrill had enough of this seesawing back and forth. *Does she, doesn't she? Will she, won't she? Fuck that!* "I don't care about the frickin' money," he shouted, then forced himself to calm down. "Did I miss something here? How did we go from hot-cha-cha to hit the road?"

"Because I can't afford to get my hot-cha-cha on."

"Afford? Are we back to money again?"

"Allow, then. I can't allow myself to surrender to my weakness again."

"Again? Like to the father of your child . . . is that what you mean?"

"Exactly. I trusted that boy . . . man . . . and it led to a whole lot of trouble, the least of which was my being pregnant with Maggie. And that's the last I'm going to say on the subject."

*For now.* "All right, but let's start over here. You are not going to quit. If you want nothing to do with me, fine." *We'll see about that.* "Consider this little kiss fest we just engaged in a lesson learned." *And, boy, did I learn a lot. Like you consider me temptation on the hoof.* "Agreed?"

She hesitated, then nodded.

"In light of your angst over a mere kiss . . ." *Mere? More like walk-off, grand slam, game-over of a kiss.* ". . . you'll probably go bonkers over my next suggestion."

She rolled her eyes. "Give it to me."

*Oh, baby! Poor choice of words!* He closed his eyes and pressed his lips together for a long moment so he wouldn't betray his take on her declaration. When he had himself under control, he said, "I'd like to move into your place."

"Shazam!" She tossed her hands in the air as if he was hopeless.

He was, of course. Where she was concerned. "I didn't mean that the way it sounded."

"My place. That's what you said. Seeing as how my place has one bedroom, what else could you mean?"

"I meant the motel. I have a serious housing issue for the employees I've brought in here. Charlie, Famosa, K-4 when he gets here, and myself. I can't keep staying at the Patterson senior citizen loony bin."

"The motel rooms aren't up to code, let alone in any condition to be used."

"I have an idea—"

"I think I've heard enough of your ideas."

He wagged a forefinger at her for jumping to conclusions. "I have an idea that would benefit us both. I pay an electrician and plumber to get three units working. Send in a cleaning crew to scrub them down, top to bottom. Buy a few new mattresses. Some basic bed linens and towels, nothing fancy. Just functional. A temporary solution to my problem. Later you can remodel and do whatever you want with the Elvis theme."

"More money I'd be indebted to you for! No way!"

"No, no, no! You don't understand. I don't know

what the going weekly rate is for motel rooms on the Outer Banks. Without any redecorating and without any amenities, let's lowball at five hundred a week, for eight weeks, times three. We're talking twelve grand. How much could the plumbing and electrical cost for three rooms? I'm thinking two thou max. Another three thou for everything else I mentioned. And the rest is gravy for you."

"What's the catch?"

"No catch. I already know a local contractor to do the work. He's fast and efficient and fair in pricing."

"I don't know," she wavered.

"It's a win-win for both of us," he argued.

"Okay, I guess. Maybe they could start on the work while we're out on the job this week."

"And you could order the mattresses, towels, and stuff online."

"You never give up. You've got to stop interfering in my life."

"Since when is kindness interfering?"

"You know what they say about kindness?"

"What?"

"It kills."

"I'm not sure that's what that idiom means."

"*Idiom?* Who uses a word like that outside an English classroom?"

He felt his face heat.

"You really are a genius or something, aren't you?"

"Or something."

"All right, then. I agree to the motel suggestion. But only three rooms. And that's the last of your interference in my life or my business."

He crossed his heart. "No more interference. No more Mister Buttinsky. No more Mister Nice Guy."

Unfortunately, it was Gus who yelled down to him now. "Hey, Geek, I signed your name for the UPS guy, but he wants to know if he should drop off this twenty-foot neon Elvis here or over at that diner. Man, you can buy anything on eBay!"

Merrill glanced toward Delilah and said, "Oops."

She put her face in her hands and muttered a bad word.

# Chapter 7

*Busyness was a form of therapy . . .*

**D**elilah spent that evening planning menus and making grocery lists for an initial two-week stint, as well as bulk purchasing for the future. Using her antiquated laptop that moved at the speed of sludge, she set up accounts at various big box food wholesalers. However, not having time to wait as much as a week for deliveries without paying exorbitant, expedited shipping charges or time to go off island to a BJ's or Costco, she accepted that, short term, she would need to shop local and hope for some bargains.

It was amazing how long her list grew.

And it wasn't just Internet ordering for the Three Saints project that consumed her time. The contractor that Merrill mentioned had come by that afternoon and gave her an estimate of $2,100 to get the electrical and plumbing work up to code in three motel units. She gave him a key to access the units while she was away.

Forget about Merrill's suggestion that she hire a cleaning service. Delilah about killed herself shoving and tugging six double mattresses and box springs out to the diner Dumpster, and she planned to spend tomorrow morning scrubbing the units from top to bottom. She had every intention of painting the walls and woodwork herself, first time the *Sweet Bells* team returned to Bell Cove. She would have started on it tomorrow after cleaning, but the afternoon had to be dedicated to shopping for food and supplies for the boat excursion.

She was on the Internet ordering towels and shower curtains and bed linens when she decided to make a call for help.

The phone picked up after just one ring, even though it was eight p.m. by then. "Blanket-y Blank, South Carolina's finest quilt store, Barbara Mac-Leod speaking. How may I help you?"

"Barb, Lilah Jones here. Remember me? From the diner? You came out to talk to me yesterday?"

"Sure. I remember. What's up, dear?"

"I've been thinking about your suggestions regarding my motel units." She went on to explain her situation, making it clear that she was still short on cash. "Do you think there's anything we can do on a smaller scale in such a short time frame? And how much would it cost?"

"Of course. We'll find a way to get it done. And as cheap as possible. But one week?"

"Two at the most."

"Y'know, I sense a bit of synchronicity here. I did a volunteer talk at the senior center in Hatteras today, and I met this woman . . . Suffice it to say, I think she might be the perfect seamstress for the job. She's older, but has a world of experience. Plus, it would do her good, to work again and feel she still has some value."

"And it would do me a favor, too," Delilah concluded. "I'll be around tomorrow if you have any questions, but after that I'll be inaccessible for a week or so. The contractor has a key and will be in and out if you need to go in for measurements."

They discussed a few more details before Barb said, "This is so exciting. I can't wait to tell Stu. Thanks so much for calling."

"No. *Thank you.* You're the answer to my prayers."

"That's what friends are for, honey."

*Oh, crap!*

"What did you say?"

Delilah hadn't realized she'd spoken aloud. "Nothing. I just dropped my notepad on the floor."

While she had her cell phone in hand, Delilah called the number for her parole officer. She'd deliberately waited until this late so that she'd get voice mail and not have to answer any questions. "Hello. Ms. Gardner? This is Delilah Jones. I know I'm not scheduled to come in until next week, but I'm calling to give you a heads-up. I got a job working for a salvaging company." She didn't mention the specific name for fear Ms. Gardner would call their office to confirm employment. "I'm still working to get the diner operational and later the motel, but this gives me a chance to earn some cash now. Anyhow, sorry I didn't call earlier, but I had to work late. I have to go out on the boat tomorrow and will be gone for about a week. If you need to reach me, you can try my cell phone, but I'm not sure there will be access. I'll check in when I get back. Bye."

That out of the way, Delilah called her grandmother. She'd already checked with her this morning to make sure she got the money wire, but she wanted to make sure her grandmother had no problems paying off the loan shark and past due bills. Or that she hadn't skipped off to the casinos.

At first, Delilah was worried when the phone rang repeatedly, but then Maggie picked up. "Hi, Mommy! Did you get me a dog yet?"

"No, I did not get you a dog yet." *And I never actually said that I would, you little imp.* "You sound out of breath, sweetie."

"Me and Gramma just came in. We were shopping."

Uh-oh. Delilah hoped her grandmother hadn't decided to splurge since she had a little extra cash, which wasn't really extra. She glanced at her watch. Nine o'clock. "Oh?"

"Yep. We went to Walmart. I got a new bathing suit and flip-flops and Day of the Week panties and a booster seat . . . and gummy bears. Gramma bought a suitcase and wait till you see the wagon—"

"Shh! Remember what I said? Let me have the phone," she heard her grandmother say.

"Oops," Maggie said with a giggle.

"What's up?" her grandmother asked Delilah then.

"A wagon? For Maggie? How cute! And a suitcase? For your Avon samples?"

"Um. Sure."

"Why did you buy Maggie a booster seat? I was going to get that when I came to pick her up. Hell . . . I mean, heck . . . I haven't even traded the motorcycle in for a car yet." *Forget about the compact I was considering. Already I need to make sure there's space for Maggie's booster seat, a wagon, her DVD player, toys, clothes . . . Aaarrgh!*

"There was a sale."

*On booster seats? Well, at least she didn't buy a dog leash.* "Isn't it kind of late for you to be out shopping?"

"I had to go to the pediatrician for Maggie's physical and the medical records you said she needs for kindergarten. The only appointment we could get was six o'clock and since we were out that way anyhow . . . what? You have a problem with us shopping? Cri-min-ey!"

"Son of a bi . . . bike! How did you carry all that stuff on the bus?"

"I managed. The bus driver helped. You think I'm too old to get around anymore?" her grandmother sniped. "I'll have you know the bus driver asked me for a date. A man with a job asked me for a date! How about that?"

"I wasn't being critical. Jeesh, Gram! Did you get everything taken care of today? The money stuff."

"Of course."

"No problems?"

"Why would there be?"

Her grandmother was being awfully testy tonight, for some reason. "Well, I just wanted you to know that I'll be gone from Wednesday on, maybe for a week or more. I should have cell phone access, but just in case, here's an emergency number." She gave her the phone number for Bell Cove Salvaging and Treasure Hunting, figuring that, in an emergency, Harry or whoever was in the office would have ways of contacting her on the open sea. She also told her grandmother about some of the latest developments regarding the motel.

"Sounds like things are going well for you there."

"Yes. Knock on wood. Hopefully, I'll be able to get to A.C. in another month and bring Maggie back here with me."

After Delilah ended the call with another quick chat with her daughter, she sat staring out the windows toward the star-filled skies over the sound. For some reason, she felt uneasy. Something about her conversation with her grandmother felt off.

She shook her head to rid it of any negative thoughts. She had enough on her plate without imagining troubles.

When the town bells began to toll in the distance, marking the hour with eleven bongs, she shut down her computer and called it a day. For a moment, she just listened to, first, Our Lady by the Sea, then St. Andrew's, then the town hall, each with their own distinctive sounds. In fact, the entire town—businesses as well as residences—had unique bells attached to their doors. Even the diner door chimed to the tune of "Don't Be Cruel."

By the time she'd showered and brushed her teeth and was in bed, it was almost midnight, and the bells would be ringing again. She didn't mind the constant exposure to bells like some folks did. After all, bells were the foundation of the town, even though the forge was floundering these days.

She yawned big and loud before shimmying under the cool sheets. Silence surrounded her, except for the whirring window air conditioner, giving her a first chance to think about her biggest trouble, a subject she'd avoided all evening by working to pan out the worry.

How could she forget about *him* when she had a twenty-foot Elvis sitting in her front yard? A visible reminder of how Merrill Good kept interfering in her life.

Six foot three of hard-muscled trouble, that's what he was, not twelve feet of neonized metal. Which was even worse. A fake Elvis she could handle. Not so much the way-too-kind, meddling, presumptuous, high-handed, intrusive man of the hour. Not to mention pure temptation.

With the body of a hardened warrior and the face of a teenage heartthrob, Merrill Good spelled trouble with a capital *T*. And not just because of all his well-meaning intrusions in her life. If she'd had any doubt about the danger he posed, the kiss they'd shared today made it loud and clear.

If she wasn't careful, she could fall in love.

And look where love had landed her in the past. But she'd managed to keep her romantic inclinations under control these past five years. Not so difficult when living in a women's prison. All she would need to do now was keep a steady path of noninvolvement. She couldn't let the man—any man—stir up her life now. Cool, calm, and focused.

Ironically, when the midnight bells began their tolls, one of the set sounded strangely like "All Shook Up."

### She wasn't Victoria, but whoo-boy, she had a secret . . .

Salome Jones was in a hurry. Lots to do and not enough time to do it. She had the double dead bolt locks set on both the front and back doors, security chains in place, and kitchen chairs placed under both doorknobs, but she was taking no chances. By tomorrow night—*it was always best to make a getaway in the dark*—she expected to be on the Cape May Ferry, heading south. Time to get out of Dodge—um, Atlantic City.

Vaping away on her e-cig, ginger flavored tonight to soothe her nerves, Sal put a lid on yet another box of the tissue-wrapped Avon collectibles she was packing up. She sat on the couch and was using the coffee table as her workstation. She had gotten some really nice boxes with lids from the liquor store down the street this morning, thanks to her old friend, Carmine Lorenzo, who'd thrown in a bottle of blackberry wine as a going-away gift. And she'd purchased a pigload of pastel-colored tissue paper from Walmart this evening so she could color code her prized Avon bottles by theme. No way was she leaving behind her collection! It would be just like Jimmy the Goon to come in with his cane and break them all to smithereens, just for spite. *Some people just don't appreciate fine art.* Or because she'd refused to go on a date with him to the Early Bird dinner at the Borgata. *The cheapskate!* Or maybe because she'd failed to pay off the total amount of her loan. *Jeesh! I gave Sharkie five thousand dollars toward my loan. I told him I'd pay off the rest later. Give a girl a break, why dontcha!*

"Gramma, why did you shush me when I was talking to Mommy?" Maggie asked as she came in from the kitchen where she'd been having a bedtime snack of Oreos and milk. She was wearing a new pair of Snoopy pj's and looked cute as a button. Sal was trying to wean her off her *Annie* fixation, mostly to no avail. *Just like her mother!*

"Our secret. Remember our secret, sweetie," she said, motioning for the little girl to come sit beside her on the couch. "You can't tell anyone we're going on vacation."

"In our wagon."

"Right. In our station wagon." Sal had used the remaining five thousand dollars that Delilah had sent to buy a twenty-year-old Buick station wagon and various other things for her road trip. Her pal, Honkin' Harvey Harrison over at Bonzo Used Cars, Boats, and Lawnmowers—every time he sold a car he honked a bullhorn on his TV ads—

had given her a great deal on the vehicle, which had only 208,000 miles on it. A "diamond in the rough," Harvey had called it.

"Betcha there would be room in that car for a dog."

"We are not getting a dog." At the hurt look on Maggie's face, she added, "Some dogs get carsick. It's better to wait till we get to Bell Cove and let your mother get you a dog." Sal should have felt guilty about passing the buck to Delilah, but she didn't. Too much other stuff on her mind.

Already having put the dog subject aside, Maggie asked, "Can you drive a car, Gramma?"

"Of course I can drive a car, sweetie!" *Even though I haven't driven one in ten years. But a person never forgets how. Right? Like riding a bicycle. Right? Which I haven't done for fifty years, except for that brief stint of madness when I joined a gym on my fiftieth birthday and fell off a stationary bike. Never again!*

"But you ran over the curb at the car lot and almost knocked Honkin' Harvey on his ass."

"Magdalene Jones! We do not use words like that."

"But that's what Honkin' Harvey said. 'That crazy broad almost knocked me on my ass.' And he stuck his finger up in the air when you waved at him."

"I'll be fine once I have a little practice. Besides we'll be driving real slow on this trip. Maybe stop at a few places along the way. Aunt Phyllis has been inviting me to come for years."

"Doesn't Aunt Phyllis live in a place for old farts? I don't think I'd like visiting a farty place."

Sal rolled her eyes. Her granddaughter heard way too much that wasn't meant for little ears. "Aunt Phyllis lives in a very nice active senior village in Maryland. They even have a swimming pool."

"Yippee!"

"We might even stop in Virginia at Busch Gardens." Actually, there was a regional convention of Avon collectors being held in Richmond, Virginia, that Sal would love to attend. Maybe she could talk Maggie into making a pact, several hours with a herd of Avon Ladies for several hours at Busch Gardens.

"Gramma! I don't want to go to no gardens."

"It's not that kind of gardens. Busch Gardens is a huge amusement park, like Six Flags. Remember when your nursery school took a field trip to Six Flags?"

Maggie smiled. "Can we go on a roller coaster?"

Sal groaned. She was getting too old for the raising of a child, and that was saying a lot. Salome Jones never admitted to being too old for anything. "We'll see," Sal lied.

"Promise?"

"I promise we'll go to Busch Gardens. That's all I'm promising. But remember"—she pretended to zip her lips—"our secret. No one should know about our secret trip."

Maggie pretended to zip her lips, too. But she

couldn't keep quiet for long. "Mommy will be so surprised to see us."

"That's for sure," Sal muttered.

### *Everybody plays the fool sometime . . .*

After sharing a few beers at The Live Bass, Merrill decided to drive by Delilah's diner on his way home to the Patterson Home for Overage Dodobirds.

*And, by the way, wouldn't Delilah's Diner be a better name than Rock Around the Clock Diner? Not that I'm going to suggest that anytime soon. My interference factor is through the roof already, according to Delilah.*

Passing through the business, then residential sector, he saw evidence of the huge Fourth of July celebration the townfolk had recently engaged in, which had carried over to the Rutledge wedding on Saturday. Flags. Red, white, and blue banners. Sprays of fake stars on the brass, bell-shaped streetlights. Betsy Ross sitting on a rocker in the town square gazebo sewing a flag. Several yard flamingos wearing Uncle Sam hats. Every kind of kitsch imaginable and then some.

Supposedly, the powers that be, i.e. the town council, had decided that the Grinch contest and its related festivities in December, followed by a massive Independence Day celebration, had brought in so much of the desirable pass-through tourist traffic they wanted that they were saving the decorations for some kind of Labor Day Lollypalooza, or some other bat-ass crazy idea. If anything else came into their radar, like Ethan Rutledge and Wendy Patterson's wedding, well, hey, they already had the ideas and decorations available. He could only imagine what they'd do when Delilah had her diner grand opening.

You had to love small towns!

He revved the engine on the Harley as he neared the diner, just because he could and because, in his newfound immaturity, he wanted Delilah to know he was out there at midnight. He spotted the twenty-foot neon Elvis standing by the front steps, unlit at this point, but, hey, it would be cool when "The King" welcomed folks to the eating establishment. God bless eBay. You really could find anything there. Not that he'd been looking for a neon Elvis. He'd actually been scoping out boat fridges when Elvis popped up.

That was his story, anyhow, and he was sticking to it.

But then, as Merrill was about to cruise around the corner, he couldn't help but notice something else. A huge pile of mattresses and box springs had been stacked next to the Dumpster.

In an instant, Merrill's good mood turned bad. In fact, he was suddenly so mad he could spit nails. Well, *frustrated* would be a better word, he supposed.

He just knew that Delilah had done all that heavy work herself. In fact, it was a logical conclusion after having talked to the contractor, Mike Somers, at the bar tonight. Mike told him that he and his men had started on the electrical and plumbing work late that afternoon, and the whole time they were there, Delilah had been scrubbing the walls and ceilings with some kind of bleach solution. So much for Merrill's suggestion of a cleaning service!

What was it about the woman that made her so stubborn, so insistent on doing things herself? It wasn't just poverty, he knew that. She could have asked him or any one of a dozen neighbors who would be more than willing to lift a hand. A strong work ethic was one thing, unbendable pride was another. Stupid! On the other hand, maybe it was some secret in her past that made her untrusting of even the smallest gesture of help.

He couldn't ask her. She'd probably blister his skin off with blue words, which she would immediately amend with half-baked clean substitutes, or kick him in his nuts, or tell him to mind his own fucking—uh, bleepin' business.

Which would be a silly thing for Merrill to do, anyhow, considering that there wasn't anything Merrill didn't know about computers. With a few clicks of the keyboard, he could find out everything there was to know about Delilah Jones of Atlantic City, right down to her medical and dental records. Hell, he could probably even get her kindergarten report card. But he'd chosen not to do a search, so far. Somehow, it felt like the worst kind of privacy invasion, like rooting through her underwear drawer. Yeah, guys and girls on the dating scene did it all the time, a little Google search even before a first date, just in case the person was an ax murderer, or a catfish looking to scam someone. Once F.U. got matched on one of the Internet dating sites with a lingerie model with Barbie-like dimensions, who turned out, with a little computer sleuthing, to be a three-hundred-pound inmate. Which was about right for F.U.

Nope, Merrill was old school. He still wanted the mystery of finding out about a potential mate through personal interaction. *Does that make me a geek? Probably. So sue me!*

And, whoo-boy, did he need some personal interaction in his life! He couldn't recall the last time he'd gotten laid. Well, yes, he could. That ballerina turned Navy WEALS newbie he'd met at the Wet and Wild last January. The things she could do with a plié! But then she'd dropped out of the program and moved back to D.C. Long-distance relationships were the pits, and one-night stands did not a relationship make.

*Like I have any relationship now!*

*Or the prospect of one.*

*Well, there was the kiss.*

*Promising.*

*Shit! I'm going to bust my ass for promises now?*

*Aaarrgh!*

*Six months of celibacy is beginning to wear on me.*

If sex was all he was interested in, he would have given up on Delilah by now. But what did he want? That was the question. An affair? A committed relationship? Marriage?

Holy crap! He didn't even know her. Was she

right- or left-handed? Where did she go to school? College? Did she sleep on her back, or her side, or her belly? Was she a morning person, or a night owl? What was her favorite movie, or TV show? Did she like music? What kind? Who was her baby's father? Was he still in the picture? And why wasn't her daughter with her now?

So many questions, and yet none of them mattered. There was just something about her that drew him. He couldn't explain the attraction. It was overwhelming, like an unending g-force attack on his body, and on his emotions, as well. That was the scary part.

And, dammit to hell, he felt like such a fool. Chasing after her like one of Elvis's old hound dogs.

When he got to the Patterson house, he tried to make as little noise as possible. The seniors were probably all asleep by now, even though they were an active group. Currently in residence, aside from himself on the third floor—*Please, God, not for much longer. Little does Delilah know, but I'm going to be occupying one of those motel units*—were Mildred Patterson and her boyfriend, Raul Arias, who was Bonita's father, an academic from Spain who was writing a book on dance through the ages.

Then there was Harry Carder, who'd moved in after his house had sold quicker than expected following the death of his wife, a beloved Bell Cove dentist. Harry's stay had been intended to be short-term, but was looking longer term by the day. Like Merrill's.

There was also Elmer Judd, a former veterinarian who shared a room with his menagerie of dogs. Elmer's cooking hobby kept them all in fine meals, different every night. The little garden he'd started this spring out back now produced a bonanza of heirloom tomatoes, vegetables, and every herb imaginable.

Mike and Ike Dorset, twin professors emeriti of psychiatry from Auburn, "escaped" recently from Sunset Shores retirement home where they'd been besieged by femme fatales whose freckles had long since turned to liver spots. Not that they didn't have plenty of their own, despite having full heads of Phil Donohue white hair. The two brothers, who finished each other's sentences, were always psychoanalyzing everyone, to the point where Elmer had a T-shirt made up that read, "Shrinks Stink."

On the female side, there was Claudette Devereaux, a former deb from New Orleans with a mysterious past. And the most recent addition, Joanna Horton, an actress who'd played the family matriarch Gloria Carstairs for thirty years on the soap opera, "As the Stars Shine," until its demise last year. Gloria was presumably waiting for her Millionaire's Row bungalow on Nags Head to be renovated, but Merrill suspected that she was just lonely after being dumped by her husband of twenty years for a younger model.

Mildred and Raul hosted dance parties for older folks here at the house several days each week, and not just for those in residence. Tuesday Tango. Wednesday Waltz. Flamenco Friday, Saturday Salsa. Intermixed with those alliterative titles for day of the week parties were some others: the Bounce, the Jive, the Electric Boogaloo, the Swing, and the ever-popular regional favorite, the Carolina Shag. Last week he'd even witnessed, and would forever have the image imprinted on his eyeballs, Raul teaching the crowd how to twerk.

The thing was, they were good. All of them. Really good! Even Harry in his wheelchair, which he was sometimes able to replace with a walker.

And they had fun.

Good to know that, at an advanced age, men and women could still get it on.

Especially since he was thirty years younger and not getting anything on, dancing or otherwise.

There was a light in the kitchen, he saw. Maybe someone forgot to turn it off. Usually a night-light in the hall was all that was left on.

He walked down the hallway to find a pj's-clad Harry sitting in his wheelchair at the kitchen table, playing solitaire. A bottle of wine and a half-full glass sat within reach.

"Hey, Harry? You're up late."

"Couldn't sleep. Usually, a little wine does the trick."

Not inclined to break his pattern of the evening, Merrill grabbed a can of beer from the fridge and sat down wearily across from the old man.

Harry said right off, "You had a visitor today."

"Really?"

"Yep. Some guy named Benjamin Good."

*Oh, shit!* "My brother? Here?"

"Yep." Harry grinned. "Staying at some mansion in Hatteras with your parents."

"How do you know they're staying in a mansion?"

"Because he told me so. And made a point of mentioning that the mansion belongs to some big shot on the Princeton board of trustees."

It was probably Jerome Dellasario from Johnson & Johnson, whose ego matched theirs. Who happened to be Ben's father-in-law.

"No offense, but your brother has the biggest pole up his ass I've ever seen. Almost as bad as my son Sterling, who thinks he shits gold."

Merrill arched his brows.

"Your brother looked at this house like it was a slum. In fact, his exact words were, 'For a guy who's supposed to be worth a million dollars due to some embarrassing invention on the Internet, my brother sure is slumming.' He was referring to you, of course."

"Of course." Merrill laughed. "Typical! I haven't seen Ben for five years." Last he'd heard, Ben and Vanessa were biophysicists doing research at Johns Hopkins. He had no idea if they were still there or what they were doing. "Kinda hoped good ol' Ben woulda loosened up by now. He inherited that elitist attitude from my parents, by the way. They think anyone with less than a master's degree is illiterate and anyone not pursuing 'high' endeavors is a loser."

"Uh-oh! Sounds like you've had some bad experiences in that regard."

"You could say that. They couldn't imagine why a person with a Mensa intellect and a 5.0 GPA from Princeton, where they teach, would go into the military."

"Pacifists?"

"Not so much that as a waste of intelligence."

Harry shook his head. "Serving your country is a waste? Pff! All those soldiers out there getting themselves killed for their freedom and safety must be imbeciles. Losers with no other options." Harry had served in Army intelligence at the tail end of the Vietnam War.

"Right. If they only knew the squids, jarheads, and grunts I've met! Between you and me, in SEALs, at least, there are some very intelligent, highly educated men, who also happen to be brave and loyal and patriotic. I'd take one of them any day over some professor who's never done anything outside a classroom." He paused. "Sorry for the rant. You hit a sore spot."

Harry took a sip of his wine and grinned. "It didn't help matters that Elmer asked your brother's wife if she'd like to dance. Today was Mambo Monday, remember?"

"Oh, Lord! Vanessa is here, too?"

"Uh-huh! And the pole up her behind was practically through her snooty nose." His grin faded as Harry explained, "She looked at Elmer like he was a dog turd under her fancy pancy sandals, and she said something unkind to Mildred when she offered them some lemonade."

Now, that burned Merrill's ass, big-time. It was

one thing for Ben and Vanessa to insult him, but they had no business coming here and offending these kind people. If they were here now, he would have a thing or two to say to them. And maybe a fist in Ben's priggish face was long overdue.

The sad thing was that Ben hadn't always been that way. Two years older than Merrill, Ben had been a great older brother. Fun. Protective. Adventurous. Merrill wasn't sure when he'd noticed the changes come about, maybe in high school when Ben had first fallen for Vanessa Dellasario, who thought she farted roses, even back then when she wore industrial-looking braces and had a lisp. Or maybe it was earlier than that, when their parents had begun pressuring both of them to become intolerant of those "inferior" to them, to associate only with friends with higher aspirations.

Merrill, a disappointment from an early age, had refused to bend to their mold. Almost everything Merrill liked had been a no-no. Skateboarding, football, video games, rock music, anything that didn't improve the mind. Ben hadn't been so determined, or maybe he was just weaker and unable to fight the tide of parental influence.

Merrill took a long swallow of beer and changed the subject. "So, insomnia? Happen a lot?"

Harry shrugged. "Ever since Julia died last year. I can keep busy during the day, but during the night I miss her so much I can barely stand it."

"How long were you married?"

"Forty-three years tomorrow."

"Aaah."

"I can't complain. Lots of people never find 'the one,' not even after repeated divorces and remarriages. I got lucky first time around."

Harry continued to play his card game while they talked.

Merrill took another sip of his beer, a smaller one this time, before asking, "How did you know she was 'the one'?"

"We were students at Georgetown. It was love at first sight for me. Not so much for Julia." He chuckled at some memory. "Julia had, in fact, been engaged to another fellow at the time."

"So, how'd you convince her that you were the better catch?"

"I made an absolute fool of myself, that's how," he said with another chuckle.

Merrill perked up at that word. "Really? How?"

"Maybe today I'd be accused of harassment, but I just wouldn't give up."

"And it worked?"

"Yep."

"Not that I did anything aggressive or slimy. Persistence, that's the key."

"And the willingness to play the fool?"

"Small price to pay for 'the one,' wouldn't you say?"

Merrill suspected that Harry's words were targeted at him. He knew that was the case when Harry remarked later, "What fool bought that tacky Elvis over at Lilah's diner?"

# Chapter 8

*Tarantism: the uncontrollable urge to dance (and not a spider in sight) . . .*

*D*elilah was happy.

And that surprised her. She hadn't realized that she'd been unhappy. And maybe she hadn't been unhappy, precisely. Not since she'd been released from prison five months ago, anyhow. Just joyless, if that made sense.

The mayor of Bell Cove, Doreen Ferguson, had talked Merrill into having a launch ceremony at noon; so, they were all biding their time with little makeshift jobs until then, anxious to get going. As Delilah stored the last of the supplies she'd purchased in the boat's kitchen, she wondered what had made a difference in her mood. Was it satisfaction over the work she'd done the past few days, both on her own diner/motel project as well as on the *Sweet Bells* boat in preparation for the Three Saints treasure hunt? Was it the knowledge that she would soon have her daughter living with her? Was it hope-turned-conviction that her life was finally taking a turn for the good? Was it simple excitement over the launch of the salvaging venture today? Or was it Merrill Good himself who made her happy?

Whatever!

She turned up the volume on the radio that sat on the counter, tuned to a South Carolina classic rock station, and found herself dancing in place to that old Bob Seger classic, "Old Time Rock and Roll."

"Now that's what I like to see . . . a dancing cook," Bonita said, as she came down the hatchway. "But, honey, you need a little more sass in your ass, Spanish style." She set her designer overnight case on the floor and danced her way toward Delilah in a combination boogie and salsa, with, yes, some ass sass thrown in.

Delilah moved from behind the counter to meet Bonita in the middle of the salon, where they both rolled their arms and shoulders, swayed their hips, and shook their booties, in perfect rhythm, while they belted out the lyrics to the old favorite. If they'd been wearing socks rather than rubber-soled sneakers, they probably would have added in a Tom Cruise sock slide à la *Risky Business*. When the song ended, they were both laughing.

And Charlie, who must have followed Bonita, stood at the bottom of the steps, her jaw dropped in astonishment. A duffel bag lay on the floor at her feet. "Holy crawfish! Is this the kind of trip this is going to be?"

The radio was now playing Aerosmith's "Walk This Way," and Bonita shimmied her way over to Charlie, giving her a hip bump. "C'mon, Charlie, loosen up. You're Cajun, aren't you? I hear Cajuns have an extra gene for dancing."

"Don't pick on Charlie," Delilah told Bonita. "She's probably shy."

"Fools!" Charlie said, encompassing them both, and then she did a perfect imitation of a Steven Tyler strut across the room with a hip wiggle tossed in.

Delilah was seeing the two women in a different light, and she liked what she saw. Maybe they would become—horror of horrors!—friends.

"So, this is where the fun people are hanging out."

They all turned to see the latest entrant into the cabin. It was Laura Atler, editor of the weekly newspaper, *The Bell*, who had been bird-dogging all the members of the salvaging team this week, working on an article about Bell Cove's newest enterprise. Delilah had managed to avoid an interview for obvious reasons. No publicity was good publicity for an ex-con. Delilah suspected that Charlie felt the same way, for her own personal reasons. Not so much Bonita, who seemingly had nothing to hide.

The DJ on the radio was speaking, now that the Aerosmith song had ended. "But we can't be talking old rock in the middle of the summer without mentioning beach music. No, I'm not talking the Beach Boys and the West Coast. Nope, we folks in the Carolinas know what beach music really means." And the song "Carolina Girls" came on.

Which prompted Laura to put her iPad and iPhone

in a laptop bag, which she set on a bench seat, and then launch into a perfectly executed shag, complete with intricate dance steps, dips of the knees, and twirls. She ended with a bow to each of them and laughed. "Now that's the way it's done!"

Delilah loved to dance, or at least she used to. How could she not, growing up with a grandmother who had been a showgirl and was always teaching her the moves? But she'd stopped dancing, she realized now, back when her world had started to fall apart. To her, dance had always represented joy, and there had been little of that. Until now. She liked how comfortable she felt with these women.

Not at all the way she'd felt about her fellow inmates at Edna Mahan, where you could never trust anyone, even a cell mate, who would give you the shaft for the least favor from a guard. And, yes, the women danced with each other on those rare breaks where music was played. But it had been a sad kind of dancing. Desperate, even.

But that was then, and this was now.

Delilah started to smile, perhaps with a smidgen of hope, as she participated in the high fives being exchanged among the new women in her life, but then they heard a loud blast of noise coming from outside. Pounding drums, then the melodious marching band version of "Anchors Aweigh."

"*What* is that?" Charlie asked.

"It appears that Mayor Ferguson got the high school band to come on short notice. I knew she was trying," Laura said, grabbing for her laptop bag.

"I thought there was only going to be the usual

good luck and bon voyage speech by the mayor, and a song or two by the St. Andrew's and Our Lady youth bell choirs," Bonita remarked.

"Does Bell Cove ever do anything in the usual way?" Laura asked.

"You've got a point there," Bonita said. "Case in point—last year's Christmas Grinch affair, and more recently the Stars and Stripes wedding."

"Well, 'Anchors Aweigh' is probably appropriate," Charlie conceded, "considering that we're going to be lifting anchor, if we ever get this friggin' show on the road . . . high seas. We're wastin' fuel idling here."

"The song's appropriate also because of Merrill's Navy background, I suppose," Delilah added.

Just then, a male voice yelled out, "Atten-shun!"

"Oh, my God! Doreen must have gotten the VFW guys to come out for a three-gun salute," Laura said. "Those old codgers are about eighty years old and haven't shot a gun since the Korean War. Everybody better duck."

Yep. *Bam! Bam! Bam! Bam! Bam!*

One of them was trigger-happy, or forgot how to count.

They all rushed to get up the hatchway then to see what was going on.

Merrill and the rest of the team—Adam, Gus, Gabriel Conti, the architect who owned Bell Forge, and Harry using a walker today—looked like deer caught in the headlights. Obviously, they were as shocked as the rest of them by this turn of events.

As expected, two dozen folding chairs, occupied

by various town folks, were arranged on the wharf before a podium with a microphone, and two clergymen, presumably from Our Lady and St. Andrew's, stood by, ready to give a blessing. But off to one side was the now-silent high school band, preparing to start up again. And to the other side, a half dozen senior citizen soldiers stood at attention with rifles. A red, white, and blue banner and other leftover Fourth of July decorations now adorned the bay side of the Bell Forge building. A satellite truck with the logo NBX-TV was parked in the lot.

And then the band launched into a new song, Lady Gaga's "Just Dance," with a strange accompaniment of bells, and the Shell Shore Dance Team came marching onto the scene with some of the scantily clad girls twirling batons and others doing gymnastic-type dance moves. What they had to do with a treasure hunting boat launch was beyond Delilah.

Just then, she noticed two well-dressed couples at the edge of the crowd, who glanced around with distaste at all the goings-on, and turned as one to walk away. Probably tourists.

Meanwhile, some others in the audience stood in front of their chairs and danced, too. Some of them might be from Mildred Patterson's dance club.

"This is outrageous," Charlie said.

"This is . . . mind-boggling," Delilah said.

"This is wonderful," Bonita said.

"This is Bell Cove," Laura said.

And that about said it all.

*Dare he hope for a shipboard romance . . . ?*

Merrill was appalled. And he was oddly touched.

Appalled, because when he'd agreed to Mayor Doreen Ferguson's suggestion of a launch ceremony for Bell Cove Treasure and Salvaging Company, he'd imagined a short speech by the mayor. Accompanied by maybe the breaking of a champagne bottle inside a mesh bag against the hull of the boat. But, no, that was for the launch of a new ship, a christening, wasn't it?

Touched, because these people in Bell Cove were well-meaning, and every absurd, outrageous gesture of the ceremony showed not just an honest communal wish for success in their venture, but a welcome of him and his company to the town. Besides, it had been funny. If a guy couldn't laugh at himself, he had no sense of humor at all.

The best part had been seeing the look on Delilah's face as she stood at the rail of *Sweet Bells* watching the band come marching in to "Anchors Aweigh." The worst part had been when he'd noticed his parents, along with Ben and Vanessa, at the edge of the crowd, looking horrified and embarrassed before turning to leave. Without even saying hello to him! Talk about *no* sense of humor! Did anyone else notice them?

It was two p.m. before he and his crew had been able to depart, but clear skies and calm seas made for a pleasant trip, and, yes, they were all laughing at what they'd left behind. In the hour or so it took to arrive at the site, five miles out, people exchanged reminiscences of the day.

"I couldn't believe that Doreen referred to us as buccaneers," Gus said. "Now, a Viking, that's another story."

"Some folks say I look like a young Johnny Depp," Famosa claimed.

"In your dreams!" the rest of them hooted.

He just laughed.

"In Loo-zee-anna, we prefer our pirates to look like Jean Lafitte," Charlie called out from the wheelhouse where she was steering at a low rate of speed, not wanting to push the engine too fast, too soon.

"Father Brad's prayer was kind of nice," Merrill interjected, "although I noticed that he mentioned the importance of sharing wealth. Do you think he's envisioning a big church donation? I do like his assumption, though, that we're going to make some big discoveries."

"From his lips to God's ears," Famosa joked. "The last treasure I cashed in on went to back alimony for my second wife. How about that little tuba player who farted every time she blew her horn?"

"She was not farting!" Bonita elbowed Famosa. "It was just the sound she made in the lower registers because she didn't have enough wind . . . um, breath."

Famosa grinned at her misspeak.

"I used to be able to do a triple flip like that dancer did," Gus said.

Bonita glanced at his six-foot-three frame and

arched her brows. "When was that . . . when you were ten years old?" She was obviously not a football fan, or she would know about Gus's antics.

"Nope. Every time I made a touchdown, I did that on the sidelines . . . until I got too many penalties for showboating. The fans loved it. Bet I could still do it."

"Please, don't," Merrill urged.

And so it went with light conversation as they settled in and got to know each other. He noticed that Delilah remained silent, listening but not sharing any personal info. Then she went down below. Soon they saw their designated spot, pinpointed by bobbing flags they'd set in place previously, and loud cheers greeted some startled birds overhead.

A map had been drawn of their licensed search boundaries as pinpointed by specific latitude and longitude lines on the open waters of the Atlantic, with the site divided into squares like a checkerboard. All of it had been programmed into Merrill's high-tech computer. They anchored the boat on the bottom left square and would begin diving there in the morning. Square by square they would move the boat, as many as six times a day, like a lawn mower, until they hit pay dirt.

Actually, it wasn't as hit-and-miss as that. He and some of the crew had already made a sweep of the site last month using side and bottom sonar equipment and a proton magnetometer, which could detect ferrous metals. With that data logged into a computer, the original five hundred or so blocks in the grid had been reduced to less than three hundred considered diveworthy. The problem was, time was money, and their permit expired one year from their starting date. That meant only four months left this year until winter set in, rendering dives impossible. If they found nothing by November, they would have to wait until April or May to return. By then, the bottom terrain could have changed, due to ocean currents and storms, meaning a whole new redo of prep for their dives. And of course, they had to get through hurricane season, which on the Outer Banks was July through December, but most likely August or September.

A cold lunch was set out by Delilah, but Merrill was busy on deck all afternoon, and wasn't able to go below until almost dinnertime. He found her alone in the kitchen chopping vegetables for a salad in a huge wooden bowl. On the counter separating the kitchen from the rest of the salon sat several loaves of garlic bread ready to go into the oven. An equally large trencher on the table held various fresh fruits: apples, oranges, peaches, plums, and grapes. Delicious smells of some kind of pasta sauce emanated from a pot on the stove.

"That smells delicious," he said, going up to the sink and washing his hands.

"You missed lunch. You must be starving. Do you want me to make you a sandwich or something?"

He shook his head. "I can wait for dinner. What's on the menu?"

"Nothing fancy. Seafood linguine with a summer salad and garlic bread. A store-bought fruit tart for dessert. I didn't have time to make anything from scratch today. Sorry."

"No cinnamon rolls?" he teased.

"Are you saying that I overdo the cinnamon rolls?" She pointed the sharp knife in her hands at him.

He laughed and put both hands up in surrender. "Your cinnamon rolls are heavenly. Can any man have too much heaven?"

"Good answer," she said, and resumed cutting tomatoes into neat wedges which she tossed into the bowl.

Delilah appeared more relaxed today. Not so prickly and quick to take offense. He wasn't sure if it was because they were away from town, or she was growing more comfortable with him and the other crew members. He wasn't about to question a good thing.

"That was some launch celebration the town held for you," Delilah remarked. "Did you expect that?"

"No, but then that's Bell Cove. I shouldn't have been surprised."

"Everyone loved it."

"Not everyone. Did you notice those two couples who walked out?"

"I did. Anyone you know?"

He hesitated before saying, "Yeah. My mother, father, brother, and bitch-in-law. Vacationing on Hatteras." He could have kicked himself for revealing that personal information. He rarely talked about his family. They were irrelevant to him.

Delilah looked at him, waiting for more.

He'd said more than enough. "On a happier note,

Bonita told me that you four women, including Laura Atler from *The Bell* newspaper, were dancing down here earlier today. I would have liked to see that," he remarked, sneaking a carrot stick from her pile and popping it into his mouth. Crunching away, he watched her face bloom with color as she gave him a little smile.

And his heart lurched. If she wasn't so skittish and he wasn't afraid of crossing a line, he would have hugged her spontaneously and perhaps planted a quick kiss on her lips. The desire to touch her was almost overwhelming. Which caused him to back off.

Once again, he wondered why he was so hot for Delilah. Sure, she was attractive. Her silver-blonde hair was held off her neck and face and piled on top of her head with some claw combs. Her bordering-on-voluptuous figure filled a plain black T-shirt and white jeans. What drew him most, though, was her face, which was innocently vulnerable, with blue eyes that seemed to be wary from some huge pain and lips which were full and rose colored, even without lipstick, and parted as if always ready to defend herself from some attack.

*Attack? Where did that come from?* Merrill wondered.

He slid onto a stool on the other side of the counter and noticed an open spiral notebook. "Your menu plans?" he asked, seeing a calendar with meal and food remarks made on particular days. Chicken salad sliders. Crab cakes. Ina's mac and cheese. Steak and kidney pie. Pulled pork. Grilled salmon. "Mind if I look?"

She shrugged.

"You might want to make room for fresh fish. Usually some lines are thrown overboard, even during the dive operations. Never know what we might catch out here. Bass, flounder, red drum, whatever."

"Sounds good. Just so it's not shark. And please don't tell me that shark tastes just like chicken. I don't care. Did you know that sharks pee through their skin? Yuck!"

He laughed.

"Do you have any particular preferences? Dishes you like?" she asked.

"I eat most anything. It's more a question of what I don't like. I've been in the military the past fifteen years. Food on the base was actually pretty good. I'm embarrassed to say that I like Spam, that old military standby, but I hate Shit on the Shingle, creamed chipped beef on toast." He grimaced and pretended to shiver with distaste. "I like anything with lemons. Lemon meringue pie. Lemon chicken. Lemonade." He waggled his eyebrows at her. "Lemon Jell-O shots."

"I like lemons, too. In fact, I make a spectacular honey glazed lemon cinnamon roll, if I do say so myself."

"Why am I not surprised?" He stole a cucumber slice this time. "Is there anything you don't put in cinnamon rolls?"

"Chipped beef," she said with a grin, even as she moved the bowl out of his reach. "Behave yourself, and I'll make you a batch of the lemony cinnamon rolls sometime."

"I'll hold you to that promise." Merrill liked this easy banter with Delilah and the companionable silence that followed as she continued to build her salad. He hesitated to break the mood. "You obviously enjoy cooking. Did you always?"

"Yep. I was raised by my grandmother. I think I told you that before. She was always working. Had to, of course. So, I learned to cook from an early age, or survive on Pop-Tarts and boxed mac and cheese."

He noticed that she didn't mention a grandfather, or a father and mother, for that matter. Those questions would come later. Instead, he said, "What's wrong with Pop-Tarts?"

She gave him a disapproving look and continued, "I didn't have many friends, with us living in a rough neighborhood and Gram not wanting me to play outside. Kids my age were reading 'American Girl' books and collecting the ultra-expensive dolls, while I was devouring the used cookbooks I bought at yard sales. I have an impressive collection, although they're pretty much useless now due to the Internet and all. The days of leafing through real books with colorful illustrations are long gone. Much easier to just google what you're looking for." She was whisking some kind of homemade salad dressing now—olive oil, raspberry vinaigrette, and herbs—when she paused, perhaps realizing that she was talking more to him now than she ever had before. "So, what did you read as a kid? Action adventure books? G.I. Joe comics?"

"Nah, my parents would have never allowed that—too plebeian. And, yes, that's a word they actually use. I'm probably ten years older than you, but—"

"Ten years older! You look ten years younger."

"Is that a good or bad?"

"Definitely good. You have the face of a teenage boy."

"And the body of a mature man, I hope."

She just smiled and shook her head as if he was hopeless.

"As I was saying, I was a precocious kid, reading way beyond my years. When other little boys were reading Dr. Seuss, which I liked . . . still like, especially *The Sneetches*, I finished *The Lord of the Rings* by the time I was six years old."

"Seriously?"

He nodded. "I'll confess something, though. My guilty pleasure, even today, is watching reruns of 'Mayberry.'"

She frowned with confusion. "You mean that old *Andy Griffith Show*?"

"Oh, yeah! I know the lines of some of the shows by heart." In a Sheriff Taylor voice, he said, "You start dating one woman all the time and pretty soon people start taking you for granted. They don't say, 'Let's invite Andy' or 'Let's invite Elly.' No, they say, 'Let's invite Andy and Elly!' See, then it's 'Andy and Elly.' 'Elly and Andy.' And then, that's when the woman gets her claws in you."

Delilah laughed and clapped her hands.

He could feel his face heat. "Anyhow, a psychiatrist would have a heyday examining my Mayberry obsession."

"Is that why you moved to Bell Cove?"

"Could be. Although Bell Cove is a half-assed version of Mayberry."

Suddenly serious, she put her whisk down—*Who knew I had a whisk, by the way?*—and said, "That's nothing. My go-to comfort movie was, and still is, the movie *Annie*. The original version."

"See, we have something in common. Guilty pleasures." He winked at her. "Who knows what other guilty pleasures we might share?"

"Oh, you!" she said, but didn't seem offended. Instead, she went on, "In fact, my daughter has apparently inherited that *Annie* addiction of mine. She watches the movie over and over."

There was a message hidden there in her words, about why she and her daughter fixated on a movie about an orphan. And how they were rescued by . . .

*Oh, no! Is that why she asked me if I ever shaved my head? Is she thinking of me as a Daddy Warbucks? I'm not that old! And I do not want to be a father figure to her.*

But then, she picked up the whisk again, and using it like a microphone, she sang, in a surprisingly good voice, the lyrics to "It's a Hard-Knock Life." Her lips were smiling as she sang and looked at him, but her eyes were sad.

And Merrill fell in love, even more than he already was.

# Chapter 9

*Me and Jacques Cousteau . . .*

After one full day on the site, no treasure had been found, but Delilah was having the time of her life. Instead of work, this felt like a vacation.

She was especially pleased because everyone raved about her meals. Not just last night's seafood linguine, but this morning's mushroom and cheddar omelets with sourdough bread, and a lunch featuring turkey, bacon, and avocado sliders with Amish macaroni salad. Tonight she would be serving a mostly Mexican feast which included tacos, burritos, yellow rice, refried beans, and decadent churros with a rich chocolate sauce.

But more than her enjoyment over cooking for an appreciative audience was her fascination with the whole treasure hunting process. Who knew that salvaging could be so thrilling! Especially for her! In a way, treasure hunting was like gambling, and Delilah had always had an aversion to gambling, growing up in a casino town and seeing the ill effects on some people. Fortunes were lost, families ruined on the flip of a card. But shipwreck salvaging was different somehow, in more than the obvious ways. Sure, the stakes were high and the risks even greater, but there was a professionalism to it that raised it above the muck. Maybe it was because so much hard work was involved. Or it could be the historical context. It felt a little Jacques Cousteau-ish.

Three dives had been made today with alternating pairs going down in tandem. Merrill and Gus. Adam and Bonita. If nothing of interest was seen and the spot was deemed a dud in terms of shipwreck remains, the anchor was pulled and the boat moved to the next block in the grid.

Even the diving itself was a time-consuming process due to all the necessary precautions. Because these were deep waters, the divers could only stay below for twenty-five minutes, Merrill had explained to her earlier, and then an hour coming back up, stopping at intervals to decompress as a precaution against the dreaded narcosis, better known as the bends. Even when they were back on board, they had to wait another two or three hours as they continued to decompress.

By late afternoon, they were about to make the fourth and final dive for the day, and Delilah was too excited to stay below. Checking to ensure that all her food was ready to be popped into the oven when everyone wanted to eat, she went up on deck. She was just in time.

Bonita and Adam were sitting on the side of the boat in full diving gear. At a signal from Merrill they bit down on their regulators and rolled backward into the water.

"I thought you guys would be wearing those skintight rubber suits like you see on TV," Delilah remarked to Gus, who was watching that the lines uncoiled without a hitch. "The ones that fit like a glove." *And I wouldn't be caught dead in. My curves get too much attention as it is. Besides, no way would my butt fit in one of those girdle-ish affairs, and my boobs would be squished if they fit at all. Em-barr-ass-ing!*

Without looking her way, Gus said, "Nope. Too cold for a wet suit at this depth. The dry suits are big and bulky, but at least your toes, and other body parts, don't freeze." Now that the line was fully extended, he glanced her way and grinned. "I can always model my tightest neoprene for you if you're interested."

She went stiff at his suggestive remark, but then, as he winked at her, she realized that he was just teasing. "Thanks, but I'll pass." She really needed to stop being so defensive. Not every man was a sexist pig, like many of the guards she'd been exposed to for five long years.

Merrill came over then and exchanged a few words with Gus. "The WAPs are surprisingly good this afternoon. I was able to do an overlay of the GODAR sets with the GrADS and see much better than this morning. Super clarity!"

"And the virtual biological sludge on the GCMS?"

"That, too."

"Cool," Gus said.

"What foreign language is that?" Delilah asked.

Merrill grinned. "Computerese."

"Hey, don't feel bad," Gus said. "I don't understand half of what he says, either."

"WAP is a wireless application protocol. Then there is Global Oceanographic Data Archaeology Rescue, and Grid Analysis and Display System," Merrill explained.

"That makes it perfectly clear," Delilah said.

Merrill chucked her under the chin for her sarcasm. "Are you saying I'm a geek?"

"Only in a good way."

"Hey, Merrill," Charlie called from the wheelhouse. "I have to go pee. You wanna spot me on these monitors?"

"Aye, aye, Captain," Merrill agreed, and motioned for Delilah to follow him. "C'mon. I want to show you something."

"Do you want to show me, too?" Gus asked, with fake sincerity.

"Later," Merrill said. "Check the fishing lines first. See if we have any big-ass fish hooked for dinner."

"Sure. I saw a school of red drum earlier today. If we're lucky . . ." Gus went off to the other side of the boat where a half dozen rods were locked in place along the rail.

"Hey, I'm serving Mexican tonight," Delilah protested.

"You never heard of fish tacos?" Merrill said.

"You get me a big fish, and I'll cook it tomorrow, my way."

"Whatever you say, De-li-lah." He flashed her a mischievous smile which said, loud and clear, that he would be calling the shots, not her. And not just about some fish.

Wearing a well-worn U.S. Navy gray T-shirt with tan cargo shorts, sockless black athletic shoes, and a Yankees baseball cap, he should have looked like a college kid, but instead he was all muscle-bound man comfortable in his own suntanned skin. The smile was almost her undoing.

If it wouldn't have appeared obvious, Delilah would have fanned herself.

"I'm gonna take a break while I'm down below, if you don't mind," Charlie said to Merrill as she passed through the doorway.

"No problem," he replied. "By the way, Harry says some guy with a Southern accent has been calling the office for you."

Charlie swore under her breath.

"He refers to you as Charlotte, not Charlie, if that gives you a clue."

"Oh, I know 'zactly who it is. That damn Beauregard Butler, who thinks he's gonna be mah Rhett and rescue me. A Southern knight in shining souped-up truck! Or else Jefferson Lee Landry. Yep, it's probably JL. That boy has been a gnat on mah backside since we were wadin' in the bayou in our diapers catchin' mudbugs. Some men never give up." On those words, she stomped off.

Delilah and Merrill exchanged looks and then laughed.

At least no one had called for Delilah, she thought

with a sigh of relief. Not, for example, her grand-mother, or her parole officer, or Davie, God forbid, sending yet another plea that she come visit him in New Jersey State Prison. Small blessings!

Merrill indicated that Delilah should sit on the high stool before a series of monitors. He stood behind her and explained what they were looking at. There were the usual things you would expect on a boat this size, stuff like you see on TV shows like *Deadliest Catch*, depth finders and sonar scanners and such. But, in retrofitting this ship for salvaging, a bunch of high-tech computer equipment had been added to the point that the wheelhouse resembled some kind of NASA operation.

Delilah watched, fascinated, while Merrill explained patiently what was happening on the various screens, including the murky one that showed two divers moving about on the ocean bottom. Several times, Adam or Bonita, it was hard to tell which was which, picked up an item and put it in one of the bags attached to their belts. Various-sized fish and slithery snake-like animals, probably eels, swam by, mostly ignoring the humans in their stomping ground.

The whole time, Merrill had a hand placed on her back, between her shoulder blades. He probably didn't realize it. He might have done the same thing if anyone was sitting here. But she was aware of the simple gesture. The heat of his palm, like a brand. An *erotic* brand proclaiming his intentions toward her. Possession.

She didn't feel threatened.

She felt comforted.

Finally, the two divers could be seen yanking on their cords, a clear signal that they were about to begin the slow process back to the top. Another dud site.

She turned on her stool, thus forcing him to move his hand.

Only then did he seem to realize that he'd been touching her. He stared at his hand for a fleeting moment as if he didn't recognize it. Then looked at her mouth. Impulsively, he leaned down and gave her a quick kiss, which was electrifying, despite its brevity and butterfly lightness.

"Sorry. I don't know why I did that. Well, yes, I do, but . . ." He shook his head to clear it.

She wasn't offended. More like intrigued. Wishing the kiss had been a bit more intense so she could examine why she wasn't offended. But then, seeing how embarrassed he was, she changed the subject. "Are you terribly disappointed that today was a failure?"

"No. Not disappointed," he said, taking a step back, as if fearful he might kiss her again, or more. "Today was more of an exploratory venture. A look around, survey the terrain kind of thing. Yeah, it would be great to make a find the first day, but it almost never happens."

"Well, I better go below. Some last-minute things to do for dinner."

"In case I didn't mention it before, you've been a godsend. I was naive, or stupid, to think we could have gotten by, taking turns cooking."

"Thanks for saying so, but I'm sure you would have survived. Canned soup and bologna sandwiches, maybe, but no one would have starved."

"Look, Delilah, before Charlie comes back, can I ask you a question?" His face was serious.

*Uh-oh!* She was immediately wary. Had he found out something about her past? Was she about to be fired? Out at sea? Were her cooking skills not enough to keep her on the crew? Was the kiss a kiss-off? "You said you were pleased with my cooking, but did I do something wrong? Get in someone's way? Fail to clean the frickin' . . . um, filthy bathroom good enough? Are you gonna make me walk the plank . . . ha, ha, ha?" she tried to joke.

"What? Huh? Oh, nothing like that. I was just wondering . . . when we're back on land, would you go out on a date with me?"

It was her turn to say, "Huh?" But then, she narrowed her eyes at him. A "date" was often a code word for something else.

"I want to get to know you better, and vice versa. On a personal level."

*No, actually, you do not.* "Are you talking *date* date here? Like in high school?"

He blushed. He actually blushed. "High school, but better. I feel as if I've approached my attraction to you in the wrong way. Came on too strong."

She arched her brows at him. "You think?"

"Maybe we could go out to dinner, someplace where we could dance, too. A club. Or something."

"You like to dance?"

"Hell, no! But slow dancing I can manage without making a fool of myself." Merrill was not only blushing now but rubbing a hand over the boat's steering wheel, back and forth, back and forth.

Delilah was touched by his nervousness; she couldn't help herself. Still, she hesitated. "Merrill, I haven't been on a date since my junior class prom. And I haven't been with a man for more than five years for reasons beyond my control. I am not the best date material." *Whoa, why did I reveal so much about myself? I'm usually more careful. Maybe that innocent, vulnerable attitude of his is a ploy he uses to get women to open up. Maybe I'm weaker than I realized. Or just plain lonely.*

"You haven't been on a date for more than five years? Would that have been with your kid's father? And for what crazy 'reasons beyond my control' have you been celibate? That's what you meant by being with a man, I presume."

He waited for her to explain, which she did not.

As for his dating question, she should have told him "Thanks, but no thanks." Instead, she said, "Ask me again when we're back in Bell Cove."

To which, he smiled.

And, God help her, she smiled back.

## *Children are gifts from . . . who? . . .*

Monsters come in all sizes, and Salome Jones was sitting next to one who sat all princess-like in her throne-like booster seat. Perched between them on the bench seat was a dog the size of a small pony, a life-size Goofy, which had cost Sal a mere fifty bucks in the ringtoss game from hell.

Looking at the little girl, a bystander might see her as cute and innocent and a joy to be around. Hah! Try spending eight hours walking around an amusement park—aka a torture arena for grand-mothers with fallen arches after fifty years in high heels. Or sitting on one kiddie ride after another till your butt goes numb and your hair looks like a bird's nest. Or playing games meant for profes-sional ballplayers when your only hand dexterity involves pulling the lever on a slot machine.

The alternative? Cajoling, guilting, weeping, brib-ing, and then pulling a full-blown tantrum that had security guards eyeing Sal like she was some kind of child abuser. "I want a dog!" she'd wailed.

Yes, there was a devil in Magdalene Jones, in fact a bunch of devilish imps, and they had all come hop, skip, and jumping out today. But payback was going to be sweet. Tomorrow was Avon day.

"Gramma," the evil one said.

"What?" Sal snapped as she drove the car toward the motel where they would be staying that night. It was six p.m. Sal wondered how soon they could go to bed.

"I love you."

And, of course, Sal forgave all.

"But I still want a real dog."

Maybe not all.

### *May the force . . . um, luck . . .*
### *be with you . . .*

A week later, they were returning to Bell Cove. No great discovery thus far, to Merrill's chagrin, but carrying a few "artifacts," which would be carbon dated to determine if they might have come off one of the three saint ships. Nothing spectacular. Several hinges, a doorknob, some brass buttons. If they were as old as they appeared to be, they might be from another shipwreck, which could be equally exciting.

Charlie was steering the boat and would have its holding tank pumped of waste material, its fresh water supply renewed, and the boat gassed up again for a return to the site day after tomorrow. She insisted on sleeping on the boat, even though Delilah had offered the use of her convertible sleep couch.

Also traveling with Merrill was Bonita, who owned a cottage in Ocracoke. She needed to make contact with her university regarding a problem with her thesis. While she was there, she would take the "artifacts" into the lab for testing.

And Delilah, who was constantly adding to the list of supplies she needed to buy, came, too. Aside from shopping and other chores, she was anxious to check on the progress of the motel renovations, which were supposedly complete, or as complete as she was prepared to go financially at this point.

Famosa and Gus had agreed to stay on the site in

the large cabin cruiser that Merrill had purchased
along with the salvaging boat. Pirates were always
an issue, even when there were no big discoveries,
yet. And, yes, both men were armed against that
possibility.

Any day now K-4 should arrive, his last SEAL
contract now fulfilled. Maybe even before they returned to the site. That extra man, especially one
dive-qualified, would help tremendously.

As soon as they arrived back at the wharf in Bell
Cove and got the gangway in place, Bonita took off.
She had a long drive to the university at Durham
where she was set to meet with her doctoral advi-
sor. Charlie helped him and Delilah load the trash
bags into the dock Dumpster and stack the laundry bags in his truck.

"So, we're back on land," he said to Delilah as she
opened the door on his truck and was about to hike
herself up on the high seat.

She turned.

"I'm asking again."

A slight pink flushed her cheeks. She knew what
he was talking about, but wasn't about to give him
a break by acknowledging that fact.

"You told me to ask again once we were back in
town."

"I didn't mean the minute we set foot on land."

He was not about to be put off by a little snippi-
ness. "Well?"

"What do you have in mind?" Poor choice of
words! The pink grew pinker.

"Dinner?"

"I have so much to do, Merrill."

"A late dinner?"

She hesitated, then said. "Okay."

"Eight o'clock?"

She nodded.

He turned to walk toward the building, before she had a chance to change her mind, which he knew she would if given a chance, especially since she was muttering, "This is so not a good idea."

"I beg to differ, babe," he said to himself as he continued walking from the parking lot into the building where Harry was waiting to update him on the business.

"For a guy who hasn't hit pay dirt, you sure are looking happy," Harry remarked from where he sat behind Merrill's desk. His wheelchair was off to the side, which was a good sign that Harry was regaining some of the strength in his legs.

Merrill sank down into a chair in front of the desk. "There's pay dirt, and then there's *pay dirt*."

"Aaah."

"Know any good restaurants for a date?"

Instead of teasing him, as one of his buddies would, Harry took his question seriously. "Well, considering the time it would take to go out of town with the ferries and all, and considering that you wouldn't be able to drink if you're driving, your best bet would be to stick around Bell Cove. Nothing wrong with the Cracked Crab."

"I suppose, but we'd run into everybody in town who'll want to stop and chat. About our progress on the boat and Delilah's diner, and—"

"Ah. So, it's Delilah, huh? Interesting. I thought her name was Lilah."

"She prefers to go by that nickname. Anyhow, you know how the busybodies will be swarming . . . and I mean busybodies in the kindest way."

"You could always call ahead and ask Tony to reserve you a table in the back of the room. You know Tony, don't you?"

He nodded. He'd met Tony Bonfatto, the owner, when he was here last Christmas. His restaurant featured a mix of Italian and beach seafood entrées. A great wine list. And a live band out on the deck, with a tiny space for dancing. "Good idea. Thanks!"

He and Harry spent the next hour going over bills, estimated future expenses, and correspondence.

"Did you see this letter from Joel Bastian, the guy up the Blue Ridge mountains who claims to have emeralds on his property the size of golf balls? Looking for someone reputable to help him dig up one section."

Merrill arched his brows. "Why us?"

"Well, most speculators would come in with heavy equipment and upheave the terrain. Mr. Bastian doesn't want his land destroyed, and the state wouldn't allow it. Plus, it's a really remote, inaccessible area. No real roads."

Merrill's eyes went wide. "He would want us to dig, by hand?"

"Pretty much." Harry chuckled. "The thing is, North Carolina really does have as much treasure in the ground as it does in shipwrecks off its coast. Something about the geology that creates gems, just like the ones you find in South America and Africa."

"Now that you mention it, I read something about a farmer on the other side of Charlotte who found a huge emerald worth a million bucks."

"Anyhow, I only mention this as something to consider for the future. You need a master plan for your company. Whether you are successful with this particular salvaging operation or not, you need to make a decision about whether you want to concentrate only on shipwreck salvaging or diversify into other treasure hunting arenas, like Jinx did. Gold mines, cave pearls, whatever."

"I'm not sure, but it's something to think about."

"And here's something else to ponder. If you do decide to branch out, you might want to increase your workforce. Perhaps delegate one person to head shipwreck salvaging. Another to concentrate on land treasures. And so on."

"Do I want to become so big?"

"I don't know. Do you?"

"I just moved to Bell Cove. Seems like I should wet my feet in this region first."

"You could do that with Bell Cove as your headquarters and perhaps just venture into North Carolina jobs, at first."

"Keep track of all the inquiries we have, along with those passed on to us by Jinx. Once we've made headway with the Three Saints, we can have a brainstorming meeting."

Merrill was about to drive Delilah's motorcycle over to the Patterson house, where a hot shower and change of clothes would be welcome. His skin felt crusty from the saltwater dives, and he hadn't shaved in days.

Before he left, Harry called out, "Good luck tonight."

Which could be interpreted as "getting lucky." Merrill was all right with that.

# Chapter 10

### A little food, a little wine, a little dancing, a little . . .

*I* kid you not!" Merrill said. "When I walked into the house today, there were eight geezers doing the most crazy-ass version of a belly dance I've ever seen. In costumes! Even the men. Bonita's father, Raul, was the ringleader of the dingbat circus."

"Belly dancing? By the over seventy crowd?" Delilah had to laugh, then revealed, "Actually, my grandmother, Salome . . . yes, Salome, like in the Bible . . . was a showgirl in Las Vegas at one time, and she's never forgotten it. 'Why walk when you can dance?' is her motto. She dances when she's cooking. She dances when she's vacuuming. She dances when she pushes a cart in the grocery store. She still does a mean kick over her head."

Merrill's eyes widened in surprise, probably wondering if she could do the same. Which she could, but would never show, or tell.

They sat at a back corner table in the Cracked Crab. A band had just set up out on the deck, but the sounds were muted by the partially open, sliding glass wall, which made conversation possible. They were sipping white wine from stemmed glasses and picking at an antipasto platter that sat on a tray between them as they waited for their meal.

Delilah wasn't sure why she'd agreed to this date with Merrill. Maybe she was just tired of being lonely, of living in her self-imposed bubble. Maybe it was time for her to relax and enjoy life, instead of always looking over her shoulder or walking on eggshells. Maybe she just wanted to be a normal, single, twenty-eight-year-old woman who could enjoy the company of an attractive man without second-guessing all the reasons why it was a bad idea.

And, yes, Merrill Good was an attractive man, especially tonight in dark jeans, a white dress shirt open at the collar, and a navy blue sport coat. He'd shaved off his week-old beard, but hadn't cut his hair, which was still short, but not military short. He was tall and well built, though thankfully not steroid muscled, and he did have a youthful face, but it was his eyes that were so compelling. Intense when he was serious, dancing when he was mischievous. Despite his apparent intelligence and advanced education, he didn't talk down to her, or anyone else.

The bottom line was that she was enjoying herself, and that surprised her. Blame it on the wine. That was her excuse, anyhow.

"The most amazing thing is the old folks were good. Really good," Merrill continued. "I should have known something was up when I heard Middle Eastern music twanging all the way out to the driveway."

"At least they weren't stripping. I think some belly dancers do both."

"Please! Don't say that out loud. It would give them ideas."

"The only one I've met so far is Mildred Patterson. She seemed very nice."

"They're all nice. In fact, they're the kindest people in the world, but they drive their own crazy train, and they're driving me crazy along with them. Seriously, I need to get out of that place."

"Or what? You'll be belly dancing, too?" Delilah asked.

"Not a chance!"

"Or stripping."

He shrugged. "That, I might be able to handle, with the right appreciative audience." He grinned at her.

Delilah wiped the tears of laughter from her eyes with a napkin, as Merrill continued to regale her with stories of his fellow boarders at the Patterson house. She agreed with him about the people here being borderline crazy but kind to the max. When they'd come into the restaurant, they'd been greeted here and there as they were led to their table by almost all the diners, including Ethan Rutledge and Wendy Patterson, who were back from their honeymoon and wanted to know all about Merrill's salvaging venture so far and the work being done on Delilah's diner and motel. It was only when they promised to get together soon after seeing their waiting hostess looking anxious that they were able to move on.

Only to be stopped by Laura Atler, the newspaper lady, who wanted the scoop, too, and her dining partner, Gabe Conti, who discussed an AC problem at Bell Forge with Merrill; Frank Baxter, who thanked Delilah for her paint order; Gus's mother, Ina Gustafson, who made Merrill promise to stop tomorrow for some Norse herring potato salad to take out to the site for her son; and so on, until the hostess pointed out their table and said they could seat themselves when they were ready. In all, it took them twenty minutes to get there.

"But I didn't finish my story about today's event," Merrill went on, after pouring more white wine into both their glasses from a carafe on the table. "When I made the mistake of mentioning that belly dancing might not be the best dance for senior citizens, one of the ladies, in a huff, told me that belly dancers have better orgasms than other ladies. Jeesh! I stepped into that one. Because they're old, these folks think they can say anything. No filters whatsoever!"

"I heard that Mildred Patterson holds dance club parties at her house, and that she has a bunch of elderly boarders living with her, but how did you end up there?"

"The house belongs to Wendy, Mildred's niece. Wendy was in WEALS, the female version of SEALs, when I served in the teams. A bunch of us, SEALs and WEALS, came here with her last Christmas."

"That's when you fell in love with Bell Cove?"

"Yep. Which was understandable, really. I'd just come off a mission in which we lost a teammate. A FUBAR op from the get-go, as in Fucked Up Beyond All Recognition. All of us were burned out. I'd been in the military for fifteen years by then. Bell Cove, with its remoteness and quirky inhabitants, seemed . . . still seems . . . far removed from the terrorism that pervades the rest of the world. A rose-colored view, I'm sure, but . . ." He shrugged.

"I know what you mean. It feels safe here." *For how long, though?* she wondered. *Everything could go south if my past becomes known.* "So, you were looking for Mayberry and settled for Bell Cove."

"You could say that."

"Do all your friends know about your Mayberry addiction?"

"Sure."

"The big bad SEALs, who surely watch things with lots of bang-bang, shoot-'em-up? Didn't they make fun of you for your less violent tastes?"

"Hell, no! I made them watch every episode with me. My house, my TV, my remote. And, truth to tell, they probably enjoyed them. Of course, massive amounts of beer flowed at the same time. Everything is better with Sam Adams."

She was impressed that Merrill could make fun of himself so easily, or be teased about some "shortcoming" and let it bounce off him like raindrops. That came from self-confidence, she decided, something she lacked big-time.

They shared a fresh garden salad with a homemade creamy Italian dressing that was to die for, and then the waiter brought their entrées. Crab cakes and a side of penne pasta with vodka sauce for her, lemon-crusted halibut with a lobster-stuffed baked potato for Merrill.

At first, they just ate in silence, enjoying the delicious food. Delilah hadn't realized how hungry she was. With all the chores she'd done this afternoon—laundry, in particular—she hadn't stopped to eat.

"So, the motel rooms look good?" Merrill asked.

"Wonderful. Well, Stu and Barb from the quilt store are coming tomorrow to hang some curtains and deliver some bedspreads. That should make a big difference. I was surprised that the contractor went ahead and painted the walls and ceilings and woodwork with the paint I had ordered from the hardware store and must have been delivered while I was gone. I intended to do that myself." She patted her mouth with a napkin and narrowed her eyes at him. "Did you have anything to do with that?"

He put up his hands in surrender. "Not me. I don't do interference anymore."

"Hah!" she said.

"You do know that I intend to take one of those units for myself."

She was about to resist, but then shrugged. As a motel owner, she couldn't choose all her customers, and she needed the income. "To get away from Crazyville?"

He didn't answer, the implication being that was only one reason. When he did speak, it was about the other two rooms that had been finished thus far. "I figure Famosa can take one, and Charlie the other, if she ever gets off that boat. Or maybe K-4 when he gets here."

"You know, you've made me rethink my plan for renovations. All along, I've been working to get the diner operational first, figuring it was the best way to start a cash flow. But maybe I should do the motel first."

"I think you're right."

She took a first bite of her crème caramel and sighed at the decadent sweetness.

He stared at her lips for a long moment before trying his cannoli.

"What? Do I have something on my mouth? I am such a sloppy eater."

"No. I just enjoy watching you enjoy your meal."

"Like a glutton, you mean."

He shook his head. "Lots of women pick at food, think it's unattractive to actually be hungry and feed the need. Which is ridiculous. There's something sensual about eating . . . and sharing a meal. Good food should be savored. As a cook, you should know what I mean."

She nodded and not just because she wanted people to appreciate her cooking. She liked to watch Merrill eat, too. He held his fork in his left hand and cut his food with his right hand, and even though he was right-handed, he brought the bites on the fork to his mouth with the left hand. Very European, or sophisticated, or something. He'd probably been taught to eat that way from a young age while dining with his parents in fine restaurants, where there were three forks and two spoons, and a special knife, just for butter, all solid silver. Nothing like Jake's Luncheonette in Atlantic City where you were lucky to get one fork, and that made of cheap stainless steel.

They exchanged tastes of each other's desserts.

"I bet you'd prefer your cannoli filled with lemon cream," she teased. *And isn't that unusual? Me, teasing?*

"Oh, yeah. Don't forget, you promised me lemon cinnamon rolls someday."

"How can I forget? You remind me at every turn." She made a face at him. "What's the deal with Charlie?" she asked then, picking up their conversation on whether Charlie would stay in one of her motel rooms or continue to live on the boat.

"I don't know much, other than what she's told us all. She comes from the well-known LeDeux family in Louisiana. I've met some of them over the years. One of my SEAL friends is Cajun, Justin Le-Blanc, whose SEAL nickname was Cage, from that neck of the bayou. The most outrageous of that clan is an old lady called Tante Lulu, a folk healer, who is crazier than any of my fellow boarders here in Bell Cove. Anyhow, it was Tante Lulu who recommended Charlie to me."

The owner of the Cracked Crab, Tony Bonfatto, came over to talk to them then. He was a thirty-something guy of obvious Italian heritage, friendly, and appreciative of their compliments on the food. He promised to get Delilah the recipe for the salad dressing.

Once he left, Merrill said, out of the blue, "Tell me about your daughter."

And Delilah's heart sank.

Could she discuss Maggie without revealing too much about her own past? On the other hand, Maggie would be here soon, and she couldn't avoid talking about her forever.

"She's adorable. Long, wavy blonde hair, more golden than mine, which she hates. She would love to have it all chopped off, given a perm, and dyed red."

"Like Annie."

"You remembered."

"Delilah, I remember everything you say."

*Okay, that is heavier than I am ready for right now.* "She'll be here next month, before school starts. Just starting kindergarten."

"You'll be glad to have her here with you."

"More than you can imagine." Tears filled her eyes, and she blinked them away.

The too-observant Merrill noticed and reached across the table, taking one of her hands in his.

The press of his palm against hers, warm and comforting, was more than she could handle now, too. But she didn't draw away. His eyes held hers, and he said, "Let's dance."

They both stood and he followed her out to the deck, where the band was playing some country song about beer and horses. She was wearing the same white halter dress she'd worn to the Rutledge wedding, the one that was modest enough in front but bare to the waist in back. Was that a mistake? When he put a hand there, guiding her, a tingle ran through her body. Definitely a mistake!

Was it a tingle of alarm, or a tingle of something alarming?

Either way, it was too late to turn tail and run. Too late to pull up her bubble shield. Too late for so many things.

Merrill turned her when they were outside on the dance floor and put linked hands on that sweet bare spot. She looped her arms around his neck.

He tugged her closer, as they swayed to the music.

She put her face into the crook of his neck and inhaled deeply of his pine-scented skin. Probably soap, she noted with what was probably hysterical irrelevance, or panicky irrelevance.

He put his mouth to her ear and whispered, "At last!"

She felt his breath through the whorls of her ear, rippling down to all her extremities, and some interesting places in between. She sighed and moved in closer. In her four-inch heels, he still had several inches on her, but they were pretty much chest to breast, belly to belly, groin to groin. Tongue in groove, in more ways than one.

She moaned.

He did, too.

And so they danced, and danced, and danced. If it could be called dancing. She couldn't say what songs were played, or whether they were fast or slow. It was magic, and it was reality, and it felt so good.

She was a woman. He was a man. It was as if they were meant to be. For now, anyway.

Thus, when Merrill leaned back and looked at her and said in a voice raw with emotion, "Let's get out of here," she didn't protest.

She was in way, way over her head and not a life buoy in sight. Who knew drowning could be so wonderfully delicious? Or was it surrender that was so sweet?

### Ah, the pains and perils of dating! . . .

Merrill was drowning in his need for Delilah, and it took every bit of his strength and skill to fight the overpowering waves of passion. One of the first things a Navy SEAL learned in BUD/S training was drownproofing. Piece of cake for an old vet like him!

*Ya think?*

*Not when you're drowning in testosterone, like I am.*

*Not that drowning of a certain type doesn't hold some appeal. In fact, I want to dive right in with Delilah, and I will, but I need to slow things down. The worst thing that could happen would be for her to wake up tomorrow and feel that I seduced her into something she didn't really want. No regrets, that's my goal.*

*But, man, it is fucking hard.*

*And speaking of hard . . .*

It didn't help that he had imprinted on his brain her words of last week that she'd been celibate for more than five years. What guy didn't consider that a challenge?

Didn't help that when she'd been eating, Merrill had recalled a time a few years back when he'd been sitting in the Wet and Wild with the guys, and he'd expounded on his theory about the way women eat correlating to the way they would act in bed. For example, women who licked their lips when eating tended to be screamers. Those who took small bites were repressed nymphos. That kind of crap. Being perpetually horny, the men had sucked up his ideas like beer, which they'd been consuming in large quantities.

It was a good theory, nonetheless, but, luckily, he hadn't shared it with Delilah. Women tended not to have the same sense of humor about sex that men did.

For the record, Merrill had noted that Delilah did both: took small bites *and* licked her lips.

*Can anyone say "Hoo-yah!"?*

But now, Delilah walked ahead of him through the restaurant, out the front door, and into the side parking lot toward his pickup truck. Which gave him a bird's-eye view of her white, Marilyn Monroe halter dress, all bare back and swishy skirt that molded her hips and backside as she moved. While her hair was silver blonde, her skin—from shoulders to waist and on both arms, not to mention mile-long legs—was golden hued after a week out on the ocean. In fact, despite the constant slathering of sunscreen, everyone had gained or enhanced their tans this week, whether they wanted to or not.

Had to be a guy back in the day who designed that dress, or a woman with a sadistic inclination to torture men. The dress design was ageless, though, he had to give him, or her, credit for that. A hundred years from now, some Space Age hot mama will be donning some version of this creation, turning her future male admirers to puddles of horniness.

While his mind was wandering, he wondered, not for the first time this evening, what would happen if he untied the knot at the back of her neck. Besides being an expert in drownproofing, he excelled in Knots 101. *Hoo-yah!*

And, hey, with that backless wonder, she must not be wearing a bra. *Double hoo-yahs!*

"Merrill," she said, turning when they arrived at the car. "Can we talk? I just want to tell—"

But he didn't want to talk now. He wasn't taking a chance that she would say, "This is a bad idea," (*when, in fact, it is good, good, good*), or "Yeah, you're cute and all that," (*kiss of death*) "but I'm not interested in you that way," (*What other way is there for a man and woman?*), or "Let's be friends," (*Yuck! Another kiss of death*) or the worst-case scenario, one she'd hurled at him one of the first times they'd met, "Get lost, sucker." Or something to that effect.

So, to forestall what she was about to say, he pressed her up against the car and put a fingertip to her lips. "Shh," he said, and kissed her. No touching—he didn't dare touch her—but kept his arms braced against the car on either side of her head. That was enough. For now.

Her lips!

*Luscious.*

*Soft.*

*Moist.*

*Parting.*

*Welcoming.*

*Sucking on my tongue, like . . .*

*Too soon.*

*Gotta stop.*

*Sinking.*

*Want more.*

*Wait.*

*Oh, damn. Damn, damn, damn.*

Somehow, he raised his head, which was light as air and weighed about fifty pounds. Could she hear his heart pounding? He was panting like a race horse after the Preakness.

She stared at him with glazed eyes and glistening lips. In shock, no doubt.

With mumbled self-flagellation, he managed to open the car door and help her inside. Once he was behind the steering wheel, and before he turned on the ignition, he turned to her. "Sorry if I came on too strong."

She shook her head. "No, it was me."

*Oh, no! She's going for the "It's not you, it's me" line.*

"I like kissing," she went on.

*Oh, okay.*

"I haven't had much, for a long time, kissing, that is, but . . ." She shrugged, and though it was darkish in the car, he would bet she was blushing. "Anyhow, I wanted to talk to you about—"

*No, no, no. Not the talk. Besides, you don't tell a guy that you like kissing if you don't mean it as a cue.* He leaned over and kissed her. Again. One long unending kiss in which he licked and nipped and sucked and thrust, never wanting to break the kiss. Mouth sex, for sure. Somehow, they ended up half reclining across the bucket seats before they heard the loud honking of a car horn, and some teenagers driving, yelling out, "Get a room!"

He was the one who was probably blushing now. *Shiiit!* He hadn't made out like that since high school.

They each straightened their clothing, and Delilah sat staring straight ahead as he drove out of the parking lot. It was only a short distance to her motel/diner property. He drove through the town proper with its hokey brass bell streetlights, a commemoration of the bells that were the foundation of Bell Cove. Didn't matter that Bell Forge was floundering as the demand for finely crafted bells went the way of telephones and vinyl records. It was still a town that celebrated bells. The stores on the square were closed, the bells having just rung the eleven o'clock hour, and only a smattering of people could be seen on the sidewalk, probably tourists doing a little window-shopping before returning to their rentals, of which there weren't very many in Bell Cove.

"Can I talk now?" she asked finally.

He was pretty sure there was a grin tugging at

her lips, which was odd, but they'd already passed through the lighted portion of town. He couldn't be certain. Besides, if she was having a good yuck, it was over his pathetic horniness.

"Sure," he said, regretfully. At least he'd gotten in two good kisses and some slow dancing that felt a lot like foreplay. That was more than he'd expected when he'd started this date tonight. He had to keep reminding himself that this was Delilah. Baby steps.

"I've decided . . . well, I'd like to make love with you."

*Whoa!* Merrill had just pulled into the diner parking lot, and he was so shocked by her declaration that he almost ran over Elvis. Swerving at the last second, he came to a screeching halt on the gravel driveway beside the motel driveway.

Carefully, he turned off the engine and turned to stare at her. He thought of a dozen things he could say to her but couldn't manage to form the words to any of them.

"Would you repeat that?" was one possibility which he rejected right away. He wasn't taking a chance that he'd heard wrong.

Or "After all these weeks of me chasing my tail over you, now you want my tail?" But, no, she might take his attempt at humor the wrong way, like he was mocking her.

Or "I thought you'd never ask," which was a lie because never in a million years had he thought that she *would* ask.

Or "This isn't some kind of payback, is it? Like

you feel you owe me?" Nope. He couldn't say that. It would be setting up a negative. And what if she did feel beholden to him. Would he reject her offer?

Glancing toward the end unit of the motels, the one he intended to claim as his own, and then toward her living quarters behind the motel office, he smiled at her and went for that old standby, "Your place or mine?"

# Chapter 11

*Moonlight becomes you . . .*

They were halfway across the backyard when Merrill stopped abruptly and said, "I can't wait." His voice was raw with emotion—probably lust. She was feeling a bit lusty herself.

Reaching behind her neck, he untied the double knot in her halter dress, with a mere flick of his fingers, indicating an expertise that was surprising. He was usually so awkward around her, fumbling for words. She should have known better because she'd seen how smooth he could be when Bonita, and other women, flirted with him.

She stood in the moonlight now, bare to the waist. She was bigger than she'd like to be on top, especially when her waist was small and her hips flared out. She was saved from being overtly voluptuous by her long legs, which seemed to balance out her top-heaviness, or what she liked to call her upper bimbo.

At least, that's how she'd always viewed her own body, uncomfortable from a young age with dubious assets that attracted the attention of males. Yes, even in middle school. But not that many males had ever seen her like this. In fact, just one. Davie, from age sixteen on, till his big betrayal. How pathetic was that? What a waste of all those good years!

She should have been embarrassed, but she wasn't. Not when Merrill was gazing at her with such appreciation.

"Why am I the only one half-naked here?" she said, and flicked her fingers at him. "How about a little show-and-tell?"

He laughed. "Because I'm not as pretty as you are." But he already had his jacket off and tossed to a nearby patio table. His shirt soon hit the mark, too.

"Oh, I don't know. You look awfully pretty to me," she said, and that was the truth. His face might be that of a teenager, but his sun-bronzed body was that of a man. Broad shoulders, a patch of dark curls, muscles, sinfully narrow waist and hips. Later, she would like to explore the scars she saw here and there. She stepped forward and was about to put her hands on his chest.

But he was having none of that. He picked her up by the waist and lifted her high, feet dangling off the ground, putting her breasts in front of his face. Which was kind of startling—and alarming. Delilah was no lightweight.

He licked one nipple, then the other, the abrasiveness of his tongue acting like tinder to a match. Sparks of intense pleasure ignited in her there creating twin aches that literally throbbed. Until—

*oh, my!*—until he took the tip of one breast, nipple and areola together, into his mouth and sucked on her. Rhythmically.

She put her hands on his shoulders to steady herself and arched her back.

He put one big hand under her buttocks to hold her in place. The other hand was doing remarkable things to her other breast.

The boy—man—must have incredible strength. He certainly was a master multitasker. She could only think, *WOW!* Then, *Please don't let me have said that out loud.*

The throbbing in her breasts moved lower and she pressed herself against his belly to relieve the ache. But wait. Her legs had somehow wrapped themselves around his hips. And that now-vulnerable part of her, protected by a mere scrap of silk, was undulating against his hardness. Which caused her inner muscles to start slow-pulsing with the start of an orgasm. With a gasp of surprise, she began keening in counterpoint to the rise and fall of her spasms, each guttural sound rising in pitch. "Oh, oh, oh, oh, oh, oh, oh, oh!" An orgasm. Then a whimpering trail of smaller sighs, "Ooooooooooh!"

She wasn't sure how it happened, but they were in her bedroom, where he'd presumably carried her. The low light from a bedside lamp gave a golden hue to the room, which was thankfully cool from the window air conditioner. Thankfully, because she was raging hot, every inch of her skin feeling the heat of Merrill's scrutiny as he set her in the middle of the room and removed the rest of her dress, including her thong. Then, he helped her sit on the edge of the bed where he undid the buckles on her high-heeled sandals.

"Don't move," he ordered as he leaned down to kiss her quickly, then stood to take off his own clothing.

She wanted to tell him to slow down, to let her savor every little thing. The toeing off of his loafers to reveal bare feet with surprisingly sexy toes. The movement of his long fingers on the buckle of his belt. The rasp of the zipper. The shrug of his hips to let his pants fall into a pool at his feet, which he kicked aside. Then two hands slipping into the sides of his boxer briefs, pushing them down, down down. Showing . . .

"Oh, my!" she said.

He arched his brows. "Now am I pretty?"

"Not exactly pretty. More like . . . amazing."

"Why amazing?" he asked, leaning down to take his wallet out of the back pocket of his pants and removing a strip of foil packets, which he lobbed onto the mattress behind her.

"Amazing that you must want me that much," she said with a giggle, pointing at his turgid penis— *really* turgid penis!

"Sweetheart, you have no idea. That's only the half of it." He waggled his eyebrows at her, then picked her up by the waist once again and tossed her up onto the mattress. He followed after her, spread her legs, then knelt between her knees.

She held out her arms for him.

But he didn't move, just looked her over, closely.

"I'm ready," she prompted, in case he didn't get the message.

"Well, I'm not."

*Whaaat?* She glanced toward his happy place and arched her brows in disagreement. "Really?"

"Sweetheart, I have been wanting you for so long that I intend to enjoy and prolong every bit of this encounter. More than one encounter, if I have my way. And by *encounter* I mean . . . well, I don't want to be too graphic. Yet."

"How do you know I haven't been wanting you, too?"

"Maybe. I hope so."

In truth, it was only between the appetizer and the entrée tonight that Delilah had decided to go all the way with Merrill. *And isn't that an indication of my lack of experience that I would think in such a high school-ish way? All the way? Next I'll be thinking in terms of first base, second base, and home runs. Jeesh!*

Bottom line: Merrill was an attractive man. She liked him. He'd made it more than obvious that he liked her, or lusted after her.

He was single. She was single.

And she did have—not exactly needs, but—wants. Long-suppressed wants.

More than anything, she was damned tired of being different from other women. Why shouldn't she enjoy herself without looking over her shoulder?

As if sensing her thoughts, Merrill chucked her under the chin. "Tell me what you like."

*Whoa! Blunt much, buddy?* "I don't know what I like." At the look of disbelief on his face, she disclosed, "I've only been with one boy . . . man . . . ever."

"And where is he . . . never mind. I don't want to know."

*Actually, you really don't. Prison is not a subject to be brought up in the midst of lovemaking. Talk about a killjoy!*

"Let's discover what you like . . . and what I like . . . together."

And they did.

### *This wasn't a game to him, not that kind of game, anyway . . .*

*D*elilah was a feast for the senses, and he didn't care how crazy-ass hokey that sounded.

*Not that I'm going to say it out loud. I'm not dumb. Sometimes my Mensa brain does come in handy.*

Looks, smell, taste, feel, sounds—yep, Delilah had it all. In one nude, sexy body. And she was all his!

*Happy birthday to me! Three months early.*

—She *looked* sensational, naked. Not all women did. *Take it from me. Whoo-boy! You know that country song about all the girls looking prettier at closing time. Ask a few SEALs about their experiences with beer goggles. The things that Spanx and makeup can hide!*

With Delilah, all that creamy skin in a curvy package spelled Male Fantasy #1. Not a diet-conscious hip bone in sight. Nor signs of a surgeon's enhancement or reduction.

And, hey, he now knew she was a true blonde. *Hubba hubba!*

—As for *smell*, there was some sweet scent about Delilah all the time. Was it perfume? Or maybe, with all the baking she did, the vanilla or cinnamon had infused her skin.

—Would she *taste* like her luscious pastries? He already knew how sweet her lips were. Strawberry sweet. And cherry hued. Like her nipples. Man, those oversensitive buds and the mounds they crested were definitely going to be retasted. Over and over again.

—He already knew from his brief strokes of her back when they were outside that her skin was smooth as silk to the *touch,* and soft. No muscle-toned body for Delilah. Not that she was fat. Not at all. Just supple. *I can't wait to see if she's malleable all over. Especially—well, you know where.*

—The topper on this sensual cake for Merrill was the *sound* that Delilah made when she was coming. Manna to a starving man's ears!

"If you don't start pretty soon, I might just fall asleep," she said, knocking him from his reverie.

"Sorry. I'm enjoying the view too much. Where to start, where to start?"

"I liked your kisses," she suggested.

"Your wish is my command," he said, and arranged himself over her on braced elbows so he wouldn't crush her. Before he lowered his mouth to hers, though, he said, "I want you to know that this isn't just a slam-dunk game for me, just another score. I think I'm in love with you."

Her eyes shot wide and she started to protest, "No, that's not—"

He put his fingertips to her lips and said, "Shh. I'm not expecting you to reciprocate." *Not yet.* And then he replaced his fingertips with his mouth and proceeded to kiss her into acquiescence and then full participation. She was wet and open to him as he shaped her lips to fit his, demanding and coaxing, teasing and devouring. If he were a true basketball fan, he would call this a full court press of the mouth, except he wasn't sure who was on the offense and who was on the defense in this exchange. Her hands were framing his face, and her legs were locked around his hips.

But he had a full court to work here, and the timer was counting down. There was a third participant in the one-on-one who wanted a goal *now*. That was the entity between his legs that had a mind of its own and had surely grown two inches in the past five minutes.

He moved down her body and back to his knees so that he could see her breasts—feast on them, actually. She lay flat on her back, her eyes closed, but her lashes fluttered open and she stared at him through eyes that were already hazed with arousal. She looked more confused than disgruntled at his move.

"Do you know how much I like your breasts?" he asked.

She blinked and became more alert. Rising up on her elbows, she glanced pointedly at a certain part of his body and said, "I can tell."

"Witch!" he chided her and pinched one of her nipples, lightly, in reprimand.

She gasped, more in pleasure than pain. "More."

He spent a long time then, a really long time (for a penis anyhow), maybe five minutes, playing with her breasts. Molding them from underneath. Palming them in rough circles. Tweaking the nipples, then flicking. Finally, using his mouth and teeth and tongue to bring her to a writhing, moaning tribute to his expertise (*even if I do say so myself*).

"Don't . . . want . . . to . . . come," she choked out.

"What?"

"Not . . . like . . . this . . . again." She grabbed for that part of him, and almost gave him an instant ejaculation. "Inside!"

"Whoa, whoa, whoa," he said, and unpeeled her fingers off his cock. Sliding even lower down the mattress, he was about to touch her exposed moistness. "Just let me check to see if you're ready."

She slapped at his hand and snarled, "I told you I was ready two hours ago."

Well, that was an exaggeration. They'd only been inside a half hour, but he wasn't about to argue with her. Not when the woman he probably loved was inviting him in. Quickly, he rolled on a condom, placed himself on the key spot, and swish, he was home. Goal!

And that's exactly how he felt. Home. Thirty-five years he'd been trekking along in life. Had this been his final destination all along? *Oh, not Delilah's vagina. Jeesh! I'm not that crude. But Delilah herself.* He thought about telling her so, but if she'd been shocked at his declaration of a possible love, just think how she'd react to being his destiny. Besides, he doubted he could speak above a gurgle in his present state, buried to the hilt in muscled folds that were spasming around him in welcome.

For a moment, Merrill lay heavily atop Delilah, forehead to forehead, trying to regain a little bit of control. He'd never been accused of firing the torpedoes too early, but he might be now. If he wasn't careful.

Once he'd taken his arousal down a notch, he raised his head to look at Delilah.

She smiled at him. She actually friggin' smiled. While he was in agony.

He straightened his arms and began the slow withdrawal of his cock, followed by the slow thrust. Over and over, at least a dozen times.

She wasn't smiling anymore. In fact, her mouth formed a little O of surprise.

This time when he was in to the hilt, and then some, he moved his hips from side to side so that he rubbed against her clit.

She whimpered and tried to arch her lower body off the mattress.

He was having none of that. He kept the pace long and slow. As long as he could.

Her whimpers turned to pants.

"Do you like that, sweetheart?" he asked.

She didn't reply.

So he did the talking.

"Spread your legs wider. Knees up. Yes! Like that."

"Do you want it faster? Ouch! You pinched my butt! I take that as a yes."

"De-li-lah, you feel so good. Like warm honey."

"Can you put your legs over my shoulders? Ouch! No? Maybe next time."

And then he was quiet as he began the short, hard thrusts that moved them both up the mattress to hit the headboard. Rolling over, she was on top now, straddling him, looking dazed and unsure what to do next.

He showed her. With hands on her hips, he lifted her up and down until she got the rhythm.

Being the one dazed now, he gave himself up to her climax which was pretty much telling his cock, "Now! Now! Now!"

In the aftershocks of their mutual, mind-blowing orgasm, she lay splatted over his body. Possibly asleep. His hands swept over her bare back and rump, caressing, comforting, loving.

Yep, he was home.

He didn't understand why or how this had happened, what had drawn him to Delilah from the get-go, but one thing was certain. He was never letting her go.

Time for a full court press.

### *Just how thankful was she? . . .*

$D$elilah was having an out-of-body experience.

It felt like she was a spirit or something floating above, watching one love scene after another—two so far. Merrill had control over the first one, turning her into a throbbing, keening creature she did not recognize. Then he led her down the rocky slope to the rough shore of the Atlantic behind her property where they swam together in the nude, a fantasy Merrill had been harboring for some time, or so he claimed. That led to the second bout of lovemaking back in her bed where she took the lead, worshipping Merrill's hard, battle-scarred body in ways that must be instinctive because she sure as sin never learned *that* from experience.

*Who is this sensual woman?*

*Was this core of wantonness always in me, hibernating, just waiting for the right man to draw it out?*

*Is that right man Merrill?*

*Is this a one-night stand . . . an affair . . . or something more?*

*Do I want something more?*

*Can I afford something more, with all my baggage?*

*Why not just enjoy the moment, and stop looking back, or peering forward?*

*So many questions!*

Merrill was fast asleep now, belly down, spread-eagle on her bed, taking up most of the room on the double mattress. She smiled at the view of his world-class white buttocks. The rest of his long, lean body was suntanned to a deep bronze, not just from their week out on the water, but from years spent outdoors with the SEALs. She also smiled, thinking that she'd had the ability to wear him out so.

Unlike Merrill, Delilah was unable to sleep, despite trying for the past hour. It was four a.m., but she was too hyped-up.

Slipping out from under Merrill's arm, she grabbed his dress shirt and padded out barefoot to the kitchen where she did what she always did when unable to sleep, or whenever she had a free moment, actually. Baking. And she barely stifled a laugh as she grabbed for some fresh lemons.

After putting on a fresh pot of coffee, she sat glazing her lemon cinnamon rolls when Merrill came out. He wore white boxer briefs and that's all, leaving all that six-foot-three muscled body open for her inspection. Broad shoulders, narrow waist and hips, long legs. His short hair was rumpled from sleep. In other words, sex personified. He sniffed the air. "Is that smell what I think it is? Lemons?"

"Yes. Lemon cinnamon rolls with honey glaze. Fresh from the oven."

"Great. And coffee, too! You are a wonder woman!"

"Wonder woman, or wonderful?" she asked, before she had a chance to check her tongue. She didn't usually make suggestive remarks like that.

"Both." He stuck a fingertip in the bowl of honey glaze and licked it. "Yum!"

She felt the lick in her own body, deep down.

And he knew it! His dancing eyes said it all.

The tease!

"It's only six o'clock. Are you sure you want to get up so early?"

"Unless you want to come back to bed with me."

"Seriously? You're insatiable."

He arched his brows at her.

"Okay, I'm insatiable, too. But I have a lot to do today to get ready for tomorrow's return to the site. Laundry's done, but there's shopping to do, and phone calls, and I need to finish up the motel rooms."

"I'll help. Then we'll have time to—" He waggled his eyebrows.

"Merrill!"

"Tsk, tsk, tsk!" He shook a forefinger at her. "I was going to say, time to come back here and let me cook you dinner, for a change. I make great grilled black and blue burgers."

"I don't have a grill."

"We'll buy a grill."

He sat down at her small table and she placed a mug of black coffee with one teaspoon of sugar, the way he liked it, along with two warm pastries on a plate in front of him. He stared at them for a moment, then raised his head to look at her, suddenly serious. "Thank you," he said.

She cocked her head in confusion. "It's just cinnamon rolls. I can make them in my sleep."

He waved a hand dismissively. "Not for this. For last night. For letting me love you. For giving me"—he shrugged as if lost for words—"yourself."

"Oh, Merrill," she said, and went over to him. Sitting on his lap, she buried her face in his neck and wept. She wasn't sure why. Maybe that was the reason for her insomnia. Too much emotion walled up, and now her defenses were suddenly giving way.

"Hey, I'm sorry. I didn't want to make you sad," he apologized once she dabbed at her eyes with a paper napkin.

"You didn't." She moved off his lap and sat on the chair next to him. Motioning for him to eat and drink, she began to explain. "I was a bit emotional because I'm the one who should be thankful. No, I'm not just saying that. You have to understand, you released me last night, with your lovemaking."

"Release? Well, that's another word for it."

"Not that kind of release, you fool. Last night was a first for me."

"You weren't a virgin."

"No, not technically. But, in some ways, I was."

He tilted his head in question. "This is all related to the one guy you've been with, your baby's father, right?" he guessed.

She nodded. "Davie . . . David Zekus."

"Has he ever been in your daughter's life? Maggie's life?"

She was surprised that he remembered her daughter's name. "Never!"

"Because he didn't want to be?"

"Because he's in prison."

He was clearly shocked.

She was shocked, too, that she'd blurted out that secret. She probably should have told him Davie was dead. Same thing.

"And when he gets out?"

"He'll never get out."

"What—"

"No, I don't want to talk about Davie anymore. He's past history. Long dead to me and Maggie. But my connection with him . . . we grew up together before we became high school sweethearts . . . and his betrayal later were more than just a 'He done me wrong' song. He hurt me more than I can say, and it changed me. Trust, or lack of trust, has kept me frozen."

"So I thawed you out," he teased.

"You could say that."

"Wanna melt some more? That tiny shower of yours has to have been made for a scarecrow, but I bet if we're really careful we could fit in together."

"Oh, I don't know . . ."

"Hey, here's a better idea. How about a game of drizzle and lick?"

"Huh? Do you mean dribble and kick?" He'd been making all kinds of ball game references during the night.

"No, sweetheart, I mean drizzle . . ." He reached over and dipped his finger in her honey glaze again, then let it drizzle in a heart shape on her hand which was resting on the table. ". . . and lick." Before she could react, he lifted her hand to his mouth and laved the sweetness off with his tongue. Holding her gaze then, his caramel eyes dancing with mischief, he asked, "Wanna play?"

"You're crazy."

"The shower would make more sense then."

"You're crazy."

"Crazy in love."

"Don't say that," she said, but she liked it. Too much. She tried to draw her hand away from his.

He wouldn't let go. "I thought you were thankful." He batted his eyelashes at her.

"Oh, so now you want to be thanked with more than words?"

"What a good idea!"

And it was, though she would have to make another trip to the laundry with the soiled sheets. As for her hair, both sets, she would need a bottle of shampoo to get rid of all the stickiness.

And as for the shower, they just fit. Barely.

When he went down on his knees before her and said he was looking for more honey to lick, she laughed, at first. Then she was no longer laughing as she reached up for the shower head to support herself in his sensual exploration.

But she got back at him when she sank to her knees and told him she was getting into this treasure hunting gig. Time for her to make her own search for gold. A gold bar, a gold staff, a golden flagpole, any old gold would do. He wasn't laughing for long, either.

By the time they were done, the hot water had run out. But they barely noticed, their bodies were so hot, hot, hot.

Merrill stayed in the shower, cold as it was, when she got out to towel dry. She put his shirt back on and ran a comb through her wet hair as she walked outside with a new mug of coffee. It was nine o'clock but the sun was already warm on the patio stones under her feet. She loved this time of the day when everything was new and dewy clean, promising sunny weather. She loved the view of the sound where a sailboat could be seen skimming the blue waters in the distance, and a fishing boat was chugging out for the day's haul of whatever the catch of the day would be—tuna, marlin, bass, shark, whatever. She loved this run-down property she'd inherited with all its potential for a better future.

That's when she heard an ominous sound. A car engine. Pulling into the parking lot.

Still barefoot and only wearing Merrill's shirt, she set her coffee cup on the patio table and walked over to peer around the corner before running inside for more decent attire.

But it was too late.

There was a big old gas guzzler of a station wagon coming to a grinding halt, filled with boxes, both inside and atop the rooftop carrier. Out of the passenger door popped a little gremlin with long wavy blonde hair, wearing a red Annie dress with white anklet socks and black patent leather shoes.

"Mommy! Mommy! Surprise!"

Delilah had no chance to run and dress now because her daughter hurtled at her with a flying leap, almost knocking them both over. Delilah hugged her little girl, kissing her face and neck and hair, over and over. "Oh, sweetheart, what a wonderful surprise!"

And someone was going to have to answer for that surprise. That someone—wearing purple pedal pushers, a low-cut silver knit shirt, blonde hair piled atop her head like a 1940s pinup, high-heeled wedge sandals, and enough makeup to plaster a wall—stepped out of the driver's seat and arched her back like a person who's been driving too long without a break. One of those electronic cigarettes hung from her mouth, which she gave a few expert, handless puffs, creating a cloud of vapor with a strong scent of vanilla.

Meanwhile, Maggie was hugging Delilah and rambling on, "Me and Gramma had a secret and we couldn't tell no one, 'specially not Jimmy the Goon, who's gonna break Gramma's legs, both of 'em, with his HurryCane, and Honkin' Harvey called Gramma a crazy broad fer almos' knockin' him on his ass with her car at the Bonzo lot, and Gramma said five bad words, and she got a ticket from the coppers fer goin' too slow, then she got a ticket fer goin' too fast, and what're corns and bunions anyhow? A truck driver called Gramma a hot mama. Isn't that silly? She's not my mama. You are. Kin I have a dog now?"

Her grandmother was indeed hobbling toward them on the corns and bunions that she'd been complaining about most of her life—all those years in high heels as a showgirl, she claimed. The e-cig was thankfully out of sight now, though the vanilla scent remained.

But then, Gram stopped dead in her tracks and looked pointedly at something over Delilah's shoulder. Delilah could guess what she saw, and it wasn't the Bell Sound view.

Leaning against the corner of the building, wearing nothing but a low-riding towel and a wicked grin, was Merrill.

"Looks like we're not the only ones with a secret, Miss Maggie," her grandmother said. "If this is what the Outer Banks has to offer, maybe I'll stay awhile."

# Chapter 12

*When Vegas came to the Outer Banks . . .*

**M**errill stared with humor at the scene unfolding before him. A ball-of-fire chatterbox and an over-age bimbo dragging on an e-cigarette had invaded Elvis Presley land. Obviously Delilah's daughter and grandmother.

Delilah Jones was like a jigsaw puzzle to him. Piece by piece he was finding out things about her, like last night's whopper of a revelation about the lifer felon ex-boyfriend. He would bet his last dollar that these new arrivals would add a few more clues to the mystery of Delilah.

"You think this is funny?" Delilah said when the little girl ran back to the car and was dragging out a stuffed dog bigger than she was, or just about.

"Don't you?" He just noticed that the car, a honkin' big Buick station wagon from another less gas-conscious era, was stuffed with boxes, and there were a bunch more bungeed to the rooftop luggage rack. What was the old lady hauling?

"Pfff! It's either laugh or cry." She shook her head at the pinup queen—who had a surprisingly hot body for a woman her age, he just noticed—as she hobbled over the gravel stones of the parking lot to stare up at the giant Elvis.

"I had a date with Elvis once, in Vegas when I was a showgirl," the grandmother remarked, to no one in particular. "By then his hunka hunka burning love had gone the way of too many peanut butter and banana sandwiches."

"Your grandmother was a showgirl?" he asked Delilah.

She nodded.

*Actually, she told me that last night. But it didn't sink in then. Whoa. Another piece of the puzzle. Raised by a showgirl grandmother.* "Cool! Bet she'll fit in great with the dance crowd over at the Patterson house."

Delilah groaned. "Oh, my G . . . gracious! You're right."

"Of course, it's a nonsmoking crowd."

"She'll convince them that it's not really smoking since no nicotine is involved."

He was bent over laughing by now.

"You do know that these unexpected visitors mean your plans for the evening have gone south."

"Oh, crap!" He adjusted the towel around his hips.

Which caught Delilah's eyes, which went wide. She seemed to suddenly realize that he was half-naked and made a hissing sound of distress. "Hurry. Go get dressed."

"You're wearing my shirt," he pointed out.

She looked down at herself and blushed. She must have forgotten her own lack of attire.

This scene out of a bad comedy, or a really good comedy, just got better and better.

"Go!" she ordered. "And while you're inside, take all those sticky sheets off the bed, and gather up all those wet towels. Pick up any, um, loose clothes off the living room floor, too."

*Sticky sheets,* he liked the sound of that. But maybe now wasn't the time to tease her. On their fiftieth wedding anniversary, though, all bets were off. "Sticky sheets" was going to be their code word for a certain activity. And, no, he wasn't going to examine why he was thinking of anniversaries when weddings weren't even discussed yet, or imagined. Talk about jumping the gun. "I assume I'm going to the laundry."

"You did offer to help," she said.

"Yeah, but then there were rewards to be had." At the crestfallen look on her face, he said, "I was just kidding. Lighten up, sweetie. Everything will be all right." He leaned down, gave her a quick kiss, and went back inside.

A short time later, he had his truck stuffed with laundry. Delilah had given him a short grocery list—not for the salvage boat, but for her family's needs today. They would do the *Sweet Bells* shopping this afternoon, but would he mind stopping at Hard Knocks, the hardware store where Frank had ordered a mini blowtorch for her to make some kind of desserts, and the Cove, a mercantile or general store dating back to the 1930s to buy a cast-iron frying pan, and, oh, could he check with Stu or Barb MacLeod at Blankety-Blank to see if the bedspreads were ready yet for the motels? Delilah kept apologizing about asking for his help. Finally, he had to tell her, "Cool your jets, babe. I want to help."

She had tears in her eyes when she said, softly, "Thank you."

*Damn! Tears over a little frickin' help! What had her life been like pre–Outer Banks?*

Another missing puzzle piece.

He would have taken off then but the grandmother, to whom he'd been introduced as "My friend, Merrill Good," solicited his help in unloading her car.

Yeah, right. He'd like to give her "friend." Maybe with a quick smack on her cute butt, which was now demurely covered by a loose sundress. But that was being petty. What did he expect? That she'd introduce him as her lover? Or something more? One night did not make for "something more." He knew that, but he'd been hoping for another night, and another.

The little girl stared at him, speculatively, through crafty blue eyes, just like her mother's. Probably wondering if he was going to be her Daddy Warbucks. Or maybe she was wondering if her mother had brought home an uncle for her to play with. Or maybe she didn't like his looks and wanted him to be gone. Bottom line, she was clearly casing him out.

He winked at her and said, "Cute duds, Annie McFannie!"

She smiled. Apparently, he'd passed the test. "I want a dog."

*Whoa! Does she expect me to get her a dog?* "That's nice. I thought you already had a dog."

"That's not a real dog," she told him with disdain, as if he might be a bit dim upstairs. "Do you have a dog?"

"Not presently."

"But you're gonna get a dog?"

"Maybe."

"Good. You can keep it here."

"Maggie, come here a minute," Delilah called from inside.

*Was I just hustled by a mini con artist?*

He went off to help the grandmother.

"What's in these things, Ms. Jones?" he asked as he hefted one of the boxes off the roof and nearly herniated himself.

"Call me Salome, or Sal," she said.

*Salome? Wasn't she the babe who danced for a king in the Bible? Delilah said she used to be a Vegas showgirl. Oh, yeah, this babe is going to fit right in here in Bell Cove!*

"They're Avon, honey," Sal told him.

"Huh?"

"Didn't Delilah tell you that I was an Avon lady for years, as a side gig, when I wasn't dancing onstage. You know, ding a ling, doorbell ringing, 'Avon, calling!' That kind of Avon."

He barely stopped himself from rolling his eyes. "Well, we have plenty of doorbells here in Bell Cove. It's a town built on bells, from way back. You should do very well here."

She smiled at him. "I'm counting on it, sugar. By

the way, I have a great men's cologne, Black Suede, that would suit you perfectly. It's on sale for only nine ninety-nine."

"Uh, I'm more into Blue Suede. Like, you know, blue suede shoes," he tried to joke.

She ignored or didn't get his jest. "Black Suede is sort of a citrusy/sage scent."

"I am partial to lemons," he conceded.

"Black Suede is promoted as a fragrance for the rugged masculine man."

"Well, hell's bells, order me a gallon then."

Another con job, he decided, with a chuckle, as he stored the boxes in the shed for her and then took off in his truck, a little black bottle sitting on the seat beside him, his wallet minus a ten spot. So much had happened in the past few hours that he didn't have time to think about the amazing night he'd just spent with Delilah. He wanted to go over every little detail in his mind.

In the meantime, he had errands to run. After loading the machines at the Laundromat, he headed for Hard Knocks, the hardware store, where he picked up Delilah's mini blowtorch and decided to buy a grill and a bunch of related barbecue accessories, which were in a window display. He put the clothes in the dryers and picked up the items on Delilah's grocery list at a nearby supermarket. Once the clothes were dry and folded at the Laundromat, he went back to the Patterson house to gather his belongings for his move into the motel unit.

While he was there, he mentioned to Mildred Patterson that Delilah's grandmother and her daughter had just arrived. He also happened to let slip that Salome had a dance background. Some of the other oldies overheard and about suffered heart attacks of excitement at the prospect of a Las Vegas showgirl joining their group. All of them seemed to speak at once, asking him questions, most of which he couldn't answer, having just met the woman.

"Do you think she can still do a high kick?" Elmer asked him as he finger combed his bald head.

"I wouldn't be surprised," Merrill replied.

"Should we invite her over?" Mildred asked.

"Sure, but you should probably wait until they settle in."

"She sounds like fun."

No doubt. "She dated Elvis a time or two, I understand. That should make for good conversation." Merrill's loose tongue was obviously enjoying a holiday.

"Wow!" Mildred said, and a bunch of senior jaws plummeted.

Merrill closed his eyes for a moment, fearing he'd witness a mass denture drop.

"I dated Ann-Margret one time," Ike said.

"You did not!" his brother Mike corrected. "It was an Ann-Margret look-alike in one of those nostalgia revues."

"Same thing!" Ike contended.

The two white-haired gentlemen, former psychiatrists, were twins, but they disagreed about everything. Personally, the whole house could use a little head doctoring.

Yep, Salome Jones was going to fit in here just right.

He was packed up and ready to head back to the motel, including the grill and groceries, when a vehicle pulled up out front. To Merrill's surprise and great pleasure, it was K-4.

"Yo, Geek!"

"You made it," Merrill said, going up and giving his buddy a man-hug.

"Yep. Finished out my contract on Tuesday and closed out my apartment on Wednesday, and here I am."

"Any trouble?"

"They tried to talk me into re-upping."

"And?"

"I was tempted, but, honestly, it's time for a change."

"Same for me."

"I'll probably need help adjusting to civvy life. I'm already experiencing a little withdrawal. It was a huge adjustment for me when I joined the teams, after Karen died. Seems I'm in for another adjustment back to a nonmilitary regimen."

K-4's wife had died of cancer. Merrill had known him from when he'd first arrived in Coronado, and he'd been a basket case of depression and rage.

"Takes time, dude. Best remedy is hard work, and there's plenty of that here. You have no idea how welcome you are. We're in desperate need of another diver."

K-4 nodded. "Any luck so far?"

Merrill shook his head. "A few artifacts that we're checking out, but nothing yet to indicate any of the Three Saints are down there. I'm hopeful, though. It's still early days."

"By the way," K-4 said, "what's with those signs I saw coming in? A Labor Day Lollypalooza?"

"This crazy town . . . what can I say? Remember that Grinch fund-raising crap when we were here last Christmas?"

"Who could forget? Even I, a stranger, got nominated . . . and got five frickin' votes. Just because I frown too much, or so someone contended."

"You do frown a lot," Merrill pointed out, and ducked when K-4 attempted to punch him. "Anyhow, the powers that be here are always looking for new ways to raise money without the town going all commercial, like other beach towns. Plus, they had all these decorations left over from the Fourth of July and the Rutledge wedding. Voilà! A Lollypalooza."

"Don't they mean Lollapalooza? Or can they just not spell?"

"It's a deliberate misspelling. And this isn't going to be a huge music concert. This'll be more like *American Idol* on the Outer Banks. A talent contest for homegrown talent. Everything from yodeling to shag dancing."

K-4 was shaking his head with disbelief.

"Yeah, I know. It boggles the mind."

"So, you got a room for me here?" He glanced toward the yellow brick and weathered shakes of the Patterson house.

"Actually, one better. At Delilah's motel. You remember Delilah from the wedding?"

"The blonde babe?"

"Exactly, but I wouldn't refer to her that way in her hearing."

K-4 grinned. "Any progress?"

"Some," he admitted, and grinned back.

"Hoo-yah!" K-4 proclaimed, then repeated that sentiment after following Merrill to Delilah's property. They both got out of their vehicles. K-4 glanced around, taking in the twenty-foot Elvis, the Rock Around the Clock diner, the Heartbreak Motel, and said, "Hot damn hoo-yah!" Immediately followed by "The only thing missing is Graceland. Or is that on the horizon?"

"God only knows!"

In Bell Cove, one never knew what would happen next.

*In the end, all you've got to do is shebang . . .*

Delilah was alternately furious and ecstatic.

Furious with her grandmother for just popping in, with no warning.

But ecstatic to finally be united with her daughter.

After making them a breakfast of cinnamon buns and more cinnamon buns, Merrill's lemon ones, to be precise, just about all she had on hand, Delilah showed them around the diner and motel. Maggie loved everything, never once complaining that she wouldn't have a room of her own yet, or that there was no television, or how shabby the furnishings were, or what was her mommy doing with a man on the premises? Her only constant refrain was, "I want a dog."

When Delilah had said "We'll see" for about the dozenth time, Maggie told her, "Mister Merrill is gonna get me a dog."

"Did he say that?"

"Not 'zackly. But almost."

"You're not supposed to ask people for things, especially people you don't really know."

"I didn't ask him."

"Really?"

"He likes me."

"How do you know?"

"Because he winked at me, and he called me Annie McFannie."

Perfect child logic!

"Sweetheart, our apartment here isn't big enough for a dog."

"Maybe we'll get a mansion."

"Not gonna happen, cupcake."

"Does Mister Merrill have a mansion?"

"No, but he has a boat."

"A big boat?"

"Yes."

"Yippee! Betcha a dog will fit on a big boat!"

More child logic!

After a while, Delilah set her daughter up on the bed with her old-fashioned DVD player and the

*Annie* movie. Almost instantly, she was asleep, the trip having caught up with her.

Which gave Delilah the opportunity to confront her grandmother, who had just finished the breakfast dishes and was sitting outside on the patio with her third cup of coffee, vaping away. The scent she emitted at the moment was something called Strawberry Smoke.

Delilah sat down with her, setting her own mug of coffee on the table. Before Delilah had a chance to launch into her, her grandmother said, "It's a beautiful property. Has potential."

"Yes, it does. With lots of hard work. And money, which I don't have. Speaking of which . . ."

Ignoring her obvious reference to the money Delilah had sent her, part of which must have gone toward the purchase of that rattletrap of a car, her grandmother puffed away for a second, then mused, "Clyde always was a strange bird, even before he went off to 'Nam."

"You weren't close?" Obviously not, since Delilah could only remember that one visit when she was a child, and Gram never talked about him, spoke to him on the phone, or got any letters.

Her grandmother shook her head and blew more smoke. "He was a lot older than me, and he was a loner type. He did love the ocean, though. And Elvis."

"You'd think, growing up in Atlantic City, that he would have settled there. Same ocean."

"After the war, he seemed to need a more remote

place. There was already talk of casinos coming to Atlantic City. I think he had an Army buddy who lived here on the Outer Banks."

"So, Gram, what's up? What are you doing here?"

"What? Can't a gal come to visit her granddaughter without having an excuse?"

"Bullshit!"

"I thought you were trying to cut down on the prison language."

Delilah bristled. "People here don't know about that, and I'd appreciate your not mentioning it."

Her grandmother made a face and puffed some more on the damn e-cigarette, creating a strawberry cloud, before saying, "Don't go getting your feathers ruffled. I may be old, but I'm no fool. I know when to keep my trap shut."

"Did you give the loan shark any money at all?"

"Of course I did. Five thousand dollars! And that's more than Sharkie deserved."

"Sharkie?"

"That's what everyone calls him. Boardwalk Bobby, remember him? He made a mint lugging people along the boardwalk in one of those rolling carts. Got a bent back and about a million bucks for all that work. Then, set himself up as a loan shark. So now he's Boardwalk Sharkie."

*Why does every question put to my grandmother require a novel for an answer when a simple yes or no would do? And, please, I'm about to puke from all this strawberry vapor.* "And he . . . Sharkie . . . was satisfied with half the loan being repaid?"

A pink flush infused her grandmother's cheeks,

mixing with the rouge that was already there. "No, but I told him I'd get the other five thou to him as soon as I could. Which would be on, let's say, the fifth of Never. But, of course, I didn't say that to him."

"And that's when you decided to skip town?"

"Yep. Just till things settle down a bit."

"So, you're not staying?"

"Are you kidding? A gal like me needs action. What kind of action is there in a burg like this?"

Delilah assumed she meant casino action. "Why did you bring all your Avon crap . . . I mean Avon collection . . . if you don't intend to stay?"

"Are you kidding? Jimmy the Goon threatened to break every one of them with his new Hurry-Cane. I tol' Jimmy I would break his false teeth and kick him in the you-know-what if he touched any of my precious treasures. But I wasn't taking any chances."

Delilah rolled her eyes. She'd done that a lot in the past few hours.

"So, who's the hottie?"

"The hottie is my boss, the one who owns the treasure hunting business."

"Ah. Has a bit of cash, does he?" her grandmother guessed, putting two and two together regarding Delilah's sending her ten thousand dollars. "Every lady needs a sugar daddy once in a while."

"Gram!"

"What? You know what they say. It's as easy to love a rich man as a poor man."

"I am not in love, or about to be."

"Well, all I'm gonna say on the subject, is, it's 'bout time you got over that loser, Davie Zekus."

"Oh, Gram. I was over him more than five years ago."

Her grandmother reached over and squeezed her arm.

"Have there been more calls from the prison?"

Her grandmother nodded. "Once a week. Every Saturday. I just refuse to accept the calls."

Davie had the nerve to not only want her to visit him, but his daughter, as well. That was going to happen on—what was it Gram said?—the fifth of Never.

Just then she saw two vehicles drive up and park in front of the motel. Merrill and some other man got out, had a discussion, pointing at the various units, then began to unload things which they carried into the first two rooms.

"Another hottie," her grandmother observed.

She supposed the man was attractive in a buff, military sort of way. High and tight haircut, muscle definition in a tight T-shirt, and shorts that showed off a set of long hairy legs. "I think it's K-4, Kevin Fortunato, a Navy SEAL buddy of Merrill's. He's going to join the salvage team."

"Your hottie is a Navy SEAL?" her grandmother asked, impressed.

"Was. Not is," Delilah told her, "though none of the SEALs identify themselves that way. All hush-hush. They usually just say military or Navy."

"Got it," her grandmother said.

"I better go over and talk to Merrill. We have a lot

of shopping to do today before going back on the ship tomorrow." She looked at her grandmother. "That's another problem. I have to go out on the salvaging operation. You're going to have to stay here until this job is over. I haven't made any plans for child care before school starts."

"A couple weeks here in the boonies won't hurt me."

"Please don't use that term when talking to people here. They would be offended." *Or maybe not. To them, it might seem a compliment.*

Delilah went inside to get her shopping list and check on Maggie, who was still sleeping. Back outside, she asked her grandmother, "Will you be okay?"

"Of course. I might even lie down with Maggie for a little beauty nap."

"This discussion is not over, Gram."

Her grandmother sighed. "I'm doing the best I can, girl."

Feeling bad, she reached down to hug her grandmother. "I know you are, Gram. You always have."

Delilah walked across the yard that separated the motel office from the units themselves. At one time, it probably had a flagstone sidewalk and pretty flowering bushes. Maybe even a fountain. Now, it just looked like a sad, neglected yard. Someday, she promised, it would look good again. Maybe she'd even plant a few shade trees, or fruit trees. She smiled at a sudden thought. Maybe even a lemon tree, to remind her of . . .

Merrill was standing in the open doorway of the

end unit, the one named "Blue Moon." He grinned at her and said, "Welcome to my humble abode."

"Humble it is," she noted after she entered. The curtains and bedspreads hadn't yet arrived, but there were crisp blue linens on the two double beds and their pillows, with a darker blue, loose-woven summer blanket folded at the bottom of the mattress.

"I don't know," Merrill said. "It looks a helluva lot better than it did when I first saw it. At least it's clean and functional. Everything seems to work."

"So much to do, though," she disagreed, sitting down on one of the beds to survey the room. "The dressers and bedside tables need refinishing, and new drawer pulls. The ceiling light is pure 1930s, and I don't mean vintage quality. I suppose I should refinish the floors, too, or put some tiles down. And those little patios facing the bay will need umbrella tables and chairs, maybe a lounger." *And I can barely afford toilet paper.*

"Give it time, babe. I'll help, and so will a lot of other people." He'd just put the last of the clothing from a duffel bag into the dresser drawers and he leaned against the wall.

"But I don't want help. I want to do it—"

"On your own, I know," he said. "You shouldn't have moved to Bell Cove, then. By the way, Mildred and her gang are anxious to help with the grand opening of your diner, when you're ready. She said to tell you that they're willing to act as waitresses and waiters to help serve the super crowds you'll have at first. Free of charge. The guys will even dress up in glitzy Elvis jumpsuits and grow long sideburns, and the ladies will wear wigs and skimpy Ann-Margret utfits." He grinned as he relayed that message.

She groaned. "See what I mean. And don't you dare mention this around my grandmother, or she'll be planning the whole shebang."

"Where's your grandmother now?"

"She and Maggie are taking a nap."

His eyes lit up. Pushing away from the wall, he walked over to the door, put the chain lock in place, then turned to her. "What say, we create our own shebang?"

She laughed. "My daughter and my grandmother are here. Your friend is next door. We have a ton of shopping to do this afternoon. You need to go into the office, and I have arrangements for Maggie's school looming. You can't be serious."

He was.

His clothes were off and folded on the other bed so fast she was lost for words for a minute—because of his speed, and he'd actually taken the time to fold his clothes, probably a military habit, and because of the really sexy body he was exposing. Yeah, she'd seen it last night, but the light in her bedroom had been dim. And, in the close confines of the shower, she'd barely been able to move her head, let alone give him a full-body appraisal. But now—oh, my!

"We don't have time for this," she protested.

Not only did they make time, but he tortured her until she choked out in surrender, "Shebang!"

*Chapter 13*

*Being a sugar daddy isn't always sweet . . .*

*K*nowing that Delilah was anxious to get back, to spend as much time as possible with her daughter before returning to the salvaging site tomorrow, Merrill did his best to help speed their errands. Trips to the supermarket; the elementary school where Delilah registered Maggie for kindergarten; and the lawyer Matt Holter's office, where Delilah picked up reversal of guardianship papers for her daughter.

He had some questions about that—why Delilah had needed to grant her grandmother guardianship for the short time she'd been in the Outer Banks, but he supposed it was a necessary precaution where a kid was concerned. Emergency medical care and all that.

He'd even bought a half dozen stackable plastic patio chairs in vivid colors of red, blue, green, and white, at the supermarket of all places! Amazing what they sold in grocery stores these days! The hard resin chairs, along with a matching chaise, coffee table, and utility stand, would serve their purpose temporarily until better quality outdoor furniture could be bought, he'd told Delilah, who protested every little purchase he'd made.

She'd insisted that they separate their orders at checkout so that he wouldn't be paying for anything going to her place, not realizing that the plastic furniture *was* for her place, not the motel units. The only thing she had there now was an old metal patio table and a couple folding chairs.

"How am I going to make a hamburger feast for me, you, K-4, Maggie, and the Glam Gram with one flimsy table and two rickety chairs?" he asked.

"Feast . . . what feast?" she sputtered, then repeated, "Glam Gram?" and had to smile, despite herself.

The unexpected arrival of her grandmother and daughter posed problems for Delilah that she refused to discuss with him. He didn't have to be a genius to see how conflicted she was about leaving her daughter so soon. He'd already suggested that she take a few days off, but she'd refused, as he'd known she would. She was bound and determined to earn that advance salary he'd given her.

A salary which he was beginning to suspect had gone to her grandmother for debts yet to be explained. He was pretty sure he'd heard the words *loan shark* mentioned.

Truth to tell, Merrill was enjoying the hell out of this whole melodrama that had become his life. Especially now that he'd scored in the sex department.

When they were on their way to Bell Forge to

drop off those items destined for the boat, Delilah turned to him and said, "Do not . . . I repeat, do not dare buy a dog for my daughter."

"Huh? What? Me?" He put a hand to his chest in fake offense.

"Yes, you! I mean it, Merrill. You've become like a good fairy. All a person has to do is rub your lantern and poof you're off to grant wishes. The sugar daddy for all mankind!"

He laughed. "I think you've got your fairies, genies, and Daddy Warbucks confused."

"Bite me!" she said, and didn't even try to correct her language, like she usually did.

"Anytime, sweetheart," he tried to joke.

She didn't smile. "If, or when, I decide that Maggie should have a dog, I'll be the one to get it."

Even though he was driving the pickup, he raised his hands, momentarily, in surrender. "Okay, okay. But there is this cute little schnauzer puppy in a litter over on Nags Head that I just happened to see on my computer this morning."

"I knew it! Don't. You. Dare."

K-4 was putting together the grill when they got back, per Merrill's instructions.

Which caused more scowls from Delilah. She stalked inside with some groceries while he unloaded the plastic patio furniture, which K-4 deemed, "Cool!" Then he went to get his laptop from the truck and placed it on the patio table, while K-4 continued to screw some side tables onto the grill, pretending not to notice the little drama taking place between him and Delilah.

On her second trip to get her personal groceries from the truck, having already declined his offer to help, she got her first good look at the grill, did a double take, then sliced another scowl at Merrill. "Could that damn badass grill be any bigger?" she asked. Again, no backtracking on bad language. "The local fire department might want to borrow it for their barbecue grill-off."

He thought about quoting that proverb about sarcasm being a poor substitute for gratitude, but figured he'd go for that other proverb: Clueless men should stop when they're ahead. And midmorning sex, after a night of passionate lovemaking, was definitely "ahead." *And, yeah, shoot me for a testosterone-loaded brain, but I meant that literally, as in giving—never mind.*

He couldn't stop grinning.

Which caught K-4's attention. He just shook his head at Merrill's hopelessness.

Back to the grill. It *was* a nifty piece of equipment, all shiny red, six feet long with enough space to grill two hundred hot dogs in five minutes, or so its label said. With the attached side tables, it was actually closer to ten feet long. It even had a—*No shit!*—built-in satellite radio, which was currently set on a country station playing a Toby Keith marathon.

K-4 had managed to find a cooler which he'd filled with ice and a dozen cans of beer and soda. Which was a great idea, considering that the temperature was still in the mideighties.

"What's that smell?" he said as K-4 handed him a cold one.

"My Prime."

"Prime what?"

"Cologne. 'Prime' cologne is for the bold and masculine man, dontcha know? An aromatic blend of lavender, spearmint, and cedarwood." He smirked at Merrill.

"Let me guess. Avon?"

"Ding-a-ling! Avon calling!"

Merrill took a long drag on his beer, which really hit the spot, and opened his laptop. He had a lot of incoming mail, but the one that jumped out at him came from Bonita. The subject line read: "Good and Bad News!"

"Uh-oh," he said.

K-4 fired up the grill, now that it was assembled and the propane tank hooked up. With a whoosh, the burners came on. He adjusted the knobs, closed the door, then sat down at the table with Merrill. "What's up?" He pointed at the laptop with his own can of beer.

"The bad news is that the objects brought up this past week are not from the Three Saints, but are from roughly the same time period. A wreck about two years later, in 1864. The good news is that they might have come from a French privateer that was attempting to swerve around the Yankee blockade during the Civil War. Which might mean chests of gold from a group of textile manufacturers in desperate need of Southern cotton."

"Like a lot of gold?"

Merrill shrugged. "Still have research to do. The ship in question was *Le Faucon*, or the *Falcon*. Not as big a prize as the Three Saints, but still conceivably worth millions."

"This is exciting, man!"

"Yeah, it is."

Before they had a chance to discuss the project more, Maggie came out, dragging a huge stuffed dog, who might be Pluto, or maybe Marmaduke. Her hair was all rumpled from a recent nap, and she looked downright grumpy.

"I don't like you."

"Wow! That's harsh. What'd I do?"

"Yer gonna take my mommy away tomorrow."

"Just for a week or so." Merrill didn't know much about kids, but he recognized how lame that answer must seem to her. A week would seem like a year to a five-year-old, he supposed, or at least a month.

"Five years without a mommy is tooooo long. Now I have her, I don't want you taking her away . . . you . . . you poopyhead."

Well, that was certainly telling him off! *But wait. Five years without a mommy . . . what does that mean? She probably just means that she's five years old, and . . . whatever!* "Where's your mom?"

"On the phone. And Gramma is paintin' her toenails. Peach passion. She's gonna do mine later."

She took great care in placing her dog on the chaise, then sat her little rump on the bottom edge, staring up at him, expectantly. She was barefoot but still wearing the red dress.

"What?" he asked when she continued to stare at him.

"Mommy tol' me to come outside and help you put together the friggin' grill." She was still giving him the stink eye.

"Oh, she did, did she?"

"What's a frig?"

K-4 exchanged a look with him and chuckled.

"It's not a nice word for little girls to use," Merrill said.

"Mommy did." More stink eye.

"Well, it was probably just a slip of the tongue."

She giggled. "Tongues can't slip." She stuck out her own tongue and tried to look at it, to no avail.

Merrill wasn't much into kids, but this one, despite her attitude toward him, was really cute. Looked just like her mother, except for the golden blonde, rather than silver blonde hair. And she had a few freckles across her nose and cheeks.

"Tell you what, kiddo. You can watch me make my world-class black and blue burgers, and if you're really good—"

She perked up at that and finished for him, ". . . you'll get me a dog?"

"No. No dogs from me. Only mommies buy dogs. What I was going to say was, if you're really good, I'll tell you my favorite story."

"Please, poopyhead, don't let it be the one about how you captured a bunch of tangos in Peru just by fucking up their computers," K-4 said, low enough that Maggie couldn't overhear.

"You already know the story of Little Orphan Annie," he started.

Maggie nodded.

"Oh, man! You're going to tell her about that porno flick, *Annie Does the Orphanage*. Not appropriate, my poopyhead friend!"

"Shh," he warned K-4, then continued addressing Maggie, "but have you ever heard of Little Orphan Andy?"

"Was he Annie's big brother, who came searching for her, forever and ever, but couldn't find her, and that's why she had to live in an orphanage, where she had a hard-knock life for five whole years?"

"Um, probably."

"Can I have a dog?"

"You expect a poopyhead to get you a dog?"

"You wouldn't be a poopyhead if you got me a dog."

"Nice try, monkey, but no bananas today."

The devious little imp frowned with confusion, then stomped inside where she yelled, "Mommy! Mister Merrill called me a monkey."

Later that evening, everything had been cleared up from what everyone agreed were the best hamburgers ever. The side salads they'd bought in the supermarket deli, along with dishes of Ben & Jerry's Cherry Garcia ice cream added to the feast, but it was his burgers served on fresh rolls with lettuce and tomato and spicy mayo that had been the big hit.

K-4 had gone off to some local singles bar to check out the action, and had only teased Merrill a little when he'd said he wasn't interested. Maggie and the grandmother were in the bedroom, which they'd taken over, Maggie already fast asleep and

Sal, as she preferred to be called, was reading several back issues of *Cosmo. Don't ask!*

Delilah would be sleeping on the pullout sofa bed in the living room. But for now, she'd come out and was sitting at the patio table across from him, going over some last-minute details for tomorrow's return to the site. He was drinking the last beer, and she had a tall glass of iced lemonade.

"Congratulations on the great meal," she said once again. "I'm going to dream about your hamburgers tonight."

*I'd prefer you dream about my other meat,* he thought and bit his bottom lip to ensure he didn't let such a crude thought escape aloud. *Really, I've been living in a male horndog society—SEALs—way too long. I need to relearn gentility. Hah! That's a word my mother liked. I'm becoming my freakin' mother. No, no, no! I will not become genteel. I will maintain my rude, crude roughness, on the inside, anyway.*

"Maybe you should be doing the cooking on *Sweet Bells.*"

"Oh, no! I'm a one-dish wonder. Besides, the team members would shoot me if you didn't come back. You promised them a special batch of your cinnamon rolls."

She nodded. "I'll make them first thing in the morning. Several varieties."

"Lemon?" he asked, hopefully. "I only got those two this morning before your visitors arrived, and I saw K-4 scarfing up the last few this afternoon."

"Yes, Merrill, I'll include lemon," she said with exaggerated patience as if he were a small child.

He was feeling nothing like a child as he gazed at her in the sundress she'd been wearing all day, the sundress that had ignited lots of ideas in his overactive brain. Oh, there was no halter knot at the back of her neck, but those thin spaghetti straps could probably be lowered by a motivated man's teeth.

"Are you ready to take off tomorrow?" he asked. *Something's ready to take off from my end.*

*Rude, crude, for sure. My mind is really in the gutter tonight.*

"Everything on my list is done," she said.

"Mine, too. All my phone calls made. Harry's been brought up to date and is well able to handle my business from this end."

"Should be an interesting week, with Bonita's news."

"Yep. I did some research earlier, and the *Falcon* would be a great discovery."

"Does that mean you'd give up on the Three Saints?"

"Not at all. We have the site until next year. Just a change of direction, for the moment."

She looked a little bit sad as she stared off toward the bay. There was a ripple of thunder in the distance, presaging a storm to come. The breeze was a welcome relief to the day's heat.

"I'm worried about you going out tomorrow," he said suddenly, into the silence. "You know, leaving your daughter behind, practically on her arrival."

"She'll be fine. I've given Gram a list of things to do with Maggie around town and here at the motel.

Plus, my grandmother has ideas for how to clean some of my diner equipment, with Avon products." She gave him a rueful shrug, as if apologizing for her grandmother's quirkiness.

"You do know she sold me and K-4 men's colognes already?"

She rolled her eyes. "That's my grandmother, but don't feel obligated to buy stuff from her. She'll con you if she can."

"She asked K-4 today if he'd like to play a round of poker. He got leery when she pulled out a case with her own chips and everything."

"She has a little issue with gambling. Living in Atlantic City with the casinos in walking distance is a great temptation. For her anyhow."

Ah, so that's where the money went. "You said that Maggie will be fine when you're gone. But will you?"

"What do you mean?"

"It's obvious how much you love your little girl and how much you've missed her, already. It's too soon to be separated again. As I've already suggested—"

She put up a halting hand. "No! I honor my obligations. Trust is important to me. I need you to trust that when I say I'll do something, I will."

"Okay, okay. I didn't mean to offend." He stood and told her, "Wait here. I have an idea."

She rolled her eyes, again.

He chucked her under the chin in passing. "Not that idea," he said, "although I'm more than willing."

He went to his truck and picked up a package

from the backseat. When he got back, he handed her the bag, which had an imprint of The Cove. Suspiciously, she opened the bag and pulled out a child-size life vest.

He hadn't sat back down, but instead stood watching her reaction.

"What is this for?"

"If you won't stay here with your daughter, then bring her with you."

"What? I can't bring a five-year-old on a salvaging ship."

"Why not?"

"It would be unprofessional of me."

"Says who? Take your kid to work day, or days. Nothing new in that."

"Your operation is a business. A child has no place in a business."

"I'm the boss. My boat, my rules."

"It would be unsafe for a child out on the ocean."

"Delilah, I doubt whether Maggie would ever be more than five feet away from you, and she'd wear the life vest 24–7. With seven adult lifeguards in close proximity, the imp would be as safe as on land."

"Thank you, Merrill, but no thank you."

"Are you crying?"

"No, I am not crying. I never cry. Why would I cry?" On those words, she stood and said, "I'll see you in the morning."

And she went back inside, closing the door firmly behind her.

Stunned, Merrill just stood there for a moment.

*What just happened?*
*Am I in trouble for trying to do a good deed?*
*Sure seems like it.*
*And I didn't even say that crude crap out loud.*
*Man, sometimes a guy just can't win for losing.*

An hour later, he was in his motel bed, propped against two pillows, his laptop resting against his raised knees. He'd already answered the dozen or so text and email messages he'd gotten from former teammates, his current team members on *Sweet Bells*, and others, like Laura Atler from *The Bell*, looking for news to fill a space in her weekly tabloid. There was also a surprising text message from his father:

> <<<Merrill: The family would like to meet with you. We will be returning home on the 27th. Dinner here at the Beach Manse before that? Call to set date.
> Dr. Martin Good, College of Molecular Biology, Princeton University>>>

Merrill had to smile at his father's sig line. Not "Father" or "Dad" or, God forbid, "Love, Dad." As for "the family," wasn't he part of that family? And the reference to the Beach Manse, the name of the place where they were staying—just a bit of the usual snobbery, as in this imagined scenario:

"Where are you staying, Mr. Good?"

"At the Beach Manse with my daughter-in-law's father, James Dellasario. You know Jim from Johnson & Johnson, on the Princeton Board of Trustees."

"And you, Merrill, where are you staying?"

"Heartbreak Motel."

Enough said!

His message back was short and sweet:

<<<Dear Dad: Be gone for a week. Shipwreck salvaging. Will call on return, if you're still around.

Love, Merrill>>>

He'd deliberately used the term "Dad" just to annoy the old man. And, yeah, he'd mentioned shipwreck salvaging as a continuing middle finger of rebellion. Being a Navy SEAL was bad enough, in his family's opinion. Being a treasure hunter had to be another notch down the prestige pole. As a final "insult," he'd signed off with "Love" at the end because, dammit, despite everything, he still loved his father.

There was a slight scratching on the door. Probably K-4 returning from his night on the town. Even though he tried hard to get on with his life, K-4 still mourned the wife he'd lost to cancer some years back. Before he had a chance to call out something like, "No hot belles in Bell Cove tonight?" the door opened. But it wasn't K-4.

Delilah stood in the open doorway, wearing a thigh-length sleep shirt with a Beach Bunny logo featuring a sexy, bikini-clad rabbit, and flip-flops, both of which she'd probably purchased at some thrift shop, as per her usual habit. Not that she didn't look as hot and attractive in her relatively demure outfit as any Victoria's Secret model, if they even had models with curves these days. Her hair was wet from a recent shower and pulled off her face into a neat braid. Her face had been scrubbed clean. As innocent in appearance as a teenager—a teenager with an adult woman's body.

"Can I come in?" she asked.

"Are you kidding?" he replied, closing his laptop and tucking it under the bed. Folding his hands behind his nape, he stretched his legs out. He wore only boxer briefs. He'd turned the AC off and opened the sliding doors out to the patio. Thunder and lightning promised a storm yet to come. It was still hot, but there was a pleasant breeze off the sound.

Delilah closed the door behind her and shifted from foot to foot, as if unsure of herself.

"I'm sorry I ran off like that before," she said.

"I'm sorry I made you cry."

"I do not cry."

"I forgot. Sorry I made you not cry then."

"Fool!" she muttered. "Listen, I owe you an explanation."

"No, Delilah, you don't owe me anything, and if you mention that fucking money, I'm gonna spank your sweet ass."

Her eyes went wide.

"Oops. I didn't really mean that the way it sounded."

She arched her brows at him, in a way that was teasing, rather than offended. *Note to self: A spank or two might be added to my repertoire.*

Leaning back against the closed door, which caused her breasts to be outlined by the tautened shirt—*and, yes, I am noticing nipples, so shoot me*—she said, "No one has ever been so nice to me before, and that's why I overreacted."

"Oh, crap! You're not going to start the 'nice' business, are you? If there's anything a man hates, it's to be called nice by a woman he wants in his bed. It's the kiss of death for the prospect of sex."

"Really? And what half-assed, clueless man sex manual did you learn that from?"

*Bad language from Delilah and the mention of sex without blushing . . . man, I am on a roll! Or maybe not. Maybe this is just the preamble to the big kiss-off!*

"You've already gone overboard in helping me with the salary advance, and, yes, I know you don't want to hear about that now. But that was just the beginning. You've treated me with respect and been patient with me on the boat. I was already attracted to you before, I admit that, even before we went out to dinner, but the way in which you behaved with Maggie . . . well, it touched me deeply."

"Even when she called me a poopyhead?"

"Even then. Believe me, I had a talk with the little imp about that kind of language," she said. "But, Merrill, for you to have offered to bring her on the salvage boat, that went above and beyond. You didn't care about the inconvenience, or what other people might think. You have a good heart. And I was touched."

He knew what Delilah was saying, even if she didn't say the words, or even recognize what was happening. Delilah was falling in love with him, just like he was falling in love with her.

He motioned her toward him with a forefinger.

She just blinked at him. Stubborn to the last, even when she was the one who'd come to him.

"Delilah, honey," he said huskily, then cleared his throat, "lock the door and come here. I'm not nearly done . . . 'touching' you."

*Sometimes love is a tsunami,*
*sometimes it is a gentle wave . . .*

And, oh, she needed touching!

Merrill stood and opened his arms to her, and she stepped forward into his embrace, gladly. Wrapping her arms around his waist, she laid her head against his chest. Even the feel of his heart beating against her ear was a touching of sorts. Everything about him was love.

And that's just what scared her so much—what had caused her to break out in sobs and run away like a silly teenager earlier this evening. His kindness—his loving—was a tender force that broke down all her barriers. No jackhammer chiseling away. More like a persistent drip, drip, drip. She couldn't resist him. She just couldn't.

She raised her head and looked up at him. "Love me," she urged.

"I already do," he replied, and lifted her into his arms and onto the bed.

Short work was made of removing her nightshirt and his briefs. Lying on her back, she reached for him, but he took her hands instead and arranged them above her head on the pillow. "Let me just look at you first."

Which he did.

For a long time.

"Do you have any idea how beautiful you are?"

"Too curvy."

"I love your curves. All the soft squishy places."

"Squishy!" She swatted at him playfully. "Well, you're beautiful, too."

"Yeah?" he said, laughter in his eyes and voice. "What part of me is the most beautiful?"

"Your heart."

"Oh, crap! The nice guy line again."

"You're beautiful on the outside, too," she conceded with a smile.

"But I don't have any squishiness."

"Hardness has its attraction, sometimes."

"Now you're talking, sweetheart." He took her hand and put it on his hardness, just so she'd know what he meant.

As if it wasn't obvious!

"I want to love you all over," he said then.

"Now you're talking, sweetheart," she repeated back at him.

Which caused him to smile, recognizing that it was unusual for her to banter so.

He kissed her then, endlessly. And not just her lips. He devoted equal attention to her jaw and eyelids and neck and the erotic whorls of her ears. Her breasts. Even her underarms and the inside of her elbows. Her belly. Skipping over her private parts. The inside of her thighs and knees. The arches of her feet and her toes.

Then back up again.

And they weren't silent kisses, either. Each stop along his journey was accompanied by softly whispered, often wicked compliments or observations.

When he licked and blew into her ears, he chuckled at her squirming body and said, "Like that, do you, De-li-lah? How about this?" He dipped the tip of his wet tongue into her ear, repeatedly, until she arched her body and begged him to stop. Or had she begged him to not stop? She wasn't sure.

He was fascinated with her breasts, and his kisses there were both praising and teasing. Who knew there were so many ways to use the lips and teeth and tongue as erotic torture devices?

"I'll pay you back for this," she warned when he'd done something particularly torturous, bordering on perverted.

"I can't wait," he said, and moved on to other places he had not yet kissed.

Several times she tried to stop him with her hands, or pull him into an embrace, but he continually raised her arms back up, above her head. "Let me," he would say each time.

And she did.

The worst part, or the best part, was when he prepared to enter her. Looking down, he said, "I love you, Delilah Jones."

She wanted to repeat the words back at him, but they stuck in her throat. Years of distrust had built up scar tissue that blocked her emotions. But she showed him.

With her hands now free, she held his precious face as he thrust slowly in, and out, of her body. With her knees bent and cradling him, she showed that he was welcome. With her hips meeting his every stroke, she followed his lead and then set a counterpoint of rhythm.

Her gaze locked on his beautiful whiskey-brown eyes, and hoped he saw there what she was unable to express in words.

But then, the lovemaking that had started out slowly and gently turned turbulent. His strokes became shorter and harder, hitting her clitoris with a rhythm that was both torture and pleasure. Her orgasm came hard and suddenly, rushing out in waves of spasms that had her stiffening her legs and raising her butt against the onslaught.

He gasped and arched his head back, the veins in his neck sticking out as he tried to hold back his own climax. But she was having none of that. She reached between her legs to the place where they were joined and squeezed him.

With a roar, he withdrew and slammed into her one last time.

And she came again.

Afterward, as she lay cuddled in his arms, the storm finally hit with pelting rain. It gave the motel room a feeling of being in a cave. Comforting. Safe.

"We're good together," he remarked idly.

"Are we?" she asked. "I mean, it was good for me, but I don't have much experience for comparison."

"I do, and, believe me, we are a good match . . . in bed."

His trailing words implied, other than bed, too.

"I just wish . . ."

"What?"

"That you trusted me."

"I trust you."

"Not entirely."

He was right, and that was a concern. That he could sense that she had secrets she wouldn't or couldn't share with him.

Time for a change of subject. "You know what I wish? I wish I had some bubble bath. With that little shower in my apartment, I've been dying for a tub to just soak up to my neck in warm bubbles."

He grinned and jumped off the bed. "Your wish is my command."

"What?"

He set his cell phone on flashlight mode and had the door unlocked before she could grasp that he intended to go outside. In the pounding rain. Bare naked.

Good Lord! She got up, wrapped a sheet around herself, and walked over to the open doorway. She saw the flashlight over by the shed, and she began to understand what he was up to. The fool!

Even more foolish, she watched as K-4 pulled in from his late-night trip to one of the local bars. When he got out of his SUV, he stood talking to

Merrill for a minute. There was laughter on both sides and a remark from K-4 over his shoulders as he ran toward his motel unit. Something about "monkey ass crazy horndogs."

She had towels ready for Merrill when he came back a short time later, soaking wet. Before he towel dried, he handed her two bottles, Avon Cherry Blossom and Vanilla Cream Bubble Delight. "Delightful as these sound, I couldn't find any lemon ones, darn it! On the other hand, I'm not sure I could handle you tasting like lemons. I would probably overdose."

He winked at her.

And he was so adorable, she almost said those three magic words. Almost. Instead, she said, "You're probably too manly for a bubble bath."

"Wanna bet?" Just before they, both of them, entered the tub, which was overflowing with bubbles, Merrill said, "You should be forewarned. Navy SEALs, whether active or retired, do their best work in the water. They don't call us frogmen for nothing."

"Ribbit, ribbit," she replied.

Which Merrill took for a challenge.

He won, hands down (literally) under water, that was.

# Chapter 14

*Treasure found in the ocean: Is it*
*Pay Dirt or Pay Water? . . .*

*H*e's a poopyhead."

*Are you talking about me, kid?* Merrill paused at the bottom of the boat steps, listening to Delilah's daughter talking on the speaker of the satellite phone he'd set up for her on the galley counter. Delilah was kneading dough with both hands in a huge bowl while she carried on a conversation. A born multitasker, like himself, he noted, always looking for commonalities because he'd noticed that the stubborn woman thought their differing backgrounds were a roadblock to any kind of serious relationship. Hah! To him, growing up in academic bigotry was no big asset.

Today, Delilah wore tight pink yoga pants and a sleeveless pink-and-white-checked shirt. He also noticed that she rarely wore tight shirts or tops. Another of her hang-ups. Obviously, he had opinions on that subject, too. Her hair was piled on top of her head with one of those claw hair clips. In other words, good enough to . . .

*No, not going there! Not if I want to get any work done today.*

For a moment, he was just fascinated by the movement of her fingers. Pressing, massaging, almost caressing the yeasty mixture to a smooth ball. He could imagine them at work elsewhere—like, maybe, on his skin, which might not be yeasty, but definitely sweaty after hours in the blistering sun. But then he could also picture his hands . . .

*Focus, man! Focus!* He shook his head to clear it, and directed his attention back to the phone call. Assuming he was the poopyhead in question, he smiled to himself, and shamelessly listened some more. He'd been under the misconception that he'd made friends with the little girl by making up that fool Little Orphan Andy story. But then, what did he know about kids?

And he couldn't really be offended. It was his fault for eavesdropping. What was it they said about eavesdroppers never hearing good things about themselves?

"He is not a poopyhead, Maggie."

*That's telling her, sweetheart.*

More kneading.

*Was it dough for bread, or maybe more of her cinnamon rolls?*

"And I told you not to use that word anymore."

*Wait till the kid hears some of the blue words that escape your lips sometimes, Ms. Potty Mouth.*

"Mister Merrill is Mommy's friend . . ."

*Oh, no, no, no! Not a friend! Not even friends with benefits. We are more than that, Ms. Delilah.*

". . . and it's not his fault I can't be there with you."

*Well, okay, then.*

"Mommy has a job so she can make money for us to live together."

*Great! The money fixation again!*

"Gramma says you could get lots of money if you'd sell that crapola diner."

*Oooooh, boy!*

Delilah sighed and muttered, "Gramma talks too much." To her daughter, she said, "That's another word that little girls should not use."

But Maggie was off on another subject—well, maybe not really, since it involved money, indirectly. "There's a bald man at Miss Mildred's house. Maybe he could be our Daddy Warbucks."

*Could she possibly mean Elmer Judd, the former veterinarian? He's about five-foot-five and seventy years old. Whew! For a moment there I thought I might have competition, some new boarder who looked like Bruce Willis or David Beckham.*

"When were you at Miss Mildred's house?"

"Yesterday. Gramma is teachin' them how ta be showgirls . . . and guys. One man fell on his bum on a high kick, but he was laughin' so hard I doan think he was real hurt. They dint call an am-boolance or nothin'."

"Oh, Lord!" Delilah said on a groan. "What are you doing while Gram and the others are dancing?"

"Sellin' Avon on a TV stand on the front porch. I made thirty-seven dollars. Is that enough for you ta stop workin'?"

"No, sweetie, that's not enough," she said, swiping at her eyes with a forearm. In an undertone, she whispered, "I'm gonna kill the old lady. I really am." Speaking aloud again, she added, "And you shouldn't be working, either."

"I only did it for a little while. Tonight I'm gonna be a waitress at the poker torn-men."

"The what?"

"Shhh! It's a secret. Gramma is gonna hold a poker torn-men right here on the patio. She even rented some card tables and folding chairs. And Mister Raw-ool . . . that's Ms. Mildred's boyfriend . . . is gonna fire up the grill fer a parr-ill-ada. That's a Spanish barbecue. We're having beef ka-bobbies and shrimp tapas."

"Where's . . . your . . . grandmother?" Delilah gritted out. "I want to talk to her right now."

"Gram-ma!" Maggie yelled so loud that Delilah had to lean away from the phone. After a pause, she told Delilah, "Gramma says ta call back later. She's laying outside in her bikini gettin' a suntan, and she doesn't wanna be half-baked."

Delilah made a growling sound, and just then noticed Merrill standing at the bottom of the steps. "Listen, Maggie. I need to go. Tell Gram I'll be calling her in an hour, and she better be there. Love you bunches."

"Love you more bunches," Maggie chirped, and the line went dead.

Slowly, Delilah turned more fully to look at him. "You heard all that?"

"Yep."

She sighed. "I'm worried. My grandmother is a wacko."

"Don't be worried. She's no more wacko than the rest of that town. And no one's gonna let anything bad happen. They take care of each other."

"If you say so," she answered, dubiously. "So, what's up? You were looking for me?"

"Yeah. We're about to start the new experiment. With the metal detector. Thought you might like to watch."

She nodded and set the bowl aside, placing a towel over the top for the dough to rise. While she washed her hands, she remarked over her shoulder, "I thought metal detectors were for old fogeys working the touristy beaches."

"This is much more high-tech."

"And expensive," she guessed.

He shrugged.

"Men and their toys! How expensive?"

"Nine thousand."

"Whaat!"

She was probably thinking that she could buy all new furnishings for the motel or high-end appliances for the diner with that amount of money. He stepped forward and embraced her from behind at the sink, kissing her neck. She allowed him to hold her for just a moment, even turned and kissed him, quickly, before shoving him away.

Although everyone on the ship probably suspected something was going on between him and Delilah these past five days they'd been back on-site, the two of them—*well, mainly Delilah*—had agreed to keep their relationship private. Hands off in public, which meant almost all the time aboard a crowded ship. Not an easy task for him. Not just the "no sex." Now that he'd had her, he wanted her. All the time. But even not being able to touch, or kiss, was difficult. He found himself catching her at the odd moment, like now. Which was not nearly enough.

"What are you making?" he asked, pointing at the covered bowl.

"Pizza," she said.

"Oh, please, God, not lobster pizza."

She smiled. "No. Not lobster pizza. Just regular tomato cheese pies with sausage, mushrooms, and banana peppers."

"Perfect," he said.

These five days back on the site this time had been pretty routine. No big finds, but some promising small artifacts that indicated something was— or might be—there. What the divers had found lots of, though, were spiny lobsters which hung around wreck sites. Another promising sign. But, man, they were all getting sick of lobster on the menu.

Spiny lobster had no claws, and the meat was tougher and less sweet than Maine lobsters. As a result, the shellfish had found their way into Delilah's lobster omelets, lobster rolls, lobster bisque, lobster tacos, lobster mac and cheese.

"C'mon. Hurry up," he said, frog-marching her up the steps, which of course gave him a good view of forbidden parts—for now. "We've stopped diving for the day, and are going to do some metal detecting," he told her.

Even with K-4, they were still only running three dives a day. They might try to squeeze four in later, with K-4 relieving one or the other in alternate dives, but what they really needed was six qualified divers to do more. But first, they needed more information.

And, actually, six divers would be excessive. Even five was a lot. Face it, while "slow and steady wins the race" was the recommended course of action, he was an impatient man, always had been. Fast and furious was more his style.

Once topside, Delilah said, "I thought you already had a thingee to spot metals."

He smiled at her use of "thingee" to describe a piece of complicated equipment. "I do. The side scan sonar *thingee* detects objects that aren't buried, like shipwrecks, and the proton magnetometer *thingee* measures magnetic fields, instead of the topographic terrain, including metal objects."

She jabbed him with an elbow for teasing her.

"This metal detector we're trying now is another tool . . . or you could say, I admit it, a new toy. Actually, these professional models are nothing like the cheesy wands you see on beaches. We drag 'towfish' from the end of the boat where their reach is very wide. In fact, we're going to run three coils. The computer will tabulate the path of the frogs, and when a target is reached, as in a high level of ferrous material, the coordinates will change color." He realized on seeing the glazing of her eyes that he'd gone off on lecturing mode, and concluded, "Bottom line—it's a gamble, just like shipwreck salvaging is a gamble. We shall see what we shall see."

At first, she just stared at him, but then she grinned and said, "I love when you go all Albert Einstein-y."

Huh? Albert Einstein was a physicist, not a computer nerd. Bill Gates would have been a better choice. *But, hey, she used the word* love *in connection with something about me. I'll take whatever I can get.* "Does that mean you'd like to come to my place sometime, baby, and view my etchings . . . I mean, computer software?" He waggled his eyebrows at her in a Groucho Marx kind of way.

"You are such a child sometimes," she said, with a laugh.

"I'll keep you young, sweetheart."

"Promises, promises. Remember, I grew up with the super saleswoman of all time for Avon products that guarantee to turn back the clock on wrinkles. Promises of eternal youth. Gram raises the bar very high on the fountain of youth. The Ultimate Avon Lady."

"You could call me the Ultimate Avon Man."

"God forbid!"

They walked toward the stern, where Famosa and Bonita were securing the tow lines, talking in an engrossed manner as they worked. Merrill didn't know if the two of them had something going on romantically, but they apparently had discovered a lot of common interests in their academic work, Famosa as a professor of oceanography at Rutgers and Bonita as a doctoral candidate in marine archaeology. There was even talk of them writing a book together.

"Are we about ready to go?" Merrill asked.

"All set," Bonita said, straightening.

Famosa stood, too.

*Is that really a Speedo he's wearing? Holy shit! It takes some kind of ego to pack your goodies in one of those skimpy things.*

Delilah looked at him and winked. Apparently she shared his view on male attire. *See, another commonality,* he almost said aloud.

Instead, Merrill raised his hand, giving Charlie the signal to start moving the boat. They would travel over the entire grid today, if they had time. Fortunately, the water was calm. Any change in the weather could affect everything on the site. The prospect of starting all over was daunting.

Merrill was especially excited to try out a new computer program he'd developed. It would take the readings from the metal detector and overlay them, frame for frame, over the previous recordings of the magnetometer. Hopefully, there would be signs of identical loads of ferrous objects. *Sometimes my Mensa brain comes in handy.* If it worked, he could probably patent his invention, and pull in some extra cash that way, in addition to the treasure.

"Delilah thinks we're like old fogeys on the beach waving our metal detector wands over the sand," Merrill remarked.

"I didn't say that, exactly," Delilah protested.

"Hey, when it comes to treasure hunting, don't discount the craziest ideas. Whatever works," Famosa remarked. "I knew a guy who bet the bank on a device that followed schools of amberjack, which tend to congregate around shipwrecks. About killed himself catching those fish live, they can get up to six feet long and 175 pounds. No teeth to speak of, but jaws like a steel clamp. Anyhow, he managed to implant GPS chips in a dozen or so of them. Everyone made fun of him, but he's sitting in the Bahamas now after a multimillion-dollar shipwreck discovery."

"That's not so outrageous, actually," Bonita said. "Shipwrecks become natural reefs to marine life. In fact, they call amberjacks 'reef donkeys.'"

Sometimes Merrill forgot that Bonita's expertise was in the marine life aspect of oceanography.

"You'll be interested to know, Ms. Doubtful," Merrill said, turning to Delilah and, without thinking, putting an arm over her shoulder, "that while some people . . . crazies, in my opinion . . . eat amberjack, they're loaded with white worms, called spaghetti worms."

"Yuck!" she said, and shrugged out of his embrace, casting him a scowl of warning.

He just grinned.

"As for that guy with his amberjack theory"—

Merrill directed his words to Famosa now—"they say 'follow the money' in crime detection. Why not 'follow the fish' in sunken treasure detection?"

"Sounds like a great title for a book," Famosa commented to Bonita.

Bonita smiled at Famosa as if he'd said something particularly clever.

*Hey, I was the one with the clever observation. Not that I want Bonita looking at me that way. Delilah, on the other hand . . .* He glanced at Famosa and then Bonita. *Yep. Something definitely going on there.*

They all headed toward the wheelhouse, where they could view the readings on the computer screen. For the next four hours, Charlie trolled over one lane after another of the grid. Everyone watched the screen with excitement, and occasionally one or the other of them spelled Charlie at the wheel.

There was reason for excitement. A number of squares in the grid showed potential, especially since they were clustered together near the center of the site. Luckily, they weren't along the edges because then there would have been the worry over exceeding their license limit or of other salvaging companies moving in to legally steal, or rather, take advantage of all their work.

By the time they all sat at the table down below, well past their usual dinner hour, eating pizza and drinking beer, there was an air of euphoria. First thing tomorrow morning, they would begin to dive the first of the six areas that looked most promising. Of course, there were no guarantees, but everyone was cautiously optimistic. All, or most of them, were dreaming of what they would do with their share of the profits if a discovery turned out to be as prosperous as they hoped, but no one spoke those dreams aloud for fear of jinxing the outcome.

By the next evening, though, the euphoria turned to jubilation. The remains of the *Falcon* had been found. Scattered by 150-plus years of battering tides and shifting sands, they'd only skimmed the surface of four blocks, but they'd already brought up buckets of encrusted gold and silver coins and bars that had to be worth millions. A piece of brass that once graced the wooden steering wheel clearly identified the find as being the *Falcon*.

Merrill had called Gabe, who owned a large percentage of the business, and Harry, who got a small cut in this one mission, telling them about the discovery but cautioning them both to remain silent. The longer they could work the site without the public, or other salvagers, knowing about it, the easier it would be for them to complete the operation. Of course, the state and some historical agencies would have to be notified, but again Merrill wanted to work, uninterrupted, as long as possible.

After dinner, Merrill brought out the champagne he'd saved for just such an occasion, and he proposed a toast. "Thanks be to God for favoring our quest. Thanks be to the ocean, and especially the *Falcon*, for giving up this bounty. Thanks be to hard workers and good friends to share the joy."

There were responses of "Amen!" "Cin Cin!" "¡Salud!" "Bonne Chance!" "Skål!" and "Hoo-yah!"

They all took long drinks from their plastic glasses.

"In the words of Mr. Spock, who was just as eloquent as my friend Geek, but more brief," K-4 said then, connecting a high five with Merrill, "live long and prosper."

Everyone nodded and took another drink.

Charlie surprised them by offering a toast related to her own situation: "Two ins and one out. In with health and wealth. Out with debt."

After they drank to that toast, Merrill opened a second bottle of champagne.

Bonita stood then, already a little wobbly. "There are good ships and there are bad ships that sail the seas. But the best ships are friendships. Forever may they be."

"Hear, hear!" everyone said, and took another drink.

"You guys are so full of nicey-nice shit," Gus said. "Here's to you, and here's to me. Friends may we always be. But if by chance we disagree, up yours! Here's to me!"

*Time to steer this party in another direction.* "I know what I'm going to do with my share of the treasure," Merrill said. "Buy a house in Bell Cove. How about the rest of you?"

Delilah stared at him in surprise.

*What? Does she think I'm going to live in a motel room the rest of my life? Or does she think I'm going to skip town? Not anytime soon, baby!*

But the others had taken his cue on changing the subject.

"I'm going to quit my job with the National Park Service and finish up my PhD. About time, too." This from Bonita.

"I like teaching," Famosa contributed, "so I won't give that up. And I like shipwreck ventures, like this one on the side. Maybe I'll buy a diving boat . . . a small one . . . and teach shipwreck diving off the Jersey coast."

"How about you, Gus? Will you give up your convenience store and gas station for the high life?" Merrill asked.

"Hell, no! I've had the high life, and it's not what it's cracked up to be. And I don't care about having a big bank account, either. Had that, too. Time to concentrate on finding a good woman and settle down to raise some kiddies."

He winked at Delilah.

To Merrill's relief, she just laughed.

"Personally, if my itty-bitty share is enough, my dream is to just finish fixing up the diner and motel and try raising my daughter in a safe, peaceful place."

"Did I mention . . ." Gus waved his hand at Delilah.

"Shut up, Goose," Merrill said, and didn't care if it revealed his feelings for Delilah.

The others laughed, thus proving his theory that he and Delilah weren't fooling anyone by their discreet actions aboard the ship.

"Personally, I don't have any dreams at all. How sad is that?" K-4 said.

Everyone knew by now that K-4's wife had died

of cancer some years ago, and he still hadn't recovered from his grief.

"And how about you, Charlie?" Merrill asked. "Guess we know what you'll do with your share."

She nodded. "My family is gonna be back in the commercial fishing business. Any money left over will go to my sister Ann Marie who wants to be a doctor."

"By the way, Charlie, I was talking yesterday to my housemate, Janice Franklin. She works in the marina office in Hatteras, and she mentioned a yacht that pulled in a few days ago. Name of the yacht was *Sweet Charlotte*. The owner was asking how to get to Bell Cove."

Charlie's face turned pink.

"Jan said that this guy looked like a cross between Matthew McConaughey and Chris Hemsworth. I think his name is . . ."

"J. L. Landry," Charlie finished for her with an exhale of disgust. "I told the fool that I'd shoot him in the nuts if he followed me."

They all gave Charlie a second look then to see what a cross between McConaughey and Hemsworth would see in their Charlie. But then, Merrill noticed that the woman was looking surprisingly pretty tonight. Her cap must have fallen off in the process of their drinking toasts, and she had a mass of brown waves spilling over her shoulders and back. Her eyes were dark and sultry under the influence of alcohol. Hard to tell what her figure was like in her usual overalls and T-shirt, but he was beginning to suspect they had a Cajun hottie on their hands and never realized it.

"Okay, here's the deal," he told the group, before they got wasted and were unable to carry out their duties. "Someone needs to be up topside all night, keeping guard. I'll take the first watch, until eleven. At two-hour intervals, we should probably change off. How about you taking over from me, K-4, and then Gus or Famosa can come on at one and three?"

"Is it really necessary?" Delilah asked. "I mean, really? Pirates?"

"Oh, yeah!" everyone else said.

"And we will have to take the boat in to refuel and flush out soon," Charlie pointed out. "That's when we'll be most vulnerable. Try as we might, word might get out, and the site will be flooded with pirates, news media, spectators."

"Too bad we can't have your friend with the yacht come park over our site," Merrill said, in jest. "Now that would be some security!"

"Yeah, but what would I have to promise in return for the favor?" Charlie scoffed, taking his suggestion seriously.

"On your back, in the sack, would be my guess," Famosa said.

Instead of being offended, Charlie replied, "On my back, in the sack, with a ring on my finger."

Again, everyone looked at Charlie with speculation. McConaughey-Hemsworh was looking for her, not only to rescue her from her money problems, not only to get her into his bed, but he wanted to marry her, as well.

*Well, well, well.*

"By the way, folks, don't go on a spending spree anytime soon," Merrill warned. "It will probably be months before we see any cash from this operation."

"Plus, it will alert the busybodies in town," Gus pointed out. "Not to mention the press."

"Right," Merrill concurred, and the others nodded in agreement.

"It's going to be hard not to smile a lot, though," Bonita said.

They all agreed with that, too.

An hour later, it was ten o'clock on a star-filled night as Merrill sat in the wheelhouse, keeping an eye on the horizon. It was silent in the way only an ocean can be. But then he heard someone approaching. It was Delilah in her Jessica Rabbit "Beach Bunny" sleep shirt and flip-flops.

*Ah, the memories!*

"I couldn't sleep," she said. "Mind if I join you?"

*Now that is a loaded question! Is she that clueless about me?* "Sure," he answered, patting the built-in, high seat next to his. "Still worried about your grandmother and your daughter? That's not what's keeping you awake, is it?"

She shook her head. "No, just too much going on in my head. Everything that's happened today, of course. Everything I need to do tomorrow, here on the boat. Then when we return to Bell Cove, so many things to do related to Maggie starting kindergarten, and me getting the diner and motel open. Then, back to the boat again."

"But those are good things, especially with the cash you'll get from this operation. One day at a time, and things will get done."

"Guess I'm just a born worrier. I've been living by Murphy's Law for so long that I just expect bad things to happen."

"Not anymore, sweetheart. You're under my good luck umbrella now."

"Is that like some knight in shining armor protecting his lady with his trusty shield?"

"Absolutely. Shield, umbrella, same thing." He leaned over and kissed her lightly on the mouth. But then, he stood and moved closer. This time he deepened the kiss. She tasted like champagne and mint toothpaste and sex.

*Okay, that last was wishful thinking.*

With a groan, she put her hands on his shoulders and opened her mouth wider.

*On the other hand . . .*

Her lips were moist, her tongue was moving against his, and she was rubbing her breasts against his chest. His stunned brain registered three facts at once: *She's not wearing a bra. Her nipples are hard. SHE WANTS ME!*

He was pretty sure his eyes rolled back in his head. *Holy shit! Talk about hair-trigger arousal!*

In a nanosecond he had his hands on her waist, lifted her off her chair, and had her up against the wall. Lifting the hem of her sleep shirt, he discovered that she was pantieless . . .

*Am I on a good luck roll or what?*

. . . and wet . . .

*Holy-frickin'-hallelujah!*

. . . and he was in!

Which surprised the hell out of both her and himself. And embarrassed him, too.

"Oops, I didn't mean to rush you like that." Embedded to the hilt, motionless for the moment, he pressed his forehead against her forehead as he attempted to count to ten—in Arabic.

She giggled—she actually giggled. "Obviously, I was ready." She flexed her inner muscles for emphasis . . .

*Wow! Can you do that again, honey?*

. . . and rubbed her breasts against him again.

*Definitely rock hard nipples!*

"Oh! My! Delilah!" he choked out.

The wallbanger of all wallbangers followed then.

He held her pinned to the wall with the press of his body, at first, his hands being busy checking out those pebbly nipples under her shirt that was pushed up to her shoulders by now.

Her hands were busy, too, tugging his T-shirt over his head.

Hers was suddenly gone, too.

*How did that happen?*

Ah! Skin against skin.

More rubbing.

Stars. Not in the sky but behind his closed eyelids.

He put his hands under her buttocks to lift her higher.

She locked her heels behind his ass.

The long slow strokes in her hot folds soon became short and fast. The wet sounds of the slip and slide was the best kind of aphrodisiac, music to a horny sailor's ears. He tried to slow their rhythm with his hold on her bottom, but she was having none of that and undulated her hips, demanding, "More! Harder! Harder! Oh! Oh! Damn!"

*Damn was right. Hot damn!*

He shot his wad in a bone-melting conclusion that was pure ecstasy. For a moment, he remained, unmoving, limp but remaining inside her weaker and weaker spasming folds as her climax ran its course. Only belatedly did he realize that he hadn't used a condom, but then she'd told him previously that she was on the pill. Even so, Merrill hadn't been so careless in years, if ever. This woman was driving him bonkers. In a good way.

Before he released himself, and her, he leaned his head back and said, "I love you, Delilah Jones." He just wanted to make it clear that while he might have come on like a raving sex maniac, at heart—well, she had his heart.

She didn't repeat the words back at him, but she did put a hand to his cheek in a kind of loving manner and she did look like she loved him.

Still . . .

**Chapter 15**

*Dum, dee, dum, dum! Trouble*
*coming, and it's not sharks . . .*

$F$or the next five days, excitement was the name of
the game on *Sweet Bells*, and Delilah couldn't help
but be caught in the wave of euphoria. But finally
they were going to return to Bell Cove for a much-
needed refueling, "flushing" out sewage, laundry,
resupplying food and other products, and general
maintenance.

In the midst of all the excitement, Delilah was
still worried about her grandmother and Maggie, whom she hadn't seen for ten days now. Even
though her grandmother assured her that she was
doing nothing illegal and promised to be more
low-key, Delilah wasn't convinced. Her grandmother wouldn't know low-key if it hit her in her
fool, Avon-powdered face.

And speaking—or rather thinking—of a differ-
ent kind of excitement, *and, yes, I mean that kind,*
Delilah was conflicted over her "relationship" with
Merrill, whom she couldn't seem to resist. *Dammit!*
First, he'd plagued her with constant interference in

her life. *Can anyone say neon Elvis?* Then he plagued her with his tempting body. *What was it they said about Navy SEALs and sexual prowess? Multiply it by ten for my horny sailor.*

*And another ten for horny ex-felons.* In Merrill's defense—not that he needed her defense—she was as bad as he was when it came to sex. Which he would probably consider a plus. Bad sex, that was. As in wild, spontaneous, uninhibited, good time anytime. *Yikes!*

Five years of celibacy were apparently taking their toll on her in terms of a sudden, ravenous hunger for the age-old game—with Merrill, anyhow. As evidenced by that wallbanger in the wheelhouse five nights ago. Or in the shower stall midafternoon two days ago when everyone had been up on deck. Or in his bed last night where he constantly had to caution her, with a laugh, to be quieter in her responses. And those weren't the only times! *Dammit!* Or should that be, *Shame on me!*

Or, *Shame on him!*

Or, *What the hell . . . Hail to the Big O!*

Merrill kept telling her that he loved her, but how could that be, when he didn't really know her? Fearing the worst, when—or if—he ever found out, she withheld her own words of love, which she knew hurt him. But how could she do otherwise? With the weight of her secret past holding her back, she wasn't free to love anyone.

Care, though—oh, yes, she did care for him. A lot! And lust after him like some kind of crazed sex addict. Maybe her grandmother's gambling gene had carried over to her, manifesting itself in her hormones, instead of deft card shuffling fingers or a slot machine arm. *Now, there's a thought!*

Next I'll be on Dr. Phil. Confessions of a felonious blonde bimbo sex addict who cooks, treasure hunts, and runs an Elvis motel and diner on the side.

Her only saving grace was that she kept busy most of the time. When she wasn't cooking or serving meals, or taking care of housekeeping duties, she was assigned the job of cleaning the silver and gold. Bonita and Famosa, whoever was available at the time, worked on the more sensitive metals and artifacts, which started to deteriorate once exposed to air.

Their success so early was attributed to Merrill's reputation for good luck. Apparently it took some treasure hunters months, even years, to recover a shipwreck. Sometimes, they never found the ship they were searching for, or even died in the process.

But those on *Sweet Bells* . . . Holy cow! Every time the divers went down, they returned with overladen bags of gold and silver coins and occasionally bronze and copper, as well, attached to their belts. Francs, centimes, and livres of the 1850s and 1860s. Finally, they started sending baskets down with the divers that they could fill to heavier limits, and those on board lifted them more easily, compared to the bags attached to the divers' belts.

Thus far, Gus and K-4 had driven the motorboat into town three times, under the cover of darkness, and unloaded the ice chests onto the Bell Forge wharf, where Gabe and Harry made sure they were locked in a secure room. An amazing ten chests so far! And more ready to go.

Only once had Gus or K-4 encountered any town folks who might question what they were doing. It had been Frank Baxter from the hardware store, who had taken up jogging of late, supposedly to impress the widow mayor, Doreen Ferguson.

"Whatcha got in them ice chests?" a huffing Frank had asked.

"Shhh! It's spiny lobsters," Gus had lied. There was a legal limit on how many lobsters one person could catch in a day. "Don't tell anyone. My mother loves to mix them with herring in her Norse potato salad."

Frank had barely hidden his distaste for that news. Apparently, everyone knew about Mrs. Gustafson's potato salad that was heavy on the little salted fishies, when it wasn't alternated with something called lutefisk.

"Should I tell Mom to send you some?"

"No, no, I'm allergic to shellfish."

But now, as the boat chugged on its five-mile trek back home, Delilah was down below, her bag packed, and the salon half-filled with trash and laundry bags to be taken ashore. Other people's luggage and duffels were there, too.

Kevin came down then. She had trouble thinking or referring to him by his SEAL nickname, "K-4." Just as she would have if asked to call Merrill "Geek."

"Need any help?" he asked.

"Not yet," she said. "Once the boat is secured, though . . . definitely."

"Any coffee left?"

"Yes," she said, and poured him a mug, which he took black.

They both sat at the table, listening to the activity up above. The stomping of feet, loud chatter, laughter.

She had a tablet in front of her on which she'd started several lists: Food (the list was enormous even though she didn't know how long they would be out next time). Supplies (such as napkins, paper towels, and toilet tissue). Maggie (school clothes, backpack, dentist appointment, guardianship papers from lawyer). Diner (remove old appliances, call gas company, fix neon sign?). Motel (cost estimate for remaining five units, reflagging patios, parking lot repairs).

The radio on the counter was playing beach music of the Carolina style with occasional interruptions to give updates on Tropical Storm Heloise, which was expected to hit the Outer Banks tomorrow. It wasn't a hurricane or anything dire like that, but high winds and driving rains were forecast for the next few days, which meant no diving. Another reason why they'd decided to head back today.

"So, you and Geek, huh?" Kevin remarked suddenly, and grinned at her.

She wasn't sure how to answer; so, she just nodded. "He's a good guy."

That she could agree with. She nodded again. "You're not going to warn me about not hurting your buddy or something like that, are you?"

He laughed. "Nah, Geek's a big boy. And I know from experience that life's short. Grab what happiness you can when you can."

"Even if it can end in pain?"

"Even then."

Kevin was a good-looking man, even with the ten-day scruff of beard he'd grown and hair over-long and in need of a trim. His eyes always looked a bit sad, though. Women must love him, sure they were the ones to heal his grief. He probably used that to his dating advantage.

*That is so cynical of me!*

*But probably true.*

"Your room at the motel is ready for you," she informed him. Her grandmother had told her yesterday that Barb and Stu from Blankety-Blank had come by and installed curtains and made up the beds with new linens and the wave-like bed-spreads. "I assume you want to stay there again."

"Yep. The Blue Hawaii suite. I expect to have hula girls greeting me when we get back," he teased.

"Don't count on it. From me, anyhow. Any hula girls will have to be by your own arrangement."

"Aw, shucks! And I was really in the mood for some grass skirt action."

"Poor you! There will be a small flat-screen TV, though. I had my grandmother buy them for the three completed units while we were gone."

"That's great, although I don't watch much television. Give me Wi-Fi and I'm good to go."

"Not even the *Andy Griffith Show*?"

He laughed. "You know about Geek's Mayberry obsession, huh? Once he made us watch a marathon of the show when we were stuck in a safe house in Kuwait. After three days of utter boredom, F.U. swore he developed a thing for Aunt Bee."

"F.U.?"

"Frank Uxley. The most politically incorrect, obnoxious frogman to ride the seas, but the guy you want covering your six when you go down range."

"Do you think you'll miss the SEALs?" she asked, though what she really wanted to know was whether Merrill would get bored with civilian life eventually and want to go back in the military.

"Probably, but, with this week's action here, treasure hunting comes close to the adrenaline rush of bang-bang ops in foreign countries."

Merrill came down then, and, after exchanging a few words about last-minute details, K-4 went back up.

"We should dock in about fifteen minutes," he said, a slow grin tugging at his lips.

Like K-4, he was looking a bit scruffy with week-old whiskers and very tan skin. He wore a ratty gray T-shirt and faded black running shorts, long legs leading to sockless running shoes, that had also seen better days. In other words, six foot three of yummy sexiness.

She realized belatedly that he was heading directly for her with that mischievous, I've-got-you-in-my-crosshairs gleam in his eyes. She stood and backed up a bit. "Not again," she said.

"Again what?" he asked with the innocence of a cobra about to strike as he strolled to her side of the table.

She moved, putting the table between them. "You know what? Someone could come down here at any minute."

"Not to worry!" He sidled closer, to the end of the table. Pretending to be looking over her notes, but knowing exactly where his target was. Target being her. "I told everyone to stay above so I could have a quickie with my honey."

"You did not!"

He winked at her. "Just kidding."

And just like that, he vaulted over the table and had her backed up, face against the wall.

He nuzzled her neck and said, "Actually, I came down to tell you that I was able to get cell coverage and talk to Harry. No one unusual hanging around. So, the news hasn't leaked out yet."

She sighed and turned in his arms, giving his whiskers a tug. "Any plans when you'll announce the discovery?"

"Hopefully, we'll have a few days to prepare. Bonita and Famosa will do more research on the *Falcon* to go with the news releases. Maybe a press conference on Thursday or Friday."

Her heart skipped a beat at that news—and because he was tracing the outline of her lips with a forefinger. She nipped at his finger and ended up sucking on the tip.

He groaned and ground his lower body against hers.

She groaned then and pushed him away. "Stop it! I can't concentrate when you do that."

He grinned.

Putting some space between them, she went back to the table and began to gather her papers. "I won't have to be involved in a press conference, will I?"

"Probably not. But they might want pictures of the full crew." He was at the open fridge now, scanning the contents, then shut the door for lack of interest.

"I'd rather not, Merrill."

He turned to look at her. "Aren't you proud of our work?"

"Sure, but I like my privacy."

He narrowed his eyes, studying her for a moment, but then he shrugged. "It's up to you, but I can't guarantee anonymity if some newshound digs it up."

She shivered inwardly at the prospect.

"Anyhow, before any of that happens, we first have to notify the state and historical societies of the shipwreck site. Find out exactly what we have in terms of gold recovered so far. Study the pictures of what remains below . . . cannons, portholes, and so on. Anything nondegradable that has survived the elements. Then put together a schedule for working the rest of the site. People in authority get their noses out of joint if they read about artifacts being taken out of the ocean without the salvagers following protocol. So, we need to get our ducks in a row, according to the rules."

"Don't other countries sometimes try to claim the treasure from shipwrecks, even when they haven't done the work to recover it?"

"Yes, but that shouldn't apply here since we're only five miles out. International waters begin at twelve miles. Of course, sometimes the original owners of a ship try to claim the goods, but the owner of this ship was a conglomerate of factory owners in the 1860s. Proving a claim would be impossible."

Since Merrill mentioned phone service resuming, she clicked on her cell phone even as they talked. Her eyes went wide with alarm when she saw a grand total of 48 calls and 66 text messages, many of which seemed to come from Ms. Gardner, her parole officer. Skimming the texts didn't provide much info, just that she wanted Delilah to return her calls.

Merrill had gone into his bedroom while she'd been checking her phone. He came back with a leather Dopp kit which he dropped next to his sea bag. Noticing her reaction, he asked, "Is something wrong?"

"No, just a lot of calls to be handled."

"They're probably like email. A mass delete should take care of them pronto."

*I wish!*

The engine slowed down noticeably as they approached the wharf at Bell Forge and Merrill prepared to go back up on the deck. Before he did, he

walked over to her again and tilted her chin up
for a quick kiss. "It's going to be wildly busy this
afternoon, for both of us. Will I see you tonight?"

He probably meant in his motel room after her
grandmother and Maggie were asleep.

She hesitated and then nodded.

His kiss then was longer and deeper before he
whispered against her mouth, "Good. I can't wait."

She couldn't, either.

*Dammit!*

"And I have something serious I want to discuss
with you regarding our future."

"Future? What future?" she tried to joke.

"You know exactly what future, babe." He didn't
smile, just stared at her, daring her to disagree.

*Double damn dammit!*

For that, she *could* wait.

### *Are secrets a deal breaker among lovers? . . .*

They arrived back at Bell Cove at ten a.m. to a calm
and pleasant reception of one. Gabe Conti. Which
had to be good news.

"Is it true? Really? Five, maybe ten million in
gold? You are fucking unbelievable! No wonder the
Navy didn't want to let you go."

"Shhh! Hold your enthusiasm," Merrill warned
as Gabe alternately clapped him on the back and
grinned like an idiot.

"Yeah. Right," Gabe said, then continued to grin. "This is the most excitement I've had in weeks."

Merrill took that to mean that Laura had dumped him again, or maybe he'd dumped her this time. Those two had a relationship much like a roller coaster. One or the other was always jumping off, then climbing back on.

After the initial unloading of the boat, Charlie drove it off to the pump station. She still insisted on sleeping on board the boat out at the site, which allowed him, Famosa, and K-4 to have their own rooms at the motel.

Bonita and Famosa went to the university. They would be researching some of the items found and preparing a press release. A list had already been prepared of all the agencies to be contacted once Merrill gave the okay signal.

K-4 and Gus were planning lunch at the Cracked Crab after a quick shower and shave. There was mention of two Victoria's Secret models in town that Gus knew from his old football days. They were here—well, in Nags Head—for a photo shoot and a few days' vacation.

And Delilah, of course, went home for a happy reunion with her daughter and a not-so-happy lecture for her grandmother regarding her alleged antics of the past ten days. Delilah took his truck with a mountain of laundry. He'd told her that it didn't have to be done right away since they wouldn't be returning to the site until after the storm hit and ran its course, which should last at least three days. But knowing her, she'd be at the Laundromat this afternoon. In addition, she'd told him he could have the truck back after today since her grandmother's station wagon was available for her use. Hah! He questioned how long that big-ass gas guzzler would last.

Whatever! He wasn't going to let anyone rain on his parade today. The exhilaration Merrill felt wasn't unlike what he and his teammates experienced on returning from a successful mission. Adrenaline out the wazoo. Besides, despite the success of their mission, despite his busy schedule for today, Merrill had tonight to look forward to. Life was good. *Can anyone say adrenaline sex?*

He and Gabe spent an hour in the storage room going over the coins and artifacts that were laid out on various folding tables. Gold and silver didn't require any special treatment for preservation, but they did require cleaning and in some cases picking away at the encrustation. Harry had been working on this himself so far, not wanting to bring in any help that might have a flapping tongue.

"Where is Harry, by the way?" Merrill asked.

Gabe laughed. "You do not want to know."

Merrill arched his brows.

"We didn't know for sure what time you'd get here. So, he stuck around the Patterson house this morning for a hot-cha-cha breakfast. He should be in anytime now."

"Is that something else I don't really want to know about?"

Gabe grinned. "Delilah's grandmother has been

leading a prebreakfast 'Wake-Up Exercise Class' that presumably gets the sap running on even the oldest trees, if you get my meaning."

"Good Lord!" And that was a prayer because he knew Delilah would be all upset and too busy keeping an eye on the old lady now to have time for him. *Goodbye adrenaline sex!* "Even Harry?"

"Especially Harry. Supposedly, he's had his first hard-on in five years just from slathering his body with some Avon crap before the morning happy time."

"He told you that?" Merrill was shocked. Harry was usually more dignified in his manner and speech.

"Hell, no! But he implied it. And he's started wearing cologne."

"That's no proof. I suspect everyone in town is wearing cologne these days, thanks to the Avon Lady who's perfected 'The Art of the (Avon) Deal.'"

"Yep."

They grinned at each other. Good ol' Bell Cove.

"So, are you done with the site?"

"Oh, hell no! We haven't begun to bring up the big guns, and I mean that literally. Cannon, cannonballs, other weapons, heavy stuff. We'll probably have to let some of the historical preservationists come down to look things over before we disturb the wreck any more than we have."

"Weeks? Months?"

"No longer than winter. If someone else wants to salvage the site more, like next spring, they can buy the license from us."

"And then what?"

"Man! Give me a break. Maybe I'll go to Hawaii for a year." He was smiling as he protested.

"I just meant, do we give up on the Three Saints?"

"No, but it will take some research . . . a lot of research . . . to see where our calculations went wrong. And then, if we have a better idea of location, go through the whole process of applying for another license to salvage."

"Harry thinks we should dig for emeralds up in the mountains."

"Hmpfh! I like the way you say 'we' and then stay all warm and snuggly back here in your Mc-Mansion."

"I'd be glad to sell you that McMonstrosity I call home, if you're interested."

"No thanks." He knew Gabe wasn't serious anyhow. Chimes was a family heirloom, sort of.

"Now that you're about to reap a few million, you can afford it."

"I was a millionaire before."

"Are you saying you don't need thirteen bathrooms?"

"When I go to the head, one toilet, one sink, and one shower are all I need."

"Yeah, but if you and Delilah get married and have a dozen kids, you might need a McAnnie-sion, Daddy Warbucks. Might even turn it into an orphanage."

"Harry talks too much," Merrill said. "Listen, speaking of bathrooms, I've gotta go take a shower and shave." He rubbed a hand over his bristly chin.

"I'm starting to itch." Plus, he had enough salt encrusted on his skin and hair from diving to fill a salt shaker.

"You can go to my place if you want."

"Nah! I'll use the shower in my motel unit. I have clean clothes there. If Harry gets here while I'm gone, tell him to hold down the fort. I know he has a lot of business to go over with me. And tell him to stop gossiping about me."

"I think it's the grandmother who's been filling Harry's ear with ideas."

He rolled his eyes. "As long as that's the only cavity being filled."

"You've been too long at sea, my friend," Gabe observed with a chuckle.

When he got to the motel, he saw that his pickup truck was missing, as he'd predicted. Delilah's grandmother, who was the only one there, affirmed his suspicion.

"Lilah and Maggie went to the Laundromat and the grocery store." She narrowed her heavily mascaraed eyes at him. "Lilah seemed awful happy. Did something happen?"

Well, that answered that question. Delilah hadn't mentioned the treasure or their relationship.

"No idea," he said. "She's probably just glad to be with her daughter again."

"Uh-huh," the grandmother said, skeptically. She was looking him over like he was a prime steak, meanwhile puffing on one of those ridiculous flavor vapor cigarettes. Apple this time, he would guess.

"I've gotta go shower and get back to the office," he said then. Really, his eyes were starting to burn with his effort not to go googly-eyed at the sight that Salome Jones presented.

The sixty-something person had her forty-something body squeezed into a pair of figure-hugging short shorts and a stretch T-shirt that showed off her cleavage almost to her waist. Long, shapely legs led to a pair of high-wedge-heeled sandals, exposing neon pink toenails. Bottom line, a woman her age had no business having a butt like that. And her boobs!

*I. Am. Not. Looking.*

Harry was at the office when he got there about noon. Right off the bat, Merrill noticed that Harry had a new hairstyle, parted on the side. And his eyebrows looked different. Didn't he have a unibrow before?

*Not my business!*

Harry had ordered pizzas and cold sodas for lunch. Glancing at the huge pile of papers on the desk waiting for his action, Merrill almost turned around and left. With a sigh, he dug in, to both the food and the work.

An hour later and only halfway through the pile of paperwork, all hell broke loose. News had broken about the treasure.

It started with the mayor, Doreen Ferguson, rushing into the office, without knocking. "I just heard. I just heard. Oh, my God! You found the treasure!"

"What? Who told you that?"

"I was having my roots done at Styles & Smiles.

That's my daughter's hair salon," she said, pausing to catch her breath. Just then, he noticed that half her hair was wet and had some reddish-brown substance plastered on it. The other half was brown and dry with a one-inch line of gray at the roots. This was not good. Even he knew that. "And Maisie Dolan . . . she gets a shampoo and blow-dry every Monday, when Francine runs a half-price sale . . . Maisie said she heard from her cousin Bruce who works at Bell Forge that you guys have been hauling gold in here by the wheelbarrow loads."

"Do we own a wheelbarrow?" he asked Harry. Before he had a chance to respond to Doreen's statement, the sound of screeching wheels could be heard in the parking lot. Looking out the window, he saw that two news vehicles had arrived, a van with a satellite dish on its roof and the logo, NBX-TV, and a black sedan with the logo, "The Bell, Where Local News Is Celebrated." Annie Fox and Sam Castile from *The Morning Show* were fighting to get past Laura Atler at the entrance.

"Where's the gold?" all three of them yelled once they got inside and noticed Merrill and Harry through the doorway that Doreen had left open.

Laura gave Doreen's half-dyed head a double take, then turned to Gabe, who'd joined the fray by now, having heard the commotion from the other side of the building. "You promised me, Gabe. You said I would get a scoop when they found the sunken ships."

Merrill and Harry glared at Gabe, who was looking like a kid caught with his hand in the cookie jar.

"Um, I was in an, um, vulnerable position at the time."

Merrill assumed he meant in the sack with his cookies exposed.

"Hah! We were having dinner at the Cracked Crab at the time."

"Yeah, but there was the prospect of . . . you know?" He waggled his eyebrows at her.

Laura was not amused.

Merrill assumed he meant the prospect of cookies.

"That is so unprofessional," Annie said to Laura. "Trading sex for a news story."

Laura inhaled sharply and reached for a stapler sitting on the desk. "I'll show you unprofessional, you crazy bitch. How about that time you were caught having sex with a fireman in a boat during Hurricane Florence, and Sam was pretending to drown in two feet of water? You and Sam here are the joke of the Outer Banks."

"Hey!" Sam protested. "There were snakes in that water. Probably."

Merrill grabbed the stapler out of Laura's hand and yelled, "Shut the hell up! All of you!" In the silence, he then said, "Sit down, everyone."

Gabe brought in some folding chairs to accommodate everyone.

Merrill explained everything to them then, in general, but he said there would be no details until a press conference in two days, on Wednesday at two p.m. And definitely no look-see at any of the gold coins until then. It wasn't the Three Saints, though, he disclosed that much, but the *Falcon*, an 1860s era French blockade runner. Merrill had originally planned to hold a press conference on Thursday or Friday, but it was hopeless to think they could hold out that long now.

"Oh, good! That will give us two days to bring out the decorations," Doreen said.

Merrill groaned.

"Will there be room enough for us to do it here? Maybe we should use your place, Gabe."

Gabe groaned.

Merrill was further alarmed by Doreen's use of the word "us" and "we," especially when she added, "The whole town will want to come."

"Ooh, ooh, ooh, I have a great idea. If you wait until the weekend for the big reveal, we could have a Dress Like a Pirate Day in Bell Cove. Tourists will love it."

*More we's!* "We're not pirates. We recovered our treasure by legal means," Merrill emphasized.

Doreen waved a hand dismissively. "Same thing. Bet we could find some big pirate chests on the Internet. Exactly how much gold are we talking about here, Merrill?"

*The sly woman! Thought she could get the deets by the back door.*

"That is a wonderful idea, Doreen," Laura said.

"No, no, no, it is not a wonderful idea," Merrill protested.

No one paid any attention to him.

"Do you still have any of those wild animals at your place, Gabe?" Doreen wanted to know.

When Gabe, an architect from Durham, inherited

Bell Forge and his grandparents' mansion in Bell Cove, he'd discovered that one of his ancestors had a Big Game stuffed animal collection. The walls and every inch of space in half the mansion was loaded with the things. A taxidermist's paradise!

"Only a gorilla," Gabe replied.

"Too bad! Especially all those fish would have made a great backdrop for our event. Imagine a whale lying there with a pile of gold coins coming out of its mouth."

Merrill's jaw dropped and, yes, he was noticing the use of "our" event.

"I never had a whale," Gabe sputtered.

"No problem. Betcha Del Brown over at The Honey Hole could get us a big fish. If nothing else we could borrow that marlin he has up on the wall of his fish shop. By the way, everyone, Del has a sale on halibut this week. Thanks for mentioning that in your paper, Laura."

Laura nodded and said, "I'm partial to his red fish. Cooked with lemon on the grill . . . yum!"

"Are you people crazy?" Annie exclaimed. "We're talking a big news story here, and you two are chitchatting about food. This scoop . . . I mean, this segment for *The Morning Show* . . . could give me the boost I need to move up to the networks."

Meanwhile, Sam was glued to his cell phone, probably texting the story around the world.

Jeesh! Merrill had to get a handle on this run-away train.

"That's it for today, folks. Sorry to see you go, but Harry and Gabe and I have work to do if we're going to have a press conference on *Wednesday*." He put particular emphasis on that day so that Doreen would get the message. No pirate nonsense!

By the time everyone left—even Gabe, who claimed to have an appointment in his Durham office that would probably keep him overnight, which was probably a lie—Merrill looked at Harry and sighed. "First things first. We need to warn the other team members that the cat is out of the bag."

"More like the tiger's out of the cage," Harry said.

"We need a plan, that's all. A strict plan of nondisclosure so that any reveals come from one source only."

Harry nodded. "The phones are going to be ringing off the hook."

"Just direct them to me, and I'll choose which, if any, to answer. Also, we need extra security on the storage room. There's a saying in historical preservation work, according to Bonita. When asked what's the best way to preserve gold, the answer is, 'Put it in a safe.'"

Harry laughed, but then he turned serious. "There is one thing I need to discuss with you."

"Nah. That's enough of that crap for today." He waved a hand toward the remaining paperwork. "We can go over that tomorrow. I need to go celebrate."

"How?"

"The best way," he replied with a grin.

"Um, that's what I need to discuss with you. Rather who I need to discuss."

Merrill tilted his head in question. "Delilah?"

Harry nodded, reluctantly.

"What?"

"She's a felon."

Merrill couldn't have been more shocked if Harry had stood up and kicked him in the gut. "No way!"

"Unfortunately, way! Her parole officer, a Ms. Gardner, dropped by last week and wanted to know if she'd reported her felony background to her employer?" Harry handed him the parole officer's business card.

That news was alarming, but then Merrill laughed. "What'd she do? Rob a bank?"

"Accessory to armed robbery and murder."

Another kick in the gut. "Impossible. Not Delilah."

"She served five years in the women's penitentiary in New Jersey."

Finally, the missing piece of the puzzle. That accounted for Delilah ceding guardianship of her daughter to her grandmother. That accounted for her five years of celibacy. That accounted for so many things.

Merrill put up a halting hand when Harry was about to say more. Rising, he began to leave. "I need to be alone, Harry." He jammed the card in his back pocket and said, "Make the calls to the other team members. We'll talk tomorrow. I'm sorry to leave you with all this, but I just can't . . ." He shrugged.

"Just one thing, my friend. Don't do anything rash. You haven't heard Lilah's side of the story."

*Her side?* Some omissions were so huge that they

amounted to a lie. In essence, she'd been lying to him from the time they'd first met.

*It's over.*

*Maybe it was never meant to be. She certainly fought hard and long not to have a relationship.*

*It's over.*

*Besides, she never said she loves me. I told her, though. I said those three crazy-ass words. More fool, I!*

*It's over.*

*But Harry says there are two sides to any story. Maybe I should ask for an explanation.*

*No, it's over.*

*It has to be.*

*Definitely.*

*Probably.*

*Maybe.*

"Another thing . . . and I know you don't need another thing at the moment, but your family has been trying to contact you all week."

They'd been trying to contact him, too. He'd just hit DELETE on both voice mail and text messages. From everyone.

"Your mother is in a hospital in Hatteras."

"What? Oh, shit!" He'd thought they were gone by now, back to Jersey. "What's wrong?"

"I have no idea."

It had to be serious. His mother was the type who abhorred strange places for intimate things, whether they be the bathroom in a restaurant or a doctor's examining room in a strange city. She would prefer her own Princeton Medical Center and longtime GP Dr. Phillips.

Once he'd left the building, he hopped onto Delilah's cycle and rode through town, aimlessly. The skies were getting darker and the wind was picking up, a prelude to the predicted storm to hit tonight or tomorrow. Which did nothing to lighten his mood.

As he rode, he thought, *Did I really think this morning that life is good?*

Talk about jinxing oneself!

*Life sucks!*

Could he forgive her? Would she even want his forgiveness? That was the question.

No. The better question was, where could a guy go at three in the afternoon in a staid little town like Bell Cove to get knee-walking drunk?

# Chapter 16

*Who was it that said trouble comes in
threes? How about fives or tens? . . .*

*I*t was a day of highs and lows for Delilah.

High, when reunited with her daughter, and the
knowledge that soon she would reap rewards from
the treasure that might finally make her financially
stable. And high, of course with the anticipation
of being with Merrill later. Maybe tonight would
be the night she would be able to say those three
magic words. She certainly felt them. High on love.
The best kind of high, she decided.

Low, when she had to deal with her grandmother
and all she'd been up to in Delilah's absence. The
woman was freakin' unbelievable.

Nobody was home when she arrived at the
diner/motel property. Her grandmother had never
been an early riser unless she had to be. Where
could they be in the morning? And what a mess the
place was! Dirty dishes in the sink. Unmade bed.
Laundry on the floor in various rooms. Wet towels
on the floor of the bathroom. Avon products all over
the damn place.

Her grandmother had never been a super house cleaner, but it had never been this bad. Not in Delilah's memory, anyhow.

In her defense, her grandmother hadn't known she'd be back so early today. But this just showed how they lived when Delilah wasn't around. Unacceptable!

There was a binder notebook on the kitchen table, the kind her grandmother always used to keep track of her Avon customers, what they'd bought, the price, the date, a notation where they would need a reorder on a certain date, or observations about the person that might lead to a sale.

"Oh, my God!" Delilah said when she flipped through the pages. Her grandmother must have sold Avon products to every single person in Bell Cove, and she was scalping them with these prices. The total must be over a whopping thousand dollars, or two.

Some of the notations read:

"Ike bgt case Wild Country body wash, tried to sneak a feel. The old fart! Twin brother Mike, much nicer, still old fart. And they're psychiatrists! Or maybe just psychos. Ha, ha."

"Melanie Lewis . . . Natural blonde, my patootie!"

"Gave Harry depilatory. No more unibrow. Dandruff problem."

"Try rosary society at Our Lady by the Sea. Pitch spiritual charms & angel fragrance figurines."

"Wrinkle creams for all ladies at Patterson house."

These were only a few of the entries. There were dozens. But then she noticed one in particular.

"Sell remaining Elvis figurines to Delilah for diner and motel. Family discount?"

*Hah! Discount for a family member! With a question mark! How about free, you old bat?*

Just then, she heard the clatter of metal on metal, a loud muffler, then an engine continuing to run when it was turned off, until it petered out. Immediately followed by car doors slamming and a young voice screaming, "Mommy! Mommy! You're home!"

She went outside and caught her daughter on a running leap into her arms. She kissed her all over her hair, which was done in a French braid (her grandmother's work, to her credit) and smelled of Avon's Wacky Watermelon kids' shampoo, her cheeks, which were sticky from whatever she'd had for breakfast, and her neck, which still carried the scent of pure baby skin, even if she was five years old.

"I have missed you so much, little girl. Bunches, and bunches, and bunches."

Wriggling down to stand at her feet, Maggie said, "I'm not little anymore. I growed an inch las' week. Gramma said so."

"Now that you mention it . . ."

"Did you bring me a dog?"

"No, I did not bring you a dog."

"Maybe tomorrow?"

Delilah crossed her eyes at the conniving little imp.

Then Maggie raced toward the back door, yelling back at them, "I gotta pee."

Delilah directed her attention to her grandmother

then. Her hair was braided same as Maggie's, but
that was where the similarity ended. She wore tight
red spandex yoga pants that would require a crow-
bar to get on and off, white athletic shoes with
pink pom-pom anklet socks, and a red tank top
with a sequined logo, "Yes, They're Real!"

She gave her grandmother a kiss on her heavily
made-up face, barely avoiding the honey-scented
e-stick hanging loosely from her lips, then sur-
veyed her unusual attire—unusual for her. "Where
were you?"

"Teaching a prebreakfast exercise class over at
the Patterson house."

"What? You don't get up till ten unless you have
to, and you once said that exercise is for losers born
with the wrong genes." *And you were smoking those
stinking e-cigarettes the whole time, no doubt!*

"Can't a gal turn a new leaf?"

"New leaf, huh? Does that mean you plan to
stay?"

Her grandmother's face turned pink. "For a while.
It's not as bad as I expected."

"That's a backhanded compliment if I ever heard
one." She gave her grandmother another once-over
and sighed. There were so many things wrong
with a grandmother in spandex, but Delilah had
much bigger concerns where the old lady was concerned. "Don't you think that, at your age, it's time
to cut back?"

"Age is relative. And, by the way, don't take this
the wrong way, sweetie, but you need an Avon
Anew Brightening Clay Mask for those frowny

wrinkles." With those words, she swanned off toward the patio, with a swing of her too-perfect hips.

Delilah refused to let her grandmother get the last word, and she stomped after her. "I saw your notebook. Are you paying sales tax on all those products you've been selling around Bell Cove?"

Her grandmother's face flushed again, but maybe it was just rouge. "Who says I have to pay sales tax?"

"The government does. Jeez, Gram, don't tell me you never paid sales tax in Jersey over all those years when you were an Avon Lady."

"I did when I worked for the company, and they took it out of my checks, but it wasn't necessary when I sold my own stock."

"It *was* necessary, Gram."

"I didn't know that."

"Ignorance is no excuse."

"Are you callin' me ignerent now? Good golly, girl, is this all the thanks I get for helping you out? Complain, complain, complain. Maybe I should go back to Jersey, after all. At least Jimmy the Goon never nagged."

"Just threatened to break a few bones." Delilah realized that she could have chosen a better time to lay out all her concerns and said, "I'm sorry, Gram. I do appreciate everything you do for me and Maggie."

After that, Delilah gathered up all the dirty laundry in her apartment and added it to the huge piles in the back of Merrill's pickup truck, and she and Maggie were off to the Laundromat. With the skies

turning grayer, she wanted to get the truck emptied before the rains hit.

They filled three of the commercial-size washers
and two of the regular ones, with Maggie getting
great delight over being able to sort whites from
colored or dark fabrics. Her stuffed dog, whom she'd
named Randy—not to be confused with Annie's
dog, Sandy, which was impossible, since this one
was more like Pluto—sat on the folding table while
they worked.

The little girl hadn't stopped talking since they
left the motel parking lot.

"Is this Mister Merrill's truck? Where is he? Will
he tell me another story? Maybe Annie and Andy
had a cousin named Lester, who was a clown in
the circus, and his mommy and daddy were lion
tamers . . . or act-o-bats."

"That's some imagination you have there, kiddo."

"Can I have a dog?"

"Can I have a magic elf who could do painting,
carpentry, electrical, plumbing, and general con-
tracting work to fix up the diner and motel? All for
free."

"Huh?"

"It was a joke, honey."

"Oh, will my new school have a playground?"

"Probably."

"Can you get me a Grinch storybook? Ms. Patterson says they have a grinch contest here at Christmas."

"You've seen the movie *How the Grinch Stole
Christmas*, haven't you?"

"Yeah, but I don't have the book. Elmer says Gramma has a great butt."

"He shouldn't say things like that to her."

"He didn't say that to her. He was talkin' to Rahool. But Gramma says that all the time anyhow."

"It's okay if a lady says it about herself, but other people . . . men, in particular . . . shouldn't say it to her."

"Huh? When I grow up, I'm gonna have a great butt."

"I'd rather you have a great brain."

"Huh?"

"You'll understand when you're older."

"Can I have a dog?"

Delilah reached across the truck seat and tweaked her daughter's chin.

And so it went the entire day, including when they walked down the street, while the machines were churning away at the Laundromat, to the secondhand clothing store, Out of the Closet.

The owner, George Saunders, took one look at Maggie as she skipped in with Delilah, and said, "Lilah, you are in such luck! Lance just sent me a half dozen boxes of children's clothing from the Hatteras shop. Some rich folks did a closet cleaning."

George and his partner, Lance, owned a dozen upscale thrift shops throughout the Outer Banks and into South Carolina down to Myrtle Beach. What didn't sell in one community did well in another.

"I just called Sally Dawson over at Sweet Thangs

to come look-see, but she has only boys . . . three growing boys. So, no conflict with you. Wanna see?"

"Of course."

Maggie was already off to the side eyeing a pair of red sparkly Dorothy (from *The Wizard of Oz*) shoes. They would probably be too big, but she could grow into them, Delilah supposed.

"They're still in the boxes in the back room, so they might be wrinkled."

"No problem."

And he had been right. The boxes were a gold mine of little girl bargains. The usual Gap and Old Navy jeans and tops, with some Kalliope Kids outfits tossed in. But then, there were a few high fashion dresses from couture designers—a pink tulle dress over black-and-white polka dots from some French boutique, and a Lanvin leopard print dress to die for. At fifty dollars each, that was expensive for a thrift shop, but way below the original prices well over five hundred dollars. George gave them to her, a repeat customer, for a combined discount price of sixty dollars. Still expensive, but Delilah figured she had to have some way to celebrate the treasure hunting success.

Not that she wasn't going to celebrate in another way tonight. Which reminded her that she hadn't heard from Merrill all day. She checked her cell phone. Nope. No replies to the three previous text messages she'd sent, either. Which was unusual for him. But then, this was an unusual day.

Back to shopping. Delilah discovered that her daughter was a mini fashionista, a born shopper.

The deciding factor on any dress was whether it passed the twirl test. Pants couldn't be so tight they would hinder running. Tops couldn't be scratchy. And orange was an icky color.

It was fun shopping with her daughter, and she even found a few things for herself. Some of them were chosen by Maggie, who proclaimed, "You have a great butt, too, Mommy."

*From the mouths of babes!*

"I heard that," Sally Dawson said with a laugh. She'd just arrived with her three little boys in tow. "Be prepared. The things your kids say will embarrass you. The trick is to embarrass them first."

Three adorable boys, with short brown hair and freckles like their mother but pale blue eyes that must come from their father, one of them missing his two front baby teeth, stood behind Sally, looking like they wanted to be anywhere in the world but a clothing store. Three bicycles were parked outside. They all smelled like something sweet, cookies probably, having come from their bakery down the street.

Glancing at Delilah's overladen shopping cart, Sally made a face. "You got here first."

"Yeah, but I left all the boys' things."

The youngest, about Maggie's age, stepped forward and said to the little girl, "I have a new bike. It's red. Wanna see it?"

His brothers gawked at him like he was either brave or crazy. They might have liked to do the same thing but they were much cooler older guys, at least six or seven.

Maggie looked to Delilah for permission and she nodded. She just knew that the next thing Maggie would be wanting was a bike.

"I promised the boys burgers and fries at the The Bay Shack for lunch if they behaved," Sally said. "Wanna join us?"

"Sure. I need to pay for this stuff, then put loads of wet laundry into the dryers over at the Laundromat first."

"Good. I should be done by then. Can't wait to hear about the big treasure discovery on *Sweet Bells*. You guys are gonna make this town famous."

"Um . . . where did you hear that?"

"It's all over town. Annie and Sam from *The Morning Show* did a news alert about it on NBX-TV this afternoon. Treasure Found. Bell Cove Riches. Or something like that. More news to come at six."

That must be why she hadn't heard from Merrill. He would be swamped with inquiries if news of the shipwreck discovery had leaked.

An hour later, and a hundred dollars poorer, Delilah sat with Sally eating delicious soft shell crab sandwiches with sides of coleslaw, while Maggie and the boys devoured cheeseburgers and homemade boardwalk fries. They would have eaten outside on the deck, except that the sky was dark gray and the breeze uncomfortable. She'd like to be home before the downpour hit.

Before Sally had a chance to grill her on the shipwreck discovery, Laura Atler, the local newspaper editor, came over to their table. "Congratulations, Lilah!"

"Well, I'm just the cook and odd job person. I don't dive."

"Still, this is so exciting! I'll have enough news to put out a special edition this week. Exactly how much gold do you figure the team has brought up so far?"

Delilah realized then that the news leak around town hadn't been specific, so far, and she wasn't about to be the confidential informant. "Gold? What gold?" She batted her eyelashes with innocence.

"What a kidder!" Laura said, but she wasn't amused. She was in full-blown newshound mode. But then she smiled. "The whole town will want to be involved on Wednesday when the press conference is being held. It will be held over at Gabe's mansion to accommodate the out-of-town crowd that will no doubt be here. All the major networks have called, and *People* magazine wants to do a cover story."

*On Wednesday? So soon? And publicity. I do not want to be involved in any publicity.*

"The town council has already met. It would have been nice to have a parade and all that hoopla, but two days is just not enough time. Even so, we're asking all the merchants in town to participate in some way. Banners in the windows. Products related to treasures or gold or shipwrecks. Anything you could do at the bakery, Sally?"

"Maybe gold dust sugar cookies. They make sprinkles now that look like real gold."

"Great! Tony over at the Cracked Crab is going to put Shipwreck Spiny Lobster on the menu."

Delilah groaned.

"What?" Laura asked.

"Nothing. I'm just not a fan of spiny lobster." *Anymore.*

"Frank Baxter at Hard Knocks Hardware is ordering in more metal detectors. People always get the fever when any kind of treasure is found, even like that class ring found over by the sound last summer. You would have thought it was a Cartier creation."

Delilah thought about the high-tech underwater metal detector that Merrill had bought and how his investment had paid off. The news media would probably love that angle on the story, and, yes, that would mean a rush on metal detectors everywhere.

"Too bad that neon Elvis of yours isn't lit up yet," Laura said to Delilah. "We could throw a gold lamé cape over him, which would be perfect. Betcha Stu and Barb over at Blanket-y Blank could scrounge up a length of lamé somewhere.

Delilah refused to rise to the bait. "Sorry. No time. Maybe next year, if Elvis is lit up by then." Then, she thought of something else. "Won't the storm be raging here by then? That should dampen the crowds coming to town." *Please, God!*

"Hopefully, the rains should have stopped by then. The latest weather forecast says it might veer north by Tuesday night. Just in case, we're having Father Brad over at Our Lady by the Sea and Pastor Morgan at St. Andrew's hold an ecumenical prayer vigil tonight for good weather."

"Isn't that kind of materialistic to pray for weather to hold an event that would benefit the town merchants?"

Laura put a hand to her chest as if Delilah had stabbed her. "You have to live through a barrier island hurricane to know why people pray for good weather here all the time."

"Sorry. I didn't mean to offend," Delilah apologized, even though that's not exactly what she'd said. A town praying for good weather in this case had nothing to do with hurricanes, but it wasn't an argument Delilah wanted or needed to engage in.

Laura nodded an acceptance of her apology and went on, "There's just so little time. We're already discussing a bigger celebration for later this summer, maybe a Pirate Gold Day for the salvage treasure in combination with the Labor Day Lollypalooza. You and the *Sweet Bells* crew could dress up like pirates and all the gold you've discovered could be on display in a huge pirate treasure chest on the town square, and a ship resembling the *Falcon* could be brought into Bell Sound, where tours could be given, maybe even stage a fake battle between the *Falcon* and whatever Yankee ship shot it down, and . . ."

On and on Laura went with plans involving a private venture which had suddenly become the town's venture, and what any of the *Sweet Bells* venture had to do with pirates was beyond Delilah's understanding. She barely restrained herself from putting her face on the table and pounding her forehead, but then she noticed Sally grinning at her and realized that some things about Bell Cove just needed to be taken with a grain of humor.

How was Merrill reacting to all this hoopla?

She checked her phone. Still no messages.

After Laura left, Sally patted her hand and said, "Welcome to Bell Cove."

Delilah and Maggie got all the laundry folded, most of which was put in laundry bags, which they dropped off at the warehouse before heading home. There was no one around the salvage side of Bell Forge, which didn't surprise her. They were probably all hiding out, avoiding the press and nosy townspeople.

She stopped at the grocery store, where folks were emptying the shelves in preparation for the storm. Even though a major disaster wasn't predicted, people took no chances. Delilah didn't, either, buying more than she usually would, considering the size of her small fridge and freezer.

Rain started coming down just as they'd arrived in the parking lot back on the diner/motel property. Maggie ran ahead of her, giggling at the warm shower, while Delilah hurried with her heaping basket of clean, folded, soon-to-be-wet-if-she-wasn't-careful sheets, towels, and clothing. Maggie was already chattering away to Gram about her new friends and burgers and fries and a wish for a bike, along with a dog, while Delilah ran out for a second trip to the truck to get the bags from Out of the Closet.

Through the now-pelting rain she saw two vehicles pull up to the motel, driven by Kevin and

Gus, who had two beautiful women with them, who were so tall and slim and gorgeous they could be models. They all ran, laughing, for the second and third motel rooms. She assumed that Gus was using Adam Famosa's room and that Adam was staying over at Ocracoke with Bonita.

None of her business.

Except that Merrill was not yet back.

And he didn't come at all that night. She knew because a panel truck marked "Stella's Wine and Cheese Bar, We Deliver," pulled up about nine o'clock before the motel. About one a.m. there was a pizza delivery. Party time at Heartbreak Motel! For some people.

By then, after two more failed attempts to contact Merrill, she went to sleep on her sofa bed. Not that she slept much.

Merrill was either in trouble somewhere. Or he was in trouble with her.

Either way, Delilah knew there would be trouble come morning.

# Chapter 17

*Sometimes a high I.Q. doesn't
equate with smartness . . .*

*M*errill drove Delilah's motorcycle directly to the hospital in Hatteras. The rain hit halfway there, and by the time he arrived, the pellets were coming down in torrents. He looked and felt like a drowned rat. Perfectly fitting for his mood!

He was shivering when he entered the air-conditioned premises and dripping a puddle where he stood at the reception desk. "I'm looking for a patient. Cordelia Good."

A nurse (he knew she was a nurse because of the name tag hanging from a lanyard around her neck, which said: Melissa Adams, R.N.), who'd just come up beside him, asked, "Do you mean Dr. Good?"

"Yeah. Dr. Cordelia Good." Man, even in an emergency his parents had to flaunt their academic credentials.

"Second floor IC unit. Room 203. The elevators are down the hall."

*Intensive care? Man, that is not good.* He felt a twinge of regret for his negative thoughts about his parents' academic snobbery at a time like this, and guilt for not answering phone calls as soon as he'd docked this morning.

He was about to walk away when the nurse said, "Wait a minute." She put up a halting hand and passed over some papers to the receptionist on duty, explaining details about an incoming patient and his special needs. Turning back to him, she asked, "Are you Lt. Merrill Good, by any chance?"

"I was," he said. At her confused look, he explained, "No longer in the military. What happened to my mother?"

"You should speak with her doctor."

"I will, but in the meantime, can't you give me a clue? Today is the first I knew she was in a hospital, and just now, the first I knew it was something serious enough to be in an ICU."

"Well, your family has been expecting you for days."

Was there a reprimand in there? Ah, so that was the reason for her snarky mood? The "family" had portrayed him as the black sheep, the unsympathetic son. "I've been away. Just got back in town."

"No cell coverage?"

*Definitely a reprimand. And out of line, professionally.* "Actually, no."

"A mild heart attack," she revealed. Her stance indicated that would be the extent of her cooperation.

She gave him a quick once-over and remarked, "You need a towel."

"Ya think, Melissa?"

Frowning at his sarcasm, and probably the use of

her first name, she motioned for him to follow her to a utility room, where she handed him several towels, which he used briskly to dry his hair and bare arms. There was nothing he could do about his sopping clothes.

He was not unaware that she watched him closely, and that she was not unaware that he was physically fit. And, yeah, a SEAL or ex-SEAL.

"Come with me. I'm going to the ICU."

She was back to being snippy again, probably because he'd caught her in the act of ogling him.

When they were in the elevator traveling to the second floor, she turned on him and said, "Wait. Are you the guy . . . the treasure hunter . . . who just discovered a billion dollars in gold in a sunken ship?"

"Uh. Where did you hear that?"

"A spot news flash this afternoon on NBX-TV."

*That damn Annie and Sam! Couldn't keep their mouths shut for a minute. Bet Laura has gone to town, too. Literally.* For the first time since he'd left Bell Cove three hours ago, he glanced at his cell phone.

"Oh, my God!" There were seventy-three text messages and forty-one voice mails. Several of them were from Delilah, a dozen from his father and his brother, but many were from news outlets. With a muttered curse, without reading or listening to any of them, he mass deleted the whole bunch.

"Aren't you worried that some of those might be important?" the nurse inquired, watching him.

"Obviously not."

When he got to the intensive care floor, there was a beehive of activity. Nurses, aides, doctors, technicians. Monitors beeping. The usual antiseptic smell of a hospital ward that he hated. Through some of the doors, he saw patients in seriously bad shape, while others were sitting up in bed chatting with visitors, though attached to a gazillion wires. In one unit, the attendants wore what looked like space suits right down to the booties; must be a case of sepsis.

Vanessa and Ben were standing outside the last room. Vanessa gave him her usual snooty look, accompanied by a muttered, "About time, asshole!" Then she gasped at his appearance. "You . . . you . . ." She pointed at his wet clothes plastered to his body, giving up steam by now. Whereas the AC had been running full blast on the lower floor, it was tropical heat up here.

"Hey, Van, it's raining outside, in case you didn't notice." He thought about adding, "With your nose perpetually up in the air like that, you better stick inside or you might drown." But then, he decided she wasn't worth the trouble.

Ben looked embarrassed at his wife's remarks, but not enough to rebuke her. Merrill held out a hand for Ben to shake. He took it. In other families, where two brothers who'd once been so close reunited again for the first time, there would have been at least a bro-hug.

*Ah, well!*

"How is she?" Merrill asked.

"Stable. Wanting to go home. They'll probably move her to another floor later today."

He nodded. "Does that mean you guys will be sticking around for a while yet?"

"Another week, at least. Van needs to get back to work . . . a project she's heading is at a critical stage, but I'll stay with Father until she's released."

*What a stilted conversation! I could be a stranger he's just met for all the warmth.* "Still at Johns Hopkins?"

His brother nodded and would have said more, but his father noticed him from inside the room, and Merrill stepped inside.

"You got here," his father said with a sigh of relief, as if Merrill's presence mattered.

"Father," he acknowledged because he knew that's what the old man preferred, but instead of going over to shake his hand, he walked directly to the bed. His mother was awake and propped up on several pillows. She might be stable, according to Ben, but she looked like hell. She had always been thin, but she appeared frail as well now.

A thin line of gray showed at the roots of her frosted brown hair, which she would hate. Instead of the silk bed jacket she wore at home on those rare occasions when she'd been sick, she had the usual white johnny coat on, the kind that opened in the back, which would be a huge indignity to her refined self. An oxygen cannula was attached to her nose, and a dozen or more wires ran from her chest and arms to heart and blood pressure monitors.

Under it all, her skin was pale, without the subtly applied makeup she'd used through the years, some stuff she'd take the train into Bloomingdale's twice a year to buy. The crap cost as much as a car payment but was guaranteed to make you look like you weren't wearing makeup.

Women! Even his mother! Go figure!

"Hey, Mom!" he blurted out, without thinking not to offend, and leaned down carefully to give her a hug.

The "Mom" and the hug were both out of the norm, but instead of the stiffness he might have expected, a stiffness indicating that once again he'd done something inappropriate, she raised her thin arms to his shoulders and hugged him back. Against his ear, she whispered, "Oh, Merrill!" and patted his shoulders, followed by another "Oh, Merrill!"

Raising his head and seeing the tears welling in her eyes, he wondered what that was all about. *She's patting my back? Like I'm the one needing comfort! Shiiit! Have I entered an alien universe?*

The moment passed and he pulled a chair close to the bed, next to his father. Ben and Vanessa came in, too, and sat on chairs on the other side of the bed. They chatted softly, mostly over her as she dozed off, mostly relating to Merrill what had happened.

"Is this the first sign of heart trouble?" Merrill asked.

"No," his father said, "she had a few minor episodes a year ago, but she was following a heart diet and getting regular exercise. Seemed to be doing fine."

"It was probably the stress that brought this on," Vanessa opined.

"That'll be enough, Van!" Ben warned his wife.

Which surprised Merrill. Usually Vanessa was the one who wore the pants in their family.

Instead of being upset with Ben, Vanessa cast a glower Merrill's way. Man, the woman had never been fond of him, but this was taking her venom a step further.

*But wait . . . is she implying . . . ?* "Are you saying that I'm responsible for my mother's heart attack?"

"No one is responsible," his father said, loud and firm enough to zip Van's already-thinned lips. "There's a history of heart disease in the women of Delia's family." To Merrill, he added, "As you'll recall, Grandma Fulton died when she was only fifty-seven."

Merrill did remember. He'd been only ten at the time, but he'd been grief-stricken. As different from her daughter, Merrill's mother, as night and day, Grandma had been a homemaker who loved cooking, and baking, and her half dozen grandchildren. He recalled her kitchen being the heart of her home, and that it had always seemed to be filled with sunshine and laughter. She'd graduated from college and taught school for a few years, but didn't consider that academic credential essential to her self-identity.

Duly chastened, Vanessa took out a biophysics

book, which she proceeded to read. A clear "Fuck you!" signal to the rest of them, mostly him.

"Do you and Van have any kids?" he asked his brother.

Van stiffened but pretended not to have heard the question.

"No. Van . . . we decided early on that our work was too important to be diverted by child rearing."

*Seriously, Ben? You expect me to buy that bullshit?* But Merrill said nothing. It was their business.

"Are you and Mother still working?" Merrill asked his father.

"Oh, yes. In fact, we were planning a trip to Russia next month for a symposium on the molecular biology of dormant particles of energy. A very prestigious, invitation-only event. Of course, we will have to decline now."

"There'll be other symposiums," Merrill assured him.

The expression was trite, and Van snickered, but his father seemed to take it to heart. "You're right. The most important thing is getting your mother back to good health."

Vanessa turned her chair and clicked a remote so that the TV that was attached to a far wall turned on. She immediately lowered the volume to almost mute. The nightly news was on. The usual Democrats hate Republicans, Republicans hate Democrats, and nothing gets done in Washington.

The rest of them continued talking.

But suddenly, Vanessa exclaimed, "Oh, my God! This is the absolute end! How humiliating!"

They all turned to look at the television. Even his mother, who'd awakened, was asking, groggily, "What? What?"

On the screen was a picture of Merrill in full white dress uniform from his Navy SEALs days. It must have been the only one those idiots, Annie and Sam from NBX, were able to scrounge up. The two of them were on the air wearing pirate hats, and Sam even had a patch over one eye. They were talking about the big story in Bell Cove and how Merrill and his crew had discovered a shipload of gold off the barrier islands, recovered from the shipwreck of the *Hawk*, a Spanish galleon sunk as a blockade runner by a Yankee clipper during the Civil War.

Merrill let out a guffaw of disbelief.

"Is this true?" his father said.

"No!" Merrill declared. "Well, only parts of it. These two newshounds are more like pit bulls on crack. Yes, we recovered a sunken ship. There is gold, but not a shipload of it. The ship was the *Falcon*, not the *Hawk*. It was a French ship, not Spanish. No pirates involved, although there might be by the time I get back to the site with all this publicity. And there were no galleons or clipper ships around during that period. Other than that, just a peachy keen news nonevent."

His father and Ben looked at him like he was crazy. His sister-in-law was hyperventilating. His mother had fallen back asleep, thank God!

If only that were the end of the newscast.

Mayor Doreen Ferguson was on the air now,

about to be interviewed on the Bell Cove town square where the bells of St. Andrew's, Our Lady by the Sea, and the town hall tower were doing their competing bell chimes of the hour.

Annie waited for the bells to quit tolling and said, "Now here's a word from the mayor of Bell Cove, where its famous bell forge has been its greatest claim to fame . . . up till now. Well, other than the Grinch Contest last Christmas. Now, tell us, Ms. Ferguson, how does Bell Cove plan to celebrate its golden discovery?"

"With much fanfare. In conjunction with the Lollypalooza set for this Labor Day in Bell Cove. Folks from throughout the Outer Banks will be coming to show off their talents, and now we're planning a pirate-themed celebration for the *Sweet Bells* crew, too. That's the team led by Merrill Good, a former Navy SEAL, who moved to Bell Cove recently and plans to make this his home."

Merrill groaned. Navy SEALs, even former Navy SEALs, did not like to be identified as such. It would be like counting coup for some terrorists to nab them and chop off their heads on nationwide TV. He would bet his left nut that he would be hearing from Commander MacLean at the Coronado Special Forces center by tonight. And since when had he said that Bell Cove was going to be his permanent home?

Doreen continued expounding on all the outrageous events being planned around his discovery, as if it was the town's discovery, and somehow linking it all in with the crackpot Lollypalooza that was already scheduled. He leaned across the bed, took the remote out of Vanessa's hand, and clicked it off.

"Hey!" she protested.

He saluted her with a quick, between-you-and-me middle finger. Hoping that no one else had noticed his gesture, he glanced around, innocently, and to his surprise, Ben was grinning.

"Well, I for one am hungry. Anyone in the mood for dinner?" Merrill said then.

Everyone agreed, except Vanessa of course.

Soon after that, they all left the hospital room together after Merrill kissed his mother's cheek, something he hadn't done in maybe twenty years, and promised to come back in the morning. He had to be in Bell Cove by tomorrow afternoon to take care of the mess apparently unfolding there, but there was no way he could return tonight. Not with the rain coming down like bullets on a motorcycle, and the ferries probably not running anymore.

He grabbed his laptop case out of the waterproof leather sidesaddle on the bike and got into a Lexus SUV driven by Ben. He sat on the backseat with his father.

"You drive a motorcycle?" his father asked, trying not to sound horrified.

He shook his head. "It belongs to Delilah Jones, my . . . um, my girlfriend."

"Oh," Vanessa remarked, from the front passenger seat. "Is she someone special? Tell us about her." She was undoubtedly looking for more dirt to add to his dirt dossier.

*The bitch!*

He thought about saying the first thing that popped into his head, "She's a felon," but he restrained himself, barely. Instead, he said, "She's the cook on my boat. She's in Bell Cove to renovate her uncle's Elvis diner and Heartbreak Motel, where I'm staying at the present. She's the single mother of a five-year-old girl." Then, into the silence, he added, "And I probably love her."

It was later that night, in the plush guest room at the Beach Manse, where Merrill was reluctantly staying for the night, that he took off his wet clothing to don a pair of sweatpants that Ben had lent him. When he emptied his pockets, he found the card Harry had handed him earlier that day. It was damp but still legible. He put it on the dresser with his wallet.

That was when he finally did what he should have done long ago. After drinking a half bottle of vodka he'd pilfered from the mansion's lounge bar, he logged on to his computer, typed "Delilah Jones, Atlantic City" into his Google search engine, and watched as fifty-seven entries came up, most of them involving the trial of one David Zekus.

A half hour later, he turned off the computer and stared into space. Delilah had been convicted of a felony, and she'd served five years in a women's prison. The Edna Mahan Correctional Facility for Women in Clinton, New Jersey. A quick search of that facility showed many newspaper articles indicating this was not a pleasant place to be. Bad things had happened there.

He couldn't think about that now.

Back to Delilah's conviction. Accessory to armed robbery and murder.

*Murder!*

Now, robbery he could understand. Or even forgive.

But murder? Of a seventeen-year-old convenience store clerk? That was a leap he found hard to take.

Something didn't add up. This was not the Delilah he had come to know and maybe love. He wasn't sure if he still did.

It just didn't make sense.

He was reminded suddenly of Harry's caution not to jump to conclusions, that there were two sides to every story. And he was right. Now that he'd cooled down a little bit, he realized that he needed to talk to Delilah. He checked his watch. It was still only ten o'clock.

He dialed Delilah's cell number, which went immediately to voice mail. Same when he called again, and again, and again, finally giving up at midnight. He decided not to leave a text or voice mail. Better to talk it out in person.

Was it possible he'd waited too long?

# Chapter 18

*It was just another day in Bell*
*Cove crazy land . . .*

When daylight, or gray light, came in the morning, Merrill still hadn't come, or called. It was raining so hard—the sideways kind of rain that made walking outdoors almost impossible—that Delilah was glad she'd gotten all her grocery shopping done yesterday. They could hole up here for days.

After a breakfast of blueberry waffles and orange juice, Delilah decided to play motel owner. She made two small aluminum trays of apple cinnamon rolls and a pot of fresh coffee, which she placed in two thermal carafes with four mugs. Barely balancing the tray in one hand and an overlarge golf umbrella (another thrift shop purchase) over her head at a tilt, she made her way across the short distance to the motel units. Under the overhang, she was able to drop the umbrella and set down the tray.

She knocked on the third door first, yelling out, "Breakfast!"

A gorgeous brunette wearing a Japanese-style

robe that barely covered her yee-haw answered. "Oh, isn't there any fresh fruit?"

"Not today," Delilah said cheerily. *What does she think this is? The Ritz?*

At the other unit, a sheepish-looking Kevin, wearing nothing but a low-riding towel, said, "Hey, Lilah, this is terrific. Thanks." He took the items from her and placed them on the dresser.

From the bathroom, a female voice called out, "Hey, Kev, would you mind bringing my shampoo? It's in my Gucci bag by the bed. I wouldn't put this Avon crap on my hair if I were dying."

*Okaay.*

Kevin winced at the woman's words and shrugged an apology, then whispered, "Sorry."

"That's okay, *Kev*," she said with a grin, about to turn away. Before he closed the door, though, she had to ask, "Do you know where Merrill is? He never came back to the motel after showering yesterday."

Kevin shook his head. "I did hear that his mother is in a hospital in Hatteras. Maybe he went there and couldn't get back in time for the last ferry. Sometimes they stop the ferry services when the water gets choppy."

"Ah, that's probably where he is."

Delilah felt better after that, knowing there was an excuse for Merrill's absence. In fact, she couldn't help herself. She called the hospital at Hatteras and asked if they had a patient named Mrs. Good.

"Yes," the hospital operator confirmed. "But Dr.

Good is still in the intensive care unit. So, no flowers, or visitors, other than family."

Delilah released a sigh of relief.

But her satisfaction didn't last long. That didn't explain why Merrill hadn't called.

But she would give him the benefit of the doubt that some emergency, maybe even involving his mother, had come up.

By midmorning the rain had tapered off and the weather forecast was revised. The storm had veered north and good weather would return to the Outer Banks by this evening. She left her grandmother and Maggie with orders to clean up the place while she went over to Bell Forge with Kevin and Gus to help Harry work on some of the gold coins to be on display at tomorrow's press conference.

Kevin's and Gus's dates—who really were models, Victoria's Secret models, no less—stayed behind. Delilah asked her grandmother to go over to those two units and change the sheets and towels around noon when the ladies would presumably be gone or at least out to lunch.

By now, the ferries must have started up again, because there was a longer than usual line of cars and trucks heading toward town. Even though this was high tourist season on the Outer Banks, Bell Cove rarely got the heavy traffic the more commercial areas did. Not so today. And there was an alarming number of vehicles representing news organizations, even the national TV networks. And was that a *People* magazine logo on that one car?

"Oh, fuck!" Kevin said, sinking down in the seat.

That about summed up the situation.

Before they even left the parking lot of the diner/motel there was someone taking a photo of the twenty-foot Elvis. What that had to do with the shipwreck discovery, she had no idea. She did not need this kind of publicity. She was the one now who muttered, "Oh, fuck!"

The first thing—or person—they encountered when they got to Bell Forge and went around to the back wharf side was Charlie, a Charlie like they'd never seen before, coming over the gangway from the boat, barefoot. Her brown hair was loose and hanging in waves about her shoulders—shoulders which were bare in a figure-hugging, midriff-baring tank top. The short Daisy Dukes were also figure-revealing.

And, boy oh boy, did she have a figure! Delilah had always tried to minimize or hide her own almost-voluptuous physique, but Charlie had been hiding a whole lot more.

Kevin and Gus, beside her, were grinning like baboons.

Not to be missed was the hunk, also barefoot, wearing nothing but a pair of low-riding jeans, who followed Charlie, apparently trying to talk her into something. All they could hear from her was, "No. No. Absolutely not!"

Every time he tried to touch her—a hand on the shoulder, a tug on the arm, a swift kiss to the cheek—she shrugged him off. But it looked as if she hadn't been doing a whole lot of resisting during the night. There were whisker burns on her face and neck and even her midriff. Her lips looked moist and kiss-swollen.

Kevin summed it up succinctly. "That gal's been rode hard and put up wet."

"I don't know," Gus said. "That cowboy's got the look of someone whose spurs have been trimmed a time or five."

Both of the guys seemed to suddenly realize that Delilah was with them and turned to apologize as one, "Sorry."

Charlie came up to them and said, "I was just comin' in to tell Harry that we need more security out on the site. All this publicity is firin' the engines on every salvager within a hundred miles. They'll be rushin' out to have a look-see, and more. There's already chatter on the Coast Guard radio that pirates are on the way. Talk about!"

"We can take my boat," offered the guy—Jefferson Lee Landry, Delilah presumed.

"We . . . *I* am not going anywhere on your yacht, J. L."

"Fine with me," the McConaughey/Hemsworth clone said, smiling at her and trying to put an arm around her shoulders, which she slapped away. "We'll take your boat."

"*Sweet Bells* is not my boat," she told him.

"Well, holy crawfish, *chère*, that's no problem. I'll buy it for you."

"You are not buying me a boat," she snapped, marching off to Harry's office.

J. L. winked at them and followed after her.

"If I'd known she looked like that, I would have dropped my anchor next to her bed," Gus said, staring at her butt in the tight shorts.

"If you had, she probably would have shot your anchor off," Kevin remarked.

Adam and Bonita pulled up then and informed them of all the work they'd been doing since yesterday. Both of them looked a bit sex-worn, too, and Delilah figured they'd been doing more than research on the *Falcon*. Not her business, although she was feeling a little left out of things in that regard. Everybody had someone, except her.

Where *was* Merrill? And when would he be coming back?

Doreen was in the office with Harry, seemingly expounding on all the activities the town would like to sponsor involving the shipwreck discovery. Harry looked as if he would like to escape. Seeing them through the open doorway, waiting behind Charlie and her beau, he waved them off to the warehouse storage room, where they already knew he needed help cleaning the gold coins, or at least some of them.

Bonita and Adam showed them what to do. Adam and Kevin began washing a pile of coins in a basin of soapy water, then passed them to Gus for a rinse in another basin of clean water, after which Bonita and Delilah dried and polished them with a soft cloth and then laid them out on white towels. Several dozen of them were soon done, gleaming beautifully, even in the windowless light of the storage room. They didn't dare open the outside doors for fear someone would come snooping, or stealing.

They all set to work, chatting as they did their jobs.

"Luckily, Adam and I were in Durham by the time the storm hit yesterday, and we were able to make all the necessary legal notifications," Bonita told them. "I expect we'll have historical experts and desk jockeys from state government pouncing on Bell Cove by this afternoon. Where's the boss?"

"Hatteras, probably. His mother's in a hospital there," Kevin told them.

"I didn't know his mother was on the island," Bonita remarked, frowning.

"I thought he was from Jersey, like me. Princeton, I think," Adam added, also with a frown of confusion.

"He is . . . was. His family is just vacationing on the Outer Banks. Mother, father, brother, and sister-in-law. Remember, they were at that launch celebration," Delilah reminded them.

"Ah! The snooty ones at the back," Gus recalled.

"Well, Merrill better get back soon to handle the PR. I don't want to do it," Bonita declared.

"Me, neither," the rest of them said.

"Where's Gabe? Maybe he could take over till Merrill gets back," Delilah suggested.

"Hah! He scooted off to his architectural firm in Durham at the first hint of Sam and Annie on the island nosing around," Gus said.

"But tomorrow's press conference is supposed to be held at his McMansion, isn't it?" Delilah mused.

"Am I supposed to be preparing food for this event? If so, somebody better tell me what kind of food and how much. And soon."

*Where are you, Merrill?*

"This has the potential to become a fucking circus." This from Adam, who was prying carefully with a pick at the heavy incrustation on one coin.

"What else is new? This is Bell Cove," Gus said.

Just then, Mayor Doreen ducked her head inside. She must have gotten past Harry's surveillance team, which today amounted to Elmer Judd and the psychiatrist twins, Mike and Ike, until Merrill could make better arrangements. Doreen's eyes went wide at the gold coins being spread out on the tables. "Do you think you'll have enough coins to fill this for tomorrow's pressarama?"

"Pressarama?" five people whispered, in horror. But then they saw the pirate chest complete with a skull and crossbones on front that she was pushing inside with a foot. It must be lightweight, probably cardboard, but it was the size of a shopping cart, without the wheels.

"Another thing," Doreen said, with a big smile. Her hair was a mass of teased brownish redness today, no doubt due to a visit to her daughter's hair salon, where the special today was half-priced beehives, all in preparation, no doubt, for tomorrow's oh-my-God-pressarama. "I know how busy you all must be, so, I ordered pirate costumes for the entire crew. Compliments of Bell Cove."

There was a stunned silence, and then someone

said, "Merrill better get his ass back here pronto or there's going to be a mutiny."

Delilah planned to be the first person off the boat.

## *Damage control for the clueless man . . .*

*I*t was late morning before Merrill was able to leave the hospital, where his mother was finally moved out of intensive care and into a regular hospital room, and it was early afternoon before he got back to Bell Cove. Traffic was heavy, and he saw the oddest thing on the ferry. An old guy hobbling into a vintage Cadillac the size of a boat with a New Jersey plate reading "GOON." Surely, he'd misread or it was a coincidence, but just then vehicles began to move off the ferry and he hopped on his bike, not wanting to lose his place.

He went first to find Delilah. He wouldn't be able to concentrate worth a damn until he got some questions answered, but when he got to her apartment, there was no one there. The door was open, a radio playing, but not a soul around. Then he walked over to the motel units where K-4 and Gus had apparently spent the night with their dates—the Victoria's Secret models. The two women were still there, along with Delilah's grandmother and her daughter.

The first model, wearing a full-body leotard, was over by the patio sliding doors being taught how to do a high kick by Grandma, also in a full-body leotard.

*Can my eyes please unsee that?*

The second model, wearing nothing but her skimpy underwear, was reclining on one of the beds with Maggie watching *Annie* on a portable DVD player sitting on her lap. "Oh, this is the saddest part," the model sobbed, dabbing at her eyes.

Maggie was patting her arm, saying, "That's okay. It turns out okay in the end."

"I wish I had a Daddy Warbucks," the model lamented.

"Me, too," Maggie said.

Rolling his eyes, Merrill marched up to Grandma. "Any idea where I might find Delilah?"

"She went to the salvage office with your buddies," Grandma said, and touched her toes, thus turning her butt in his direction.

With burning eyeballs, Merrill left the scene but not before he noticed a wastebasket overflowing with empty wine bottles and several foil condom wrappers. He was pretty sure Delilah would not approve.

When he got to Bell Forge, he saw that *Sweet Bells* was missing. Hopefully, Charlie had taken it back to the site. With all the publicity they were getting, he should probably get more patrol boats out there, just to be safe.

To his shock, he soon discovered that he already had a security patrol of his own. Elmer Judd and the twin psychiatrists, Mike and Ike Dorset, were walking around the outside of the building carrying rifles.

"Shot anyone yet?" he joked.

"Just a few reporters," Elmer said, and then laughed at Merrill's gasp. "Just kidding."

The scene was ludicrous, really. Elmer was bald and about five-five, very much resembling that comic book character. On his suspenders was a star-shaped badge, which might be misinterpreted as something denoting the authority of the law but was, in fact, a veterinarian's club honorary award of some kind. Mike and Ike, in camouflage, were much cooler with macho rifle holsters over their shoulders and handcuffs hooked onto their belts. The Mutt and Jeffs of Merrill's policing efforts? Was that the best Harry could do in his absence?

Should he fire them on the spot, or play Andy Griffith and be more accepting of his very own versions of Barney Fife?

Gabe pulled up then, and his eyes about bugged out. But then, he grabbed Merrill by the arm before he could go inside. "You have to do something. They're turning my house into a pirates' den."

Merrill started to ask him what he meant by that, but then decided he really didn't want to know. "Your problem, my friend. I have enough of my own to handle, apparently."

When he went inside, Harry was motioning frantically for him to come into the office. With a cordless phone to his ear, Harry mouthed that he would get to him in a moment. Instead of waiting, Merrill went into the warehouse storage room to find Delilah.

She looked up from the table where she was helping polish gold coins. When she saw him, she smiled. It was a warm, completely open smile. One a guy could delude himself into thinking was a loving smile of welcome.

He just couldn't return her smile. Not yet.

Her smile faltered, and she tilted her head in question.

Everyone had something to say to him, or questions to ask, all of them speaking at once.

"Where the hell have you been? My voice mail has shut down from an overload."

"Any estimate on when we'll see some cash?"

"I've got a sketch of the *Falcon* being made into a banner. Should I pay for it in color?"

"Did you know the mayor wants us to wear pirate costumes at the press conference?"

"How's your mother?"

"The Southern Society of Historical Reenactors wants to know if they can participate in our Celebration of Gold during the Labor Day Lollypalooza? I didn't know we were having a Celebration of Gold."

Merrill ignored them all, for now. Reaching out a hand to Delilah, he said, "Come outside with me for a minute. We need to talk."

The room went silent.

She hesitated, then put her hand in his. "Merrill, what's wrong? Is it your mother? I've been so worried."

"No, my mother's all right now. They moved her out of the ICU this morning."

"Why didn't you call when—"

Merrill had no opportunity to answer just then. Thankfully. Harry had wheeled himself out of the office and into the wide corridor where Merrill was leading Delilah toward the outside door. When Adam and Merrill had formed a partnership, they'd renovated the Bell Forge building with an extra-wide hallway to separate the forge operation from the salvage office and warehouse. Even through the thick walls, Merrill could hear the forges running and workers talking.

Harry looked at their joined hands and smiled. "Ah, I'm glad to see you took my advice, Merrill. There's always two sides to every story."

"What story?" Delilah asked.

"You know, honey, about your felony." Harry looked with pity at Delilah.

Pity was the last thing Delilah would want. Merrill knew that much about her.

"How did you know about that, Harry?" she asked stiffly.

"Uh-oh," Harry said. "Have I spoken out of turn?"

Delilah wasn't bending a bit. In fact, she yanked her hand out of Merrill's grip and folded her arms over her chest, waiting, stoically, for Harry's response.

"Oh, Lilah, I wouldn't hurt you for the world," Harry said, "but I felt obligated—"

"It's not Harry's fault," Merrill interrupted. "Let's go outside and talk there." He tried to take her hand again, but she was having none of that. In fact she edged away from him, as if repulsed.

"No, let Harry speak."

Harry glanced uncomfortably at Merrill until he nodded.

"Your parole officer came here," Harry disclosed. "A Ms. Gardner."

"When?"

"Last week."

"And?"

"She wanted to know if you had reported your felony background to us . . . your employer."

A flicker of something like fear appeared in her eyes before she turned to Merrill. "And when did Harry tell you about this? No, let me guess. Yesterday, before you shot out of town. That's why you haven't called. You judged and found me guilty, without even giving me a chance to explain."

*Like you haven't had weeks to explain before this!* "Explain now. Come outside and let's talk."

"Eff you!" she said.

He winced. "Hey, don't put me on the defensive. You're the one who kept secrets. You're the one who served hard time for accessory to robbery and for-fuck's-sake murder."

Suddenly, he realized that there was an odd silence, followed by a whispered gasp of "Murder?"

That latter came from Mayor Doreen, who must have just come in from outside. But also witnessing this news were Elmer, Mike, and Ike, behind the mayor, as well as K-4, Gus, Bonita, and Adam, from the other end of the corridor.

Delilah looked with horror at all the people, then at Merrill, her expression showing how wounded she was. With a sob, she bolted for the door and ran outside, pushing past the mayor and the three loony guards.

He ran after her, catching up with her where she stood, puzzled for a moment. She must have realized that she'd come with K-4 and Gus and left Merrill's truck back at the motel. In other words, no transport. But then she headed for her motorcycle.

"Wait, Delilah. I didn't mean for anyone else to know."

She ignored him and swung a leg over the seat.

"I was upset. I needed some space to think before confronting you about it." *Maybe* confront *isn't the right word. Too late now.* "Give me a break, sweetheart. I was in shock." *I still am.*

She searched around for the keys, which were in his pocket. She wouldn't look at him, and he knew why. Well, one reason why. Tears were brimming in her eyes, and she wouldn't want him to see.

He took the keys out and handed them to her. Still not looking at him, she fumbled, trying to fit the key in the ignition.

"Delilah, I know there must be an explanation. I want to know what happened to you. You wouldn't commit murder or be willingly involved in a murder."

"How do you know that?"

*Because I love you. Love knows.* But he didn't say that. Instead, he repeated, "We're both hurt here, Delilah. We can work it out."

The tears were streaming down her face when she finally looked directly at him. "One day too late. Leave . . . me . . . alone!"

She roared off.

Merrill would have liked to follow after Delilah immediately, but he was waylaid by three news trucks pulling into the parking lot in tandem, as if they were in a race.

Holy shit! It was a shipwreck discovery, not an alien landing or some monumental hurricane disaster.

Just then, the NBX-TV satellite van skidded onto the gravel lot, too, and Merrill thought about dragging Sam and Annie out and beating the crap out of them. Those two nitwits were the ones responsible for this mayhem.

But he took a deep breath and stood his ground. He noticed that his rifle squad had come out to stand behind him.

"Okay, folks," he addressed the newspeople and cameras. "Unless you have business with Bell Forge, this is, from now on, considered private property. No Trespassing signs are about to be posted, and you will be arrested. Or . . ." He glanced back at the three old codgers behind him. "My security detail will be given orders to shoot, and I understand they are crack shots."

The three guys were surprised at his words, but they straightened with pride and made sure everyone saw their rifles.

"You can't do this," Annie Fox yelled. "It's illegal."

"Do I look like I care, Ms. Fox?"

"We just want a story," a woman with a *Newsweek* logo on her shirt said.

"I understand that, and we'll give you all the details you want at the press conference tomorrow at Chimes, the home owned by one of my partners, Gabriel Conti, who also happens to be the owner of Bell Forge. If you want a story in the meantime, how about discovering the interesting history of this town, which was by founded by the Conti family, who've made some of the most famous bells in the world?"

That piqued their interest, or at least diverted their attention. Of course, Gabe would not be a happy camper.

Something occurred to Merrill then. Sure as gossip moved at the speed of sound, word would already be spreading of Delilah's notorious past. If the news media got wind that one of his crew members was a felon, they would be running in that direction. Even though it had nothing to do with their discovery, the press was always looking for a "color" angle. He didn't care what they said about him, but he would like to protect Delilah from that kind of crap if he could.

If he had a choice, he would have gone after Delilah right away, but there were things he needed to do with Harry first. And then another alarming thought occurred to Merrill as he recalled the flicker of fear in her eyes when she found out that her parole officer had been here. Would the fact that Delilah hadn't reported her felony to her employer jeopardize her parole? Could she be sent back to prison?

*Oh, my God!*

*This is a freakin' nightmare.*

So, the first thing he did when he got back to his office was pull a business card out of his wallet. He punched the number into his cell phone, and then said, when a woman answered, "Ms. Gardner?"

"Yes."

"This is Merrill Good, owner of the Bell Cove Treasure and Salvaging Company. I understand you spoke with my business manager, Harry Carder, last week. He might have mistakenly given the impression that Ms. Delilah Jones had not informed us of her felony conviction. That is not true. Ms. Jones gave me all the details before she was hired."

"Are you sure about that?"

"Why would I say so if I were not?"

"Why now?"

"I've been out of town for the past ten days and had no info on your visit until yesterday."

"Are you involved with Ms. Jones?"

"I don't think that's any of your business, Ms. Gardner. All you need to know is that she is my employee, and a very good one at that."

There was silence at the other end.

"Does this mean Ms. Jones is no longer in trouble?"

"That's not the only trouble she has," Ms. Gardner murmured.

"What did you say?"

"Nothing? I'll make note of your call into my records, Mr. Good. It's commendable that you would give a hardened criminal a second chance."

Was that sarcasm he detected?

"Thank you for your time, Ms. Gardner," he said with an iciness that was the best he could garner in terms of politeness.

"Good for you," Harry said. "Do you think she'll suffer for my slip?"

"I don't know." At the very least, the fallout would mean the entire town knew of her background. "But don't blame yourself. I'm on it now." Merrill was not without powerful friends from long years working for Uncle Sam and higher-ups in government. He wasn't above calling in some markers, if need be.

He spent an hour with Harry, making a list of business matters and calls that needed to be answered ASAP, in order of priority. At the end of that time, he told Harry, "I need to go out for a while. You go home. I'll come back later this afternoon to take care of the rest."

Harry nodded. "You're going to make things up with Delilah?"

"I hope to." He grinned then. "Guess you're going to have to drop me off. Delilah took her bike."

Harry grinned back at him. Even with a wheelchair, the old man was able to drive. Merrill helped him, though, folding up the wheelchair and putting it in the back of the SUV and then watching as he used a walker to get to the driver's seat.

When they got close to the diner, Merrill said, "Uh-oh!" and asked Harry to slow down.

"What's up?"

"See that Caddy over there on the street in front of the diner?"

"The one with the Jersey plate that says 'GOON'?"

"Yep. I think it might be some loan shark jerk up to no good with the Glam Gram."

"Sal? Someone followed her here from New Jersey?" Harry was clearly more than interested.

"Might be. As I recall, there was a mention of breaking legs with his cane."

"Whaat? We can't let that happen. Let's go back to the forge and get those rifles."

"No. No weapons necessary. But I might need your help."

Harry eased his van onto the parking lot. Everything seemed to be quiet. Merrill's pickup truck, Delilah's motorcycle, and the Glam Gram's tank were there, as well as K-4's and Adam's vehicles parked in front of their motel units. But no one was about.

But wait. Merrill thought he heard a noise coming from behind the diner. It was Maggie and she was crying, "Don't you hurt my Gramma, you poopyhead."

"Stay here and call Sheriff Henderson. Tell him we have a potential criminal event taking place here."

"Gotcha." Harry was already speaking in his phone before Merrill opened his car door and grabbed one of Harry's crutches from the backseat, saying, "Hey, Bill. Elvis diner. ASAP. Crime in progress." The sheriff must have said something, and Harry replied, "Yeah, you better bring an ambulance, just in case."

Merrill walked softly up behind Maggie and lifted her up from behind, putting a hand over her mouth. Into her ear, he whispered, "As soon as I set you down, run to your Mommy. Do you understand?" She looked at him over her shoulder and nodded.

The "goon" was snarling at Grandma. "You stupid bitch. I tol' you Sharkie wouldn't let you get away without payin' off your tab. Now you owe another five thousand, and I got orders to hurt you real bad if you don't cooperate."

The second Maggie hit the ground and ran back toward the motel apartment, shrieking, "Mommy, Mommy!" Merrill swung the crutch against the back of the assailant, who had a terrified Grandma pinned up against the diner, with a four-pronged cane pressed against her windpipe.

The guy dropped to his knees, the cane falling to the ground. "Ow, ow, ow! Oh, fuck! Oh, damn!" Merrill immediately had him facedown, with his foot pressing against the guy's back. "I got bad knees, asshole. Now, they mus' be broken. Call a doctor. Call an ambulance. Ow, ow, ow!"

"Bad knees are the least of your problems, buddy."

Meanwhile, Harry had somehow managed to hobble over to the diner and was holding a sobbing Grandma in his arms. Sirens were wailing in the distance. K-4 and Adam, both half-dressed, came running out of their motel units, followed by two women, who wore even less clothing. And then there was a horrified Delilah coming out of the back door of her apartment and staring at the scene unfolding before her.

This on top of the scene back at the forge, when her secret had been disclosed, had to have Delilah feeling frightened, and alone. He wanted to go to her, but held back, wanting to deal with this creep and the police first.

Bill Henderson handled himself in a surprisingly professional manner for a small-time sheriff. By talking to Delilah's grandmother and getting some documents that showed her original loan of two thousand dollars a year ago, of which she'd repaid five thousand, but was now presumably up another ten thousand again.

Henderson read the man, James Goodson, aka Jimmy the Goon, his rights and then told him, "You are facing some serious jail time, Mister Goodson. We do not appreciate extortion here in North Carolina."

"I wasn't extortin' no one," Jimmy protested. "I was just collectin' on a loan."

"Did I mention that loan-sharking is illegal, too?"

"I want my phone call. Sharkie will have a lawyer here faster 'n you can say, 'What the hell?'"

The sheriff shoved Jimmy none-too-gently into the backseat of the patrol car and said, "You'll get your call when I'm good and ready. This is Bell Cove, my friend, not Atlantic City. We're like Frank Sinatra. We do things our way."

"I knew Frank Sinatra. He used to hang out at The Five. That's the 500 Club in Atlantic City."

"Yeah, and I knew King Kong. He used to hang out at the Conti mansion."

"Huh?"

Delilah and Maggie were over by the ambulance where an EMT was examining the Glam Gram who sat in the open back doorway of the ambulance, swinging her long dancer's legs in the same full-body leotard she'd had on this morning, puffing away on an e-cigarette that smelled a lot like aged bourbon. Harry was holding her hand, he noticed. And the Glam Gram was clearly enjoying all the attention. When it appeared as if she wasn't having to go to a hospital but was having her neck wrapped in some kind of gauze bandage, Merrill walked back to talk with the guys.

"Excitement follows you everywhere, my friend," K-4 said. "I can't wait to see what happens next."

"Me, too."

"Wanna come in and have a beer?"

"Nah. I need to talk to Delilah first."

"Oh, boy! Sure you don't need fortification? I might have a half bottle of tequila left."

He shook his head. "I need a clear head for this."

"My advice? Take her to bed, screw her silly, and then talk."

"Has that ever worked for you?"

"No, but it's gotta work for someone."

Merrill went into his motel unit, where he showered and shaved. He called to check on his mother, and his father said she was much improved since this morning. "When will you be back?" his father asked.

"I don't know. Everything is going crazy here. I have a press conference tomorrow. And all kinds of business matters that have piled up during the ten days I've been gone. If there's any change, let me know."

"I will," his father said, "and, Merrill, we appreciate your coming."

*Oh, shit! Make me feel guilty, why don't you?*

He ordered a pizza, and when it was delivered, he carried it over to Delilah's apartment.

"Hello, Merrill. Thank you so much for your help today," the Glam Gram said from where she sat at the kitchen table playing a game of solitaire, still vaping bourbon. She'd lost the leotard and was wearing some kind of silky black robe that had a band of red feathers along all the edges. A thick swathe of white gauze was wrapped around her neck, which would probably impress the hell out of the seniors tomorrow. "If it weren't for you, I might be dead by now."

He wouldn't go that far.

Maggie, who'd been sitting on the sofa watching *Annie* on the small TV that the Glam Gram must have bought in Delilah's absence, just then looked up and squealed, "Pizza! Yippee!"

Merrill set the pizza box on the table, on the other side from the cards, and Maggie came running over, demanding a piece. He put one on a plate for her and another for Grandma, then took a piece for himself.

The door to the bedroom was closed, and he assumed Delilah was in there. *Is she hiding out from me?*

*No, Delilah would come out punching, if she had some-*

*thing to say to me. That's the problem. She obviously doesn't want to talk to me.*

*Well, tough toenails, toots! We're gonna talk if I have any say, and, boy, do I have a lot to say!*

"She's mad at you," Grandma said.

"No kidding!" He took another slice and wondered if he dared ask if they had any beer in this joint, or even a frickin' soda.

Sensing his thoughts, Grandma got up, went to the fridge, and came back with two beers.

"So what's up with Delilah?" he demanded.

"She was worried sick about you last night. It was storming real bad here, and you weren't answering her calls." She shrugged and stacked all the cards together, having apparently lost that round with herself, then began to shuffle them like an expert croupier.

"Wanna play a hand?"

He laughed at the apparent hustler. "Not a chance. You'd clean me out in a casino minute."

"Wanna watch *Annie* with me?" Maggie asked, patting the sofa beside her.

"Maybe some other time."

She had pizza sauce around her mouth and was pretending to feed the crust to her stuffed dog. Narrowing her eyes at him, she asked, "Did you get me a dog yet?"

"I never said I would get you a dog."

"Betcha my Mommy would like you better if you watched *Annie*."

He actually considered that possibility for a moment.

"Betcha she would like a surprise dog."

*What a little con artist!*

Finally, he'd had enough. He went over and knocked on the bedroom door. "Delilah, are you decent? I'm coming in." When he opened the door, he was shocked to find the room empty.

He turned and demanded, "Where is she?"

The conniving old lady blew out a thick cloud of bourbon vapor and said, "Gone."

# Chapter 19

*Sometimes, just a hug is enough . . .*

*O*n the last ferry back to Bell Cove that evening, after spending more than an hour with her parole officer, Ms. Gardner, in her Nags Head office, Delilah was alternately furious and frightened.

Furious, because Merrill had gotten her into this mess. Oh, to be fair, *he* hadn't reported her to her parole officer. She's the one who'd been lax in notifying her contact in the department that she had a new job. Well, no, she actually *had* given notification of her new job by a cowardly voice mail before going out on the *Sweet Bells* expedition. Where she'd been lax—and, yes, deliberately so—was in failing to notify her employer of her prison record before the hiring.

Frightened, because even such a small thing as failing to notify an employer of a prison record could nullify parole and result in a convict being remanded back to jail to do additional time. And what about Maggie, then? Oh, Lord! The prospect of losing her child to the system was beyond frightening to Delilah. It was terrifying. She doubted they would appoint her grandmother as guardian again. They would consider her a whack-job, with all her talk of Vegas shows, and slot machines in Atlantic City, and Avon products out the wazoo. Instead, they might place Maggie—oh, who knows where? Inadvertently with a sex pervert, maybe? Or with some hairy-armed guy with a heavy hand? Or with some religious nutcase who lived in a compound? Or with . . .

No, she couldn't think of all these things.

As she sat in her car, waiting for the ferry to cross over into Bell Cove, she relived her conversation with Ms. Gardner:

"I understand that you notified your employer of your felony status," Ms. Gardner had said.

"I did? I mean, of course I did."

"When I first talked to the office manager at the salvaging company last week, I got the impression that he had no idea of your background. But Mr. Good informed us this morning that he had been well aware of your parole status."

*He did? Oh, thank God!* "Of course, he did."

"But our first suspicion that you'd failed to notify your employer of your background led us to do more investigating. We are concerned, very concerned."

*What's with the "our," "us," and "we" business?* she'd wondered, immediately followed by the ominous words, *"more investigating"* and *"very concerned."* She'd taken a deep breath for calmness and asked, "So, you're satisfied that I informed my employer?"

"For now, but of course that led to further questions."

*Oh, my God!*

"Did you send a wire for ten thousand dollars to your grandmother in New Jersey?"

"Yes."

"Where did you get that kind of cash?"

"It was an advance from my employer. I sent it to my grandmother for moving expenses for her and my daughter to come to Bell Cove from New Jersey."

"That's a very unusual employer who gives a new employee such a generous advance!"

Delilah had ignored the sarcasm in that remark, barely.

"What is going on in those motel units of yours? There appear to be a number of men and women going in and out. Are you by any chance running a brothel?"

Delilah had gasped with outrage. "Are you serious?"

"Serious as sin. And what is happening out on that boat for a week at a time? Men and women shacked up together? I'm telling you, Ms. Jones, this does not look good. Are you perhaps involved in a house of ill repute, or rather a boat of ill repute? Ha, ha, ha!"

"That's not funny, and I don't think Mr. Good would think so, either. Are you prepared to face a slander suit in court?"

"Are you threatening me, Ms. Jones?"

"No, but Mr. Good is in a better position to defend himself than I am. I doubt he would appreciate the implications you're making about his company."

"Hmpfh! Is your grandmother by any chance involved with loan sharks?" The parole officer had moved on.

"What?" *Oh, my God! I am screwed if this comes out.*

"Does your grandmother have a gambling addiction?"

*Screwed to the wall and shot full of holes.*

"And smoking. Do you think it's acceptable to have a smoker in the house with a young child?"

"She doesn't smoke. She vapes." That argument sounded lame, even to Delilah. "I object to your slander. My grandmother is a churchgoing woman who has taken good care of my daughter while I dutifully fulfilled my prison sentence. If you have problems with her, perhaps you should be complaining to the authorities in New Jersey who approved her as guardian while I was in prison."

Ms. Gardner had ignored her protest. "And this is the person . . . a smoking gambler with a shady past as a showgirl . . . you've chosen to care for your child in your absence while you are high-flying off on some pleasure boat?"

"Now just wait a minute. My grandmother is perfectly capable of caring for my child in my absence. As for high-flying and pleasure boat, *Sweet Bells* is a salvaging vessel, pure and simple."

"Hmpfh! Do not leave Bell Cove for the time being. I expect a further investigation will result in a hearing to determine temporary guardianship of your child, and possible revocation of your parole."

On those terrifying words, Delilah got up to leave. Under her breath, she said, "Go fuck yourself, lady!"

Before the door slammed behind her, she was pretty sure Ms. Gardner heard her, if the quick intake of air behind her was any indication.

When she got back to Bell Cove, she would consult with her lawyer, Matt Holter. Well, first thing in the morning. It was too late now.

To say she was terrified was to minimize her mood as she finally exited the boat and drove back to Bell Cove. She was half-dead with weariness when she drove onto her property and turned off the engine of the tank passing for a car that her grandmother had purchased. It continued sputtering even when the ignition was off, until it came to a dead silence.

But that wasn't the end of her day from hell.

When she stepped out of the car, Merrill was standing there.

"Oh, babe, you look like hell," he said.

With a choked laugh, she reciprocated with, "Well, I'm not so happy to see you, either."

"I didn't say that I was unhappy to see you. I just said that you look like you could use a friend." He opened his arms to her then.

She should have walked away.

She should have told him to shove it.

She should have said she didn't need his aggravation.

Instead, she stepped into his embrace and murmured, "Thank you, friend."

Sometimes, all a girl needed was a hug.

### *Trust me, baby, I have plans . . .*

**M**errill led Delilah into his motel unit and then directly into the bathroom where he started to fill the tub with warm water, pouring in a dollop of some Avon bubble crap she'd left there. Immediately the small room filled with the sweet scent of flowers.

Meanwhile, Delilah stood frozen in the middle of the bathroom. By the looks of her, she must have had a hell of a day. No time for questions now. Later. But, man, he'd like to slay some dragons for her at the moment. To knock some sense into the person, or persons, who'd put that defeated expression on her face.

*Please, God, don't let me be one of them.*

He was still pissed at her over the felony conviction, and, oh, my God, five years' hard time in a women's pokey that he'd learned by a quick Google search was no country club designer prison. What kind of hell had she experienced?

First, he undressed her. It was a sign of her miserable state that she didn't even protest. When she was naked, he tested the water, which was covered by about a foot of bubbles. He might have overdone the dollop.

He helped her in, then rolled up a towel to place under her neck so that she could lie back.

"Aaaaah!" she sighed with appreciation.

He pulled over a hamper and sat down on it, next to the tub.

"Tell me," he urged.

"I'm afraid."

"Don't be. I'm going to help you."

"But I'm an ex-con."

"I know."

"You were mad about that."

"Confused more than mad. Do you want to talk about it?"

She shook her head. "Not now."

"Okay, tell me what happened today that has you so upset."

She did. Haltingly. Stopping to answer questions when he didn't understand.

"Let me help you."

She nodded, bending forward so that he could shampoo her hair.

That's not what he meant, but he figured he could explain later.

When she was clean and wrapped in a towel, he wet-combed her hair, then carried her into his bed and crawled into the bed behind her, still fully dressed, though wet from his ministering to her. She was asleep before he even pulled the blankets up over them both, spooned together.

He lay like that for a long time, thinking. Merrill's high I.Q. came in handy at times like this. His brain worked like a computer, and he soon had a plan.

Getting out of bed, carefully, so as not to wake Delilah, he pulled out his computer and set it on his lap while he sat on a chair with his feet crossed on the end of the bed.

He needed a plan to protect Delilah and Maggie. If her daughter got into the system, it would be hell to get her back out. So, number one, get the kid in a secure location until the legalities could be ironed out. And he couldn't send her anywhere alone. That meant that the grandmother would have to be with her.

He checked his watch. It was ten o'clock. Going into the bathroom, he closed the door and called his father. "Dad, I need a favor," he said, the minute his father answered. He'd forgotten to say "father," rather than "dad."

But apparently it didn't matter because his father answered, "What do you need, son?"

Without going into too many details, he explained that his fiancée's daughter and grandmother needed a place to stay for a few days. He hoped to make that little lie about a fiancée become the truth shortly.

"Bring them here," his father said, without question. "There's plenty of room."

Good thing Vanessa was gone by now. She'd have a bird on meeting Salome Jones. Merrill wasn't sure that his mother wouldn't react the same way. He couldn't worry about that now.

Next, he checked North Carolina marriage laws and found out that there was no waiting period, not even a requirement for blood tests. Just get a marriage license at the courthouse and find someone to perform the ceremony. Easy-peasy. He figured that marriage was the safest way to protect Delilah. Convincing her—now that was another story.

After that, he looked into adoption procedures, but that would take much longer. A good lawyer should be able to protect Delilah's rights in the meantime. If she was protected, and if there was one thing Merrill Good had learned as a Navy SEAL it was protection. Whether country or person, that was his specialty.

Some of these government employees liked to wield their power, though, and he wasn't taking any chances of Delilah or Maggie staying here in the open like sitting ducks.

Now, convincing Delilah that all these things needed to be done—that would be a challenge. Merrill smiled. There was nothing he liked better than a challenge. And planning—hell, he was an expert planner, whether battle plans or plans to fight government bureaucrats, he was in his zone.

Leaving the motel unit quietly, he went next door and told K-4 what he needed to do and asked for his assistance with a few details. Next, he walked over to the apartment behind the motel office. There was still a light on, and he could see through the sliding door that Delilah's grandmother was sitting at the kitchen table with some kind of green crap on her face that looked like hardened concrete. She was painting her fingernails yellow, of all things.

He assumed Maggie was asleep in the bedroom. A radio on the counter was playing some oldies but goodies music.

He knocked lightly and was waved in.

"Salome, I need your help," he said right off.

He sat down at the table opposite her, and after he'd explained the situation, she asked, "And it's all right with your parents if Maggie and I go stay with them at their place?"

"It's just a summer place they're renting, and only my dad would be there. My mother is in the hospital."

"Oh, I'm sorry. Is it serious?"

"Pretty much, yeah. Her heart."

"Oh, my goodness. Listen, dear, my face is cracking. I need to go wash this stuff off. Wait here. Have a soda or something. We don't have any beer left, or alcohol of any kind."

"That's okay. I need to keep my brain sharp," he said to her back, although he probably could use some caffeine. Maybe later. He couldn't help but notice as Salome walked away that she was wearing some kind of sleep outfit that looked like it would fit in a harem. He wondered idly what Delilah would look like in one of those.

When she got back from the bathroom, her face scrubbed clean and showing every one of her sixty-some years, she said, "I could always stay at the Patterson house."

"Yeah, but I'm not sure that Maggie could be hidden there, and, besides, it would put them in a touchy legal situation if they lied about the child in the event authorities came for her."

Salome put a hand to her chest. "Do you think it's possible that they would actually do that? Take her from me, or her mother?"

"I do. And I'm certain that Maggie would be terrified with strangers."

"Okay, I'll do it."

"The first ferry doesn't leave until six a.m. We'll leave here at five to give us extra time. Pack enough for several days. Make it appear like a fun, surprise trip so that Maggie won't be scared."

"Are you going to tell Delilah ahead of time?"

"Not if I don't have to."

"Oh, boy!"

There was a tablet and pen on the table that Salome had been using to keep score of her games. While Salome was packing—she would wake Maggie at the last minute—he began to write the note he would leave for Delilah, assuming she was still asleep by the time he left for the ferry, *please God!*

*Delilah, sweetheart:*

*I've taken your grandmother and Maggie to stay with my parents on Hatteras for a few days, just till we've ironed things out with the state. I've left a message with Matt Holden to meet with you later today to ensure your parole won't be revoked. Don't be mad that I didn't consult you first. Trust me, we can work this all out. I'll be back in time for the press conference at two. I'd like you to come, but I'll understand if you want to lay low for a day or two. If you need anything, ask K-4. Trust me.*

*Love, Merrill*

Even though she was awakened early so they could make the six a.m. ferry, Sal—that's what Delilah's grandmother asked him to call her—sat in the passenger seat next to him, smoking, rather, vaping away. Same thing, as far as he was concerned. Even if it was lemon-scented today. The woman was going to ruin his appetite for lemons.

Meanwhile, the Little Annie clone (yes, she was in full red dress orphan outfit today) sat in the high-backed booster seat in the rear of his pickup like it was a bloody throne. Her stuffed dog sat next to her like a royal subject.

The little girl didn't stop talking for one minute. Everything merited comment. Usually no response was necessary. The sign at the edge of town, for example, announcing the Labor Day Lollypalooza. "Gramma is gonna dance with the Old Codgers Club in the talent contest," she informed Merrill, which was news to him. First, that they'd given their group a name, or that Salome was a member of the group, or that they'd entered a talent contest.

*Can life get any better than this?*

"I'm gonna sleep over with three boys next week."

*Okaaay.*

"I hafta pee."

"Wait till we get on the ferry."

"Do you live in a mansion like Daddy Warbucks?"

"No, but my parents do. For the summer anyhow."

Salome's eyes went wide at that and she mouthed at him, "Really?"

"Yeah. It even has a name. The Beach Manse."

"Wow! I shoulda brought more Avon products. I could probably sell out my stock in that kind of neighborhood."

*Please don't be doing your Avon Lady shtick there.* But then he amended that thought to, *Why the hell not? Go for it!*

"Your Mommy's in a horsepital?" Maggie asked. "Does she have a boo-boo? I could kiss it and make it better."

*I'd like to see that. She'd probably have another heart attack. My mother doesn't do touchy-feely.*

"Mommy was crying yesterday. Did you make her cry?"

*Oh, Lord!* "I hope not."

"Did you see that bird? It pooped right on the rail."

"That's what birds do."

"Bobby Dillon pooped his pants one time in nursery school. P-U! Teacher had to open the window to farm-a-gate the room.

"When I grow up I'm gonna be a dog groomer or an astronaut."

"Good choices, kiddo. And diverse!"

"I know what divers are. They have them at the pool at the Atlantis Hotel.

"Are you gonna marry my Mommy?"

"I hope so."

That got Salome's attention, big-time. She turned slowly to look directly at him, after blowing more lemon vapor.

He winked at her. "I can only hope," he said with a shrug.

"Do I gotta call you Daddy then?"

"Only if you want to."

"Sometimes you're a poopyhead."

"I know. It's a guy thing."

"Mommy says that's a bad word."

"It is, for a little girl."

"You mean, it's okay for big people to use bad words?"

"Not really. You should probably use a substitute word. Find something else about the person you don't like that isn't so offensive."

She probably didn't understand a word he'd said, but she surprised him by saying, "Sometimes Gramma says I'm stubborn. Are you stubborn sometimes?"

"I am."

"Stubb-head, that's a better word then, right?"

"I suppose so."

On and on she went till his head started to ache. He hadn't slept yet, and it was catching up with him. Maybe in the car on the two ferry rides back to Bell Cove he could catch a catnap or two.

Salome handed Maggie her portable DVD player and told her to watch that for a while. From then on until they reached the hospital parking lot, he kept hearing, over and over, "It's a Hard-Knock Life." Sometimes Maggie sang along in her high-pitched, tone-deaf, kiddie voice, which was more like shouting than singing.

He was amused, the first two or three times he heard the song. After five or six, he was rolling his eyes at Salome. "Does she ever get tired of it?"

"Nope. Earplugs help sometimes."

When they got to his mother's hospital room on the third floor, his mother was sitting up in bed, looking much better, or at least she'd lost her on-death's-door pallor. His father, who was reading the *New York Times* in a lounge chair at the foot of the bed, stood when they entered. He had to give them credit, their eyes only widened a bit on seeing the guests. Maggie in her bedhead hair (*Someone forgot to comb her hair. Holy hell! Should it have been me? Is that what I've taken on here?*) with her portable DVD player in one hand and dragging that huge, bedraggled dog in the other. And then there was Salome in white capri pants, a "Hot (Grand) Mama" T-shirt, wedgie sandals, and about a gallon of makeup, which she'd applied in the restroom on the last ferry ride.

He introduced everyone, and before he could stop her, Maggie dropped the dog, put her DVD player aside, and crawled up on the bed next to his mother, advising, "Scooch over."

His mother, too stunned to protest, did as she was asked and Maggie cuddled up next to her. He doubted anyone in her life had ever told his mother to "scooch."

Maggie was fascinated by the cannula that came out of his mother's nose and asked, "Does it take out all the snot?"

His mother actually let out a snort of laughter and said, "No, my dear. It brings oxygen . . . fresh air . . . into my body from that machine over there."

"Oh. So you can breathe better?"

"Yes, dear."

"You're Mister Merrill's mommy, aren't you?"

"I am."

"Are you gonna be my gramma when my mommy and Mister Merrill get married?"

All eyes shot to Mister Merrill then.

He just shrugged.

"I guess so," his mother said.

"That's good. I don't have a gramma. Just a great-gramma, but I call her Gramma 'cause Great-gramma is too long to say." She looked at Salome in case no one knew who she was talking about. "What should I call you? I can't be calling two people Gramma, can I? Because two people would answer at the same time, and that would be confusing." She giggled at her own words.

"You could call me Grandma Good, I suppose."

"That would be silly." Maggie giggled some more. "That would be like I have a good gramma and a bad gramma, and my great-gramma isn't bad at all. Only when she swears at the slot machines. Swearing means bad words. Mister Merrill says I shouldn't call him poopyhead anymore 'cause there's a better word. Now I call him Stubb-head."

"Stubb-head?" his mother sputtered.

Maggie nodded. "Sometimes he's stubborn."

"Tell me about it!" his mother remarked, looking pointedly at Merrill.

"Call her Nana," Merrill's father suggested. "That's another name for grandmother. It's what I called my grandmother."

*Really?*

Time to put some brakes on this line of talk, but before he could speak, Salome came to the rescue. "Come down from there, Magpie. You've done enough talking for now." Salome helped Maggie get off the bed and then addressed his mother. "Listen, Mrs. Good, we're not going to be any trouble at all. It will only be for a few days. You won't even know we're around."

*That is doubtful.*

Thankfully, Salome had left the e-cigarettes in his truck. They would have given his mother another heart attack, and his father his first one, no doubt.

"That's all right. Merrill explained the situation to my husband, and we want to help in any way we can," his mother said.

He hadn't told his father everything, but enough to know that Maggie was in danger of being taken into foster care. He was relieved to know his mother would cooperate, too. Luckily, Ben had returned to Maryland to join Van. He wasn't so sure they would have been so compliant, especially Van.

"Well, I'm gonna help you, too," Salome said to his mother. "Don't take any offense, sweetie, but you've got a line of snow on your roof that shouldn't be there. I can take care of that, lickety-split, and

without going to any fancy pancy beauty salon."
His mother glanced to him and his father for help,
but Salome was already searching for something
in her purse, which was about the size of a barge.
Out of it, she pulled a small case of what looked
like crayons. "Touch-up sticks," she announced. "A
woman's guardian angel in times of beauty stress."

Holding one after another of the sticks next to
her mother's head, she smiled and said, "Wall-ah!"

He assumed she meant "voilà!"

"See. A perfect match!" she told his mother, who
was actually looking pleased, after looking at herself in a hand mirror that Salome also pulled out of
her purse.

"In fact," his mother said, "thank you. I've been
so embarrassed. I had a hair appointment the day
I had my heart attack, and my roots were showing
even back then. I can't believe you did it here in a
hospital room."

"I have other things to show you, too. Did I mention I'm an Avon Lady? Merrill told me you're a college professor. Well, between you and me, it don't
matter what a woman does for a living, whether
she's a showgirl like I was one time, or a lawdy-
dawdy, high-falutin' egghead, she wants to look
good."

*Oh, my Lord! Did she just call my mother a lawdy-
dawdy, high-falutin' egghead, uh, intellectual?*

To his surprise, his mother smiled, and his father,
behind him, snickered.

And Maggie, already engrossed in her DVD
player, remarked idly, "I like eggs."

*Earth to aliens: Is this bizarro-land, or what?*

He had to leave soon after that in order to get back to Bell Cove in time for the press conference. Maggie got suddenly teary-eyed near the end, clinging to his neck when he lifted her for a hug. "I doan wanna stay without you."

*Oh, crap!* "Listen, Annie McFannie, did I mention that the house where you're going to stay has a swimming pool?"

She raised her tear-streaked face. "It does?"

"Yes," his father interjected, "and I believe there are some children next door who are looking for playmates."

She perked up a little bit more but was not yet convinced to let go of her death grip on his neck.

"I'll have your mommy call you this afternoon."

"She will?"

"Yep." He took a deep breath and tossed in the zinger. "And if you're a good girl, when this is over, I will get you a dog."

*Bingo!*

She raised her head, smiled, and struggled to get down.

*A dog? Where did that come from? Delilah will kill me.*

Then Maggie took his father's hand and asked, "If she's Nana, what are you?"

His father puzzled for a moment and then said, "Poppa."

*Yep, bizarro-land.*

On the way out of town, he noticed a strip mall with a men's store as its anchor. Going in, he told the guy, whose name badge read: Jerome Erlick, manager, "Listen, Jerome, I have a half hour tops in which to buy a suit, dress shirt, and tie. Price is no concern. I have black loafers that I can use, but better toss in a pair of black socks just in case."

"But the tailoring that would need to be done . . ."

"No time for that. Get me something as close to my size as possible, ready to go."

In fact, Jerome turned out to be a wonder man, in terms of style. Merrill couldn't ask for a better choice or fit than the black Boss suit he was sold with a pristine white shirt and a tie with black stripes against a red background. When he was about to leave the store with the garment bag in hand, Jerome said, "It just occurred to me. Aren't you the guy who discovered gold in a shipwreck off Bell Cove? I saw your picture on TV last night."

"That would be me."

"A former SEAL, huh? Thank you for your service."

He nodded his acknowledgement of that common refrain, one that didn't get old, even to hardened warriors.

"So, this is for the press conference today?"

"Nope."

Jerome raised his eyebrows.

"I'm getting married today."

# Chapter 20

### A *surprise* WHAT? . . .

$A$t eight o'clock that morning, after waking from the sleep of the dead, Delilah read Merrill's note once, and then two more times. *Trust him*, that's what he asked of her. The guy who'd walked out on first hearing of her prison record because he needed space to think?

*Trust him?*

Never trust a man who needed space, for anything. That was her philosophy.

Besides, they hadn't even talked about the details of her crime. Would he walk out again when he heard everything?

*Trust him?*

He'd taken her daughter somewhere without her permission.

*Trust him.*

And her grandmother, the traitor! How would his parents—intellectual snobs, that's how he'd described them—react to the Glam Gram?

*Trust him.*

She sighed. What choice did she have?

But once again, he was interfering in her life. She wouldn't be surprised to find another Elvis staring her in the face when she walked outside, one singing "Suspicious Minds," or some such thing, to reinforce Merrill's exhortation to trust him.

There was no Elvis when she left the motel unit and walked over to her apartment, just warm sunshine after yesterday's rain. The storm had apparently ended early and veered in another direction, as later predicted.

The apartment was a wreck due to the apparently hasty departure. She spent an hour cleaning up and then called Harry to ask if she was supposed to be preparing any kind of food or drinks for the press conference.

"I actually don't know. The mayor and her gang seem to have taken over with some god-awful pirate theme. You could give her a call but she'd probably talk you into some Anne Bonny outfit."

*Over my dead body!*

"Why don't you just get one of those cheese or fruit tray things at the supermarket with some bottled waters or sodas, just in case?"

*I can do better than that.* "Sure."

"Lilah, I'm truly sorry for any trouble I've caused you. I have a big mouth."

"No, Harry, it's not your fault. It would have come out eventually."

"Well, I feel real bad about it."

"Don't. I'll see you at two then." She looked up the number for Stella's Wine and Cheese Bar that she'd noticed making a delivery to Kevin and Adam and their Victoria's Secret babes, and called to place an order to be delivered to the Conti mansion by one, at the latest. Luckily, they weren't busy this early in the day and were more than willing to take the order, and, yes, they could fill in the trays with crackers, fresh fruit, and other finger foods. She didn't even wince when told the bill came to four hundred and twenty-five dollars. Merrill, or the company, would be paying for it.

What next?

She figured she could stop at the supermarket on the way to pick up some bags of ice and paper products, although she suspected that Doreen would have pirate, or Fourth of July, napkins and such.

Her cell phone rang when she came out of the shower. It was Maggie.

"Mommy. I'm swimming!"

"You are? Where?"

"The big pool at our house."

"Which house would that be, honey?"

"The . . . what do they call it?" She was speaking to someone else who was in the room with her. Maybe Gram. But, no, it was a man's voice. "Poppa says it's the Beach Manse."

"The beach mansion?"

"Nooooo. The Beach *Manse*."

*Same thing, sweet pea.* "Who is Poppa?"

"He's Mister Merrill's father. We went to see Nana in the hospital. Then Poppa brought us here to the Beach Manse."

*Nana? And Poppa? Oh, my! I foresee a disaster in the future.* "Where's Gram?"

"She's outside with the neighbor lady, eating horse doors and drinking singing-poor-things."

It took Delilah a moment to realize that she meant hors d'oeuvres and Singapore Slings. "I miss you, pumpkin."

"Me, too. Gotta go. It's my turn to play Marco Polo in the pool."

The line went dead, and Delilah just stared at it for a moment. *Guess that puts me in order of my daughter's priorities.* But, actually, Delilah was glad Maggie was okay with this temporary separation.

When she came out of the shower a short time later, there was a missed text from Merrill:

<<<On my way>>>
<<<Meet u @ Chimes>>>
<<<Wear MM dress>>>
<<<Please>>>
<<<Trust me>>>

Delilah tried to call him back, but she got an "out of range" message. He'd probably turned off his phone just so she couldn't give him a piece of her mind. Then she puzzled over the letters *MM.* Oh, he meant the Marilyn Monroe halter dress. But why? She would have thought the press conference was informal.

She did as he asked, even though she would probably look like a fool, especially if Charlie was there in coveralls. But Bonita would be dolled up for the cameras, no doubt about that. Not that Delilah was going within a mile of any camera, not if she could help it.

When she got to the Conti mansion, driving the old station wagon, it was early. Only one o'clock, but there were already a dozen vehicles and a number of news vans. She saw Gus and Adam, who were both dressed casually, darn it! They came to help her carry her supermarket purchases inside while she went over to the Stella's panel truck, which had just pulled up.

The pocket doors that separated the two huge drawing rooms on one side of the mansion had been opened to create one extra-large space. A dais was set up at the front with long tables and chairs and microphones, and several dozen folding chairs were arranged in rows down below. Having lived in Bell Cove for several months now, she was not surprised to see a pirate theme going on, or was it some convoluted shipwreck scene? No, it was pirates, she decided, on seeing that the enormous stuffed gorilla, a prize from a wildlife safari of one of Gabe's ancestors, had been rolled into the room. On its head was a red bandanna tied at its nape biker style, or was that pirate style? There was a patch over its one eye. A kid's swashbuckling-type sword was taped to its one hand.

The decorations were heavy on skulls and crossbones. Some barrels had "Grog" written on their sides. A number of canvas kite-type things hung from the ceiling that Delilah assumed were supposed to be ship's sails. And, yes, some of the townsfolk were dressed like crazy-ass pirates. An enormous pirate's chest was filled to overflowing with shiny gold coins, with two pirate guards with rifles standing on either side of it, the twin senior citizens, Mike and Ike. When she walked up to them, they addressed her with, "Ahoy, matey!"

What was really nice, though, was the enormous banner hung behind the dais depicting a sepia-tone sketch of the *Falcon*. The work of Bonita and Adam, she was sure. There were press kits sitting on a number of the chairs, also the work of Bonita and Adam, who had been busy beavers, apparently.

Delilah moved to the long, glassed-in sunroom off to the side, which had probably been screened-in porches at one time. There were several folding tables there with white tablecloths on them. That's where she directed Adam and Gus and the caterers to put her purchases.

She hadn't had time thus far to feel like a sore thumb in her dressy clothes, compared to the others. But then, she noticed Kevin, who was in a dark jacket over a dress shirt and tie, and jeans and athletic shoes, but still he was clothed more like her dressiness than the rest. Bonita wore a black spandex dress that hugged her curves and would have fit in anywhere. She guessed it was that kind of affair where everything goes in terms of attire.

She set everything up, and a couple of townspeople asked if they could man the table. In fact, they set up several other tables with skulls and crossbones and leftover Fourth of July paper products. They carried in a number of large ice chests, which they just slid beneath the tables for now. Holy cow! There would be enough food and drink here for an army—or a dozen bands of pirates.

It was a sign of how anxious she was that she could joke with herself like that.

When she peeked out into the main room, Delilah realized that the whole town must have shown up. Aside from the press in the first few rows, who were being bossed around by Laura Atler, the local newsperson, every seat was taken, and folks were lined up against the walls. Many of them gave her little waves, which surprised her. By now, everyone should have heard about her felony status. Instead of judging her, not having heard actual details— even Merrill hadn't heard those yet—they seemed to not only be accepting, but supporting her. Was that possible?

Gabe Conti, owner of Bell Forge and Merrill's business partner, owned this big mansion. He sighed on first viewing all the pirate nonsense going on, especially when he saw what they'd done with his gorilla. But then, he'd shrugged and laughed.

Ethan Rutledge came in with his wife, Wendy; his mother, Eliza; and daughter Cassie, who walked with a limp but was supposedly going to have an operation soon. There were a number of potted palm trees around the room, thanks to his landscape nursery, no doubt. Must be this was supposed to be a pirate's island hideaway or something.

The mayor and her troop of helpers, responsible for this unusual press conference, a pressarama, were all in pirate gear. Even her daughter, Francine, the hairstylist; and her husband, the sheriff, Bill Ferguson. Bill came up to her and whispered, "Don't you be worryin' about that goon guy. He's been extradited. Not only is he gonna pay for attempted assault here, but he has warrants a mile long back in Jersey. He'll be seeing a lot of time."

"Thank you so much."

He shrugged, as if it was nothing. "As for that other thing, I saw that Ms. Gardner and her cohorts snooping around here earlier . . ."

*Here?* Delilah glanced quickly around the room. *That's all I need. I knew I should have stayed away and lain low. Too late now. At least Maggie is safe.*

". . . but you're not to worry," the sheriff went on, patting her on the arm. "No one's gonna revoke your parole, not while I'm on duty."

*OMG! Are we gonna have a shoot-out at the pirate mansion?*

*More nervous joking! Stop it, Delilah. This is serious.*

"Besides, once you get two senators, a federal judge, and a governor involved, these overzealous state clerks are gonna think twice about overstepping their bounds. Of course, the wedding will cement the deal."

"Senators? Governor?" she asked in confusion. "What wedding?"

"Anyways, your man must know people in high places." He waggled his eyebrows at her before going to sit with his wife.

"My man?" she asked, but he was already gone. It didn't take long for her to realize that Merrill must have been at work, even while he was gone, on his handy laptop or cell phone. The man—not *her* man, *the* man—just could not stop meddling in her life. But she couldn't be mad at him for his interference in her latest problems. Not when they involved Maggie. Still . . .

On and on the craziness went. The seniors from the Patterson house were there, some of them in fancy dance attire. Were they going to give a dance demonstration, or something? But wait. Glancing out the window, she saw a van double-parked outside and some people getting out, carrying instruments. The logo said: "Nostalgia." It was the popular Outer Banks classic rock band that had played at the Rutledge wedding.

This situation just got weirder and weirder.

Then there were the merchants she'd met in town. And Ina Rogers, the church secretary from Our Lady by the Sea. And was that Father Brad from her church, wearing vestments? Why? Was he going to bless the gold or something?

*Self-joking again! Oh, Lord, my brain is going to melt with all this nervousness.*

Matt Holter, her local lawyer, came up to her at one point and said, "I know you planned on coming to my office this afternoon, but it won't be necessary today. I brought some paperwork for you to sign. If I need more, I'll let you know." He pulled some folded papers out of the inside pocket on his suit jacket and handed her a pen, pointing to the bottom of several pages marked with an X where she should sign. She could swear that Merrill's name was on one of them, still waiting for his signature.

Ordinarily, she wouldn't sign anything without reading the whole thing, but Matt was talking the whole time, and she just said, "Will you give me duplicates of this?"

He looked surprised and said, "Of course."

The odd thing was, when he walked away, he went over to the priest and showed him one of the papers. Was Father Brad going to be a witness to her character in foster care proceedings, or something? He really didn't know her that well.

Her new friend, Sally Dawson from the Sweet Thangs bakery, came in carrying a huge box of what must be bakery products, which she handed to the folks manning the other tables in the sunroom. Sally, with her brown hair spiked up for the occasion in a pixie-ish haircut and some out-of-character makeup, which still allowed her freckles to show through on her face, looked very pretty in the peach-colored dress she'd bought at the thrift shop the day they'd had lunch. She came over to give Delilah a hug and whispered against her ear, "Good luck!"

An odd sentiment, unless she had heard about her foster care and parole worries. "I may need it."

Just then, Kevin was about to walk by. She grabbed him by the arm and asked, "Have you heard from Merrill? He should be here by now."

But Kevin, who'd stopped dead in his tracks,

was staring at Sally as if he'd been gobsmacked. "Who . . . are . . . you?" he finally asked.

"Kevin, this is my friend Sally Dawson. She owns the bakery in town. Sally, this is Merrill's buddy, Kevin Fortunato, or K-4."

"I know who he is. Ex–Navy SEAL," Sally said, raising her ski-jump nose in the air. To Kevin she added, "And don't be giving me that look."

"What look?"

"That I-want-you-baby and I'm-so-hot-how-can-you-resist-a-buff-guy-like-me?"

Kevin laughed. "What are you doing later?"

"Nothing involving you."

"Why?"

"I don't do military men. One was enough."

"Do?" he inquired with amusement. Then, "I'm not in the military anymore."

"Once in the military, especially Special Forces, it's in your veins. Danger. Excitement."

"What's wrong with that?"

"Listen, Mister Macho Man, go play with your Victoria's Secret model." Apparently the whole town must know about the goings-on at her motel during the storm. "This single mother has enough to do with three children."

"The model is gone. And, by the way, I love kids."

"What a load of hooey!"

"I think I'm in love."

Sally laughed.

Delilah walked away while the two continued to banter. Sally wouldn't be able to resist a man like

Kevin. Wait until she heard about his dead wife. She'd be down for the count within a day—a week, max.

And then Merrill showed up, and this whole press conference thingee could get underway. He saw her and smiled.

Oddly, that smile calmed her down, and she knew everything was going to be all right.

Making his way toward her, Merrill was stopped by several people who had something they wanted to talk to him about, including Matt Holter, who had him sign some papers, as well. She wasn't sure if they were the same ones that she'd signed or something else.

Merrill looked so good, and thankfully was dressed more in line with what he'd asked her to wear. A black suit with a white dress shirt and tie. Very, very nice!

"Been shopping?" she asked.

"Yep. Like it?" He did a silly little runway spin to show off his outfit.

"Of course."

"You look good, too," he said, and leaned down for a quick kiss. "I have plans for that dress, later."

"I bet you do."

"You smell good, too. Is that an Avon product?"

"No, it's Ivory Soap."

"My new favorite."

"How are Maggie and my grandmother?"

"Unbelievable! I'll tell you about it later. My parents have been transformed. Suffice it to say, those two are miracle workers."

*Whaaat?*

But Mayor Doreen was already up on the dais, announcing the beginning of the press conference. For the next hour or so, the team, along with the mayor, all sitting on the dais, gave presentations on their discovery and what would come next, taking questions at the end. Delilah managed to stay off to the side with Gabe and Harry, although when it came time for pictures, they joined the others.

It was actually a fun event. Serious stuff when Bonita and Adam gave a history of the *Falcon* and how it ended up at the bottom of the ocean, but much laughter when they talked about the expedition, including the surfeit of spiny lobsters. Finally, Merrill said that the press conference was over, that they would pose for some photos, and in the coming weeks would be available for more interviews, including some special events at the same time as the Lollypalooza over Labor Day weekend. Apparently, the author of a book on shipwrecks, including the *Falcon*, would be doing a book signing then.

Mayor Doreen said, "Thank you all for coming, but we need you to clear the property, except for those invited. We have another event about to take place."

"What event?" one of the reporters asked.

"A wedding," the mayor announced with a big smile, but then said, "Oops!" when she noticed the wince on Merrill's face.

Merrill looked at Delilah.

She looked at him, puzzled. But then, she understood.

*He wouldn't.*

"You wouldn't!" she exclaimed.

*And how could he, anyhow? A secret wedding? Ridiculous! People needed marriage licenses and stuff, didn't they?*

Suddenly the papers she'd signed and the priest in vestments began to make sense. And somehow all the chairs had been arranged so that there was a center aisle. Stu and Barb were unrolling a runner from a huge bolt of white fabric down the center from the end of the room to the dais. A florist was coming in with baskets of flowers, pink and white roses. The table on the dais was being made into an altar with candelabra and a gold ciborium, which held communion hosts in a Catholic Church. Off to the side, the band was tuning up with that famous shag dance song, "Carolina Girls," which was a must-have anywhere along the beaches, from the Outer Banks to Myrtle Beach. On the other side, bell choirs from both Our Lady by the Sea and St. Andrew's were setting up for some kind of performance.

It almost looked like preparations for a wedding, and a wedding reception.

"You wouldn't?" she said again, staring at Merrill with accusation.

"Let me explain," he said, trying to make his way to her through a crowd of guests who were attempting to ask him more questions.

That's when she bolted from the room, almost knocking over Long John Gorilla, a keg of grog, and two palm trees.

That's when she realized that Merrill Good had pulled off the ultimate interference in her life.

That's when it was all over.

*There were many ways for a man to sway a woman to his way of thinking, but the best way was . . .*

**M**errill had his work cut out for him in the damage control department.

Rushing after Delilah, he caught her heading toward the back of the house. She was in the hallway just off the kitchen when he pulled her into the butler's pantry. Yeah, they had butlers in the days when this old mansion had been built.

She backed up to the window at the far end of the galley-like room. There were marble-top counters on both sides, one of which had a sink for washing the fine china and sterling flatware that would be stored there. The cabinets, top and bottom, were a dark cherry with an aged patina. "Leave me alone."

"Not until I have a chance to explain." He moved closer.

She put out a halting hand. "You interfered again!"

He ignored the halting hand, and reached out with his own right hand, cupping her cheek. "I did, for the best possible purpose."

She bent her face away from his hand. "And that would be?"

"Because I love you."

"Bullshit!" she exclaimed, and he could tell that she didn't like that she'd let that foul word slip, but she was too proud to take it back.

"I do. I love you so much I can't think straight."

"Were you thinking straight when you planned a surprise wedding for me?"

"Probably not. But in my defense, I just started the process and it kind of got out of hand."

She leaned left when he tried to kiss her neck.

When that didn't work, he went directly for her mouth.

She ducked down and under his arm, heading for the door, which he'd fortunately locked behind him. He yanked her back and held her tight in his embrace until she stopped struggling.

"I love you, Delilah," he said, kissing the top of her head.

"You don't even know me. You don't know anything about why I was in prison." She was speaking against his neck, and her breath felt warm and sexual.

But he couldn't go there. Not yet. "What I discovered over the past twenty-four hours, after behaving like a cowardly jackass, is that love doesn't set any barriers. It's unconditional. It either is or it isn't." He had her pressed against the door, and his hands were cupped around her buttocks, rubbing softly against the silky fabric.

Instead of shoving him away, she sighed and arched her hips against him just at that spot which was showing the biggest sign of his affection at the moment.

He saw stars.

"You say that now, but what if . . ." she continued.

How was it that women could turn a guy's brains to a testosterone blob and still carry on a conversation? "See, you're looking for roadblocks, and I'm looking to take them down." That didn't sound so bad for a guy who was drowning in blob.

"That doesn't make any sense."

At least she wasn't struggling anymore. So, he picked her up by the waist and set her on the counter, stepping between her dangling legs. It put his body at just the right level it wanted—needed to be. But not yet.

"Here's the deal, sweetheart. You had, still have, two critical problems. They could take your parole away at the least provocation. And they could put Maggie into foster care at the least hint of an issue, real or imagined. I figured that marriage between you and me, with my eventually adopting Maggie, would be a way of permanently stopping the clock on any overzealous parole agents. We would be a family." He couldn't resist then. He rubbed the palms of his hands over her breasts bringing the nipples to obvious peaks.

She made a small gasp.

And she was listening.

So, he plowed ahead, both in speech and action. "I would continue working for the treasure hunting company. You could get the diner and motel going." He raised the hem of her dress up to her waist and tugged off her panties.

She shifted so that he could tug them the rest of the way off.

"And maybe we could build a house out there on the bluff overlooking Bell Sound." At the same time—God bless multitasking—he unzipped his pants and pulled out one very excited symbol of his rising affection.

Her eyes went wide, whether at what he'd said or what he was showing her, he wasn't sure.

And wasn't about to ask.

"You've been doing a lot of thinking, and planning, without consulting me."

"Yeah, I have, and I admit it's partly because I feared you would object because, face it, you've never said that you love me."

She said nothing.

He decided to change direction and reached up to untie the bow at her nape, letting the fabric drop to expose her breasts.

"Have I told you how much I like this dress?" he asked in a voice husky with arousal. "Have I told you how much I like your breasts?"

Then he showed her by licking, then suckling first one breast, then the other. When he leaned back, he saw that the nipples were moist and rosy and turgid with the female equivalent of a hard-on.

She was breathing heavily through parted lips.

But she still hadn't said that she loved him.

She still hadn't agreed to his plans.

"How can we get married without a marriage license?"

He waved a hand airily. "Matt took care of that."

She leaned forward and was about to kiss him, but she paused. "You mean those papers I signed were an application for a marriage license?"

He could feel his face heat with guilt. "Maybe."

"Don't those applications have to be made in person?"

"Matt knows people."

She nodded her understanding and kissed the side of his mouth. Not nearly the kind of kiss he wanted, but at least she wasn't shoving him away.

"Speaking of knowing people," she started to say, the first time he took his tongue out of her mouth and came up for a breather.

*Honestly, how can I be dumbstruck and practically babbling like an idiot and she just keeps talking, as if we aren't about to engage in world-class monkey sex?*

"Do you really know some senators and a governor who are going to put the press on Ms. Gardner?"

"Hell, no. It's a case of six degrees of separation. I know someone, who knows someone, who knows . . . well, you get the picture." His cock was at the brink of the happy tunnel, but first he rubbed against that part of her that looked like it would like a little attention.

She almost shot off the counter on a long groan. And then—amazingly—she resumed talking. "And so you decided that I would be pleased with a surprise pirate wedding?"

"No, no, no! I fully intended that we would get married at town hall later today. It's just that once people in Bell Cove get wind of something, they just run with it. I had no idea it had gone so far. And speaking of going too far, I'm about to explode if this keeps up much longer."

"What are you waiting for?" she asked with mock sweetness and shimmied her butt forward a bit, encouraging him to enter her.

Not yet. Oh, not by a sexy minute was she going to have him without paying her dues first.

"Tell me," he urged.

She raised her chin haughtily.

He touched her clit with his thumb.

She gasped and tried to close her thighs, but he was already there, spreading them apart.

"Tell me." He fluttered her clit with his middle finger.

She made a gurgling sound, and he was pretty sure her climax was starting. Either that or her eyes were rolling back in her head for no reason.

He rubbed his lips across hers and plunged his tongue inside, then slid out slowly. "Tell me."

She opened her eyes—eyes that glistened like blue crystals—and looked at him. "I love you."

He almost cried out with joy, and maybe it was with the sheer torture/pleasure of thrusting in and out of her spasming folds until she said, almost in a shout, "I love you, dammit. I love you, love you, love you."

After her breathing slowed down and he could stop panting, he kissed her, then leaned his head back so that he could look at her. "Does this mean we're getting married?"

"No, I have quickies with any ol' guy who asks, in a pantry, outside a ballroom with about a hundred people listening."

"Will you marry me, Delilah Jones?"

Just then, all the bells of Bell Cove, the two churches, and the town hall clock tower, rang out the hour. It was almost a mystical moment, a sign of approval from above.

That's when she said, "Yes, of course."

# Epilogue

### *Long John Silver couldn't have done it better . . .*

*D*elilah Jones and Merrill Good were married in a surprise wedding that afternoon at the Chimes mansion in Bell Cove, which had been amazingly transformed into a wedding chapel, then a reception hall in the twenty-three minutes the couple had been missing. Ina Rogers, the church secretary, timed them, to Delilah's mortification.

The fact that it had a mixed pirate/Independence Day theme didn't seem to bother anyone. There were both Blackbeards and Uncle Sams on the dance floor later.

Delilah wore a white Marilyn Monroe halter dress that everyone said was as good a wedding dress as any they'd ever seen. A circlet of pink roses, a gift from the local florist, Rosie's Posies, sat on her silver blonde hair. Somehow, the neat upswept hairdo she started the day with was loose and full about her face during the ceremony, a face which not a few people noted was dusted with a whisker burn or two.

Merrill was handsome as sin in a black suit; all the ladies said so. He never let go of his bride-to-be's hand until the ceremony was over, as if he feared she would change her mind.

Kevin "K-4" Fortunato and Sally Dawson were best man and matron of honor. It was hard not to notice the attraction between the two of them, Kevin's obvious lust, hers more lust-hidden-by-hostility. Bell Cove-ites predicted another wedding in their future, maybe even during the Lollypalooza celebration.

The band played lots of shag dancing songs because, after all, this was the Carolinas. Delilah and Merrill would learn eventually. They also played some Elvis songs, and encouraged folks to visit the Rock Around the Clock diner once it opened.

Merrill, when he gave a toast, said, "Today was a day for celebrating our discovery of gold on the *Falcon* shipwreck, but I've discovered my greatest treasure is right here beside me."

The only thing missing was Maggie and her grandmother, Delilah said.

"We could always have a second wedding later and include them," Merrill suggested.

"Bite your tongue," she replied, and glanced around to make sure no one had overheard. Otherwise, they would be part of the Lollypalooza weekend, too.

Later that night, Merrill showed Delilah a new use for Avon Skin So Soft.

She showed him some things that made a hardened Navy SEAL, or ex–Navy SEAL, say, "Hoo-yah!"

# Author's Note

Dear Readers:

Merrill "Geek" Good's story has been a long time coming. I hope you liked it.

Way back in 2004, I got the strange idea of combining Vikings and Navy SEALs. After all, there are so many similarities. Fighting men. Brave. Attractive. Work well in water (Frogmen, anyone? And longships!). Sexy. Great senses of humor. Thus was born the first of my Viking Navy SEAL novels in *Wet and Wild*, followed by *Hot and Heavy*, and five others.

From the start, Merrill "Geek" Good was an important secondary character in all those books. A genius with a Mensa I.Q., Geek graduated from college at a young age, bringing a unique perspective to the elite Special Forces. And, despite his youthful appearance, which he played for all its worth, he was sexy as sin.

For years, I wondered what kind of woman would finally land this brilliant rogue. Would she be a PhD? Would she be a female SEAL, or engaged in some kind of military, like he was? Would she be movie star beautiful, or plain?

Finally, I think I found the perfect match for him in Delilah Jones, an ex-con who barely graduated from high school, in this book, *Life, Love and the Pursuit of Happiness*. And I love the backdrop of the Outer Banks of North Carolina.

We got a hint of Merrill's intention to leave the teams in the first book of this new Bell Sound series, *The Forever Christmas Tree*, and, of course, we'll be seeing more of him and Delilah in the third book of the series, where he will continue to treasure hunt and she will finally launch her rock-and-roll-themed diner and Heartbreak Motel.

I love to hear from you readers, and I respond to all mail at shill733@aol.com. You can sign up for my mailing list on my website at sandrahill.net, or get news on my Facebook page at: Sandra Hill Author.

As always, I wish you smiles in your reading.

*Sandra Hill*

Don't miss the next book in the fun and sexy Bell Sound series by *New York Times* bestseller Sandra Hill

# A HERO COMES HOME

**Coming January 2020 from Avon Books!**

## Also by Sandra Hill

### Bell Sound Series
THE FOREVER CHRISTMAS TREE

### Cajun Series
CAJUN PERSUASION • CAJUN CRAZY
THE CAJUN DOCTOR • THE LOVE POTION

### Deadly Angels Series
GOOD VAMPIRES GO TO HEAVEN
THE ANGEL WORE FANGS
EVEN VAMPIRES GET THE BLUES
VAMPIRE IN PARADISE • CHRISTMAS IN TRANSYLVANIA
KISS OF WRATH • KISS OF TEMPTATION
KISS OF SURRENDER • KISS OF PRIDE

### Viking Series I
THE PIRATE BRIDE • THE NORSE KING'S DAUGHTER
THE VIKING TAKES A KNIGHT • VIKING IN LOVE
A TALE OF TWO VIKINGS
THE VIKING CAPTIVE (formerly MY FAIR VIKING)
THE BLUE VIKING • THE BEWITCHED VIKING
THE TARNISHED LADY • THE OUTLAW VIKING
THE RELUCTANT VIKING

### Viking Series II
HOT & HEAVY • WET & WILD
THE VERY VIRILE VIKING • TRULY, MADLY VIKING
THE LAST VIKING

### Creole-Time Travel Series
SWEETER SAVAGE LOVE • FRANKLY, MY DEAR...

### Others
LOVE ME TENDER • DESPERADO

## "Me_____? Do I need to call an ambulance?"

Her face was so close, he could feel her breath on his lips. Like a kiss.

*A breath kiss?*

He liked the sound—rather, the thought—of that.

And so he did what he shouldn't, but what he'd wanted to do since the first time he'd seen her. He put hands on either side of her face and tugged her the few remaining inches closer. Then he locked lips with her in a kiss that was sweet and seeking and innocent as a hello.

But, hello, her lips were parted in surprise . . .

*Yay, me!*

. . . and because fifteen years on the teams had taught him to grab any window of opportunity before it disappeared . . .

*Seize the day!*

. . . or because maybe she'd been wanting this as much as he had . . .

*Okay, that's a stretch.*

Well, for all those reasons, and then some, the sweet kiss turned wicked. Wicked good.